BROADSIDER

The Siege of The Behemothis

Lilith Antoinette

Text Copywrite © LIlith Antoinette 2020

FOREWORD AND ABOUT THE AUTHOR

Firstly, thank you for picking up a copy of Broadsider! It has been a thrill and a huge learning experience to write from start to finish. Writing a novel is a huge hurdle for anyone to do. So having a reader like you take a peek at the story inside makes me eternally grateful. Broadsider is set in a far future where humanity has grown beyond some of its physical and mental limitations. But humanity still has to face challenges of living in a new interstellar environment. In the book you will find a new language and new technologies. There are lots of different people, planets, stellar phenomena, and (best of all) spaceships!

I've been writing science fiction ever since I was a child. Ever since I first saw movies like Star Trek The Motion Picture, TV shows like Battlestar Galactica, and video games like Mass Effect. I've always wanted to create my own varied and exploratory sci-fi story. After so many years of writing, I never found the time to focus my work and put it out for other people to see. Finally, I started the blog "Orchestrators of the Universe" in 2019 so that I could start to share. This book, and much more, is a culmination of all those efforts.

In 2020, the year from hell, I turned 25 and I knew I had to put my work out there. There was no better time to finish this book. So here we are! Broadsider! I hope you enjoy the novel. It was no small feat to put together, and I hope you enjoy the time you spend with the places and characters as much as I did while writing them.

Thank you to my wonderful partner Alia, my friends and family, and everyone who continues to support me in my writing journey.

THE AMADELLAN FLU

It is an inarguable fact that most people believe in a reason to exist, whether it be a religion, a personal goal, or a responsibility to another person. For Katsina Lucas, it was her ship, with every person on board. She had never considered it before, but deep in an unmapped region of space, away from home, Katsina paused and thought for a moment about her circumstances. Though she had every reason to, she never dipped her head or shrugged her shoulders. She did, however, let out a sniff and sigh during her morning routine while taking a moment here and there to wipe her nose. It was hard to concentrate on getting set up to work when a flu was going around aboard an enormous spaceship, but that didn't mean work wasn't going to be done. Katsina leaned back into her chair and closed her eyes to consider returning to her quarters for the rest of the day. A selfish idea, one she very rarely gave attention to, but today she was tempted without knowing why.

"Morning Katsina," a smooth voice said from behind her, "still sick?"

"No, I miraculously recovered in the last ten hours," Katsina replied, opening her eyes to look around at Marshal, who took up his seat behind her.

He was regal, with practically glowing skin. Katsina still, after fifteen years, couldn't figure out what made his skin look so flawless. Her skin was never as well maintained; with each part of her body having at least one or more bright pink scars, she gave up trying to. In her mind, it could have been something to do with his brown hair, wavy and long enough to shape his strong jawline, unlike her kinky and coiled mess that fell around her face sporadically. Maybe it was his aquiline nose that reminded her of a greek hero. Last she checked, he had the shoulders of one so it would make sense if that was what he turned out to be. Her most common thought was about his nails; she had never met someone with perfect nails like his. Her nails matched the rest of her hands, mangled, hardened and almost always smelled of engine fuel. There was nothing else Katsina looked at as much as him each morning. He was her first point of contact each day he was on duty.

"Ooh, grouchy huh?" he said jokingly.

"How could you tell, Mr. Richmond?"

"Call it my Ligai-Navajo intuition. Here," he said, passing an orange cup over Katsina's shoulder, "it's not a cure but it will help."

"Oh yeah, lets just all talk about our ancient earth heritage again, why don't we? Pale Native American hanging out with a black Lagosian on a spaceship billions of miles away from the planet that made up all those words in the first place. Did Rutheo tell you she's Irish?" Katsina scoffed.

Taking the cup from him and sipping gently, she winced at the heat of the coffee Marshal had made for her. It soothed her throat, cleansing its scratchy stinging walls.

"Rich blend from a Richmond; is that three shots?" she asked.

"Ligai Navajo are Botanican by the way. It's not an earth thing. You know it's three; how else are you gonna wake up and win the fight?"

"Yeah well, very funny. I'm awake, Marshal, and we're going to win the fight. How was shore leave?" Katsina asked, taking another sip of the brew.

"I love your lack of passion about heritage. My shore leave..." he paused, "Yeah, yeah, it was good; spent most of it at home up in the hills. Why? You miss me that badly?"

"Oh yeah, of course. Ship's been a mess," said Katsina, feigning distress, "What can I say, Commander. I can't be a fit captain without you."

"Oh and you think *I'm* funny. Maybe if we were still homosapien I would have half believed that. You ready to wake them up?" Marshal asked with enthusiasm.

"Alright then."

Katsina lifted herself out of her chair, forgoing the comfort for now. She brought up her index finger and tapped on the back of her neck, just behind her right lobe twice in succession, it sounded a low singular *beep* in her ear. Before her a series of lights and images began to appear, not on a screen or monitor, but in her very eyes. What they formed was her personal Heads Up Display, or HUD, tinted with orange hues. It showed the date and time, her various biological functions, a user interface system, status bar and more for her to utilize. The time read 05:55 in her bottom left corner, meaning she had two hours and five minutes before having to plug in and start her shift officially. Past her HUD, the ship's bridge could be seen. A massive oval domed room which housed over one hundred computer stations, all of which circled around a large Augmented Reality, or AR, display. Katsina's position overlooked the domed room from a balcony that stretched forward from the back wall on the second floor. The room itself was adorned with polished black wooden banisters and flooring held together by white metal beams. It was in stark contrast to many modern day spaceships, making it wholly unique. The chairs and computer stations were accented with different shades of orange and turquoise to match the ship's official colors.

Each desk had a variety of monitors of different shapes and sizes, with each modular desktop purpose-built by the people assigned to that station to suit their needs. The lights on the dome of the ship we're always a bright fluorescent white that only dimmed in an emergency; there was always something in wartime that caused them to dim, but this week the theatre of war seemed quiet. The sounds of chattering voices began to grow louder as Katsina looked down at the shift change downstairs, watching the crew greet each other and go about swapping positions. Katsina waited for the noise to taper off, before plugging a small cable into a Graphene

Fiber Ceramic Composite, or GFCC, port that rested underneath her ear. A little flash of light on her HUD notified her that she was connected to the ship via her neural link. Her half synthetic, half organic mind became one with the ship's systems, allowing her to take up the intercom system and make the morning announcements.

"Good morning, Space Carrier Behemothis," she called out in a cheerful tone, "this is your Captain speaking. As of this morning, we are now seventy-seven weeks out of space dock in what is the most advanced Broadsider that's ever flown. Good news is there is no news. That's my bad joke attempt for the day over with."

Katsina paused, and looked around the bridge at her crew, all gazing up at her. She took a sip of her cooled coffee before cracking a smile.

"As always, please look over your roster for any changes. We do still have one squadron of operators out in the field searching for the space cruiser Roverdendrom, so let's keep an eye out for them. May the t'sßolfél bring 'em back in one piece. Any major developments or notifications that may arise throughout your day, please forward them to First Officer Richmond for review; give him some work to do now he's back from RnR. Have a good day. Let's win the war. Ride the lightning."

A disjointed series of claps and shouts from around the bridge sounded as Katsina pulled the cable out from the back of her head, letting it retract to a dispenser that hung from the ceiling. She walked away from the balcony's edge and passed her first officer on the way to the automatic doors that led out of the bridge.

"Marshal, she's all yours. If you need me I'll be in on the tarmac," she said, putting the empty cup down on the armrest of the captain's chair.

The doors slid open before her and Katsina left the bridge in Marshal's capable hands. Before her stretched a busy, tall, and crowded hallway that looked closer to a main street in a small town, only bigger. It was lined with shopfronts, coffee houses, and social spots for the crew. The high ceiling was adorned by flat canvases hanging from an Edwardian era glass canopy. On each canvas was an AR display of ship updates, advertisements, and bulletins of various colors. The main hallway connected multiple major decks of ship; it led to every section, and was frequented by the crew every day. Surrounding her was a bustling crowd made up of her people and more. Men, women, people outside and around the binary, all dancing around her to attend to their respective posts. The energy was always a comfort; it showed Katsina how the ship was doing each day just by the sound of the people in it; it even smelled good. That morning she heard laughter, some coughing, but mostly laughter. People trading jokes and stories from the end of one shift to the beginning of the next, it was never dull. She stopped at the scent of cinnamon coming from a cafe in one of the storefronts, and picked up a second coffee for herself. The cafe was quieter than usual.

"Probably with half the crew calling in sick today," she thought.

Katsina took up a stool and asked the coffee machine to make her favorite blend. The small steaming contraption sitting on the bar was an older model. The cafe owner, Barry, insisted it was better than any 'modern garbage' the service industry could make in the modern day. The rugged thing rumbled to life, grinding coffee beans instead of printing them. It was an object of antiquity, like most things in Barry's cafe, including Barry. Katsina slipped off of her stool, coffee in hand, and continued on with her walk, greeting various people along the way.

"Captain."

"Good Morning."

"Mornin' Sir"

The Captain visited the ship's hospital, crew housing, engineering, the recreational center, both cargo bay houses, and every other section that made up the Man O' War Space

Carrier Behemothis. At the end of her round she finally reached her destination, the spaceflight deck; a large open space that ran the length of the colloquially called Broadsider. The strip was lined with tarmac floor plating separated by a metal framework each lifted by hydraulic actuators to adjust for landing and launch pressure. Over a kilometer and a half in length, two hundred fifty meters wide and fifty meters tall. It was the ship's entire purpose, to house and deploy ships from scouts and fighters, to as large as frigates and cruisers. The carrier could host dozens of other spaceships on her tarmac, transporting them through space at interplanetary speeds reaching as fast as three-hundred and fifty million kilometers an hour. The Broadsider was held up by its large aerospike propulsion system, fueled by 16 individual Schwartzchild Kugelblitz wheels. It used the energy harnessed from human made black holes to propel itself from one star system to the next and beyond. Each black hole, created at the center of each wheel by focusing light, was not an infinite source of energy, but rather a balancing act of supply and demand. Like a water well: in that people always needed water, but should never let the well run dry. The Behemothis was the fastest spaceship humankind had created.

    Katsina crossed the wide tarmac, closing her coat against the hot bellows of wind produced by a nearby aerospike rocket engine. The clattering sounds of tools and the whirring of different ships of strange and wonderful shapes and sizes hummed in her ears, while the lights of the AR projected runways colored her vision. This was the life of her ship, and she could never help but crack a smile each time she ran across it. Katsina looked about her as she jogged, noticing a large portion of the deck was empty. On the other side of the strip, she found herself up against a large metal door, atop a platform, with a cable dispenser next to it. Katsina opened the flap and pulled on the cable, similar in shape but smaller than the one she'd had in her head earlier. She clipped the wire into her forearm and used her neural link to activate the door.

A low *rumble* and a series of loud *ticking* sounds signaled the gears of the garage, which began to wind up and open for her. Katsina stepped back and took a glance into the darkness, noticing a severe lack of illumination. Considering how badass it was to open her personal garage on her personal section of the spaceflight deck, on the ship that she ran, the fact that it didn't light up for her was slightly disappointing.

"Great, another one?" she grunted.

"Morning Captain," a voice shouted over the noise behind her. "How's the head?"

Katsina turned to see a mechanic walking towards her, covered in grease and sweat, but smiling. His jumpsuit was missing the long sleeve with protective padding, leaving his arms on display and his elbows with fresh scrapes. He had a bushy mustache the size of her hand that concealed his entire upper lip. The wrinkles around his bushy eyebrows lined his face with wisdom. He was a man who had seen more than her, with scars to show for it.

"Morning, Howard, head's fine," she called, returning the smile. She reached out her hand to pull him up onto the platform. "You start early or you on late?"

"Oh, I'm on late, missy. McKinney is out with Amadellan, so I have her shift split between me and Ron."

"Good work, I'll forward some lieu time to the engineering officer for you," Katsina said, dipping her head in under the door.

"Thanks, you need help working on the Amber Eyes today?" he asked, ducking under the door to peek in.

"No thanks, Howard. I think you have enough on your plate, huh?" She clambered across the dark space she had entered.

"Well alright, I'll be further down the tarmac if you need me, and mind your head!"

"Thanks, Howard, thanks," she called after him.

Katsina double tapped her neck, and accessed her HUD controls. She fiddled with the settings of her ocular sensory implants, making it easier for her to adjust to the darkness. Eventually her new settings let her see again, and she looked around her messy, overcrowded workshop for a large metal frame. She turned around to look up at the ceiling before smacking her head and falling backward into a tool chest on the floor. Hitting the dirty, oily floor with a thud, Katsina groaned while pulling a wrench out from under her hips.

"Oh you mother- Son of a- ugh," Katsina thought, rolling onto her stomach and putting her head in her hands.

She flicked up her HUD controls again and sent a call to the lighting engineer on duty. Katsina guessed it was a fuse after all. She waited, groaning, as her implant connected her to the wireless blue network. Stretching all around her, the blue strands of the net could be seen and heard by everyone who chose to connect to it. Hundreds and thousands of threads connected everyone on board via a collection of quantum entangled receivers and transmitters. It was a beautiful sight, maintaining the honesty and cooperation of everyone from each of the three human planets. The only planet and people not connected were the Yggdrasilians, their enemy.

Katsina clambered her way up to her feet and dimmed her ocular implants again, leaving her in darkness. She rubbed her forehead, sighing at the dull pain that ached when she touched it. This had been the third time in as many weeks that her hangar bay had no lights, even though she had changed out the bulbs twice. She wasn't going to hear the end of it from Marshal, and she was sure he was going to love telling her how wrong she was. She was convinced a few weeks before that it was a power surge.

Eventually, there was a flicker, and then a full wash of light filled the room, showing Katsina a sight for, literally, sore eyes. Illuminated from above by the floodlights and below by the light platform it was hovering over was the Amber Eyes, Katsina's personal fighter ship from her old commission. Before she was a captain, before she was thirty-five, and before she was handed a gigantic spaceship, Katsina was a fighter pilot first. The ship was a DeWiart class, known for durability and heavy armor plating. Its curved cylindrical body was hidden behind the folded wings that clung to it like petals to a bud. It's usual twenty five meter length was cut short by some missing parts, which was Katsina's job for the morning: restoring its length.

Stepping around her bay, she plugged a chip into her neck, connecting her to the platform controls. It showed all the information about the battered, out of shape fighter ship as it slowly began to rotate with her. On her HUD, Katsina could see small dots of light around the ship, highlighting issues that needed attention, parts that needed replacing. Her last deployment in the Amber Eyes had been years before, which seemed too long ago now. It had crashed, and mangled itself on the surface of a moon. She had been restoring it ever since. The Amber Eyes was an old model, decommissioned after hers had crashed, but after collecting on a few owed favors, Katsina had been able to keep her ship from being added to the recycling pile. Instead she was allowed to store it in her docking bay at home, before finally being promoted to captain of her own ship, and being allowed to take it with her anywhere. She ran her fingers over it's hull, tracing the scratches and dents with her nails. The glass nose cone of the Amber Eyes was the only thing she was going to be able to replace before her shift, since it was easily interchangeable with newer models. Katsina pulled up the wingspan controls, and allowed the ship to unfurl, like a blossoming flower, around her in the bay. One of the four wings was badly misaligned with a considerable hole ripped into it. Its Kugelblitz wheel housing was cracked, and one of the magnetic levitation plates was missing. Other than that, it was flight capable, and Katsina only needed another day or so to finish it.

"Well, least we can be sick together, right?" Katsina said, pulling on a pair of gloves, and linking her personal playlist to the fighters speaker system.

***

Before long, Katsina resorted to enlisting Howard for his help in getting the new nose cone fitted onto the cockpit frame of the Amber Eyes. She never usually asked for help, but Howard Crawford always offered when he saw her working, so why not let him? The two of them chipped away at the alignment process for a solid hour before eventually a loud *fump* let them know they had gotten it on properly. After another set of bolts and seals were aligned, they were able to drill the giant glass cone into place; to Katsina's relief. She toppled down from the roof of the fighter ship and tossed a bottle of water to Howard. He sat on a set of tire sized gears, wheezing after all the effort.

"You need me to take you to the hospital, old man?" Katsina asked, sliding down onto the light platform to inspect the belly of the ship.

"No ma'am, just, catching my breath," he managed.

"Good, 'cause I think if you clock out too, I'll be the only one left standing on this ship."

"Ah, it's only the flu, Captain. Everyone will be right as rain in a week or two," said Howard reassuringly.

"Yeah," Katsina paused, "I just think this is a weird time for everyone to be sick, don't you think?"

"Why? Ha, in case the Yggdrasilians catch us with our pants down? It's not our fault you've been spreading it around."

"Hey, I got it from Marshal, so don't you go pinning it on me. Can you blame me for being overly cautious?" Katsina asked.

"No, no I can't, but after all the scrapes we got through over the last few years I think you should give yourself more credit. How long have we been working together, Kat? Six? Seven years?"

"Six. You round up too much," Katsina said, tugging on a loose cable in the belly of the fighter, letting out a grunt between her words. "Why?"

"And how about you and Marshal?"

"Since we started at the university. I'm still not hearing the point."

"My point is that you've picked the best people you knew from the 'Abernathy' to be on this ship with you, and they've turned out to be a very capable crew. You should be more confident in your achievements, and their abilities," Howard explained. "I've been in the military most of my life. I've seen more than a few combat missions in the war. t'sßolfél! I remember my life before there was a war, but nobody wanted an older man serving on their ship after we served on the Abernathy. Nobody wanted a mechanic who didn't have optical implants or a HUD to help him fix things. They thought I was a disadvantage because I didn't grow up with those things. But look at me now, serving on the greatest ship we've ever built, helmed by the youngest captain in the fleet. You should be proud of that, if nothing else."

Katsina pulled herself out from under the Amber Eyes, and rolled onto her elbow to look up at the aged mechanic, who had a warm smile on his dirty face. A kindness radiated from that smile, one that was reminiscent of a nostalgic family holiday, or a Nollaig night. Katsina sighed and smiled back at Howard, and cleared her throat: "Alright, fair, we have a good crew, but we still have a lot to prove. Once the squadron gets back from retrieving the Roverdendrom, I'll feel a lot better. Mara's been out there longer than I expected," Katsina said, glancing down at her HUD, "Oh man. Okay, Howard, I have to go, briefings and whatever. Can you lock up for me?"

"Aye, Captain. Go ahead." He stood up to help her to her feet.

"Thanks, I'll make sure you get a few more lieu hours," Katsina shouted back, before running across the tarmac towards the stairwell to the main hall.

Keeping up the momentum of her sprint, Katsina took a shortcut through the recreational center, slipping from one Augmented Reality Theater to the next, each one playing different scenarios and movies for the crew to enjoy in their off hours. Through the entrance to the last theater a door led to the zero gravity ring, where friendly ball games and sports were played. Katsina tugged on her messy black hair, which was greasy and knotted from her time on the tarmac. She pulled it into a tight bun around her head, and slipped her jacket over her shoulders. Finally, she slipped her Captains Affix from her back pocket and clipped it to her shoulder. It lit up with the insignia of the Behemothis, and she was finally ready to start her duty shift on the bridge.

The double doors *whooshed* open as she slowed down at the top of the grand stairway and Katsina finally made it to her captain's chair with under a minute to spare. The bright lights of the bridge were glaring compared to the one's on the tarmac, making her call into question where exactly she was more comfortable. At that point, nowhere was comfortable for Katsina, as her coughing caught up with her after her sprint.

"Hey, Captain," one of the petty officers said.

"Nick of time, huh?" Marshal chuckled, handing her a tablet.

"Morning, Yeah. Uh huh, what are we working on?" Katsina said, snatching the tablet from him in her wheezy state.

"Well, we've got one group of Yggdrasilian vessels limping it's way back to their system from the edge of the front, we've been asked to keep tabs on them since we're closer. We have a medical aid ship asking to dock with us and restock on supplies, plasma burn kits in particular; they should be here in about two days before heading to theater lines past the redemption wheel," Marshal explained, while Katsina slumped in her chair, skimming over her passover data and copying it to her personal drive.

"Alright. Plenty of plasma burn kits to go around. Make

sure they get any maintenance they need, and have a look over the report that Sarah uploaded for you earlier," Katsina said, glancing over at Marshal with a grin.

"A report? From Sarah? I didn't ask for a- oh no, you didn't," he said, gasping at his own HUD.

"Oh yeah, she said she wanted a reason for you to talk to her, so I requested a report be drawn up," Katsina said.

"Well, aren't you a savvy space dog. Honestly, I thought you'd try to set her up with Rutheo," Marshal said with a laugh, running his fingers over his brow.

"I told you she likes you. You just have to learn to trust me more," Katsina said, standing to look over the balcony.

"Who says I don't trust you?" Marshal paused, "Uh? Kat? Kat, what's wrong?"

Katsina was mesmerized, and unwilling to take her eyes off of what she was seeing. A crew member down bellow, who had tears welling in her eyes, her face crimson red, and her hands over her mouth. Alice Wesley, a relatively young but creative crew member, talented in everything to do with intergalactic signals and quantum communication. She had stood up from her station, gathering the attention of those around her without wanting to. She turned and left her monitor behind, picking up only her tablet from the desk. She started walking towards the staircase, which led her to the balcony where Katsina, Marshal, and other members of the crew were working, catching the eyes of everyone in the oval room along the way. Katsina, sniffed back her illness, and dropped her relaxed attitude, realizing it was time for her to start being a captain again.

Alice Wesley reached the top of the stairs, and stood before Katsina pulling her blonde locks behind her ears. She cleared her throat.

"Captain," she sniffed, "Good morning."

"Good morning, Alice. What's happened?" Katsina asked. A lump formed in her throat, she couldn't imagine what was wrong. But there was only one thing that could have happened, the thing that Katsina had in the back of her mind the entire day. A wisp of dread had begun to cloud her mind.

"We, uh, we got a frequency from a Delta Operator, a distress signal," She said, her voice cracking. She held out a tablet to Marshal, who took it from her gently.

"I tried to extrapolate as much as I could, but there's very little to go on. They're gone, Captain," she said, tears beginning to stream down her cheeks from her pale blue eyes.

Katsina looked into those eyes, a wallowing set of windows into her sadness. The young woman had two friends on the Delta Operators flight team. As far as Katsina knew, almost everyone on the ship had a friend on that team. Two of Katsina's closest friends, Mara and Michael, were Captain and Commander of that team. Katsina reached out and put a hand on Alice's shoulder.

"It's alright, it's alright," she repeated, softening her tone to comfort the woman.

"Alice, did anyone else hear this message yet?" Marshal asked urgently, making Katsina look around at him in confusion.

"No sir, just me and you," Alice said, her voice still broken.

"Let me listen to that," Katsina said, reaching for the tablet in his hands.

"Captain, we should take this in the war room," Marshal warned.

Katsina, taken aback by his words, asked: "Do we need to mobilize?"

"No, I just think it's best we hear this in private," Marshal said, walking towards the steps on the opposite side of the balcony.

"Alright. Alice, you're with me, come on."

Down the stairs, behind a set of mirrored doors under the balcony, was the war room. Inside was a large round table and multiple display screens, as well as a large AR map of the region they were in. On the AR map was the image of a large black hole, and the disk of light surrounding it, all around the large black spot there were wisps of starlight, but no actual stars. The deep was a region of space that was particularly empty in the milky way. Next to nothing inhabited it. The room was empty, apart from the three who had just entered. Eyes followed them until the glass doors closed again. Katsina walked Alice to one of the chairs around the table, and took one for herself. Marshal seemed to be working on his HUD until a flashing image appeared on the AR map floating above their heads.

"As we can tell from the flight paths of the Delta Operators, they had made it to the last known location of the Roverdendrom. From what the log shows here they engaged with Yggdrasilians and pushed them back to this position here," he said, pointing at a second dot to pop up on the map. "According to this distress signal, it was sent from this location here." A third dot appeared on the map above Katsina's head. She looked up in disbelief, bringing her hand to her mouth and standing from her seat to change her view of the image.

"That can't be," she said, gazing at the little green dot, which sat just inside the accretion disk of the black hole in the middle of the room.

"Flight log specifies that Mara's ship, the Raptor's Claw, took some hits, but intentionally flew into the singularity, 'INSI-3178 Comedenti', in an attempt to reach the Roverdendrom here," he said, pointing at a line connecting the two points.

"It, uh, it looked like the rest of the squadron had jumped through space without activating any thrusters or boosters," Alice said shakily. "As if something pulled them through space. That's when the Raptor's Claw traveled into the accretion disk."

"Moving through space without thrusters? What was the distress message?" Katsina asked, still in disbelief.

"Audio log is as follows," Marshal said, pulling up the audio player menu.

Katsina looked down at the tablet on the table, reading the transcript while she listened.

> Delta squadron, respond, Delta squadron this is Operation Leader, please respond. Delta squadron can anyone respond, making our way to the rescue site please respond. Mike... Michael... please..."
> Error Systems Critical
> Arrived at destination
> Fuel Critical
> Engine Failure
> Weapons Failure
> Manual Controls Failure
> Gravity Well Failure
> Autopilot Failure
> System Failure
> Error__
> Er__or

Katsina leaned forward on the war room table, listening to the message repeat itself. She glanced at Alice, and back to Marshal, both of whom had somber expressions on their faces. Eventually she looked back up at the map above, watching the little green dots pulse as the message repeated again. Katsina had spent the entire evening the night before, and the entirety of her morning, worrying about an outbreak of the Amadellan flu on her ship. All while her Delta team had been cut down by something out in The Deep. Though she had every reason to, she never dipped her head or shrugged her shoulders. Instead, Captain Katsina Lucas left the war room to inform her crew.

MOBILIZE

The silence on the bridge was uncomfortable, almost sticky to Katsina's ears. She took in the pale and concerned faces of her crew. The Behemothis normally had one announcement from the captain each day before the crew began their work, any announcement made after that always meant something bad had happened. Katsina's morning announcements on shift change gave her the opportunity to speak to everyone aboard, otherwise news and updates would take longer to circulate. Katsina shifted her weight to her left foot, before pulling herself into a commanding stance. In the almost eerie atmosphere around her, many began to realize what was about to happen. The gentle beeps and wisps of the computer stations around the room started to grow louder in Katsina's mind, before she finally sniffed back her flu and cleared her already strained throat. She projected her voice over the crowd from the Captain's balcony, her mind linked to the ship's intercom so that all could hear.

"Last night, or more accurately, eight or so hours ago, the Delta Operation team was lost to an overwhelming Yggdrasilian force in The Deep. As of now we have no survivors and only one distress signal was retrieved."

Shock and awe fell upon the faces around her, some people even disappearing in the crowd to sit down. Katsina expected to hear whispers or even gasps, but instead there was silence, before more than one member of the bridge crew could be heard cracking into tears. Their sniffs and hums echoing across the dome, the first of many who began to well up. Katsina gave them all the time she could, before having to continue her address.

"The trajectories of each ship as well as any astronomical data regarding their space flight will be forwarded to all officers and teams rostered for today. Please take note of the immediate changes on each of your passover log's. What we need to do now is to inform our superiors on Terra Botanica, and move into the Deep to retrieve survivors. This will be our first loss fighting this war together on this ship, but I don't have to point out that we've already lost enough. So please, I must ask you to continue your work. Let's find out what happened to them. Let's win this war."

She didn't expect the usual upheaval to her rally cry. It wasn't as if she delivered it with her usual enthusiasm anyway. The bridge crew began to break up, each member returning to their station, albeit slowly. Katsina watched Alice Wesley, who was making her way back to her post, before she felt a hand tap her upper arm lightly. It was Marshal.

"Should I give her the day off?" he asked, flicking his eyes in the young woman's direction.

"Offer it to her, but don't force her. We've all seen this before. If people need time they know they can take it," Katsina said in a hushed tone, keeping her eyes on Alice. "You know she's only new, Mara recommended her."

"Mara has good eyes for people, she de-"

"Had," Katsina corrected.

"Katsina..." he sighed, leaving her side to walk down the stairs. Katsina turned to follow him.

"Sorry," she said, almost whispered.

"It's fine. I recommend we mobilize the Zeta Operators; we can meet them at the debris field after we tackle the repair and resupply of the hospital ship."

"I'm taking the Beta Operators into The Deep tonight. We'll find out what happened and bring back what we can. I'll need you to hold your position here and tell the Admiral I'm indisposed," she said, without a hint of inflection.

Marshal stopped his descent, and Katsina could feel his eyes on the back of her head as she passed him. There wasn't much on her duty slip, or even her passover, to keep her in any way occupied for the rest of her shift. For her, flying out to find out what happened was the only thing she could do.

"Kat, it's just a search and rescue. You don't have to jump into every scrap," he said, following behind her.

"It's a search and rescue for a search and rescue, Marshal. If I went the first time maybe we wouldn't have to go out this time."

"If you went out last time, Captain, you would have been the one that we lost."

Katsina closed her eyes in recognition of his words, while another droplet fell from her nose. He was right, but she didn't care. She looked over to the crew doors that lead to the stairwells, longing for her chance to get into the cockpit of the Amber Eyes. But Marshal was right, no matter how little she cared. So Katsina turned around and followed him back up the steps to the balcony. She reached her seat and plugged in, making herself look over the entire crew roster for the Delta Operators. She knew each of their names, but had trouble remembering all of their faces. Apart from three, she noticed she hadn't spoken to any of Delta Operators recently. The bright lights of the bridge became irritating as Katsina read. Eventually she unclenched her hand, realizing she was digging her fingernails into the leather armrest. Another droplet landed on her jacket, she was dribbling again. She leaned down, found herself a ragged cloth hanging from her belt, and blew her nose. The sinus congestion was more than enough for her to give up on the day, at least after everything she had seen and heard. The time crept by, slower than she craved, making it unbearable to look around her at the faces of her crewmen. It had only been an hour or so into her shift, so she leaned forward and unplugged from the ship. The snapping sensation on the back of her ear when removing the cable was always a satisfying feeling that Katsina associated with the end of each shift, but unplugging so early brought no such satisfaction. She dipped her head, rubbing her palms into her face.

"*Still oily,*" she thought.

She glanced through her underarm towards Marshal,

who was writing up his report, something she would have to do later that night. Katsina rubbed her eyes one more time, and leaned back into her chair, now that she knew the faces of everyone gone, it was time to write the condolence letters. Katsina plugged back in.

***

"Katsina?" Marshal's voice blipped into her ears, "You still there?"

Flicking her eyes open, adjusting to the lights, Katsina leaned around to look over her shoulder. She saw Marshal leaning forward in his seat, eyebrows raised. She blinked again, changing her focus back to the information on her HUD, a half written letter. She yawned, and shuffled in her chair, it had been a few hours of letter writing, followed by a brief sickly doze.

"Yeah, I'm still here, t'sßolfél," she cursed, pushing her fingers into her eyes.

"It's fine, you were only snoring for five minutes," Marshal said, a kind smile on his face.

"Only five? Why did you let it go on for five?" Katsina moaned, unplugging from her seat, and standing to stretch.

"It was a little funny. Any crew member that walked by couldn't help but stare at you."

"Thanks Marshal. Did the Admiral receive your message?" Katsina asked, lifting herself as high as she could, feeling the pull in her back. "We've been here for 6 hours, surely they have enough time to get back to us."

"Well the first fleet is engaged on the Ygg's border. I can't imagine Krauss has much time right now. I'm sure they received it, but time dilation is a bitch," he said, standing to join her.

"When did that happen?"

"Sometime last night in their part of space. We only received the contact message a few minutes ago."

"And you left me here to sleep?" Katsina asked, looking at him dumbfounded.

"Actually it's why I woke you; here's the message," Marshal said, handing her a tablet.

"I can't wait for these types of things to be integrated into the HUD system. Tablets really should be a thing of the past by now," Katsina said, looking at the semi transparent piece of plastic, it had two creases in its flat surface, giving it the ability to fold in half in either orientation, making it easier to use for different tasks. The message from the admiralty office, which flowed down the chain of command, was brief but serious. Another battle with heavy losses just one star system away was a stomach curdling thought.

"Well let's just hope he kills some Yggs huh?" Katsina said, handing the tablet back to Marshal, "Notify Beta Operators to assemble for mobilization, and get onto Rutheo, I want her as my engineer."

"As you're first officer, it's my obligation to tell you that you do not need to partake in this deployment," Marshal said, in a hollow tone, knowing his words would have no effect. He stretched his cheek, wiggling his nose about awkwardly. She knew he meant well, but so did she.

"Thanks Marshal, but I'm not on shift anymore," Katsina said, putting her hand on his shoulder."You have the bridge. I'm going to get my helmet."

"Aye Captain, ride the lightning," he said.

"Ride the lightning. Don't crash my Broadsider."

Katsina pulled her coat over her shoulders and looked back down from the balcony one more time. She saw Alice, the woman was still working at her computer screens. Her blond hair pulled into a tight bun behind her ears. Her implants glistening in the lights. In fact not a single person had left their shift after hearing the news; if anything it seemed to only make them want to work harder. Katsina clicked her tongue, and a sly grin stretched over her face, she knew she had chosen a rock solid crew. On her way out of the bridge she raised her left hand to Marshal, who clapped his own hand into it. Katsina briefly squeezed his fingers before letting go, and making her way down the main hallway.

It was lunch time for the doctors and nurses of the hospital on the upper decks of the ship as they flooded into the main hall of the Behemothis, filling the various cafes and food stalls. The entire ship had heard the news about the Delta Operators by now, and it had already had a negative effect on morale. Katsina noticed that not everyone wanted to say hello, and some even ignored her when she passed.

"*Weird*," she thought, wondering what else she could have done for those affected, but she had no ideas.

Katsina pushed that idea out of her mind, knowing just how capable her crew was for these situations. Instead she continued walking, with her chin up, not letting anyone see that the loss of her crew mates affected her. The sea of white coats was left behind her as Katsina took a left down one of the eight main stairwells that connected the ship's upper and lower decks. The steps, made of solid steel, were lined with yellow and black paint stripes which blended together as Katsina's eyes glazed over. She didn't exactly see the point of them, all the colors ever did was distract her in her step. This led her to remember a time when ships had elevators, and all the problems they caused with gravity and motion sickness; this made her grateful for the stairwells. On the next floor, Katsina passed the barracks of her ship on Deck C, various crew quarters and housing for everyone aboard. Walking down what could easily be called a street on a spaceship, she noticed a warm light flickering on a yellow wall, a candle. She stopped for a moment, looking at the crew quarters name tag.

"Aaron." She said out loud, taking a step back. He was a popular but nervous engineer that she had learned to respect. He was a talented man, making him a perfect candidate for the mission. She had never been to his crew quarters before, he had always come to visit hers. He was lost to The Deep with the others.

The candle light, though out of place this deep in space, was a kind sight to see. It's open flame provided respite, a moment for Katsina's absent thoughts to cease. She glanced around the corner of the wide corridor to see that there were more of them, candles at every other doorway.

"*A Memorial,*" she thought, making a mental note to personally thank whoever arranged it.

Katsina continued her walk towards the ship's port bow housing, where her own quarters were located underneath the dome of the bridge. She arrived at her door, a heavy piece of orange painted steel decorated with her captain's insignia, which matched the one on her affix. Katsina plugged into the entryway, and the door slid open for her to enter. In a large room made entirely of tempered glass plating there was a bed, kitchen, bathroom, dining table and chairs, just about every modern stylish convenience a captain would need on a ship. The glass wasn't transparent, but instead it slowly changed colors from a pale white to pumpkin orange. If Katsina wanted to see outside from her bedroom floor, she would turn the glass lights off, but she saw enough of space every day, and opted for the comfort of the lights instead. On the walls around the bed were framed pieces of paper, commendations, graduate degrees, and so on.

The recognition of her achievements were the only things Katsina really liked to decorate her room with, as it really wasn't a personal space for her. In reality, her personal space was in her fighter because nobody was allowed there but her. She could have had the same rule for her quarters, but she didn't care for the room enough. It was tidy, as always, apart from an old ragged teddy bear that sat on her pillow in her bed. It had brown fur, wearing a red t-shirt that had the word "Riley" written across it in cursive. It was the only other thing that she took with her onto the Behemothis other than her fighter ship, and a slightly bent small scale model of the USS Enterprise E on her bedside table. Almost everyone had a Riley bear as a child; even more had model spaceships, but very few adults had either. Katsina was one of those few. Even though her Riley bear didn't walk and talk like it used to, she still kept it. Even though the model ship was from a bygone era of optimistic science fiction, she still kept it. On the other side of her bed was Katsina's helmet, which she snatched up before leaving again.

The Tarmac whirred with the sound of engines and the clattering of tools as Katsina walked across it towards her ship. The Amber Eyes wasn't fully specced for a spaceflight, but she didn't care. In fact more and more throughout the course of the day Katsina found herself caring less; her thoughts growing apathetic as she wondered who could be responsible for what had happened. She held her head up, nodding to any and all who greeted her as she passed the myriad of fighter ships lined up to launch into space. She clanked helmets with one or two in solidarity, noticing the somber expressions many of them had from the mornings news. Towards the back of the hanger something louder than any spaceship engine was going off, and it sounded angry. Before Katsina even made it to her side, she was already smiling at the sound of Rutheo's voice.

"What do you mean you lost it? Is that some kind of joke I'm not getting? Is it a spacer thing? Or a terran thing?"

"What's going on, Rutheo?" Katsina asked, ducking under the wing of her ship to find two pairs of legs protruding from the hatch of her Amber Eyes.

"Oooooh, now you're in trouble Marty," a small, but angry voice echoed. "Wait till she sees *this*."

Out of the hatch of the fighter ship came a short girl wearing a set of blue and orange overalls, typical Behemothis colors. With her brown hair in a messy bun and just about every inch of her pale skin covered in dirt or grease, Rutheo stood only five foot seven inches compared to the average 6 foot 6 of anyone else her age. Rutheo had a toothy smile, one that could knock a person down if they saw it on a good day. Her eyes, though brown like almost anyones, had a distinct resemblance to the blend of coffee that Katsina liked the most; they were darker than any other. Her pale white skin was what really set her apart from the rest of them as the average person would jump at the sight of her in a dark room. Ivory would be an understatement for Rutheo, in fact, any description would be an understatement for Rutheo. For she was a lot more than words could handle.

"You're not going to believe this. Martin over here can't seem to find the only t'sßolu'ou thing I own in your ship," her thick Celtic accent bellowed in Katsina's direction.

"The coffee machine?" Katsina asked.

"Exactly!" Rutheo said, flailing her arms about her head.

"Come on, Ruthie, I swear I was just cleaning the thing. I didn't throw it away or anything," Martin's voice called from inside the Amber Eyes. Rutheo looked up at his dangling legs, a streak of lividity in her eyes. She snatched her hand onto Martin's foot, and pushed him into the hatch, causing him to land the hard way on the floor of the ship inside.

"It's Lieutenant Rutheo McHugh to you!" she said with a huff.

"Well that's definitely going to help him find it," Katsina said, eyebrows raised.

"Don't you start. Kat, it's the twenty-ninth century, everyone and their mother, and their mother, and theirs, drinks coffee. It's been a human tradition for well over two thousand years. So if we're going out there after the bastards that got Aaron then I'm bringing the faisaheßul coffee machine."

"I'm not starting, I installed the coffee machine in the aft compartment above the first aid kit," Katsina said calmly, with a sly grin. Rutheo's face shifted, and she let out her own smile upon finding out where her precious little machine was.

"You didn't," she said, showing her perfect teeth.

"I did," Katsina grunted as she lifted herself into the Amber Eyes. "Come here, I'll show you."

"Oh yeah, now we're talkin'. Marty you're off the hook for now, I'll catch up with you after," Rutheo said happily.

Martin made his way awkwardly out of the airlock on the opposite side of the ship, taking care to avoid Rutheo's rambunctiousness as he did. The inside of the Amber Eyes had been completely remodeled since Katsina had taken command of the Behemothis, but it still reflected everything about her. From the colour scheme, to the computer system, the fighter ship was all Katsina. On the bow hung two chairs over the clear glass nose cone that Katsina had installed just a few hours earlier, one directly behind the other. From the ceiling hung a series of cables, each with a different color piece of tape wrapped around the jack dangling on the end. The interior itself was lit by a series of orange LED lights lining the floor and roof panels, which gave the ship a warm, welcoming glow throughout its cylindrical space. Each section of the ship's body was connected by massive inter-locking ball bearing rings. Katsina dropped her helmet into her seat, and pulled the hatches shut with a clank. Rutheo had already lunged to the aft section behind her, and ended up letting out a moan at what she saw.

"Kat, this thing is so high up, you could have put it in this section the other way around," she said, stretching her hand towards the small machine in the wall.

"Well I had to make a call. Do I make the medkit your height or the coffee machine your height? I'm the captain after all, had to make an example for health and safety," Katsina said, teasing Rutheo.

"There's health and safety, but there's also health and sanity. I'm pretty sure coffee falls under your five-a-day anyway so really I think y-"

"Five-a-day is a twentieth century myth Rutheo," Katsina said, picking up a cup and tossing it in the short girls direction. Rutheo scoffed, and held out her hand to take the second cup from Katsina.

"You boot her up, I'll make the joe. Coffee is engineer's work."

Katsina left her to her musings, and opted for the chance to have another coffee made for her. Rutheo pulled a large red toolbox across the floor of the module to use as a step while making the warm brew. Katsina returned to her seat at the nose cone, which was frosted with an orange tint for their privacy, just like her bedroom. She noticed a small imperfection in the glass, a grease smudge of some kind. Dropping to one knee, tutting with irritation, she ran her finger over the smudge.

"Brand new and no one can keep it clean for a single day," she thought.

Her chair was probably the only thing Katsina hadn't had stripped from the inside of the ship since she brought it aboard the Behemothis with her. It looked ragged, with wear on the leather armrests, and a large scorch marked hole just above the point where her right shoulder would rest. It was a remnant of the last time she took the ship out to the theatre, and she liked having it there to remind her. Katsina let out a sigh, and ran her fingers over her shoulder, feeling the small bumps along her skin. An old ache still sat there, weighing on her upper arm. It was annoying at times, but still not as annoying as having the Amadellan flu. Katsina climbed into her chair, and pulled a cable down from the ceiling. She closed her eyes, leaving only her HUD in her sight, and slipped the cable along the back of her neck until she felt the satisfying magnetic pop of the port behind her right ear.

"Time to wake up," she whispered.

The display in her eye blinked and multiple new menu options appeared on her interface. The ship let off a soft hum behind her and a vibration ran up her back, letting her know that it still had another fight left in it. The humming began to grow and the vibration gave way to a ferocious roar from the engines as Katsina opened her eyes. The orange tinted frost had cleared and through the glass Katsina could see the tarmac in front of her, as well as all the other fighters ready to launch. The strip was almost devoid of people, apart from two spacecraft handling officers who were directing ships into their positions for launch. Katsina wrapped her fingers around her flight controls, feeling the ship breath with her. Whatever she was about to face outside, she was ready.

"She doesn't start half bad huh? You think that wing will hold up?" Rutheo said, holding a mug out to Katsina over her shoulder.

"Not bad at all, she can fly with three. You ready for this? Oh, that's hot," Katsina said, taking the coffee from her.

"Ready as I'll ever be, 'snot my first fight and I'll be bolloxed if it's my last," Rutheo said with a scoff.

"You think with how long we've been working together, that we would have been on a fighter mission before now," Katsina mused before taking a sip of the hot coffee.

"What with you being a captain and all now, I didn't expect you to ever crawl into one of these things again. So, I guess I'm happy I have the chance now, before you become a rear admiral."

"Rear admiral huh? Let's see if we can get to Delta first, ha."

"Right... yeah." Rutheo's voice dropped at the prospect of what they had to do that evening, prompting Katsina to rotate her chair to face her. The normally smiley girl had grit her teeth, staring at the floor with a glimpse of fear in her eyes. She lost someone as well, everyone had, and everyone was coping differently. Before Katsina could say anything, a communications request popped up in her HUD, it was from Marshal. Katsina thought of ignoring it, but instead accepted the link.

"Evening Katsina," he said, his voice in no way as kind as it normally was. "I'm about to give the briefing, is there anything you want me to add?"

"Not for now. Go ahead, we're ready when you are." Katsina said, rotating back to face the rest of the ships before her.

"Alright, but before I do, I have to tell you Kat; You don't have to go out there by yourself and get them. You're needed here."

"I'm not out here alone, we've already talked about it."

"Fine, I don't know what I could have said to convince you anyway."

The link went dead for a moment, and Katsina waited for the briefing to load in her HUD. It was simply a short speech from Marshal along with accompanying documents and required reading for the spaceflight. Katsina opened the document, and listened to it using the auditory implants in her ears.

As you are all aware, this morning we learned that Delta squadron was found, and defeated by a superior enemy force while searching for the Space Cruiser Roverdendrom. Your mission is to find and retrieve any and all remains of those missing, as well as follow the flight path of the Roverdendrom to where it was last seen in the event horizon of the supermassive black hole marked on your star maps. The deep sector is dangerous, and the evidence says that there are enemy ships within it. Keep your wits about you and come home. Ride the lightning.

The briefing ended, and Katsina heard the engines of the other fighter ships growl ahead of her, eager to fly.

"Ride the lightning," Katsina thought, as the handlers signalled the first ship to launch.

One by one, in front of her and Rutheo, the fighter pilots and engineers of Beta squadron drove their ships at incredible speed out of the hangar door at the end of the strip. The boom that erupted almost instantly from the fighters as they broke the sound barrier was deafening, but that was if one didn't have the auditory implants to allow them to process it. As the fighters passed through the atmospheric shield that held the pressure of the tarmac stable, Katsina contemplated Marshal's words. Was it best for her to stay behind? What if the Yggdrasilians took another swing at her people? Soon it was Katsina's turn to fly, the Amber Eyes being the only ship left on the tarmac. It was about time she slipped on her helmet. She leaned forward, gripping to the controls of her ship, linking the focus of her computerised mind with its inner workings. She became one and the same with the technology.

"Mobilize," Katsina said, inciting her ship to leap from its place above the ground.

The Amber Eyes shifted and folded about her, her own seat dropping a few centimetres from the ceiling, adjusting to her weight as the gravity of the ship slipped behind her. Katsina was thrown back in her helmet, and her heart erupted in her chest at the sensation of being fired like a speeding bullet from the barrel of the biggest canon in the universe. It was a sensation she would never tire of, one would never forget. In seconds, the tarmac bled away in her vision as the hangar exit grew larger in her framed view. Without her eyes having a chance to adjust, Katsina was thrown into complete darkness, apart from the flickering lights of the ship's and stars in front of her. The Behemothis was already a hundred kilometres away, waiting on the edge of the Deep, and it was only getting further.

"Alright everyone, let's get into a series of V formations. I want a lead team to fan wide and keep us posted." Katsina said over the squadron wide comm link.

"Aye captain."

"Taking point."

"McCauly, you always take point! Let someone else do it for a change!"

Enthusiasm and healthy comradery were the responses that rang across the quantum waves, music to Katsina's ears. Flying sent a shiver of excitement up her spine like nothing else, and flying in a team was even better. She watched the other fighters promptly form into their own V wing formations around her. To her it was a beautiful sight to see, ships riding the waves of empty space around them, swimming in the stars.

"It's like Tír Ná nÓg," Katsina heard from behind her.

"What was that?" she called back.

"Nothing, Kat, it's an Irish thing, so it is," Rutheo said with a chuckle.

It was the first in a long time she had been in space, or at least in space on what wasn't the equivalent of a small moon.

"Yeah I get it, I should teach you some Niger-Congo, my ancestors spoke that," Katsina chirped.

"Ha, as far as I remember only one of our languages isn't dead, pal. Irish is spoken across all the four pillars. Besides I thought you hated ancestry."

"Out of tradition only. You think t'ßiensorta would have fully taken over by now. Communicating the old way feels awkward," said Katsina.

"Computer generated purpose built languages can't stand up to the naturally developed real thing. Speaking of awkward, heard your setting Sarah up with the Commander. Hilarious," Rutheo said.

"What's funny about it?"

"I thought you were going to put a word in for me is all," Rutheo joked, "she *is* from my department. You could say I would have liked you to make a queer-y"

"That was an atrocious attempt at gay humor, but I loved it so you get a pass. Ruthie, when have you ever had trouble getting a date?"

"Oh yeah, your right I guess. Sarah's pretty though," Rutheo said, her words quieting to a whisper.

"You okay?" Katsina asked.

"Yeah, just thinking about something old Howard was saying to me last week. You ever hear of that ship that went missing on Yggdrasil all those years ago?"

"The Leviathan class one? The World Discoverer?" Katsina asked.

"Yeah, that one. Howard said that it could still fly, and

it was big enough to be a city in space. Here look at this article," she said as a message popped up on Katsina's HUD.

Katsina opened the link to an article from the archives aboard the Behemothis, and glanced at it's contents.

> Of all the treasures lost to the depths of the galaxy, none were as tragic as the loss of The World Discoverer The last of three Leviathan class ships, the only three to exist. The ship had been dry docked and declared a historical preservation site in 2778. While the other Leviathan class ships were decommissioned and recycled, "The World Discoverer" remained in dry dock until its mysterious disappearance in 2810.

The article spanned hundreds of pages, and contained endless conjecture on the fate of the lost ship. Katsina closed it, finding it uninteresting compared to flying her ship. She heard Rutheo sigh behind her. For Rutheo it was a fun mystery that they could talk about while flying, but to Katsina it was just another piece of history that wasn't as important as finding out what happened to her people.

"Howard likes telling ghost stories, Ruthie. Don't let them distract you," Katsina said, keeping her eye on her drift and roll functions.

"I was just thinking; where could a ship like that hide? We have telescopes all over our solar systems and the redemption wheel. The only place we can't see into is The Deep. What if th- what the hell is that?" she said, her voice morphing from thoughtful to alarmed.

"What's what?" Katsina asked, checking her screens.

"Emergency comm link from Marshal, putting it on you HUD."

Katsina looked down in confusion at her HUD to see a small red light blinking on her interface, it was Marshal, on a secure distress line. Katsina's heart dropped and she immediately blinked to open the commlink.

" ...epeat I repeat, all stop. Incoming vessel on sensors.

Katsina I repeat, all stop you have a vessel incoming at intersolar speed..."

"What, wait Marshal what's-"

Before she could finish her sentence Katsina's proximity sensors began erratically beeping and alerting her to an incoming object, something massive on her radar. Faster than a comet, larger than a small moon. It was too big to be deflected by the shielding of her fighter, and it was heading straight for them. If it was going to play chicken with them; they would lose.

"Captain we have incoming, Man O'War class, serial number: MOWSPCA-003x16," Rutheo called ahead, a sliver of panic in her voice, "It's right on top of us. Another Broadsider!"

"All fighters disperse, evasive manoeuvres. Disperse," Katsina immediately said in response. She knew exactly who it was, and she wasn't going to be happy to see him.

Katsina looked to her left to see it arrive, right off her port bow. A massive ship, arriving in a bolt of lighting before her very eyes. The experience of seeing a space carrier arrive out of such incredible speed was jarring to say the least, it could easily make most people space sick. It took the other fighter pilots just a second to move out of the way, but she knew that just another second was all that was needed for them to be swallowed up in the lightning storm that was the ship's arrival. Before her, a wall of metal, hanging from 16 Kugelblitz wheels, was the Man O'War space carrier: Insurmountable. Its size and shape matched the Behemothis in every way, as a sister ship should. It being one of 3 of its kind, the Insurmountable was a terrifying feat of spacecraft engineering. One that, just like the Behemothis, should not be underestimated.

Katsina noticed a blip on her HUD, the only thing catching her eye and ears with the display of sheer recklessness she just witnessed, behind her she heard panting, and before her she saw her ships scrambling in every direction. In all the confusion, she answered the comm request.

"Well well, off somewhere, Katsina?" a sarcastic and scratchy voice said over the short space between their ships.

"Just decided to take a stroll, stretch our legs. What about you? What brings you here, Morann?"

"Ohoho, I'm glad you asked, Kat. I'm here to take you in," the shrill voice said in a cheery tone. "You're wanted as a betrayer to the pillars of humanity. On orders from Admiral Krauss; you and your ship are to return to Terra Botanica to make landfall."

DETAINMENT

Katsina's brow creased against her helmet, and an uncomfortable twist curdled in her stomach. The captain of her sister ship, the Insurmountable, Deacon Morann was a commanding individual. Katsina remembered him from her time before taking command of the Behemothis, and what she remembered was not pleasant. Before her, he was listed with the most medals, the most commendations, and the longest list of confirmed kills in humanity's war with the Yggdrasilians. Katsina stared at the outer hull of the Insurmountable, processing what was just said. Morann was not a friend but also not a liar, in fact nobody had been a liar except the Yggdrasilians for hundreds of years. She had no intention of ignoring the seriousness of his claims.

"I'm going to need to see your command orders and warrants for arrest, Morann," Marshal's voice called over the waves, joining in on their connection. In Katsina's viewfinder came another ship over her left shoulder, arriving on a bed of lightning, the Behemothis.

"Ah, Marshal, good to see you. Thank you for joining us. I have members of the military police on board. They request to dock with Behemothis to relay what you're asking for," Morann said, the sound of triumph in his words. Katsina saw the docking request pop up on her HUD, and glanced back at Rutheo, who was frantically clacking away on an old keyboard.

"You in yet?" Katsina asked in a hushed tone.

"Nearly there. Accessing the satellite array," Rutheo said, "In. We have his communications, downloading now."

"Good, get it to Alice Wesley, tell her to look over the command comm links and to find out if they're legit."

"You think he could be lying?" Rutheo asked.

"Nobody lies, Ruthie, but it's very coincidental that we lose people and then Morann turns up to arrest me," Katsina said, pulling her helmet off of her head and sliding out of her chair, "Behemothis this is the captain, we're coming in. Prepare for landing."

"Aye Captain; the tarmac is yours."

"Good, we can all discuss this in a more civil fashion," Morann said, before disconnecting his link to Katsina and Marshal.

***

In the war room, under the lights of the AR map, which still showed the trajectories of Katsina's lost team. Morann and a team of military police awaited Katsina's arrival, while seated around the table were Marshal and Alice.

Katsina didn't hesitate to make herself known to the faces that watched her enter through the frosted glass door, all faces but his.

"Captain Morann, welcome to the Behemothis," she said, opting to forego pleasantries. "Before we continue I will need to see your warrant document."

Morann, wearing a captain's winter coat, finally turned around. His captain's affix, like Katsina's, rested on his right shoulder. It looked smaller on him than it did on her, his shoulders broader and taller than hers. He was lined and frayed with his age, or perhaps it was the toll the war had taken on him. His dark eyes, almost as black as his pupils, were piercing under any circumstances. The way his face stretched as he grinned to meet Katsina's gaze showed that he rarely smiled. It truly didn't fit him. His short, receding hair was a patchwork of grey and black, complimented by a stubble which met it at his ears. His yellow teeth, lacking any uniformity, appeared behind his thin lips. He held a single key in his hands, a small red item which could be inserted into both a computer and a compatible human's port to share information. He twirled it in his slender, boney fingers, before handing it to one of the burly soldiers next to him. As he lifted his arm, his coat fell open to reveal a brown leather strap across his chest. It held to it an autoholster, and inside of it; a pistol with a golden grip.

    The large man, wearing a band that signified his position as a member of the military police, walked around the table and handed Katsina the key. Already Katsina didn't like the idea of these people on her ship. She made her attitude apparent as she snatched the key from his hands, which were easily the size of her head. Though spaceflight had made the entire human race taller, this man was gargantuan. Most likely the tallest person she had ever seen, he looked to be the captain of the police force. He had one green eye, the other one reassembling a white marble in his other socket. It was surrounded by cellular stitched lines, telling Katsina that at least half of his upper skull was synthetic. It could have been from a war injury, or a voluntary tech upgrade. She didn't want to know. He was menacing to say the least, thought she tried not to judge. He had no hair on his greyish skin, he must have been from the southern hemisphere of Botanica. Where people mostly lived in underwater towns, their skin was a direct result of sunlight that had been filtered through the water. One thing Katsina noticed was a thin silver chain around his neck, and a collection of rings that hung from it. Each ring looked to be part of a set, they all matched the one that was on his finger.

    "No need to be feisty now," he droned. "I'm Captain Rendell Kessler. I'll be in charge of your custody."

    Katsina ignored his comments, and slipped the key into the back of her neck, just underneath her own memory core. A small, almost unnoticeable sound in her ear let her know that the data was loading. It appeared on her HUD, where she selected and opened it. She skimmed the document over, while taking note of Kesslers name and face for future reference. She was more preoccupied by him than the warrant for her arrest.

    "...and due to mounting suspicions of sabotage of your

fellow officers and your ship, you are hereby summoned to a hearing for betrayal of the pillars of humanity..." she read out loud, a grave sound in her voice.

"I'm glad you understand. You see, you were the only ship assigned to retrieve the Roverdendrom. The Ygg's found out about that operation, and over sixty people have been killed, as well as the Roverdendrom not being retrieved and instead lost in a singularity in The Deep. There are very few people who knew about your assignment."

"This is a farce. The Ygg's were expected to be in the theatre. Why suspect a decorated individual to commune with the enemy?" Marshal asked, in awe at what he was hearing.

"There are doubts among the Admiralty Board as to whether or not she should have been assigned this ship at all. Many are of the opinion that she's bitten off more than she can chew. Not to mention the rising belief that we have a spy in our midst," Morann mused, waiving his slender fingers about himself as he spoke.

"*She* has a name," Rutheo barked. "You think you're being funny coming in here? We've all lost people, good people, and you want to throw accusations at the Captain?"

"Enough Ruthie," said Katsina before thinking to herself; *"She'll get in trouble speaking to him like that."*

"Oh well look at you, plucky. I like that," Morann said. "Perhaps Commander Kessler could teach you a thing or two about knowing your place."

"The Behemothis is to rendezvous with the hospital ship McCambridge in two days, we can hardly make landfall and make it back in time," Marshal said, in an attempt to diffuse the situation. Rutheo and Morann didn't break eye contact.

"The Insurmountable will remain here to aid in the restock of the McCambridge. And meet us on Botanica before your hearing ends," Morann responded.

"I thought you were here to take me in, Morann? Why wait here?" Katsina pointed out.

"Oh no, no you misunderstood. The Insurmountable will remain. I however," his gaze finally lifted away from Rutheo and fell to Katsina, "am taking over command of the Behemothis and returning you to Terra Botanica."

Morann sidestepped around Rutheo, catching her shoulder with his as he went. Kessler took up his position in front of Rutheo, a judgemental look on his face as he stared her down. He was bigger than her, but Rutheo didn't break eye contact. Katsina knew what was coming, and stood resolute at Morann's approach. He raised his left hand, and unclipped the affix on her shoulder, ripping it from her possession.

"Katsina Lucas you are hereby stripped of your rank and shall be held in a confinement cell until sentencing before military council. You will not wear your Affix going forward unless your rank is restored. It will be returned to you upon release from confinement, but you will not wear it. Do you have any words to add in this regard?" Morann commanded, the official jargon of her arrest reeking in his tone.

"Yes, for the record," Katsina said plainly, holding her shoulders back and her chin high. She refused to look at Morann any longer.

"Speak now, then."

"In a search for the Roverdendrom, one of our squadrons blipped through space without generating any thrust in their engines. Something else moved them. The Ygg's must have something new. A technology we don't know about. That technology killed members of my crew and I'm going to find it".

"Ha, alright then, be dramatic," Morann said, while Kessler sidestepped Rutheo and approached her with a set of handcuffs.

Katsina kept her eyes on the map over her head, the black hole at its center, along with the last coordinates of the Raptor's Claw. The small red dot, orbiting the singularity forever before falling in, burning to cinders under the strain of its power. Through the image she could see the immovable expressions of horror on Marshal and Rutheo's faces as the MP restrained her and uninstalled her heads up display drive from the back of her neck, as well as her communications implant. Without them her detailed view of everything she was used to seeing fell away, the signals dancing about the ship, the date and time, her messages, bodily status, and everything else to do with herself and her work that she was almost dependent on seeing every day. The room fell into obscurity, the detail she had once seen in every small thing taken from her. Her hands had been restrained, stopping her from running her hand over the back of her neck, the sensation of having an implant removed being more uncomfortable and itchy than she remembered. She wished she could scratch it. Above all, drenched in the blue light of the war room, Katsina finally felt her sickness taking its toll on her.

***

The days weren't long. In fact they were only slowed down when Katsina ate. Otherwise she exercised enough to knock herself down for half a day, sleeping as much time off as possible to avoid the flu she had truly fallen ill to. It travelled down her body, moving from her head and nasal to her ears and throat, before it finally arrived in her lungs. The cough was the harshest part; it kept her held down from exercising properly, causing her to gasp wildly more than once a day. She was allowed a visit to the hospital twice, where a kind nurse named Kara gave her a supply of three medicated implants to slot into her medical support ports on her lower back, each doing its own work to fight the illness. Other than that, she had no contact with anyone. The confinement bay on deck 36 was empty apart from Katsinas cubicle, in fact she was the first person to ever be confined aboard the Behemothis since its construction. This irony was something she contemplated each day, before doing her morning stationary jog. The cell itself was a rectangular black box, with a single round hole in the wall large enough to fit a person, the hole was padded, and contained a shelf for any personal effects or books one would request, not that anyone really read books after humanity stopped printing them. Katsina, however, appreciated books, and preferred reading them over having a tablet in her hands, or a display in her eyes. Therefore, the only thing in her cell that wasn't Black was a book she requested. It was a thick slab, with a red leather bound cover and a gold printed text on the front. "A History of Law in The New Solar Systems Vol. XVII" was not a particularly exciting read, but it did give Katsina something to fall asleep to when she was bored beyond reprieve. She would have listened to her own personal library, or even played music in her ears. But without a HUD implant, a person has no interface to interact with, leaving a lot of her personal media out of reach.

    Confinement itself wasn't actually confined, it was an open and well lit space, far from what prisons and brigs aboard ships used to look like hundreds of years ago. The space was ample and modular; Katsina had everything she needed apart from human contact. The guard at the door was a member of the military police, but luckily not a member of the team Morann had brought with him. His name was Hann Mao, a tall man of Asian descent with an entire cultural history tattooed to his body. He was assigned to the Behemothis on launch day. His uniform bore a pin that noted him as a distinguished Lieutenant Junior Grade. He also wore on his Affix the Horizon medal of honor. Something Katsina didn't even have. He was a good man by known standards. The only thing stopping him speaking to her now, was the law he was tasked with keeping. The only time he could interact with her was if Katsina was to make a request or if he was ordered to. One day he found a way around this rule by deciding to begin reciting the rise and fall of the Japanese super powers in his personal diary. This meant that, when Katsina wasn't exercising or sleeping, she could listen to him. She appreciated his efforts, but it did slow the time down a little, keeping her awake more and more each evening.

At least the sickness was passing and she wasn't left to her own thoughts. More and more each day she appreciated Lieutenant Mao.

The journey to Terra Botanica was made at intersolar speed, the fastest any ship could go. A ship at this speed could cross the Sol system in just an hour. But for going between star systems, it took more than a week. Before the latest ship propulsion techniques, which were developed after the beginning of the war, the same trip would have taken months. The war seemed to prompt a technological race between the Yggdrasilian people and the rest of humanity. A race which the rest of humanity was winning, albeit just by a hair. Had the planet Yggdrasil not begun the first human war in centuries, humanity would have most likely remained complacent in regards technological advance. Like on an old ocean cruise ship, traveling on the Behemothis was like not traveling at all. Inertial dampening fields lining the interior of the ship's hull helped the entire ship sleep while it hurtled itself across space. The hum of the walls always made her contemplate the physics that were at play. She remembered a famous quote by an ancient spacecraft scientist that worked on the first ever Kugelblitz drive; "After the completion of my machine, there will be only two things in this universe faster than the human race; Light and Guardians who we will one day reach." Katsina was fond of that quote, but couldn't remember what year the scientist, Lintang Sartika, had said it. Katsina began to regain strength to spite her flu, which was something she counted on before meeting the Admiralty. These people were to decide her fate and the last thing in her mind that she needed was the cough of a century. 'A severe chest infection' was what she was told by the doctor the day before, no longer a flu. She could deal with a cough. It wasn't the worst thing; it was the brain and muscle aches of a flu that really annoyed her.

It was the last day of her confinement, and someone finally came to visit. To her dismay, it wasn't a friendly face. Morann wasn't one to be casual, every action was calculated to be theatrical, even his entrance to a room. Katsina heard him before she saw him, and felt it best to maintain composure, instead of ignoring him and continuing to read her law book. He appeared before her with Kessler behind him, the hulking man framing Morann in her eyes.

"Trying to find a loophole before sentencing are we?" Morann said, his voice slightly muffled by the glass separating them. Katsina closed her book, and stood to attention.

"No, just passing time," Katsina said.

"Why is that? Are you lonely?" he asked, leaning on one foot and inspecting his nails as he spoke. Katsina glanced towards the door, and saw that Hann Mao was no longer at his post.

"No, I just like to read. Why? You want some company that isn't a walking mountain?"

"Captain Kessler is excellent company," he said, a splinter of annoyance in his mouth. "I also like a good story, and you know I can't wait to read the ones that will come out after all this is over."

Katsina began to feel warm, a flush of anger heating her neck and cheeks. Behind her back she tapped the tips of her fingers off her thumbs, counting the impacts. Morann tutted, and stepped back and forth in front of her cell, clicking his heels off of the black wooden floor.

"Hmmm, stubborn you are. Just like on the Alia moon, eh?" he egged.

"I don't understand your insinuation," Katsina replied, preferring to focus on her breathing instead of her conversational etiquette. She was providing the bare minimum, which was less than Morann deserved.

"You don't? Oh come on, you won us an entire theatre, remember? The medals you got? The promotion to captain? Everything you have? This ship?"

"Captain, I do not understand the question," Katsina repeated.

"You refused a retreat order that would have spared the

lives of thousands of people, and instead gambled the entire third fleet off of the assumption that the Yggdrasilians had little to no munitions left for the engagement. Isn't that right?"

Katsina finally understood. He was attempting to get under her skin, unintentionally agitating himself in the process. Little did he know he had chosen the wrong person to pick this game with. Katsina simply nodded.

"Correct Sir", being her only verbal response. She began to tap her fingers together at a slower pace, slowing her breathing with it. In training she was taught to give as little information in interrogation as possible to a member of the enemy forces, though Morann was not a member of the Yggdrasilian war effort, he certainly wasn't her ally.

"Why the hell does this guy have it out for me?" she thought, the question was hard to answer, she would have to pry it out of him. But that meant giving him the interaction he wanted, instead of forcing him to pull teeth, which she enjoyed making him do more.

"In your report you detailed your decision as follows," Morann said, his eyes glancing upward to look at his own HUD, "'it was well known that Yggdrasilian warships have limited capacity for EMP rods and tungsten pellet reserves, and instead were designed for structural integrity and expansive shielding along the outer hull to prevent broadside and boarding. We were cornered on the southern hemisphere of the moon, and the Yggdrasilian forces could have won the day. Upon hearing their own threat to 'destroy the remnants of the third fleet should the allied forces not retreat', it was clear to me that they were low on rounds to fire, opting to bluff instead'. Well, well, what a gamble you made."

"A calculated and reasonable assumption," Katsina added, keeping her gaze on a single point on the glass. "Ygg ships schematics are common knowledge; it was easy to extrapolate that they were unable to finish the fight. If they could have killed what was left of us, they would have."

"Your refusal to follow a direct order by a superior officer was overlooked in light of your 'reasonable assumption'," he said, making quotation makers with his hands.

"As far as I remember you were on the moon that day too. I don't remember seeing you in the trenches with the rest of us though. Maybe you weren't on Knife's Edge, manning ground-to-space rail guns in the face of certain death. You already have my report; why ask about it now?" Katsina said, deciding to confront him directly, but still not looking.

"Why? Oh, no reason really, I just was curious about it. I understand it was the first time you got many people killed and got away with it," Morann said, before turning on his heel to leave the confinement bay, "This time though, it looks like your luck ran out. You won't be getting away with it this time. We make landfall in the morning, don't sleep in."

"Morann," Katsina called out, making him pause at the door, "my fighter was shot down that day, I had a pellet wound the size of a golf ball in my chest. That wound was my excuse to not fight back that day; what was yours?"

Morann didn't look back, which worked in Katsina's favor. He and Kessler had left her alone. She finally fell back into her alcove in the wall, trying to stifle the coughs she had held back the entire time. Morann had almost won his attempt to make her lose her cool. Had she not been ill, he would have had no chance. Katsina shook, partly from the coughing, partly from the anger. She had never met someone who had criticised her so badly for what had happened that day.

"What in the name of ßolfé is up with that dude?" she thought while regaining her breath.

The coughing was overwhelming, causing her eyes to well up. After gasping one last time, she stood up and wiped her brow, glancing around the corner to see if Mao was back at his station. He wasn't, instead there was a member of Morann's entourage sitting, staring into the distance.

"Probably watching a movie or something, lazy bastard."

Katsina circled her cell, walking off any frustration left,

before dropping to the ground to perform as many push-ups as it took to make her fall asleep again. She'd had enough of the day, and began to hate the confinement deck.

***

On the southern hemisphere of Habitable Biome 002: Terra Botanica, on the continent of New Amir, in the port city of Los Ange, Katsina was being escorted down a hallway in the planetary council building. An important political and economic meeting place where the three major powers conversed over the fate of mankind. First, the Religion of the t'ßolfél, a church which spanned across the four planets, uniting man's belief systems into one faith that incited humanity to search the stars for a coveted alien species known as the all seers, the Orchestrators of The Universe. Secondly, the Military, a more relevant power since the beginning of the war and the most important leg in man's trifecta of organisation focusing on defense against the Yggdrasilians. Third and finally, the Government, a collection of ministers, elected representatives, and continent leaders who managed the socioeconomic development of human culture. Katsina had only been in the building once before; it was to receive a medal for what she had done on the Alia moon. This time around, she feared she would be stripped of that medal and disgraced in front of humanities three respected institutions.

Katsina was being led to a smaller court chamber in the hands of Kessler, away from the eyes of paparazzi and other onlookers who had gathered in the building's atrium. She opted not to look around her, and instead focused on the steps she took, counting them. Eventually the corridor led somewhere, a room which was well lit, but poorly painted. The Admiralty Court room was beige.

"Of all colours," Katsina huffed. The tables and chairs, as well as the podiums at which the council members sat, were classically fashioned. Court and government furnishings seemed to stop changing after the twenty-first century. Another example of heritage. The council podium was a semicircle which ran around the outer wall of the room, while in the concave middle, were two tables, one for the defense and another for the prosecution. Between them was a podium at which a chosen witness would stand to speak, while behind it, stretching upwards to meet Katsina's feet; was the rest of the auditorium which was already bustling with hundreds of people.

"*Well faisaheß,*" she thought.

Katsina let Kessler lead the way through the crowd, not wanting to make eye contact with anyone. Most were probably there to watch it go down without caring one way or the other. The stretch of time it took her to reach her allocated seat at the defense table was an uncomfortable and seemingly never ending experience. The entire room smelled of old paper and injustice, every surface looked freshly dusted, the chamber had probably never been used. The voices and sounds of shuffling feet reverberated off of the chamber wall, elevating the noise to an irritating volume. Katsina glanced down at her hands, which were held together by the set of magnetic cuffs clipped to her wrists. The cuffs were simply two slender oval shaped beads, which could be programmed to magnetically hold two or more objects together indefinitely. Had Katsina wanted to try and escape the two cuffs holding her hands together, Kessler could simply think of them getting tighter and they would obey. It would have been a bloody mess.

A somewhat peaceful chime sounded throughout the chamber, and the room began clattering about to their seats. The sound of chairs scraping and the heat of the room increasing gave Katsina enough to be irritated about, that was until she saw the line up of the Admiralty. The board itself was made up of six Fleet admirals, each with a companion captain. The group of twelve people represented half of the third fleet's command. The Behemothis belonged to the third fleet, meaning that if the court was convened to penalise anyone else, Katsina would have been on the board with her own admiral. But it wasn't Katsina up there, it was Morann who entered the room. Katsina didn't take her eyes off of him and his companion officer, both talking in a hushed tone as the board took their seats in the row above. He was Fleet Admiral Stanislov Krauss, the man whose presence confirmed that the rest of the Admiralty was of no importance. He was thin as anything, sickly pale from his time as admiral. Dressed in his formal black coat adorned with medals and a golden chain bearing the symbols of the Guardian race. His shoulder Affix glistened in the light of the room. It had the most prongs of any that existed while medallions detailed with symbols of the t'sßolfél faith hung from its base down his biceps. His age was sewn into the wrinkles around his eyes, his nose. But it could be seen in the fingers more than anything else, a brown canvas of skin pulled tightly over a rigid and bulbus set of knuckles. Katsina had known him for most of her life, but each time she returned to Botanica he was staggeringly older. The gravity of the planet aged him much faster than other admirals who served in space. Though they at one stage served on the same ship, with the same rank; Stanislov Krauss simply aged faster.

"*Time Dilation,*" Katsina thought.

Katsina wrinkled her nose at the idea of someone like Morann on the board, someone who had something against her. What it was that he had against her, she was yet to find out, making her huff under her breath. She glanced to her left at the prosecution table, where no one sat, and then to her right, where no one was sitting with her, the only person in her immediate personal space was Commander Kessler. She peered around the room, looking for at least one supporter, before she found Marshal and Rutheo. Both were in their dress blacks, sporting the golden pin of the Behemothis. Marshal gave her a curt nod once she met his gaze. Rutheo, as enthusiastic as ever, waved her hands above her head and threw Katsina a set of finger guns. Katsina couldn't help but snicker at Rutheo's antics, but she had laughed at an inopportune moment, the court had quietened down as she went into a fit of laughter.

"This hearing is now in order, when you are ready to join us, Miss Lucas." Krauss boomed, in a commanding tone that rang with the impatience of a teacher in an imperial school. Katsina straightened herself, coughing through the laughter. In an attempt to gain back her composure she closed her eyes, breathing slowly to prepare herself.

"Ahem, my apologies, Admiral," she said.

"I'm sure you understand the situation, and why you are here?" he asked. The court had fallen completely silent.

"Yes," Katsina said, reigning herself in to prepare for the confrontation at hand.

"Then, why must you laugh? Do you think the accusation of military negligence, or worse, betrayal is a laughable matter?" He asked, already framing the questions against her. Katsina, who once found herself sitting next to him in that very spot, realised he was not her aid this time around.

"Fine then," she thought.

"No, I do not. What I do find funny is the fact that you decided to waste valuable time and resources to get me here and accuse me of something I didn't do. What's this anyway? A trial? In a society where we all share and maintain a balance of honest communication and a consensus of history and intelligence. The last time a crime was committed was when the Yggdrasilians started shooting people years ago. Or have you forgotten who the real enemy is?"

The hushed whispers returned to the courtroom in wake of Katsina's comment, which was exactly the reaction she needed. She was known to everyone in the room, and her best chance at a defense was to remind them who she was.

PROCEEDINGS

It had been the longest, most argumentative day of Katsina's life. The hearing itself was easily associated with the pulling of teeth, at least to her. Not a single person could give her the answers she had wanted the entire day, or at least the one answer she really wanted.

"Who the faisaheß is accusing me of this?" she had thought throughout the whole day.

In any other hearing she had ever heard of or read about, it had never worked like this. The board spoke endlessly over the essential seriousness of the crime instead of providing evidence and deliberation of motivations. It was as if honesty, the inescapable aspect of human existence, had been perverted. The admiralty practically suggested that it was because Katsina wanted it to be, giving her the ability to commit a crime.

"How ridiculous," she thought.

No one seemed to want to be reminded that crime practically ceased to exist when humans began to form a consensus by sharing thoughts and experiences for historical record. Of course being the first to commit a crime in a generation would draw a crowd, a jury, a defence, and a prosecutor. But nothing of the sort was present here, apart from the crowd. The admirals didn't seem to listen, they just talked repetitively about a narrative of conspiracy.

"You may now present your defence," Krauss said in an impatient fashion.

Katsina looked up, breaking her hazy dead stare to look about the room at the rest of the board. They all gazed, expectantly, after hours of talking at her, not with her. Katsina slid the chair back as loud as she could, and extended herself to the ceiling in a loud and exaggerated stretch. To Krauss' and the rest of the board's distaste, she let out a loud yawn before clearing her throat.

"Hmmmhm, sorry Admiral," she said, rotating her head around her shoulders, "I'm just a bit out of sorts. The Behemothis has been in the field for months now, out on the edge of The Deep; fighting to keep this planet safe."

"Your point?" another admiral asked.

"No point really, just that it's strange being back on real gravity again. They say you can't tell the difference when you're up there. But you can."

"I fail to see any relevance to what you are accused of," he said.

"Well if you let me speak maybe you'll hear it," Katsina shot at him, causing another bustling of whispers around the circular chamber. The Admiral seemed taken aback, but no retort came from him. Katsina stared at him, eyebrows raised. She tucked her hair behind her ears with both hands, her mouth hanging ajar with contempt. He still had nothing to say, but she didn't break eye contact until he dipped his head.

"As I was saying, the gravity; it's nice to have it back. You can ask anyone who's been off world, even to Horizon or Crescent, and they will tell you they miss the gravity. The feeling of being home. My crew talk about it every day."

"Miss Lucas," Krauss raised his voice, "I ask that you explain your actions preceding and following the loss of the Delta Squa-"

"I'm. Not. Finished." Katsina said, not as calmly the second time, her voice sang louder than his. She noticed Morann leaning over, whispering into Krauss' ear.

"When you're done canoodling," She said, just loud enough to catch the ears of those closest to her. The room fell into snickering, and more whispers.

"Captain Morann attests that you should be allowed to finish your tangent. Though I don't see what the point is. Continue," Krauss said, again in chastisement.

"Why thank you, any more interruption and the uninitiated would assume that this court is in some kind of nineteenth century witch hunt. Any number of people who are scholars of our heritage could see that," Katsina said, glancing about at the lack of defense.

"So, like I said, the feeling of home is special to us, all of us. Ever since we came to the stars and settled these four planets we call home. Botanicans like me who are fighting the Yggs across this pocket of universe are doing it so that we can all come home and feel that again. The ground under our feet. We're doing it for those on Crescent, who can't fight alongside us yet, for the Horizonians, who have lost more than any of us. And lastly, my crew fight for everyone in this room, to try and make a safer galaxy for us all to live."

The room was held silent, she had them. Katsina could muster only a few last words before her mouth would run completely dry, she wished she had a HUD, to help her come up with something better. But this was all she had, and she needed to end it with a punch. She was panting, leaning forward to drive her point home.

"And so, in the name of all those who want to go home, I reject any and all accusations of treason or military negligence and I urge this board to help me put a task group in place to find the weapon that took my squadron from me and send me back out there to finish this war. Because just like last time, it looks like I'm going to have to do the heavy lifting again."

"Preposterous."
"No way."
"She can't be serious."
"The Arrogance."

Just a few of the replies she had gotten to her comments, before the room erupted in argument around her. The Admiralty found it hard to bring the room back to order, especially with Rutheo stirring up support for her captain in the back of the room. It was obvious to Katsina, that the court wasn't prepared for her to muster such support so early in the process, but as far as she was concerned, they had no evidence as of yet. It was a popularity contest so far, and she was prepared to win. It took time for the people to eventually quieten down, but there was a new energy. A call to arms against the idea that Katsina was a traitor to her people. She herself sat down and leaned back in her chair, feeling right at home controlling the situation as if she were in control of her own bridge on the Behemothis. She tilted the chair onto its back legs, balancing herself, a posture of defiance.

"You speak of a weapon that your people encountered in the Deep? What kind of weapon?" onf of the admiralty asked.

"Clearly it's a bid at misdirection. Miss Lucas is using this weapon as a counter claim in her evidence," Morann said, leaning forward to address the admiral.

"Then take it into evidence, Captain Morann, have the Insurmountable investigate."

Morann leaned back into his seat, swapping glares with Krauss before speaking again.

"Aye, Admiral. It will be investigated."

"This hearing is adjourned until tomorrow at ten hundred hours. Adjournment now at Twenty-Seven Hundred and Twenty-Two. Good evening," Krauss growled, unswayed by Katsina's display.

The room began to clear, and Katsina was escorted through a side door by Kessler. The hallway she was being led down was small and quiet, far away from the crowd of support she had just garnered. She didn't mind, instead of her head being down she clocked it to one side, letting herself smile for the first time in a few days. Past the sets of glass doors she could hear the chatter in the other hallway, and wondered if Rutheo was out there, winning more people over for her. Eventually she came to a concrete stairwell, which led down to the hanger that she had arrived in before. On the landing pad sat one of her own ships fighters, and a smaller space shuttle to bring her back to the Behemothis. Back to her confinement for another night. Kessler shoved her towards the shuttle where two military police officers awaited her.

"I'm sure you can handle her, mind you, she's feisty," he said, turning back to the stairwell.

Katsina stood facing two young men, who looked clearly flustered by her presence. They seemed to try to not look at her, and in doing so, did not notice that she was unable to clamber into the raised shuttle while cuffed. She sighed as she walked past them, gearing up to climb aboard the shuttle without the aid of her hands, before a small zapp emanated from the cuffs on her wrists. She had been let free of them. Katsina turned to look at the MP who had freed her, the cuffs rolling around in his hands. He was square jawed, with a typical set of brown eyes and skin like any other northern hemisphere Botanican. His cap was hanging offside a little more than a beret should, revealing the notches in the top of his ears for his implants. Glistening a deep dark coal black against his skin. What Katsina took a moment more to notice, were the droplets on the edge of his eyes, also glistening, revealing a pain she didn't notice before.

"I uh, had a brother on the Alia Moon, he said that if it wasn't for you, he wouldn't have come home," he mumbled.

"What's his name?" Katsina asked, surprised one of them had finally talked to her.

"Jared, his name was Jared. He wanted to serve on your ship, but he was assigned to the Roverdendrom," he said, his head dipping.

"And what's your name?" Katsina asked, reaching inside for her empathy.

"James, uh, I'm James. He said you were a war hero. The best of us."

"Hi James. I'm Kat, and Jared was the best of us too," she said, softly as she could.

"That's what you guys were doing right? You were sent to find him?" James said, holding back tears.

"Yes, we were going to get them," she said, putting her hand onto his shoulder, "and when this is over, we will."

James looked up, and sniffed back the sadness that still seemed fresh for him. A grief stricken person, just like she had seen in Alice a few days before. Katsina kept her hand on his shoulder a moment longer, before gently squeezing it to let go again. She turned to climb into the shuttle ignoring the other MP, who was clearly taken aback by what his superior had done. James and the other one, Portman was written on his badge, followed her in, sitting either side of her. James kept his gaze straight ahead as he clipped into his harness. Katsina felt tired enough to get some sleep on the way back to her ship.

***

The shuttle journey had already taken too long. Katsina noticed that they weren't launching into space, the rocket booster hadn't ignited. Instead they were flying somewhere in the atmosphere. She snapped out of her sleepy emotional state to keep an eye out for the window to her left. The port city of Los Ange was a marvel to look at. Built into the side of a three kilometer high cliff on the oceans edge, it was a particularly unique example of human architecture. The towers that lined the already raised coastline looked smaller than those of other cities around the planet, but only because much of their height was cemented into the rockface. Los Ange was a vertical city, as opposed to the usual horizontal designs of other great cities like Port York on Terra Horizon. A haze hung around the shuttle, allowing Katsina to see only the lights of the city below her and the flashing lights of the spacecraft. A mist had rolled in from the ocean, one that blanketed the region.

"That's a crazy fog tonight," James said over the noise of the shuttle.

"Yeah, been waiting on this one to roll in for a while now. It's probably gonna last a few days now that it's here," said

Portman.

"I forgot what the fog was like," Katsina said, leaning over James to look into the gloom.

"Don't get much out in open space, huh?"

"Not really, apart from gas giants and dense nebulas, we don't really see this kind of atmo. You ever go out there?" she asked.

"No, I'm a boots on the ground type. But if I got assigned to space I would go, I just don't seek it out," he said timidly.

"Space sickness?" Katsina asked.

"Yeah, how'd you know?" James said, a smile cracking on his face.

"I know a former astronaut when I see one," she replied.

"Commander, I think it's time you stop talking to the prisoner," Portman chimed in, causing an awkward pause in what would have been the most pleasant conversation Katsina had all day. She cocked her head to one side, training her eyes critically on Portman.

"I'm sorry, he's your superior and you want to speak to him like *that*?" she said, a low growl emphasising her words.

"Captain Lucas, it's alright, it's against protocol for us to fraternise," James said, in an attempt to de-escalate.

"Fraternise? Woah now. Chasanichennwan t'sai, we don't even use that rule on the Behe-"

"That's enough," Portman said, producing a set of cuffs of his own, and what looked like a lipstick case from his front pouch. "It's bad enough you've been allowed out of your cuffs, I won't allow you to throw your weight around here."

"Oh, okay, tough guy over here. Listen, if you use that sonic inhibitor on me, pal; I will kick your goddamn implants through the back of your head," Katsina said, sliding onto her feet with a malicious intent.

"You will sit down and you will shut up," he said, raising his voice over the jet engine.

"Alright then come on. Make me," she replied, finally losing the patience she had maintained all day. It was in

Katsina's informed and impartial opinion that his implants looked as if they needed adjusting anyway.

"That's enough," James called, stepping between the two. "Soldier you will stand down."

"Or what?" asked the younger man, angry and huffing at being put in place, "What? You're protecting her now? She lost hundreds of us to the Yggs and for what? Her own glory? You heard what she did."

"I'm protecting you, Portman, you ignorant son of a bitch. You think she really willingly killed so many? So she could kill even more? And be named a war hero? And your plan of action was to what? Fight her?" he said, causing Portmans face to turn bright red. "Sit down before she throws you out the airlock. You think I'd be able to stop her if she tried?"

"He's right you know, choose wisely," Katsina said, glancing down at her nails nonchalantly, making a mockery of the young soldier. Katsina remembered being put in her place before; it was uncomfortable, but every young soldier had a similar defining moment of humility.

The rest of the flight went with no issue, but also no conversation. So Katsina didn't get what she wanted in the end, however she did get to keep herself cuff free for the rest of the awkward trip. The fog outside seemed to get thicker as the city fell away into its depth. The shuttle flew into the Highlands behind the cliffs, far beyond the city. Katsina rubbed her jugular, imagining the worst case scenario had the sonic inhibitor been used on her. The device was harmless, but could remove one's ability to vocalise for hours by overriding their vocal cord control implant. A highly uncomfortable, and enraging device for someone like Katsina, who made it a priority in life to use her words as best she could. It was another of humanity's 'humane' weapons, designed to reduce mortal harm in war time. Katsina thought that weapons like the inhibitor were the reason the war had raged for so long.

The darkness thickened and the shuttle began to slow. Katsina considered, albeit briefly, that maybe she had made a mistake by challenging Portman, surely it was going to come up at the overly public procedure being held the next day. She'd spent most of the day seeing little to no evidence against her, instead just list after list of every regulation she had broken before, without a single mention of her achievements and the results of her insubordinate actions. Not five months ago she'd been receiving the height of praise from the Admiralty board, and now none of them even acted as if they knew who she was. She knew the public would remember her. That's all she had to go on considering the political process was to be slanted against her. As she contemplated, Katsina ran her finger over the base of the back of her skull, there a thin metallic strip inside a ceramic frame could be felt. It wasn't cold; like any implant it maintained the same temperature as the body, but unlike other implants, this one was the key to life as humanity knew it. Katsina knew that as long as she had her memory core, the implanted artificial intelligence that merged with her mind as a child, they could never convict her. All of her memories, everything she had ever done or said was kept stored in her core, linked to the quantum network. All she had to do was make them look at it, and see she was innocent. She wondered why they couldn't just skip to that part.

    The shuttle slowed even further, and began to hover over another set of flashing lights, a landing pad. Katsina rubbed her palm over her memory core, and prepared to get out. The noise of the actuators and hydraulic pumps controlling the landing gear began to sound around her, and a gentle thud and scrape bounced her in her seat. The engines came to a quiet hum allowing Katsina to hear a small whirring noise next to her. It was James, holding her handcuffs.

    "I'll have to put these back on now, Captain."

    "Kat, just Kat, no worries, James. Do what you need to do," she said reassuringly, holding out her wrists. The oval beads snapped into shape either side of her wrist, clipping them together.

    "Hopefully these don't give you carpal tunnel, I heard

they're a bitch for that," he said.

"I've had a lot worse than carpal tunnel. I think I'll be fine," Katsina replied with a smile.

The sliding hatch curled open letting fog seep into the compartment. It was cold, and wet upon Katsina's skin. Two soldiers could be seen on the platform in the veil, waiting to bring her inside the facility. James gripped her arm, not to hurt her, but to help her down out of the shuttle. Without a word he and his colleague climbed back into it, sliding the door closed behind them. Katsina was led through the fog away from the landing pad by the other two soldiers, to what looked like a doorway inlaid into a wall of rockface. Behind her the shuttle's engines powered up as it lifted into the sky, a low drone could be heard fading away as it disappeared. Leaving Katsina without an ally to her name once again.

"Well this is ominous," she joked, glancing around her at the two soldiers, "Let me guess you guys are playing the part of the two soldiers at the beginning of Hamlet right?"

No reply came from them, instead they just kept walking, their heavy boots clapping off of the concrete below.

"Tough crowd," Katsina said, feeling a knot curl up in her stomach.

The rock face doors fell into the floor, while a pad protruded up to cover the gap. The brightly lit facility inside was impossible to see through the fog, which made Katsina uneasy about going inside; she didn't know what to anticipate. What would meet her? A prison? Or a holding cell? Katsina braced herself and clenched her fists, feeling a shove of the soldier behind her. Coaxing her to go inside. She had no implants to see or hear anything in the distance. She was unable to make a plan. Her nails dug deep into her palms and she felt flushed. Her breath quickened, and the soldier gave her a great push. She passed through the fog, waiting to fight whatever was ahead of her inside the rocks.

"Captain!" a happy voice cheered, "Jeez, I thought you weren't going to get here at all in that fog."

Katsina tripped and fell into the arms of the voice, someone shorter, and more hot headed than she was. She looked up to see the wild bushy brown hair of Rutheo, her locks hanging from her smiling face.

"What the-"

"I know right?" Rutheo said with a giggle, lifting Katsina up out of her stumble. "It took more than one favour to get you out of having to stay in confinement but hey I put in a few words and sure look. That's it now, so it is."

"Oh you're the one who did this, eh, Rutheo?" a low voice called from down the corridor. The voice had a smooth tone, soft, but the underbelly of a spaceship Commander always came through; no matter how polite he tried to be. It was Marshal. Katsina let out a deep sigh of relief.

"Captain, sorry for the long trip out to the mountains, but I wasn't going to have them take you back up tonight."

"Marshal," she said in awe. She dived from Rutheo's arms to his. "Thank you, but where are we? I thought I was being brought to a base or something."

"Ha, your welcome. Not a base, no. This is my home Kat, and I wanted you here, where I can keep an eye on you."

"And *I* get to congratulate you on ripping the court a new one in just a few sentences! Wow that was awesome. They were trying to smear you with tar and feathers out there, but you were like 'Nope, I'm running the show! you can't handle the truth'," Rutheo said, giddy with laughter.

"That impression is astounding Rutheo, but who are these guys?" Katsina said, poking her thumb at the two military policemen standing by the now closed doorway.

"They're the terms and conditions, armed guards all around while you're under house arrest until the court reconvenes," Marshal explained.

"Great, more the merrier. How did you swing this?"

"I'll tell you over food. You must be starving," he said, throwing his arm over Katsina's shoulder, leading her down the hallway.

"Why not, been on a confinement diet for ages. You better be really cooking, First Officer," Katsina teased.

"Of course I am, we don't have food printers in my house."

"Sweet, love cooked food, haven't had it in ages," Rutheo chimed, catching up with them.

Though she had never been to his home before, Katsina found Marshal's to be nostalgic and comfortable. The entire house was built into a rock face, much like the towers of Los Ange were on the coast. Marshal had his own quarters on the Behemothis display images of marble rock surfaces around him, which turned out to actually be AR images of the walls of his home. Katsina ran her fingers over the smooth surfaces which had speckles of yellow jewels reflecting just under the polish. They were all caked with dust. It looked like weeks of it. Katsina wondered why he hadn't kept up with his chores over his shore leave. He was always a domestic disaster in her mind. The hallways themselves were unnecessarily tall, but felt grand and reminiscent of the halls of the Behemothis. Lining the walls were photos and holographs, depicting many of Marshal's medals and promotional ceremonies, as well as images of the ship's he had served on. One image caught Katsina more than the rest, an old photograph, taken from the eyes of a documentary reporter. It was of Marshal and Katsina, standing at a luminescent table, the light from its surface highlighting their features. On the table below them were AR images of the Behemothis under construction. Katsina grinned at the sight of it; it was a moment she would not easily forget. She was fresh out of the hospital not four days before the photograph was taken. She still had bandages on her neck and her arm was still in a cast. She was sporting her newly awarded Captain's affix, seeing her new ship for the first time. The smile she'd had when she knew she would be able to help humanity win the war with such a machine, and with Marshal at her side, it was the happiest she had been in her career. It felt so long ago now.

Down a set of birch steps they entered a wide open living space, a living room, dining area and kitchen, all in one open hall which glistened with the slight golden yellow hew. The counters and surfaces were all carved out of the same stone, the extravagant chairs adorned with wonderful cushions and blankets. It looked picturesque, making Marshal's home a warm and inviting place. Hovering above their heads were glowing yellow orbs, glowing in the space and giving it the heat it needed. Smart home technology of the time had developed past voice operation, and instead worked with a person's communications implant, making a neural link with a person and their home. One thing that seemed missing, that was common in every home, was a food and drinks printer. In its place, an ancient cooking stove, and a myriad of pots and pans to accompany it hung overhead. The island in the kitchen space had already many types of vegetables and meats littered around it on chopping boards, while something could be heard sizzling away in a pan on the hob. The noise was another nostalgic feeling, and Katsina finally relaxed her shoulders.

"I hope you like Bolognese," Marshal said, stepping around the island to pick up a spatula. "Ruthie, grab that garlic and throw it in there."

"Yah."

Katsina took her time to take in the surroundings. They were so different from the floating city she had been calling home for the last months; she wanted to remember it. It felt good to be on, or in this case, in, solid ground. As perfect as it was, something did not fit in the living room. The real stand out object that didn't match the rest of the yellow and white marbled space, was a large green pine tree, which was decorated to the point of grandeur, with baubles, bows and floating glowing orbs dancing in its branches.

"It's already Nollaig celebration?" Katsina said aloud.

"Yeah, turns out the calendar on the Behemothis was a bit behind, according to the planet's time it's been winter for 2 months," Rutheo said.

"Crazy huh, Kat? Time dilation is a bitch," chimed in Marshal.

"I didn't even think of my gift ideas yet," Katsina mused, "We're gonna have to reset the ship's clocks before it departs again."

"It will be taken care of. She's in dry dock as of an hour ago for some work. Meanwhile half of the crew, apart from who's at your hearing, are on shore leave," Marshal said, getting business out of the way.

"And the lost Delta Squadron's possessions? Have they been delivered to their families?"

"Yeah, the Admiralty board arranged delivery and condolence packages a week ago for everyone but Mara. Heard they were even offering shore leave for other family members in different units as well. Like their splitting up our crew or somethin'," Rutheo said.

Katsina hung her head and remembered Mara's status as a war orphan, no relatives or next of kin. She thought of Mara's other friends, most of them we're on Delta squadron, or in Marshal's living room. She wondered about Mara's possessions, who would they be given to.

"That's just a rumor, Ruthie. That's not a standard protocol," Marshal corrected her.

"I'm just saying. That's what I heard."

"Do either of you think that what they are saying about me is true?" Katsina cut across. Turning away from the glowing tree to look at her shipmates.

Marshal stopped chopping, and glanced at Rutheo, they were both frozen, contemplating their answers. It took more than a moment, which grew longer as Katsina waited to hear what they thought. She knew her ship and crew would be behind her, but after all she had heard that day, something made her think that the worst was happening. Maybe the admiralty we're trying to take the support of her comrades away, making them think she was a bad person.

"You've made brash decisions before, but you never sacrificed the lives of anyone for nothing. You hate our enemy as much as the rest of us. We don't know how the Yggs were able to get to them, but it's not because of you," said Marshal, before picking up the blade and continuing with his vegetables.

"I can't imagine you'd do something to hurt any one of us. You've done some crazy shit, not always to regulation, but never to hurt any of us," Rutheo added, her eyes falling to the floor at the thought of those that were lost.

Katsina noticed a change in tone, and realised she was bringing their reunion downhill. She glanced at the arch leading to the hallway, the back of a soldier could be seen, waiting for her. Before she could encourage anymore dreary conversation, she strode across the room to one of the Kitchen cabinets and began rummaging.

"How about I set the table?" she said, trying to change the subject.

"Look at you, hands on as always," Marshal said with a grin. "Plates and bowls are in that one on your right, and wash your hands."

"Perfect, I'm gonna grab us a bottle of something strong," Rutheo said excitedly, bouncing away from the stove towards a glass display case of bottles.

"Not too strong, Ruthie. We have a witch hunt to attend tomorrow," Katsina said, hoping her dry humor would lighten the mood again.

The pasta wasn't exactly as soft as Katsina would have liked it. In fact in her opinion it was undercooked, but she knew that opinion was wrong. In reality the meal was perfect in every way, even the wine, though sweeter than expected, was perfect. What really made the whole experience was the fact that she was on solid ground, eating real food, with real friends. Not something she expected to be doing while under house arrest on order from the Admiralty board. The callous and unfair court case could wait until tomorrow. Katsina decided to revel in the opportunity to not be a captain for an evening. It was a different experience to see Rutheo and Marshal in such an informal space, even though she had always done her best to be an informal captain while on board. It was just different, and for the better. A warm light orb hovered over the table as the three of them ate, while Marshal boasted about his cooking skills. Rutheo joked at every opportunity, even making a point to make fun of some of Katsina's more embarrassing moments when she was younger. The plates were soon empty and all they had left to do was finish the large emerald bottle. Perhaps it was the Horizonian fruity red wine, or even the freedom of not being in charge of the operation. Whatever it was, Katsina was happy to be there, even under the circumstances.

"Alright, that's it. You two are boring me to death," Rutheo said, jumping up out of her seat. "I'm going to bed."

"Awe come on Ruthie," Katsina moaned.

"How can you call trading card collecting boring?" Marshal said, exaggerating his shock at her words.

"I get it, you collect weird little childrens cards," Rutheo said, stretching her arms over her head, "but seriously I'm knackered. I'll see you guys in the morning."

"Fine be that way, all the more trading card talk for us," Katsina teased.

Rutheo had a stumble in her step as she made her way to the front hall, giggling as she went. Katsina watched her until she disappeared, her long hair the last thing that could be seen as Rutheo turned a corner. It had been more than two bottles of wine by the time the night was coming to an end. Or the morning was coming to a beginning. Katsina didn't care which. It was almost freeing not to have the time and date in her eyelids every minute. Instead of seeing the digital world, she saw things just as Howard the mechanic described them, not as sharp, but a little more real. There was something about using non-augmented eyesight, there were more shadows, and more mysteries behind them. One shadow in particular caught her attention, the one that Marshal's brow had cast over his eyes as he leaned forward.

"She's pretty great," he said, a half cocked grin on his face.

"Yeah she is, good kid," Katsina added.

"Kid? Aren't you two the same age?" Marshal asked.

"Yeah, but time dilation puts us four years apart now. I'm older. But not as old as you are," she teased.

"Oh it's like that?" he said, raising his eyebrows.

"Oh it's like that, Commander Richmond," Katsina said, feeling the tingling sensation of being drunk in her cheeks. "Man that stuff is pretty good."

"The wine? Oh yeah, it's pretty good. For a second I thought you were blushing."

"Me? Blushing? Ha, like you could tell. Why would I be blushing anyway?" she asked.

"I'll let you keep thinking about the answer to that question while I make us some coffee," he said, getting up from the table.

"Oh, is it Bailey's? Please tell me you have Bailey's."

"You know it, Rutheo picked it up earlier today."

Katsina watched him as he made them another drink, her cheeks still burning. She had an uncontrollable smile that very few people had ever made her have. Marshal was one of those people. Katsina rested her elbows on the table, face in her palms, admiring the man she knew she could always put her faith in. Her eyelids hung tired, a yawn escaped her throat, but that didn't stop her from staying up an hour or so longer. Marshal didn't bring up her blushing again, he wasn't lying when he said he would leave her to think about it. It was on her mind as they sat together, talking about everything, and nothing. All but one of the lights in the room dimmed as they spoke. The warm glow of the last orb over their heads encased them in a bubble of yellow, just for the two of them. Katsina didn't remember falling asleep.

SENTENCING

Katsina, though currently being charged as a criminal, thought that if anyone should be arrested it should be the MP Officer who woke her the morning of her third day of trial. It had been three days of nonsense since she landed in Los Ange. Day two had gone just as sluggishly and painfully as day one, with little to no evidence being presented against her. Not to mention her extreme lack of sleep and a head pounding hangover were also at play. The entire second day she heard hearsay, first hand accounts, and the stories of the families who had lost people "because of her". She hadn't bowed her head once, not until she had arrived back to her room at Marshal's home. Never had she accepted personal defeat, but the second day was a very close first time for her, so she slept it off. She had avoided Marshal since the late night they'd had. She touched her hand to her cheek anytime she thought of it, eventually she remembered falling asleep at the table, and being carried to a double bed afterward. She couldn't come up with any ideas on how to talk to him about it. Instead she focussed on the witch hunt.

"You have a court appearance in one hour, Miss Lucas," a gruff voice said, tapping the door over and over.

"Yah, okay, okay," she replied, groaning under the comfort of the sheets, "I just need a few minutes to shower okay?"

"Make it brief."

"Make it brief, pfft. You know it's still *Captain* by the way," Katsina snorted. She couldn't believe the attitude her fellow soldiers and officers had been presenting her with since she had made it home. She'd never wanted to be famous or infamous; she had preferred that people just be as kind to her as she was to them.

"First I'm a war hero and now I'm a war criminal,

faisaheßul bheibhenel," she thought.

Katsina rolled to her left and found her footing on the warm glowing tiles of Marshal's guest room. She had them set to the same orange glow that her windows of the Behemothis had, just for the comfort of the lights. One of the light panels on the wall displayed the mountain range around them, the snowy peaks and jagged curvature glowing in the sunlight of the early morning. Underneath the light panel was an old and rugged piece of furniture, Italian Baroque in its carving style and beautifully restored. It matched the rest of the furniture in the room, and in extension; the rest of the house.

Katsina saw no point in getting into the formal dress jacket and suit pants she'd had printed for the courtroom. That morning she didn't care much at all for what was going to happen, be it a guilty charge or not. No matter what, she knew that it was a campaign against her and not an official proceeding. So she would give it no credence. She reached into her duffel bag, tattered by its many years of travelling with her, and pulled out her jumpsuit to find something more casual. Another knock on her door from the MP. Katsina found a pair of new enough jeans and a tank top, certainly inappropriate enough to make her point to the board. While slipping the tank over her head she caught it on the lip of her empty comm implant port. A slightly uncomfortable tug had her stuck for a moment with her hands dangling over her head. She reached back, trying to undo the snag, while her mind wandered to the idea that she really hated clothes that weren't her uniform, her jumpsuit, or her captain's coat. With a yank in the opposite direction, Katsina pulled the tank back up off of her head and tossed it to the floor while letting her curly locked hair fall down around her shoulders.

Instead of answering the now rapping noise which was nearly taking the door off its hinges, Katsina glanced down at the floor, where her jumpsuit and captain's coat lay, and over on the italian carved table; her affix and goggles. The things she would really need to make an escape attempt, but that wasn't the idea. On the table, next to her usual effects, was her affix. Pulled from her shoulder weeks before. She was told not to wear it again, and she understood why she shouldn't. But that wasn't going to hold her back.

"So what's this then?" asked the MP, staring after Katsina as she marched out of her room and down the hallway.

"Rutheo, you up?" Katsina said, ignoring the MP and striding into the kitchen to find her titular technician.

"Yah, I'm here. Oh, looking good, Captain. Very, uh, informal," she said, eyeing Katsina, "Jumpsuit and captains coat? You sure that's a good idea?"

"Miss Lucas, you can't be late for this proceeding, we have to-"

"Hey, hey, relax pal. She has a minute, okay?" Rutheo said, stepping up from her seat at the kitchen island, a show of force at its least subtle.

Katsina didn't have much time, but her last chance at really turning around her situation would have to be left with Rutheo.

"Any word from Alice?" she asked in a hushed tone.

"She said she's going to forward her findings when she can. Here's hoping it's today."

"I'm sure she understands the urgency," said Katsina, letting her eyes wander to the Nollaig tree in the corner. "If not today, another is fine. A prison sentence doesn't scare me, it's just a matter of waiting."

"Then you won't mind getting yourself together so we can get on with it?" the MP cut in.

"You have some weird privacy issues, so you do," Rutheo said, stepping between him and Katsina.

"Alright Ruthie, I'll see you and Marshal there."

Katsina manoeuvred around Rutheo, pulling her shoulders back while presenting her hands to the MP, who *clacked* the cuffs to either side of her wrists.

The crisp, cold breeze that gently buttered the mountain in snow and sleet was a stark difference to Marshal's warm and cosy hole in the rockface. The mountains in the distance stretched to the horizon, as if the entire continent was a folded tectonic napkin. In the distance, towards the city, an immense orb levitated in the sky. The omnisphere of Los Ange, the centre of the Guardian church's faith in New Amir. The mountains under it reminded Katsina of the sound waveforms she used to be able to see in her HUD, which prompted her hand to run over the back of her neck, feeling the empty sockets where her implants once sat. She turned to the MP, waiting in the portal to the shuttle for her to accompany him.

"You ever not had your implants?" she asked.

"No, never," he said.

"It's excruciating," Katsina said, "to not see the mountains in all their glory, to not hear the wind and it's song. That's what they're trying to do to me."

"Ma'am?"

"Never mind. Let's do this."

Katsina turned away from the beauty of the mountain range, and slipped into the shuttle to strap herself in. She didn't want to, but she gazed out of the port window at the snowfall, wondering if her plan was really going to come together. Another fog was beginning to roll in.

In the shuttle, a familiar face awaited her, James, the Commander who she hadn't seen since her first court day. He smiled, and closed the hatch as she sat down. The soft rumble and a jolt signaled they had leapt from the platform and began racing through the air. She realised after settling in that it was just the two of them and the pilot, no Portman. It gave her an idea, something she thought would really make the Admiralty sweat. Instead of being brought in her usual back entrance, Katsina felt it was time to take the entire public charade a bit further. While coming over the horizon, Katsina saw the large spiraling towers grow from the distance, like grass growing from a fresh layer of snow.

"Whats say we put her down at the courthouse entrance?" Katsina said aloud.

"What?" James blurted.

"I mean, it's a shorter trip for you and we can show the public what kind of criminal I really am. That's what they're going for with this right?" she said, slowly leaning back from the window to look into James' eyes, giving him her most devious smile.

"So? Whatcha think James?" she asked him. He didn't answer her, but he did blink once or twice, clearly using his own HUD to communicate with the pilot. A small grin ran over his face as the shuttle began to dip right, breaking their scheduled flight path. Katsina had more support in the Military Police than she realised.

"I see what you're doing now," James said, looking down at the front of the courthouse. "Smart."

"Thanks, here's hoping it works."

On a wide open courtyard, sheltered in an alcove of the cliffs under the central governing tower of Los Ange, stood hundreds of people. The crowd divided down the middle, the occasional MP or Police Officer walking the line between them. From what Katsina could make out, both groups of people seemed to be in peaceful protest to the opposite side. The landing platform was empty, but it looked like it was going to be a hard walk from there to the entrance to the courthouse. The shuttle hovered over the platform for a moment, before a *plinking* noise sounded on the hull; hailstones.

"Are you sure this is what you want to do? Admiral Krauss wants you in Admiral Selvins office straight away. They're peaceful now but seeing you wearing that affix could cause a riot," James said over the sound of the hail.

"Krauss' demand can wait. They're human beings; I'm sure they're smarter than that," Katsina said, gesturing for him to open the door. The shuttle hovered over the platform, and Katsina prepared herself to face the storm.

James unlatched the door, revealing two more officers waiting just outside to escort Katsina through the protest. She guessed James had informed them. Atop the steps of the courtyard leading to the building's atrium, she could see her objective, a podium for a press conference. Her chance to speak to the public depended on her reaching it. One of the guards reached out a hand to help her down, but Katsina wasn't going to be seen receiving it. She hopped, landing squarely on her left knee, and noise erupted from the crowds. She touched her hand on the pale marble slates before lifting herself to allow them to see her. One half seemed to cheer in support, the other, that was a different beast.

"Traitor!"
"Murderer!"
"Lucas!"
"Justice!"
"Take it off!"

Maybe Katsina had misjudged the situation, the crowd was more heated than she'd expected, but she had faced more unpleasant things. With one guard behind her and the two in front, she cocked back her head and moved up the middle of the protesters, keeping her eyes trained on the entrance to the courthouse where the media outlets swarmed about the podium. Through the shouting and persecution, a small few voices made it to her ears, words of support, cheers of happiness. The sounds reminded her that she was still supported by some people, and that her Affix still meant something. The storm of snow began to bellow at her back, almost as if to push her forward, to get her through the rowdy and unforgiving crowd in the courtyard. It was the wind itself that carried the voices of support to her ears; the nature of the world held her up. It was her home and it, over all others, knew of her innocence. Nothing was going to take that from her.

A grunt to her left, followed by a shove which knocked her back into the MP behind her, made Katsina brace herself for something she hadn't expected. A man pushed through the crowd, close enough to touch Kastsina's shoulder, he was going for her affix.

"You don't deserve it!" he yelled, "Say what you like, but

the Orchestrators know what you've done, you traitor."

Katsina glanced him up and down, as a police officer pushed him back. In his hand was another Captain's affix, smaller in size, with less display medals lining its inner strip. The affix seemed to be charred, and missing pieces to its shoulder mounted coupling. The man himself was shorter, hunched over, and older than any other protester that she'd seen. His face was red with anger, while sadness filled his eyes, a pitiful, angry set of eyes. Even with the hail beating against his face, his tears flowed freely.

"Captains die for their ship Lucas. They don't betray them. They die for them," he moaned, while the soldiers and police pushed him back beyond the barrier.

Katsina didn't take her gaze away from the affix he held, her mind had drifted to the fate of its owner, whoever it was.

"*Get it together,*" she thought, blinking a few times to retrain her gaze on the door at the top of the steps.

What was really just a two minute walk was more reminiscent of her push on the Alia moon; it certainly took the same nerve to accomplish it. The wind picked up, and the shouting of the agitated people of Los Ange began to echo in it's bellows. Another stumble as another woman collided with the soldier to her right, followed by an upheaval in the crowd behind them. The screaming and shouting got louder, but it was no longer in hatred or support for Katsina, it was instead cries of panic and fear. Another person collided with Katsina, and another, toppling her to the ground.

"*What the hell,*" she thought, landing on her side.

"Lucas, Lucas get up," James shouted. The fear in his voice confused her, so she raised her hands for him to lift her from the tiles.

"Get inside, get her inside," he yelled, pushing her up the stairway away from him.

The entire courtyard had erupted in chaos, people bolting in all directions away from the sudden noises of railgun fire. Another MP grabbed Katsina, and dragged her up the steps, shoving people out of their way. It was as if Katsina had been thrown into a pit of wolves. She tried to regain her balance, only to be thrown off again by another incoming bystander. Before she could recover she tripped over another person tumbling down the steps ahead of her. Katsina fell and her head collided with the stone steps, sending a jolt of pain up the middle of her face. Before she even had time to process the impact, she was jerked to her feet again and pushed over the person she had tripped on, only to land again face down, this time at the top of the steps. Katsina rolled over to lift herself, realising she had lost her guard. She knew she had to manoeuvre herself, but her hands were quite literally tied. She shoved one knee under her chest and lifted herself up, stumbling over another person to find something to hold her up in the mess. A warm sensation washed down her chin and neck, while copper seemed to flood her tongue. Katsina finally made it to her feet and turned around to look back at the crowd below her. She'd thought they were rioting over her arrival, but it wasn't a riot, it was a sacking.

In the distant fog, over the horizon of the ocean, a ship approached. A massive space vessel, Destroyer class. Katsina's mouth fell open at the sight of it.

"Where... How..." she thought, as a flash of light erupted from the vessel.

The light tore through the sky above her, and she fell to the ground as it crashed into the buildings over her head. The noise was deafening without her implants, and the initial shockwave blew her back towards the doors of the courthouse. The entire crowd of protesters before her had been flattened by the shockwave. Katsina's breathing sped up as her wide eyes glanced frantically around to find an MP to release her. There couldn't have been a worse time for her to be locked in shackles. Rubble crashed into the courtyard around her, while more flashes of light from high above rained down on the ship in the distance. Fighter ships whistled over Kastsina's head, rocketing towards the enemy, their rail guns flashing along the way. Another loud boom, and a flash of light cut through the sky, removing the rockface to Katsina's left from the cliffs. The courtyard below her started rumbling. The smell of smouldering rock reached her nose as the sky above began to change color, turning a menacing black and red. She gave up on finding an MP, and instead turned to the large red doors of the courthouse, one of which had already fallen away from its hinges by those struggling to get inside. That's where she needed to be. Regardless of what they had done to her, Katsina was determined to get inside to protect the Admiralty board.

***

    Getting through the crowd wasn't easy. Even more than earlier, the sweat glistening on Katsina's skin reminded her of the anxiety she'd had the day she fought on the Alia moon. Los Ange was one of the two major port cities on the continent that had building yards for ships, military weapon factories, and all the defenses needed to protect both. It should have been the last place the Yggdrasilians would have tried to attack, as such a move was a guaranteed loss. This didn't change the reality of the situation, a ship had made landfall and fired on the densely populated city, and directly at the courthouse on the day of Katsina's sentencing. It lit a spark in her, and she pushed her way past those ahead. Inside the building there were hoards of people being directed by public officials, marines, and police officers. There was a makeshift area for wounded, and three soldiers who, like the rest, seemed scared out of their minds as they huddled in a corner. Katsina did her best to go against the flow of people, and stumbled her way over to the three men.

    "Hey, hey, I need one of you to unlock these," she called, holding her hands over her head to catch their attention. One of them, wide eyed and pale, raised his hand out to her and drew a pistol from his hip. He was younger than the other two.

"Don't move, Lucas. Get on your knees." he shouted.

The screaming and moaning of the crowd elevated at the sight of his weapon. And Katsina held her hands out ahead of her.

"Okay, hey, relax. I'm getting on my knees, just put the pistol back in your holster," she said, adjusting her tone to talk him down.

"This was you wasn't it? You and your Ygg buddies couldn't stop at one squadron now you want women and children too?" he shouted, his voice breaking under his own fear.

"I didn't do this. I'm not resisting; put the gun down," Katsina said, keeping her eye contact with him. He was shaking, not focused on her, distracted by the random bystanders who were running back and forth between them.

"Shut up. Stay down," he cried. The room around them shuddered. *Booming* could be heard among the screams from outside. Dust and pieces of rock fell from the ceiling above, the archways began to crack.

"You're scaring these people, we need to get them to safety," Katsina said, keeping her voice calm.

"You- you're not my commanding officer... I said shut up. Shut up. Shut up!"

Katsina lifted her hands over her head and spun around at the sight of his muzzle flashing. Amongst the noise of the shuddering building and falling rubble the horrified screams of the people around her followed the echo of the gunshot, but nothing hit her. She peeked over her shoulder to see the body of another soldier crumpled on the floor, his decorative tattoos telling a story of the ancient world.

"Mao..." Katsina said aloud, arriving at his side.

His eyes were quickly rolling back into his head. His jaw clenched with the pain. The hole in his chest was bleeding profusely, but Katsina put pressure on it all the same. His grunts of pain soon sped into gasps for air, his eyes closing.

"No, Mao, come on," she said, her eyes following a small trickle of blood that ran down over his badges. Washing his achievements away with him. His breathing stopped, and Katsina sighed.

"Why did you do that? Why did you do that?" She repeated.

She glanced up at the soldier that Mao protected her from. He still had his pistol aimed, and he clamped his lips at the sight of the slain brother in arms, before one of his comrades tackled him to the ground, fighting for control of his weapon. Another sound collided with Katsina's eardrums, setting her hearing into a continuous ringing. A sway of the crowd pushed her over as the hall became flooded with more people from outside. Katsina scrambled, climbing up and around a wooden reception desk to find her bearings. She held onto a brass lantern that hung from the left hand wall.

"Captain," a call from across the room found its way to her. "Captain!"

Katsina barely heard her, but found her in the sea of people. Rutheo stood in the doorway, clinging to one of the columns in an attempt to not be swept into the stampede.

"Rutheo! Where's Marshal?"

"What?" She called.

"Marshal! Where is Marshal?" Katsina yelled across the river of people. It looked impenetrable. But she couldn't risk losing sight of Rutheo.

"The port!" Rutheo replied eventually, "He's going to the Behemothis."

"The ship? " Katsina was puzzled.

She wondered what Marshal was thinking, making his way to a space carrier when the fight was down there on the ground. The room began to fill, causing people to fall under the feet of others. Katsina spotted the soldiers who had confronted her and glanced to Rutheo, pointing in their direction.

"Okay, Ruthie, get those boys up. We need to help these people get out."

"Alright," she said, slipping down from her perch into the wave. "Hey, hey, get up..."

Her voice trailed away as Katsina's eyes fell onto a man among the people below her. In his black captain's coat, and a fresh new gash across his forehead, Deacon Morann walked with a significant fury in his wake. He lifted his arm, aiming his own pistol at Katsina. She knew what he thought, so she couldn't run, he'd shoot her if she did. She had to raise her hands in surrender, knowing there was no way to convince him amidst the danger.

"Lucas!" he said, "Hands on your head."

"Captain!" Rutheo called, struggling to get around the crowd. Katsina thrust her hands towards her.

"No, Rutheo. Help these people get out."

"I said: hands on your head!"

"Morann, don't," said Rutheo.

"Ruthie, get back," Katsina shouted.

Rutheo stopped, looking at Katsina with confusion in her eyes. Her brow creased in sadness before the figure of Commander Kessler appeared from the crowd behind her, snatching her into his arms.

"We caught you and you decide to kill us all," Morann said into Katsina's already throbbing ear. Pulling her down from the desk, he said: "No more trials, time for sentencing."

"I didn't do this, Morann," Katsina said, watching the pain on Rutheo's face as Kessler pulled her away.

"Sir, we have an emergency evac waiting past the Library."

"Good, let's go then."

"Morann, what about these people?" Katsina said defiantly.

"Captain! No! Let her go!" Rutheo shouted one last time. Katsina lost sight of her as more people fell into the atrium, while she was pulled in the opposite direction, through a wide wooden doorway guarded by heavily armed men.

Katsina kept pace with Morann and his companion, leaving behind the crowd in exchange for a temporary forward operating base established in a tall boardroom. Amongst the soldiers and commanding personnel were members of the Admiralty board and their chosen captains. The broken tables and chairs had been piled onto one another to build a makeshift barricade to deter civilians from entering. The tall windows of the room had all been shattered, their remains blanketing the floor in shards to be trampled by the men hiding underneath the window sill. The AR generated images displayed on the wall for the Admiralty board were of the enemy ship, as well as multiple faces of other commanding officers discussing the situation. Katsina felt it best to keep her head down, knowing that everyone in the room would most likely share the opinion that Morann had of her.

"Admiral we're en route," he said, waving his hand in the direction of the circle of men.

"Ride the lightning," one of them replied.

On the other end of the room Katsina was pulled into what was left of a ruined library, where a shuttle had made a jagged landing atop the ruined shelves and books.

"Where are you taking me?" Katsina asked.

Morann looked back at her, his lips pressed in a hard line.

"We're going to the Behemothis."

THE WHITE WHALE

Surrounded by shuttle and fighter craft, Katsina watched the city below. It was burning. The cannons and guns that hung from the city walls continued to fire at the enemy ship, which still floated in the distance, laying waste to Los Ange. What was left of the courtyard on which she'd landed had collapsed into the sea under the city. She closed her eyes, not wanting to see anymore. A thud on her shoulder jolted her eyes open again, making her look around to Morann, who had kept his hand on her bicep during the entire take-off sequence.

"You will watch this," he said menacingly, triggering a flash of resentment in Katsina's mind. He snatched her jaw with his other hand, tilting her head around to look at the sacked remains on the cliff side.

"Seventy-seven thousand dead, twenty-eight fighters and two cruisers lost."

"Let go of me," Katsina said, noticing a smear of red on the window she had touched.

"No, you will watch."

Another ship, only a few hundred metres away, fell from the sky in flames, plummeting to the water as the city grew smaller and smaller in the distance. Katsina could see her own breath cling to the window, the condensation beginning to drip along, beading on the cold surface around a red smear. The speed of the shuttle eventually pushed her back into her seat. A shiver ran up her spine as they broke past the atmosphere into the space above. The clouds covered the battle beneath them, allowing only the flashes of gunfire to break through the thick grey layer. Eventually only the sound of the shuttles engines could be heard, the battle faded away. It was just Katsina, Morann, and whoever was sitting in the cockpit of the shuttle ahead of them. She had her eyes trained on the steel wall ahead of her, refusing to look at him. He kept his eyes on her, burning a hole in the side of her cheek. She didn't want him to be satisfied by her gaze; she knew what he wanted, and he was doing his best to incite her to do it.

"Six of them were captains," he said, his voice breaking through the discomfort. He finally caught her off guard, forcing her to close her eyes in a painful expression. "Two of them were admirals."

"That's a lie," Katsina replied, opening her eyes to set her stare on him. He was searching for something in her face, perhaps a glimpse into her thoughts. That's what she was attempting herself after all.

"Selvin and Arius. The first shot hit Selvin's office, They both died instantly."

"ts'ßolfe…" she muttered.

"There aren't enough of us to captain the fleet," he droned. "We've promoted 3 first officers, but they're just field promotions."

"Why are you telling me this?" Katsina said, tilting her head back towards the window, her eyes watching the stars rising from the planet's horizon.

"Richmond will be taking over command of the Insurmountable. I'll be taking over the Behemothis. My first officer, Dawson, will be taking over command of the Monica Bay. I won't have you anywhere else in this galaxy other than in my sight, so you're coming with me," he said begrudgingly.

"Scared to be a captain with no first officer; is that it?" Katsina asked, rolling her eyes. The shuttle rattled as it broke orbit, and the gravity holding her in her seat was left back on the surface of the world.

"Shut up. You're no first officer. You're no captain," he said, reaching over to Katsina and pulling on her shoulder, her affix detached from her jacket. The second time he took it from her. "To think they even gave this back to you after they arrested you."

"I have a right to my affix. Until they level a sentence

against me I'm st-"

A *smack* of cold metal knocked into Katsina's face, her head belted off the wall behind her. She opened her mouth in protest, before another strike caught her mouth, then another. Her hair was pulled to one side, before a final blow collided with her chin. The pain from falling on the steps on the ground spread up past her lip, through her nose, into her left eyebrow. She opened her eyes to see her Affix, bloodied in Morann's hands.

"You think I give a damn about your rights anymore? You and those faisaheßul Ygg friends of yours must really think you can fool the rest of them. But not me."

"I don't know why you think I scuttled the Roverdendrom, or my own squadron, but your demented," Katsina said, catching his gaze with her own determined stare. The burn of resentment began to grow in the back of her mind to the point of her teeth grinding off of each other in fresh blood.

"We'll see," he said, before glancing to his left. "Good. Begin docking and let's get out of here."

"Wait what? We're leaving?"asked Katsina, her voice cracking as her lips began to swell.

"The Behemothis is to rendezvous with the Insurmountable to search for your so called enemy weapon in The Deep. Admiral Krauss' orders."

"That's ridiculous, Morann. The fight is here. The enemy is here."

He didn't reply to her, and instead focused on the screens in his eyes. Katsina turned back to look down at the planet, the flashes of light still glowing through. The fight was there, and she clenched her fists at the suggestion of missing it. Suddenly the planet, the stars, and the rest of the universe disappeared, covered by the hangar walls of the Behemothis. Their shuttle had covered an immense distance in the short time they were on board, before settling down on the tarmac. Katsina felt the jolt in her tailbone as the shuttle struck the landing with force, making it the second roughest landing she had been in. Which she counted herself lucky for. The airlock to the shuttle opened, and Katsina was pulled from her seat by Morann, who had no hesitation in handling her. The tarmac was a mess, with ships and people flying and running in every direction. Behind them more and more shuttles, carrying people away from the conflict, slid into the hangar door as the Behemothis moved further out of the solar system. Botanica, the small green marble, was getting smaller. Another shuttle, smeared and charred with marks from battle, rushed overhead, rattling as it struggled to stay up. Katsina began to pay attention to the pain that was shooting through her face and head, and lifted her hand to touch her mouth, where the pain hurt the most. Before she could feel her lips, Morann snatched her hand away from her face, pulling her in his direction across the bustling landing strip.

"Jeez you coulb just askib," she said, or tried to say. Her words sounded slurred and not as cutting as she normally liked. She ran her tongue about in her mouth, feeling around for the problem, the taste of copper was rampant and overwhelming. She spat a wad of red onto the floor.

"Rancid," Morann mumbled.

What came out wasn't a projectile, but instead a drool that ran down Katsina's chin.

"Must you be so disguising? You're an embarrassment," Morann said, glancing back at her.

"Fubb you Moranb," she spat.

Out in the central corridor of the ship, personnel were running in all directions, a far cry from the usual experience Katsina had while walking towards the bridge. She looked about at her usual haunts. No one even looked in her direction as she was being pulled forward by Morann, whom they greeted as Captain. Apart from the pain that began to pulsate in her face, she felt another slight pain, deep in her chest. Not a pain exactly, but a tense pull on her diaphragm. It was more of a feeling than a pain. An empty feeling. The stairway to the bridge was a harder climb than usual, considering she wasn't climbing them on her own accord. As the doors slid open, she glanced around at a chaotic and excessively loud dome, with one voice commanding over the rest. It was Marshal.

"Marbal," she bumbled, "Marbal whas habbining?"

Morann let her arm go, giving her a chance to move on her own, which she suddenly realised was not the best idea. She stumbled on her own step, and her vision started to blur. She was dizzy, spinning on her own feet.

"Woah, woah, Kat," Marshal said, catching her in his arms. "What the hell happened to you?"

"Ask himb?"

"Can I get a medic up her please?" Marshal raised his voice, looking around the room for anyone in reach. Katsina noticed the shock on his face, his lip forming a hard line.

"Whaa? Is ib bad?" she asked as he sat her down on her captain's chair. The pain began to overcome her, a headache which pulsated through her vision.

"How did you let this happen?" Marshal shot at Morann, who was behind Katsina.

"I found her like that. Maybe she should be more careful in a fire fight," he said, less than caring.

"You are a real piece of work, Morann," Marshal replied, returning his attention to her. "Kat, lean your head back let me see it… Okay, it's swollen, it's probably going to scar."

"Captain," another voice said, "let's have a look."

A light flashed into Katsina's eyes, making her squint through her already swollen lids. She felt a touch on her cheek, the warmth of fingertips, but it sent a shooting pain across her mouth, making her flinch.

"Shhhhh, das sore," she groaned, finding it harder to differentiate lights and shapes from one another. Waves of sleep began to wash over her, and she began to let them sweep her away.

"It's alright Captain, we just need to stop the bleeding. Sir, I need to get her to the hospital to minimise the damage."

"She is to be transported to a confinement chamber. You can give her something to reduce the swelling then," Morann could be heard saying casually. Katsina could no longer see.

"But the scarring will be severe without a tissue stitcher. We have to take her in as soo-"

"Doctor, you're dealing with a war criminal and a member of the enemy's forces. She doesn't require your aid in the slightest."

"Are you mad?" Katsina heard Marshal say, before she succumbed to the dark.

***

Katsina groaned, and rolled over in her bed, only to realise all too late that it wasn't a bed. It was the cubby hole in her Confinement Chamber and she had just fallen out of it, landing on her side, making her wince. It caused her a lot more pain.

"Faisaheß," she moaned, before sliding her hand up the wall and gripping the cubby for support.

She plopped down on the padded circular hole in the wall, and ran her left hand over her face, it was still swollen, but not as badly as before. But a coarse, and sandpapery line of crust ran from her forehead downward. She followed the line with her fingertip, ignoring the searing pain that it caused her to touch it, it was a wide open scab which ran around her nose before finishing on her top lip, which was where the pain was centred. Katsina could feel her finger slip into the gap in her lip, which was split on her left side. Lifting her top lip gently, Katsina ran her index finger across her top row of teeth, feeling more of the thick scab inside her lip and what felt like a lumpy mass on her gums, more damage. She caught her finger on something sharp and pulled her finger out of her mouth in fright. Looking at the small bleeding prick in her finger she was reminded of a papercut she had gotten long ago. Her tongue lifted up to explore the sharp object only to realise that it was what was once one of her teeth, it was broken into a sharp point, leaving a gap in her smile just by her canines.

"Great," she said, before letting out a wince at her lip moving.

Katsina leaned around to see her surroundings; the Confinement area was dark, the lights dimmed for her to sleep. The only light in the room came from the glowing strip which lined the clear wall separating her from the rest of the ship. All was quiet apart from the ship's hum as it rode the Kugelblitz wheels through space. For a moment Katsina imagined a steam engine train, soaring through the universe on steam power. For a moment she forgot everything that had happened, before the sight of the bombs that the enemy ship fired at Los Ange flashed across her mind. Katsina sprung up and headed to the doorway, looking out of her cell to see the guard station, with no one at the post.

"Ugh, where the hell is everyone," she thought.

Suddenly a flutter of light lit up across the room, coming from strange angles, where there should have been no lighting at all. What looked like the glitching of a computer screen began to confuse Katsina, before it stopped, and floating in front of her, in her very eyes, were words displayed in red.

Set up complete. Launch interface? Y/N

"What the?" Katsina stammered before realising what she was looking at.

She looked at the small digital Y, and thought about selecting it, which worked. Before her eyes stretched thousands of digital blue threads, dancing about her as everyone and everything on the ship linked to one another. She looked down at the ground, noticing the true detail of the dust particles that littered around her feet. Everything was in high definition for her, and she felt like she could finally see again.

She lifted her hand up to the back of her neck, and felt her once empty port's had implants in them again. She was whole, for the first time in weeks.

"Not bad huh?" Marshal spoke in her ear softly.

"Marshal, how did you swing this?" Katsina said aloud to her first officer who wasn't there. She looked about the room and found a thread of information that connected her to him. Unlike the typical blue string of light, her connection to him was red, a glistening red string that stretched further than she knew the ship could reach. He wasn't on board.

"Where are you?" she asked.

"Just eighty or so kilometres away from the starboard bow. I'm on the Insurmountable."

"The Insurmountable?"

"Yeah, we made it halfway to the Deep Sector. The Insurmountable met us before we passed by the Alia moon," he explained.

"How long have I been out?"

"About six days. You were kept under sedation and treated for your injuries. The sedation wasn't my idea. You had a hell of a hit to the head. The swelling was crazy."

"Yeah it still is. That t'secheashin has a mean right hook. He hit me with my own affix."

"Bheibhen. I knew he did it. Are you gonna be okay?" he asked, his voice as soft as satin.

"I'll be fine, I'm always fine."

"Is there anyone with you?" Marshal asked, hushing his tone, "because I have some news."

"No, no. I'm alone."

"Good. You're going to be released under supervision soon, and you'll be put on an intersolar nav station where Morann can keep an eye on you. There aren't enough of his people to run the ship, so he's using ours. I don't recommend you cross him while you're there; you're already in enough trouble. He doesn't know you have a comm implant or a HUD, so keep it that way. You can see the comms of others, and access your library and body controls, but you can't be seen by others and you should only establish a comm link with me. I've embedded a special algorithm to let you send me messages."

"Well, that's a lot," Katsina said, beginning to pace the room.

"Yeah sorry, I just can't stay on long. Dr. Foye is the only person aboard that knows about your implants. I trusted her to put them in for you. And you need to know, Morann has no first officer. So he can't be challenged," he said, an inclination of suggestion in his tone.

"Yeah, but Marshal, I can't hide my HUD. And what special algorithm? That's illegal," she said, keeping her eyes on her feet, ignoring the pain in her lips as she spoke.

She couldn't take her hands off the back of her neck, the feeling of having her implants again making a world of difference to her. But the idea of lying, and not being able to tie her hair into a bun again, sent goosebumps down her back.

"I understand," he sighed, "but they already think you're a criminal and I can't let you be treated like one for something you didn't do. I'll figure a way out of this for you; just give me time. Kat, I have to go, Insurmountable is making a manoeuvre towards a suspicious craft a few AU's from here."

"Be careful then. And congratulations, Captain," she said with a smile, a painful smile.

"Ha, it's just an emergency field promotion. You can call me that when I earn it, Captain."

"Ride the lightning, Marshal."

"Ride the lightning. Talk soon."

Katsina watched the thread connecting them disintegrate from her eyesight. She ran her right hand from the back of her neck to her cheek, staring at the point in the wall where his voice should have been.

The glass panel to her left shifted and opened wide enough for her to step out of her confinement. She had only gotten her ankle clear of the glass before it shut again, leaving her free, but still alone. Katsina felt a breeze run up her leg, and looked down to see that the legs of her jumpsuit were torn in more than one place, and we're still stained from her time on the ground.

"Jeez, not even a change of clothes," she thought.

She slipped off her jacket and wrapped it around her waist, pulling it into a tight knot on her left hip. Tying it up, she felt an ache in her side which prompted her to unzip her ragged suit. From her shoulder to her backside, Katsina was wrapped in a serpentine bruise, which looked like it had been only made yesterday. The deep red marks around it caught her eye.

"Hemorrhaging?" she wondered, running her fingers over the dark strip.

"Busy playing with yourself?" A small but arrogant voice called through the opening doorway. Katsina glanced up, and braced on her right foot defensively. But she immediately relaxed upon seeing the long brown curls and pale porcelain face of Rutheo.

"Playing? Nah, that's more your thing," Katsina said, buttoning herself up.

"I can't believe you're alive," Rutheo said, colliding with Katsina as her tone changed to relief. "I thought he was going to shoot you."

"Hey, it's alright. I'm here," Katsina said to her saddened engineer. "It wouldn't have been the first time someone tried to shoot me that day anyway."

"Wait what? What happened?" Rutheo said, leaning back in surprise.

"Han Mao. Someone tried to shoot me. He dived in the way," said Katsina, her mind reaching back to his body in her hands.

"T'sßolfé..." said Rutheo. "He would have been in Command of the MP's..."

"I know, but he jumped in front of a bullet for me..." Katsina said, a sorrow in her voice as she spoke. She looked at the guards desk, where he sat day after day reading for her, before she realised something was missing on her shoulder.

"Rutheo, Morann. Does he still have my affix? It wasn't on my shoulder when I woke up."

"Um, well… It's safe, I just don't think you're gonna be happy about it."

"It's alright, Rutheo, where is it? He hide it?"

"No, uh… He didn't, but it's safe I swear," she said, her voice breaking with nerves.

"Rutheo," Katsina said, placing her hands on the small girls shoulders, "where is it?"

Rutheo braced herself, and looked up into Katsina's eyes, regret detectable in hers. Katsina noticed rings around her eyes, deep black pockets inlaid into a gaunt face. A bruise trailed down her neck under her jumpsuit. Rutheo looked unwell.

"Ruthie, what happened to you?"

"You're needed at your post on the bridge, and the Captain wants to speak with you."

***

The walk towards the bridge was worse than before. The main hall was deserted, with none of the cafes or restaurants open. The entire area was abandoned, with no sound but a single repeating message playing over the comms, and displayed on every AR surface that hung from the ceiling:

Remain at your assigned post.
Remain up to date with duty roster changes.
All non-military personnel are to attend combat training in the AR theatre section.
All recreational activities suspended until further notice.

"What is this? A dictatorship now?" Katsina muttered, glancing at Rutheo for comment. But Rutheo kept her eyes forward, refusing to acknowledge her remark. "Rutheo? Ruthie?"

"The Captaincy has always been a dictatorship, Kat. It's

just a matter of malevolence or benevolence," she said in a hushed tone.

Katsina stood still, watching Rutheo walk ahead of her, as if what she'd said was in no way shocking or controversial. The small girl didn't move with her typical excitement, instead she seemed reserved, subdued. Katsina looked around at the tables and chairs that had been left empty, the various cups and plates, some still with food on them, left on the counter of her usual cafe. The smell was less than gag worthy, but it was getting there. Katsina turned down her nasal sensitivity settings, allowing her to breathe without the discomfort.

"Come on," Rutheo said from ahead of her.

The lights on the bridge had been dimmed, no longer bright and warm like Katsina liked it to be for the team. The entire space matched the lighting of the war room, as if the ship was already engaged with the enemy.

"Ah, so nice to have the convict turn up. The face doesn't look so bad this time Lucas," Morann said, stepping out of Katsina's seat, his arms raised. He rested his foot up on the armrest of the captain's chair, antagonistic as always. He rested his arms on his knee, and inspected Katsina, "You look terrible, you should get a shower."

"And a stitcher," Katsina said. "What do you want?"

"Oh yes, your post is waiting for you down below, as we are short staffed we need everyone we can have. Consider it penal labour," he said, vaguely gesturing to the computer stations underneath them.

"We're short staffed because you left the planet with very little of the crew able to return to their posts," Katsina cut across him.

"I won't hear talk like that on my bridge hereafter; it incites poor morale. I'm giving you the courtesy to collect your belongings from your previously assigned quarters. You'll be staying in housing on Deck C, a former Delta Operator's quarters I believe. Does the name Mara Johnson ring any bells?"

Katsina didn't reply to him, because again she knew what he was trying to do. He was very good at it - at winding her up. She didn't let her expression change, however her heart; she felt that drop into the sinking pit of her stomach. The messy and crowded room seemed to have come to a halt upon Morann's question, people stopped walking and working around them. Katsina felt eyes on her from all angles, especially Rutheo's. But the only eyes she focused on were Morann's, which were searching her again, peering into her mind to find a reaction that she refused to give. It was at that moment she noticed a golden glint on his shoulder, bearing a recognisable symbol that she'd bore for the past months during her service. It was her Affix, scratched and frayed like the rest of her clothes, but attached to Morann's jacket. Technically it should be there, as he was in command, but he had his own Affix for that, bearing his own ID and symbols. Katsina understood why Rutheo didn't tell her. She probably would have lost her cool at the idea of someone else using her Affix. But in that moment she couldn't let it get to her, not in front of the entire bridge.

"Fine then," he said reluctantly, "If there is nothing else you're dismissed. Report to your post in thirty Botanican minutes for duty."

"Thirty minutes to C deck and back?" Rutheo entered. Although hesitant, she still stepped forward, positioning herself somewhat between Katsina and Morann.

"I don't remember you having to be here any longer engineer. I've had Mr. Kessler speak to you twice in this regard, should I call on him a third time?" Morann said, raising his voice. Katsina recognised that tone, she'd used it before, to correct any insubordination that had come up. It was the voice of a captain. Rutheo seemed to freeze.

"Ruthie. It's okay."

"That's enough, Lucas," Morann turned back to her, "Speak when spoken to. Understood?"

Katsina recognised the authority, and realised she was

in no position to challenge such a basic order. She had spoken out of turn, which was something she didn't mind her crew mates doing with her. But Morann was clearly a different type of commanding officer.

"Aye... Sir," she inevitably said.

"Good, off you go. Engineer... Uh, Ruthie, back to your position, I want the Battery Pylon calibrated by the day's end."

"Aye, sir," Rutheo said, dipping her head in submission.

Katsina turned on her heel, refusing to let her composure fall before leaving the bridge. Even though everyone had returned to their work, she could still feel Morann watching her. The frosted glass doors closed behind her as she and Rutheo made their way back down the steps to the main hallway. Rutheo had nothing to say, and neither had she. It was a somber walk for them both, until Katsina noticed that Rutheo still walked with her even after they passed the service stairwell to the engineering department.

"And where are you going?"

"With you, don't worry. I have Crawford on my shift," she said with a cheeky smile.

"Old Howard?"

"Yeah, so I'm free to help move your things."

"Rutheo, you know I don't have many things, most of what I own is in the Amber Eyes."

"Well, duh, I'm just following orders to stay with you when I can."

"Whose orders? Marshal's?" Katsina asked as they clattered down the stairway to Deck C.

"Yep, he wants you to be safe. And as far as we both know, you're not in the safest place in the universe," she said, losing her usual joking tone again.

"The Deep doesn't scare me, Rutheo. It shouldn't scare you either."

"The Deep isn't what makes it unsafe. It's Morann. Kat, he has it out for you. He genuinely thinks you sent all those fighters to die. They all think you lied."

"Yeah well he can believe what he wants. It's not like he can do anything about it right now."

"Except make your life a living hell while you're here, and it's not what he believes, Cap, it's what he's willing to do with it. He looks at you like he's lovey-hatey obsessed with you or something, it's creepy."

The two didn't say much along the crew quarter streets. Katsina noticed that the memorial candles that had been lit along the houses had been cleared away. It made sense to her since it had been weeks since she was last down here. It was just as quiet along the streets however, as if people were still mourning. The entrance to her quarters underneath the dome of the bridge was already open, with a single brown box sitting in the doorway. Katsina dropped to one knee, noticing the frames that were placed carelessly in the plastic box. One of them was her commendation of valor that once hung on her wall, another was her third graduate degree from the University of Los Ange. The frames, and the glass panes, were broken. Her Riley Bear sat ragged as always.

"Ah, come on," she said, digging her hands into the box and pulling out a piece of the old plastic spaceship figurine. "My model Enterprise; someone snapped the nacels."

"Captain... look," Rutheo said.

Katsina looked around to see her standing in the captain's quarters, which were lit with a deep red and black light from the wall panels. On the wall was mounted a large skull, a skull that belonged to an enormous creature with teeth the length of Katsina's forearm. Below it Katsina recognised an old weapon, primitive by modern standards, a bowgun.

"What is it?" Rutheo asked.

"Coelurosaurian Saeloun Theropod," Katsina said blanky, peeking under the jawline to see the inside of the massive skull.

"Uh, Irish please?" Rutheo said, remaining in awe.

"I don't speak Irish. It's a Tyrannosaurus Rex, not a real one though. It's a cloned creature made from the DNA of giant

Earth creatures that existed millions of years ago," Katsina said, stepping under the jawbone of the skull to inspect it's innards.

"And this thing was alive once?"

"Yeah, probably in the twenty third century. There was this movie that inspired actual cloning science in the late twentieth century, all about dinosaur parks. These animals were an experiment that led to being a huge tourist attraction in United Korea. They were hunted in enclosures by enthusiasts," said Katsina.

"How do you know all this stuff?" Rutheo asked.

"I took earth histories as an elective for my second degree; hated it. Dinosaur breeding and hunting was banned soon after there were too many accidents recorded. Well, they weren't really accidents, just bad hunters who ended up being hunted."

"But why does Morann have one?" asked Rutheo, before ducking underneath the skull to join Katsina.

"There, look. That's a scrape of a bowgun bolt on the inner gum line. Someone hunted and killed this thing," Katsina said, pointing at the carved wound.

"Morann?"

"No," Katsina said. "Most likely it's an heirloom, this stuff is too old to have been done in the modern day But I wouldn't put it past Morann to be the sport hunter type, even though it's illegal."

Katsina stepped out of the giant skull, and looked about her old quarters, the space, which was once empty, was now filled to the brim with animal parts. Things that looked like 'trophies' from old earth hunting expeditions in the past, almost like a museum by its impressive collection size. One object that stood out from the rest, Katsina noticed, was a framed photograph. She walked around a large ivory tusk to get a better look at the printed image. It wasn't in 3D or digitally displayed; it was a piece of photographic printing paper in a frame. In the picture stood a young woman, with light brown skin, wearing a service uniform for the medical division of the Military. She wore a first officer's badge, and a similar Affix. Her eyes were beautiful, with an unbelievable natural yellow glow. Her hair, tied into a bun behind her ears, was a deep black with wisps of silver. That, and the short wrinkles around her eyes gave an air of wisdom to her beauty.

"Do you know her?" Rutheo asked, joining Katsina to look at the photo.

"No. But she must be important, she's the only non-trophy item in here."

"Maybe we should go. I don't think he wants us to see these things," Rutheo said, her nerves beginning to show through.

"No Ruthie, it's the opposite. I think he does want us to see these," Katsina said, lifting up the picture frame, "Look here, at the back…"

"It's a pin, a first officer pin?" Rutheo said, running her fingers over the back of the frame.

"It must have been hers. Can you scan it for-"

Rutheo had already pulled up her HUD in front of her eyes to scan the object ID number.

"Aardashini Morann, MIA?" she said, confused.

"Morann?" Katsina said, mirroring the confusion.

"They were related?"

"No, She has a traditional North Indian name. Morann has a traditional North American name. Besides they don't even look like each other, she must have been his wife?" Katsina said, puzzling over the photograph.

"She went missing during her commission?" Rutheo asked.

"Yeah but it doesn't say when. If she's missing then how is her ID pin here?"

"This is so weird. Kat, we should go. Place is giving me the creeps."

Katsina didn't respond, and instead puzzled over the identity of the woman in the picture. She remembered something, somewhere about her, but couldn't remember when, meaning she hadn't a clue where in her personal data files to search. Finally she set down the frame, and saved the images she remembered of the photograph and the pin to a folder in her HUD. She glanced over to the door to see Rutheo standing outside, with the plastic brown box in her hand. She thought about telling Rutheo about having a HUD and comm implant again, but quickly heeded Marshal's words about telling no one. Katsina realised she had little time to return to her post, and joined Rutheo to drop off what was left of her broken things in her new quarters.

"I think I get it now, Rutheo."

"Get what?" she asked.

"I think I know why Morann has it out for me. It's just a hunch, but I know it has something to do with that woman."

"So you don't think it's just because he thinks you ratted us to the Yggs?" Rutheo asked, sounding confused.

"Exactly, I think there's a bigger reason for all this. His behaviour makes so much more sense. Like he's chasing after some kind of revenge. And he thinks it's me he has to exact it on."

"Sounds like some Captain Ahab type shit," Rutheo said jokingly, trying to break whatever tension was building in Katsina's theory.

"Your right, Rutheo," Katsina said.

"Wait. I am?"

"You are. He's Captain Ahab, and he thinks I'm his white whale."

THE SEARCH FOR AARDASHINI

Along the streets of the crew housing Katsina puzzled over the significance of the woman in the photograph. Rutheo pondered with her, but the two of them hardly spoke. Normally Rutheo spoke her thoughts out loud, but since she had released Katsina from confinement she was eerily silent. As if something had scared her, probably Morann, or was it Kessler?

"Next floor up," she said absent-mindedly. "Mara's apartment is just across the street."

Katsina only nodded, not really paying enough attention to engage with Rutheo. She was different and uncomfortable to be around.

Arriving at a red door with a black triangular symbol on it, Katsina finally snapped out of her thoughts. The symbol was that of a talon, curled around a star. It was the symbol for Mara's fighter ship, "The Raptor's Claw" which had only just undergone a refit before it went missing. Katsina oversaw the refit herself to install a new and improved weapons system to the ship. Something that she thought would have given them an advantage in the field, a plasma based weapon passed down from the admiralty board. She remembered disagreeing with its use on her ship, but refusing orders wasn't her job. Considering the fact that Mara hadn't come back from the deep, Katsina felt a pang of guilt for thinking the refit would have made a difference.

"Cap?" Rutheo said.

"Sorry, I was just thinking about something." Katsina said, realising she had drifted back into her thoughts again. She shook her head lightly, snatched up the GFCC cable and reached to the back of her ear to find an empty port. Katsina plugged in.

The door slid out of the way to reveal a cluttered entrance to what was once Mara's apartment. The corners of the room were illuminated with warm orange tones, reminiscent of Katsina's quarters. The room itself was a living room, with an older digital view screen lining the left wall. The original furnishings that were provided by the Behemothis were all removed and replaced with cushions and what looked like the universe's only surviving pull out couch bed. Instead of the standard issue work surfaces, Mara had moved 3 craft tables from the engineering section to her living room with Katsina's permission just after they had left the dry dock. The tables were littered with machinery and circuitry, while a 3D printer, which looked to be on standby in the middle of a print, stood in the corner.

The kitchen area, which could be seen through the wide archway in the wall, was bare. Void of any signs of use apart from the coffee grounds dusted about the pot on the vintage induction stove. Above the kitchen archway protruded a balcony with no railing, *"Why?"* Katsina thought. It connected to the living room space via a small set of steps built into the right hand wall. The walls themselves were pale greys of the steel plating that lined the entire ship's superstructure. The grey color pallet was broken up by Mara's picture and posters, and contrasted by red and black flags draped from any and all hanging points available.

"You'd swear she was a squatter and not an actual resident of the ship," Rutheo mused, looking around at the engine parts on the tiled floor.

"Well she did spend most of her time in her fighter, grease monkey she was."

"Like you then," Rutheo said absently, in an attempt to be funny before she tilted her head to one side. "Hey, what are those for?"

"What?" Katsina asked, following Rutheo's gaze. Some of the ceiling panels had been removed, and cables dangled from gaps down onto the bedroom balcony. "Well, of course she has no ceiling."

Katsina dropped her box on a nearby table, and clambered up the thin stairway. The living space was small, which was standard when it came to quarters. Perhaps it was why she never felt at home in her own captain's room. It always felt too big. On the balcony, where there should have been a service-issue single bed, was a large double mattress atop a wooden frame in the middle of the floor. All the cables that had been hanging from the ceiling rested on the sheets, converging into one helmet shaped object.

"Is that... A VR headset?" Rutheo asked, giving Katsina a small fright from behind.

"Jeez, do you ever make noise? I can hardly see a thing without my HUD. Tap me on the shoulder next time," she said with a sigh. "Yeah, it's a VR kit."

"Sorry, that's cool though. I haven't seen VR in years; stuff is kinda old. Didn't they used to fly ships and watch movies in those things?"

Katsina stared at the helmet, wondering why she didn't tell Rutheo about her new HUD. Surely she could trust her? What would she have to lose? Rutheo would do nothing to hurt her.

"They did, but that was before we developed reinforced plating and AR filters. Nothing could beat the haptic and synaptic feedback that a pilot had with their ship via neural links. It's like what we have implanted in our eyes except it's outside."

"Inside out eyes, weird." Rutheo said. "What's it doing here?"

"I dunno, probably a personal entertainment setup," she said, before noticing a small blip on the smart home tablet that was lying on the bed. "Oh, shit."

"What?"

"Duty roster update," Katsina said, snatching up the tablet and flicking it open. She searched her name and found it under 'IT - Quantum Communications'. "Shift started 2 hours ago."

***

  Katsina left in a rush, and sprinted towards the bow of the Behemothis, crossing over multiple sections until she made it to the ship's battery pylon tube. A very dangerous shortcut, but one she was willing to take. The ship's battery pylon was an enormous rail cannon that ran the length of the Behemothis. It was charged to fire a single tungsten rod that could rip through any material it touched using the energy generated from the ship's Kugelblitz engines. This, as well as the ship's ability to carry multiple other ships, is what made the Behemothis such a deadly weapon in the theatre. Should the ship ever use the battery pylon, the shaft which held it in place would heat to an incredible temperature, and become magnetically charged. This would cause any magnetic material, like the intricate wiring of a person's implants, to cling to the cylinder to the point of flattening. For any person that was inside the Pylon shaft, that would mean certain, painful death.

  Katsina climbed the cylinder walls and found the maintenance hatch she needed. Poking her head up through the hatch she found herself underneath the AR display pool in the middle of the bridge floor. Above her was the ship itself, on display for everyone on the bridge to look at. She glanced around the room, hoping no one had seen her, and quickly scuttled under one of the many work stations until she made it to the Quantum Technology Communications, or QTC, section of the bridge. She found an empty desk which had no personal belongings and a standard issue computer station, obviously laid out for her. One or two of the other bridge crew around her had finally noticed her presence and quickly returned to their work or organised the clutter on their desks.

  Katsina felt a knot in her stomach, realising that her being there was most likely awkward for the people who used to work for her. With the allegations against her in mind, she was surprised no one had thrown her a dirtier look at that stage. She turned her attention back to her monitor, and logged into the system using her name and password. A slew of mail had been left after her weeks of not being connected to the ship's system. Personal and work emails, crew rosters, maintenance updates, budget requests, magazine requisition orders, and much more. Katsina plugged herself into the desktop port, and synced her system settings, which made the monitor match the HUD in her eyes. She glanced about her, to make sure no one noticed that she was staring into space, remembering what Marshal said before. She didn't notice anyone else looking her way, until she caught sight of the one pair of eyes that were cutting across the bridge to find hers. Above her, on the bridge balcony, was Morann. He was waiting for her.

"Uh, Captain Lucas..." A shy voice sounded, making Katsina break eye contact with Morann. She turned to see Alice Wesley, standing over her, holding her personal tablet close to her chest.

"Alice," Katsina said while she extended her hand, touching it off the blond girls shoulder, "It's good to see you."

"You too, uhm.. I'm really sorry, but according to the updated roster you're two hours and thirteen minutes late to your post," she said with a nervous tremble. Katsina leaned back in her chair, realising the position she was in.

"I'm assuming you're my commanding officer here, right Chief?"

"Y-yes, Captain."

"Okay, so just call me Kat. It's okay, I'm not the captain of this ship right now. Pretty sure I'm like a petty officer or something," she said in an attempt to put the shaken woman at ease.

"Yes, you're listed as petty officer fifth class," Alice said nervously. "The Captain has mandated that any breaches to the duty roster must result in a docking of lieu hours and an exemption from rostered break times."

Katsina threw a glance back up to the balcony, where Morann was still watching. She forced her anger back down her throat and smiled politely to him, which made his face curl in frustration. She turned away from him, and gave Alice her smile instead.

"Don't worry Alice, it's okay."

"I'm sorry, he's made me do it to three other crew members. He said if I don't follow his orders he'll find someone who will. I know he changed the roster to make you late but there's nothing I ca-"

"Alice," Katsina said calmly, "It's okay."

"But if you aren't allowed a break that means you won't get to eat and that's ju-"

"I know, I know. He's trying to put you in a difficult position. Don't let him. Just follow his orders, I'll be fine," Katsina warmly said.

"But it's not fair..."

"I know, but for now we just have to work with it. I assume you have a list of comm's you need me to monitor right?"

"Yes," Alice cleared her throat, "We have 13 inter solar quantum packets that need to be logged, dated, and decoded. Each packet contains just over twelve terabytes. I, uhm, I'll need a report on your progress in the morning."

"Perfect, I'll get started," Katsina said, maintaining her smile.

"I'm sorry Captain," Alice said. There was a pain in her voice that Katsina had just wishing she could help. But there was nothing more she could do; Alice had already walked away.

***

It had been a while since Katsina had decrypted and sorted information packets. Most likely it had been in her third year of senior university, more than seven years before.

It would have been easier to do if she had free use of her HUD and other implants, but as long as she had them hidden under her hair, out of sight, she couldn't. This made doing her allocated tasks much more difficult than it had to be. Perhaps Morann gave her the one job he knew she would have the most issues with completing. It would support her suspicions of him being her personal Ahab.

The day went by slowly. Which was the worst kind of day to have on an empty stomach. It felt as if it had been days before that Katsina had woken up in her confinement cell. But in reality it had only been ten or so hours and there was still a lot of the day left to go. Katsina focused on her work and channelled as much of her energy as she could into ignoring the rest of the bridge crew that were returning from their two hour lunch break. The clambering of footsteps was familiar, but missing something, something she couldn't put her finger on. A tap on her shoulder made her jump slightly as something slipped into her lap. Katsina caught a glimpse of Alice, who was walking away as if she didn't see her. In her lap there was a small brown box made of plastic, it had the orange insignia of the ship, which she recognised from her own captain's affix. She glanced back to look for Alice, who had disappeared into the crowd. The little object was a lunch box, from the ship's rations store. She remembered them from her training, but never saw the need to use them. Humanity, even after the war started, had more than enough of everything, so the use of rations was in her opinion defunct outside of emergencies.

Katsina ran her fingernail under the clip, and pulled up the lid on the box, inside was 3 foil covered bars. One labeled Banana, another apple, and the last was a small surprise, Pomegranate. Pomegranate was a flavor exclusive to upper officers, which as of now was above her rank. Under the foil packets was a small piece of paper, which had scribbles on it.

"In Pencil?" Katsina thought, *'Who the hell uses pencils anymore?"*

She pulled the shred up from under the rations, and

read the only word on it: 'Captain'.

"Captain?" she said out loud.

"Yes, Lucas?" Morann's shrill and condescending voice cut through her train of thought. Katsina immediately thrust the lunchbox under her top and around her side, not the most comfortable place but not somewhere he was going to see it either.

"What seems to be the issue then? First you're late now you can't work without interrupting a commanding officer?" Morann said, strutting in her direction, gaining everyone's attention with his sharp and loud steps.

"Nothing, I just… am having difficulty decoding this entire packet. It would be easier if I had my HUD to access my Operating System."

"Yes, well, we all know that criminals in modern society aren't allowed such privileges. It's against the law. What would the public think when they find out a traitor was using such a thing?"

Katsina spun about in her seat to look at him, her eyes burrowing into his. He wasn't wrong, but neither was she. He was still wearing her affix.

"Under regulation; I have a right to the proper equipment to complete my assign-"

"And under the oath of captain I have the right to override any and all regulation as I see fit," he announced, bending down to meet her eye level, his hands still in his pockets. "I don't know how you ran this place, but when I got here I saw a circus, not a warship."

Katsina realised what he was getting at yet again, attempting to get a rise from her. Instead she just returned his stare, but didn't match it's loathsome intent. Morann was critical of her, almost expectant of an outburst. Katsina simply countered with an ever so slight judgemental glare. One that no security footage would ever recognise, but one that Morann definitely noticed. He wanted a show, but she wasn't going to give him one.

"Fine then," he whispered, before straightening up. "Now listen here," he announced to the bridge. "This ship, this crew, has already seen and heard enough of how lacking it has been in regards to the war effort. Your captain is a traitor, your service to her has been a lie. There is a war going on outside that nobody is safe from, and it is up to us to win it. Finish your shifts, and remember who the enemy really is."

Morann's monologue had the eyes of the entire bridge on him. Looks of confusion, exhaustion, and fear faced in his direction. He kept his chin in the air the entire time, waving his hands between his words to emit his commanding presentation. Before returning to the balcony above he whispered angrily to Katsina as he stormed by.

"This ship is mine."

A sullen silence fell over the bridge again. It sounded like people were afraid to breath, let alone discuss their work with each other. The environment felt empty, devoid of positive ethic and devoted camaraderie. Which was the last thing Katsina would want for her team. The rest of the day went along without theatrics from Morann, but it wasn't without its challenges either. Katsina knew that, if she were to use her HUD to help her decode the signal packets, she would be caught. But she also sighed more than once at the prospect of decoding the packets manually using a keyboard. The *click clacking* sounds that it made forced her to grind her teeth. She knew she would have to resort to not meeting the completion deadline, and take whatever consequences come from it. Whatever it was, it would be better than having her HUD taken away again. Living without it could be comparable to living without your eyes, being blind to everything there was to see and do in the universe. Katsina sighed again, and exhaled slowly, but not loud enough to let people see her frustration. That's what she had to really keep hidden. As far as she could tell, not everyone was against her, regardless of Morann's claims. Her shift finally ended, and she had just a few hours to rest before she had to be back on duty again, the roster had been changed a third time.

The ship's entertainment areas were a ghost town to walk through. The AR arena was closed; the theatres were all but boarded up; and the beautiful augmented signs that normally were on display were all missing. Barely two threads of data were being streamed in the entire main hallway of the ship. The walk back to her quarters was lonely, even though she was surrounded by other members of the bridge crew. Some of them were her crew, others were new, probably Morann's crew. None of them spoke to each other, let alone her. She spotted a man named Aker Castle who worked on navigation. But he looked different to her, he was normally lit up after a shift, talking about 'riding the lightning' of the Kugelblitz and 'feeling the ship move' to his touch. He was clean cut and always organised, with impeccable attention paid to his uniform. But watching him walk aimlessly, she could see he hadn't shaved in a week. His clothes wrinkled, unironed. His eyes were sunken in his head, as if he hadn't slept at all.

Katsina dipped around two others and nudged him with her elbow.

"Mr Castle. How was she running today?" she asked with a smile.

"Uh, I-I don't think I should be talking to you," he replied, not looking at her. Katsina felt eyes on the back of her head, and looked around to see the crew glancing away in any other direction as they walked.

"Sorry, I just wondered how the ship was doing, you know her better than anyone so it wa-"

"Please, please stop talking to me," he blurted. "You're going to get me in trouble."

She stopped walking, and watched him and the rest of the off duty officers walk away from her, continuing their trip home in silence. Katsina had never seen or worked with anyone who would allow such a cloud loom over their entire ship.

"The faisaheß is Morann thinking, making them act like this?" she thought.

She considered confronting Aker, she even clenched her fist in the thought that he would be so dismissive. But instead she returned to her assigned quarters.

Mara's apartment was still a mess, no different from when she dropped off her things. Once the door clicked shut behind her Katsina immediately tossed her jacket onto a chair and pulled out the rations box from under her arm. The box had left an outline on her chest from where she had kept it safe all day, the box itself was covered in sweat, and it smelled like her. She only realised, at that moment, that her most recent shower was more than a few days before. In Marshal's home. Before the attack. So the lunchbox went with her to the shower while she stripped the rest of her clothes off, leaving a textile trail in her wake. In the bathroom mirror Katsina caught a glimpse of herself as she was about to take a bite out of the apple flavored ration pack. The long vertical scar that nearly divided her lips down the middle looked raw, stretched even.

"No wonder people were staring" she thought.

She traced the cut with her left finger, feeling the tightness of the skin around it. It was sore to touch, but she couldn't help but lick at the splits in her lips where the gash went through. The stinging sensation as she widened her mouth to pull the little cuts open was, for her, a reminder that she could still feel something after the day she'd had. As far as she could tell, she had felt nothing for most of the day, apart from the small glint of something positive when she first saw the rations. Which she had finally started to dig into.

The shower wasn't the most comfortable to sit in, but then again what shower was? And the rations didn't taste like much, especially being soggy from the water. Katsina needed to wash the day off, eat something, and sleep. What she didn't realise was that she was about to do all three in Mara's shower. She felt herself dozing off, but genuinely didn't care, she just needed it. The hot water was soothing and refreshing after everything she had seen. With the lunchbox empty, and the rations working their magic to keep her energy levels up, Katsina drifted away watching the numbers in her HUD tumble up and down. Eventually it flickered off as she closed her eyes.

***

She was standing in a dark room with glittering walls, like twinkling lights had been poked through the navy and purple wallpaper. Katsina glanced around, far off stars and planets shone in the distance. She turned around to see the room had changed, not in shape or color, but it was larger than she remembered. Hanging from the ceiling on thin strings, floating in space was the Raptor's Claw, Mara's fighter ship. Katsina immediately ran towards it, her feet getting wet as she ran. She looked down on the floor and saw herself in rippling black water, her image slightly bent and distorted. The water swelled up to her waist, so she slowly trudged her way forward. Arriving at the bow of the ship she peeked into the nose cone of the Raptor's Claw and saw Mara and Aaron sitting on the glass.

"Mara!" Katsina said, relieved they were alive. She banged on the glass, but they didn't notice her. They were ignoring her, she could tell that they weren't asleep, their eyes were wide open.

"What the..."

A loud noise behind Katsina made her spin around and pin her back to the Raptor's Claw. It was deep, gut wrenching, petrifying to the ear. A sorrowful groan from the depths of space. It eventually halted, leaving only the sounds of trickling water, before a soft knock on the glass behind her made her jump a second time. She leapt back, a human skull, sat atop the shoulders of a fighters jumpsuit with Mara's badge on it, staring at her. Even though it didn't have any eyes, she knew it was looking at her. The skeleton rapped its bony knuckles off of the glass, while pointing away in the distance to Mara's left. She didn't want to turn around. A sinking feeling was taking her over. The water in the starry room began to rise.

The skeleton's hand began to bang faster and harder, while the rest of its body didn't move, the finger on the other hand still raised. Short of breath, Katsina finally spun around to see something. At least she thought it was something. It was dark, and far away, blocking out some of the stars. She couldn't make out its shape. Another deathly, haunting, sound came from the distance where the black spot was. Katsina felt it looking at her, she knew it had seen her. The spot began to grow, and the sound increased.

"But there's no sound in space," she thought. *"There's no sound in space."*

The sound was unbearable. The water had risen to her shoulders, forcing her to swim. She looked over her shoulder to check if the Raptor's Claw was still there, and it was, only it was almost submerged like her. She swam to the tail fin of the ship, feeling the monster of the deep growing larger and faster behind her. She dived under the water, and saw only the lights from the fighters angular wings, and the glowing hue of the nose cone. She swam down to the airlock, and pulled at its handle. It wouldn't move. She looked around, desperate, but there was nothing but black under the water around her. The water didn't hide her, but it was hiding the monster chasing her. Katsina needed to get into the ship, so she swam around to the nose cone, intent on convincing the skeleton to help her. But it was no longer there. Instead of the skeleton, or Mara and Aaron's frozen bodies, Katsina saw a familiar face. Aardashini Morann, sitting in the pilot's seat, looking down at her through the thick glass. Katsina gasped at the sight of her, inhaling water, not understanding what was happening at all.

"You need to find me, Katsina..." Aardashini's voice echoed.

Katsina suddenly fell backwards, and jumped awake from the horrible dreamscape. She gasped, and found herself still soaking in water. The trickling sound of the shower running over her was the only thing from the dream she recognised. She immediately stood, slipping and catching herself from a fall on the way up. With a *whack*, Katsina knocked off the shower and stumbled out of it, holding her face in her hands along the way. She was short of breath, panicked, and fuming with adrenaline.

"t'sßolfé," she gasped.

Attempting to process her dream, She glanced around the dark crew quarters, adjusting the brightness in her eyes to match it. Katsina had never had a dream like that before, in fact she never had a troubled sleep. Dreams were a rare occurrence in people since the installation of memory cores at a young age. People's minds simply no longer needed to dream.

"A... A Nightmare?" she said.

Dying off, Katsina recorded all she could from the unconscious thoughts of the dream to her memory core. Memory cores, which housed half the human personality, were the AI counterparts to the human brain. The synthetic symbiote to the organic form. One thing memory cores never processed were raw dreams, as they were created by the mind in its memory making process. The memory core of a human's mind worked much quicker, and stored information instantly. A person could only record what they remembered from a dream manually, that was if they ever had a dream to begin with. Katsina had never had a dream before, let alone a bad one. She wrote the experience off as a side effect of not using her HUD for so long, and crept up the steps to the bed on the balcony. She moved the headset that she and Rutheo had found earlier in the day to one side, and collapsed onto the sheets to bury her head in the pillows.

Of all the things she could have dreamt about, she dreamed of Aardashini Morann, the woman in the picture frame. Why? And why did Aardashini tell Katsina to find her? She didn't know, but she did know that as soon as she started her next shift, she was going to find out.

IN MEMORIAM

    The ship's live intercom signaled, waking Katsina abruptly. In her ears she heard Morann's voice, condescending as always, making the ship's morning announcements. She rolled over and pulled up her HUD to check the time, 5:50. She ignored Morann's words, muting the sound of his voice to leave only the hum of the ship. She couldn't imagine having to listen to him each day without her HUD. The inability to mute him would be a nail in the proverbial coffin for her patience. It was how he wanted it anyway, to exclude her, so for one morning she was going to let him. Katsina pushed her face into the pillows, letting out a small groan. Upon opening her eyes again she noticed a message in her inbox, in the top right corner of her eye. It didn't have a title.
    "Malware?" Katsina thought.
    But malware typically was disguised as personal messages or admin notifications, and wouldn't be encrypted. This message wasn't flagged, so she opened it.

Kat, conflict at home is over.
The Ygg ship was sunk but they still don't know how
it got through the planetary defenses.
There's someone making moves behind the scenes
giving the Yggs more and more chances to get at us.
Watch your back. Morann's people aren't the friendliest.
All the captains are shook up. People are suspicious.
As far as I can tell Morann and a few others on the board are
trying to pin these events on you.
Don't reply to this message.
Keep your head down.
M

    Katsina read the message multiple times, trying to find any other information she could between the lines. The transmission date and location was scrubbed from the log, Marshal covered his tracks to send it to her.

"Clever t'Secheashin," she muttered before rolling out of the bed.

The floor was cold, and covered with the wires and cables that ran to the headset on the floor; it must have fallen out of the bed as she slept. Keeping her eye on the time, Katsina pulled a uniform from one of the dispensaries downstairs. The clothes didn't exactly fit; Mara was slightly shorter than her, but she didn't have time to pick and choose. Her shift started in a half hour. Before leaving she looked back at her Captain's jacket, still stained with the blood from her face, still missing her affix, and decided to leave it behind. The last thing she wanted was to draw attention to herself, especially with what she had to do that day. She thought of messaging Rutheo, but knew the message would be flagged immediately; if only she knew how Marshal got his message to her. How did he find a way to lie to the system? She closed the door to Mara's quarters, and flicked her HUD out of her vision before setting off towards the ship's main hallway.

It sounded like Morann's address to the crew was still going on, as people seemed distracted on the way to the bridge for shift change. They were all staring off into space, their eyes focused on their HUD's and Morann's words. Katsina knew that she wasn't meant to hear the address, because she wasn't meant to have a HUD. An interesting turn in her opinion, to be able to hear him without him knowing. Other than the hustle and bustle of the people going to and from their shifts, the ship was eerily quiet again. The eyes of the people leaving the bridge to return home seemed to be sunk into the back of their heads, just as Aker's had been. They were pale, and dreary to look at; it made Katsina clench her jaw, and curl her fists up in her pockets. For her, this was the worst thing that could have happened to her crew.

"Captain," A voice whispered behind her, making Katsina tilt her head. "No no, don't look; it's me Alice."

"Alice?"

"Shhh, don't talk; just listen. It- It's important."

Katsina didn't respond, but instead slowed her pace slightly. She tilted her head down to conceal her eyes. And used her HUD to tune her ears to hear Alice more clearly.

"The comms you asked me to look into on Morann's ship, they checked out. But I found something from weeks before, a signal that wasn't part of our Quantum network."

Katsina kept her head down, focusing solely on her words.

"And the thing is, it happened again. It was filtered through our ship's background noise. Someone is transmitting messages off of our network."

Katsina's jaw fell and she let out a small gasp before loudly coughing to cover up her actions. She cleared her throat and rubbed her ear, hoping Alice would get the gesture.

"I still can't trace it, but I'm meeting Rutheo later, in the cafeteria. I'll see you then."

She watched as Alice quickly overtook her and walked away, noticing that there were one or two people looking in her direction. Katsina wondered if they had heard what Alice said; if their ears were tuned to listen as well. She didn't recognise their faces, just their uniforms, the men were from the 'Insurmountable' crew. Just as she remembered Marshal's message, the men looked away and turned a corner towards one of the stairwells. It was clear that she was being monitored, both digitally and in person, by Morann. That made her research into his relationship with Aardashini all the more perilous. Katsina glanced up to one of the many sensor strips that ran along the ship, this one lined over the doors to the bridge. Knowing that someone, somewhere was watching her through it; she curled her lip, and waved slyly before walking through the doors to the dome.

The bridge crew was reserved, just as the day before. People didn't greet each other, they just sat down and began their work. Up on the balcony, there was one helmsman and no one else. Morann's shift must not have started. This gave Katsina a moment of opportunity. She crossed the floor towards her desk, making a point to pass around the large holographic projection in the middle of the dome. She never really cared about interrupting the projection before, but now wasn't the time to be conspicuous. Katsina landed at her desk, and logged in to her unfinished work from the day before. Scrolling down through the information packets, Katsina found the most difficult line of code she could and clicked on it. She flagged it as unrecognisable and forwarded it to the commanding officer on duty before sitting back and waiting. After just a minute, a slim man with a gaunt face appeared silently next to Katsina, not what she had expected. She could only describe him as an insect, with his large eyes and lengthy forehead coupled with his small chin and jaw.

"A mantis," she thought.

He was clearly at the end of his shift, and not a member of her crew, the circles under his eyes showed he had been up more than enough hours of the night.

"Uh, yes, Lucas. What's the issue here?" he said in a slightly annoyed tone.

"Yes I just am having trouble recognising this string of code here. I think I need to take it down to the Archives to retrieve a manual and decode it." she said, feigning innocence and ignorance alike. Katsina knew what the code was meant to be, however rusty she was. But it was a perfect chance to get to the archives if she just pretended.

"Hmmm, this packet was meant to be finished yesterday, do you have a report on your work from last night?" he asked.

"Sorry, I didn't actually get your name? We must not have met before, I'm Katsina," she said, holding out her hand to him.

The man flinched slightly, and took half a step back while fidgeting with his fingers. He stared at Katsina's hand for a moment, wrinkling his nose before clearing his throat.

"Toboggan is my name, and I know who *you* are. No need to introduce yourself. Please, can you link to me your report on last night's work," he said, the irritation beginning to seep through his teeth.

"Oh, haha, I would, but that's a funny story. So, I don't actually have a HUD right now so I can't access my interface to send or receive messages or any other menus for my subsystems. You have no idea how much of a nightmare it's been to keep track of the PH levels in my-"

"Yes, yes, I get the point," Toboggan interrupted. "But with the work unfinished, I will have to sanction you for a disciplinary."

Katsina's heart dropped into her stomach, her plan was about to fall through. Toboggan flicked and swiped on his tablet before turning it to her.

"Finger print, please."

"Wait now, surely you can make an exception," Katsina said. "It was my first day yesterday at this packet and I have no HUD so of course I cou-"

"The rules are there for a reason, Lucas. Please present your fingerprint for disciplinary action."

"Look," she said, dropping her pleasantry. "I just need an hour downstairs to get this work done. Giving me a disciplinary isn't going to get my work done faster."

"Ship MP's have been notified of your refusal to present your fingerprint. Please present it before this is escalated further," Toboggan droned, seeming uninterested in reason.

"Are you kidding me?" Katsina said, standing out of her chair. It was another notch that cut into her, another straw on her back. Normally she could deal with red tape, but red tape on top of everything she had been dealing with was more than enough to anger her.

"Is there an issue here, Chief Petty Officer Toboggan?" a nervous voice entered. It was Alice Wesley, whom Katsina really needed.

"Yes, this one doesn't want to present her fingerprint

fo-"

"Yes, I heard you say that part alright. However you've been relieved for about fifteen minutes now. You're off duty. I'll deal with Petty Officer Lucas." Alice said, with a hint of confidence that Katsina had never seen before.

Toboggan paused, flicking his eyes back and forth between Alice and Katsina critically, before tapping his tablet to Alice's.

"Your passover. I'm sure you will deal with Miss Lucas accordingly. Otherwise I will have to report you both to the captain," he said.

"As far as I remember, Chief, you're still fresh off of being a petty officer first class. You can report any grievances to me via the proper channels so as to not waste the captain's time," she replied, a spike of irritability emanating in her tone.

"Yes, Chief. Eye's set on the Commanding officer role I see," he muttered angrily, before turning his face and leaving them both in silence.

"Woah. What did he mean by that?" Katsina asked, puzzled.

"What the hell are you thinking?" she asked, flicking her hair as she spun her attention back to Katsina.

"What?"

"Are you trying to get us both in trouble. I knew you couldn't get the work done in time but why did you flag a piece of code? It's like you want to get in trouble," Alice said in frustration, keeping her voice as low as possible.

"Listen," Katsina said before checking around them, "I need to go down to the archives. There's something there that I need to *decode this packet.*"

"Decode the... Oh. Um." Alice mumbled.

"I just need an hour," said Katsina.

Alice glanced around herself, her face worried as always. She quickly fiddled with the tablet in her hands before looking back to Katsina.

"I won't be able to grant you any longer."

"That's fine. I'll be back in no time," she said, meeting Alice's nervous gaze. "I'll tell you all about it later, it's just that I'm so *behind on this packet*."

"Understandable, please report to archives to find the relevant data you need to complete the task," Alice said, handing Katsina a tablet with her data packets.

Alice left with her tablet, to go and address another officer who flagged her. Katsina sat back down for a moment, letting the relief wash over her. She exhaled slowly, and felt her pulse return to normal. She even wiped a bead of sweat from her temple, not remembering the last time she had felt that nervous. Had it been another minute, she most likely would have been back in confinement. Katsina wondered what Toboggan meant, and she slowly came to the conclusion that she would have to check the morning address later that day. She obviously missed something. Considering all that had happened, she knew she would have to make it up to Alice; for everything the girl had been doing to support her. But that time would come. For the time she had, she had research to do.

***

The archives of the Behemothis, a vast room full of towering computer data nodes, was the only place Katsina thought would be where her answers were buried. The only noise that filled the space was that of the cooling baths filling and emptying with water, keeping the heat of the hard drives at an appropriate temperature. Among the many junctions were hexagonal desks that were dwarfed by the immense size of the Archives towers that surrounded them, stretching from floor to ceiling. Each tower would rise and fall into its pool of cooling water, causing a waterfall each time it re-emerged. The entire room was one of many supercomputer nodes that linked to the quantum network. It was both a library of human history, and a support structure for the web that connected all of humankind. Katsina found her way to the tower she needed, avoiding eye contact with anyone else in the archives along the way. The tower ID was named "Ancestry and Citizenship".

The archive of human history was made up of every human memory core that had ever lived and died since humans had reached singularity, fusing their minds with synthetic ones. Every recorded memory, event, and first hand account of history was embedded in the servers shared among the three human planets. In essence, all knowledge that ever existed was contained in this area of the ship. Human legacy was the wealth of the universe. Everyone's efforts to make their lives and the lives of those around them better was the sole intent of the ancestors who left earth. It was a goal shared by every person ever since. The only lives that were no longer recorded were that of lost souls, those who never returned from space. Before the war, Yggdrasil was part of the Archive, until they segregated their planet from the shared network, leaving Crescent, Botanica, and Horizon to record history as completely as they could. If anyone, anywhere had come across Aardashini Morann, their memory of her would be here.

Katsina sat at the desk at the base of the tower and took a moment to take in the height of the room. Very few things made her feel small; space itself, seeing a planet from orbit, but this room, and the exabytes of data surrounding her. She could see and hear all of the information around her, she just needed to plug into it. Time was of the essence.

"I need to get started," she thought.

Katsina looked around her, making sure no one was in earshot, or in a visual range to see her link to the database. She leaned over the pool of water, and focused her eyes onto the archive ID. Latching onto one of the many cables hanging from the tower with her index finger and thumb, she led the cord to the back of her neck, and plugged in. Katsina's eyes widened, and an entire menu of memory and history appeared before her eyes in her HUD. She pretended as best she could not to see it, and instead glanced down to the tablet in her left hand. To any onlooker she was doing her work manually, or at least that's what she hoped. Immediately she found the folder named Military Personnel and entered the keywords she needed, "Aardashini" "Morann" "Rank" and so on. Most of what came up was the lineage and personal histories of Deacon Morann and his family's legacy. None of which she was interested in. She pondered for a moment, wondering if it might be a good idea to look into Morann's life. Perhaps to find an answer as to why he had it out for her. Katsina bit on one of her fingernails, keeping her eye on his personal life and history. She chewed her nail before letting go of it, and her idea.

"*Not this time.*"

Among the many data files, Katsina finally scrolled over the one name she was searching for, "Aardashini Chakrabarti/Morann" was listed under known affiliates in the Morann family folder. Not the first place she would have guessed, but it made sense as to why Rutheo didn't initially find her the first time she looked wirelessly. Having a different second name to what her Military ID badge had listed was a suspicious thing to change about a person's history. Katsina exited the Morann family folder, and rearranged her search parameters to include "Chakrabarti". A new flood of family names and individuals with the same name came into view, making her scroll until she found the right person. The woman in the picture finally appeared before her, listed as 'killed in action', or KIA.

"*KIA?*" Katsina thought, remembering Rutheo saying that she was missing, not killed. Katsina looked down on the file and began to copy the data on the woman until she spotted a familiar name. Her name.

Katsina looked up at the sound of the second wave of morning announcements from Morann.

"*His shift must have started...*" she thought.

She knew she was close to her time limit, but wasn't satisfied in just copying the data to read later. She hovered over her own name, and clicked on it. What began to play was a memory from Aardashini's perspective, where the centre of her eyes were focused on a younger figure, a tall man with an angry face. It was Morann.

***

"...she's wrong, we need to retreat. There's not a hope in hell that a wild assumption like that can turn the tide here. Even if they don't have rods we c-"

"Deacon, think about it, they haven't fired for over 3 hours now. When have you known them to let any of us just walk away. This moon belongs to everyone, they can't take it. We can't let them."

"I won't let you do something so reckless. If this Lucas person wants to go down in a blaze of glory then let her," Morann said, strutting back and forth in the tent that Katsina had been thrown into, holding his hands over the back of his head. Katsina recognised it immediately. It was a medical resupply tent in aid of the soldiers defending the Alia moon. At an outpost for fighter refueling and treatment of crashed pilots. She had been there. She tuned out Morann's morning address that played in the real world to keep herself focused on the new memory she was living.

"She has sound evidence, and you can't tell me to not help her," Katsina remembered.

"Oh I can, I'm your commanding officer Aarda. These troops are under my command, and this refueling outpost is to be abandoned as we retreat from the enemy. Those are my orders." Morann said furiously, almost pleading. He raised his voice over the sounds of the people outside the tent, people chanting. A chorus of war cries led by one person.

"I'm not one of your crew. I am your wife, and I command my own people. You can tell me what to do all you like,

Deacon. But you can't stop me from taking this moon back."

Katsina, as Aardashini, looked down at her hands, they were dirty and scarred, as if just healed from fresh wounds. The blood on her uniform could have been hers or the blood of others; Katsina couldn't tell.

"Arda," Morann's sullen voice sounded, making her glance back up to him.

"I have to go," she said.

Morann ran his hand over his mouth, pulling on his cheeks. A light in his eyes seemed to fade away, a face of disbelief changing to a look of utter defeat.

"Please, don't go," he muttered, turning his back and clasping his hands to the back of his neck. He sniffed loudly, his voice cracking.

One of the bloodied hands pulled on the curtain to the tent and she left Morann behind. She stepped out into an emerald trench, carved out of pale green stone. Up a hill of the trench to Aardashini's right, standing above the rest of the soldiers who congregated in the wide carved out vein, was a bloodied and ragged woman who held a rifle over her head. The woman's clothes were torn, her body caked in muck and green dust. Through Aardashini's eyes, she looked up into the eyes of the woman; they were wide, rabid, almost savage in how they looked across the trenches towards the enemy ships in the distance. She was shouting an angry and vengeful song. Rallying Aardashini and the troops of the Alia moon to move over the no man's land towards the Yggdrasilians. Katsina barely recognised the person chanting on the hill, but she knew who it was at the same time. It was her.

Katsina stepped back, and ripped the cable out of the back of her neck, disconnecting from the server and the horrifying image of herself. She bumped into something behind her and spun around, gasping in fright, only to see the table. Katsina stanced for a confrontation, only to realise she was all alone again in the brightly lit, blue tinted archives of the Behemothis. She placed her palms on the cold table, contorting her breathing into deep gasps for air. Her heart was racing, just as it did on that day, while a cold bead of sweat ran down her nose. She let herself crouch onto the ground, keeping her fingers hinged on the table for support. She had to let herself calm, slowly allowing her breathing to return to normal. Her heart pounded in her chest regardless, panic struck her. Eventually she looked back at her HUD, shifting focus from the floor to the time of death that she had copied from Aardashini's folder. Aardashini Morann died on the Alia moon in the final push that Katsina led to defeat the Yggdrasilians. She never knew her, but she fought with her. The woman Katsina didn't recognise supported her on the day she became a war hero, and died for her efforts.

"Some war hero," Katsina whispered to herself under the table.

US AND THEM

"Where have you been?" Alice's voice cut through the ambient noise of the bridge. Katsina almost didn't react and she just barely caught what she had said. She stopped, blinked slowly, and rubbed her eyes with her palms before turning around to face Alice.

"Captain?" Alice asked. "What's happened?"

"Sorry, just had an issue accessing the Archive using the tablet. I'm sort of not used to this stuff. Sorry about that," Katsina said in an attempt to keep her voice from cracking.

"Seriously, are you okay? You look like you've seen a ghost," Alice said, her concern beginning to show.

"I'm fine. I didn't get *that report* ready for you in time. I still have a lot of packets left," Katsina said, emphasising her words in an attempt to change the subject. Alice let out a defeated sigh.

"You understand that I need to report that to the Captain directly. We don't have a first officer to report to."

"It's fine," Katsina said. "If it's okay with you, I'd like to go over some of these with you *at lunch*?"

"That's fine, I can show you some shortcuts to help you work."

"Perfect, I'll see you then," Katsina said in a lighter tone.

"Are you sure you're okay?" Alice asked. Katsina glanced around, noticing the onlookers to their conversation.

"Yeah, I'll see you later," she said with a smile.

"Alice," A rugged and familiar voice approached. It was Kessler, "Captain needs you upstairs."

Alice threw a confused glance over Katsina's shoulder before leaving. She was left with only her work, endless lines of code she still had to manually decrypt on the screen in front of her. Katsina's eyes glazed over, and she became preoccupied with the memories she had seen in the archives. She shrugged her shoulders forward, leaning into the work she knew was futile to complete. But she did it anyway, wanting to think of anything else instead of Aardashini Morann.

As much as she hoped she would distract herself, she hardly got a thing done. Haunting her mind the entire time she typed was the disturbing image she saw of herself in Aardashini's memories. Her outline against the red and smokey sky felt burned into her vision. As if she had looked into the sun for too long. Eventually footsteps began to bustle against the white plated floors around the isles of computers, signaling to Katsina that she could finally break away from the work, and her thoughts. As always the period of walking between places on the Behemothis was disconcerting and borderline physically uncomfortable. She resorted to keeping her head down, again, and not speaking to anyone after what happened with Aker Castle the day before. Focusing on her feet meeting the floor, eventually she found her way to the cafeteria of the ship, where she had barely ever set foot before. Considering the vibrant cityscape that each of the Broadsider's were built with, which included restaurants, AR theatres and more, Katsina never saw the need for the crew to resort to using the military subsidised cafeteria, let alone the rations that were stored there.

The space itself should have been brightly lit, with every few sets of tables divided by flats depicting images of home for people to see through their AR filtered eyes. But the flats were just that, flat, grey, and divisive. The lights were dimmed, leaving the space to feel uninviting. Katsina made her way around the partitions towards the kitchen pass, hoping to see a lunch that she knew wasn't there. The Kitchen on the other side was impeccably clean, with the ovens still covered in the plastic they were delivered in. Not a galley chef in sight, a sad way to see a place that would have been a creative space for the culinary staff to work. The only vending machine or food printer that was on and working was the ration distributor, which had a long and depressing looking line of people waiting to eat their assigned food of the day. Katsina couldn't feel hungry after seeing it, so decided to search for Alice. The crew were sitting mostly apart from each other, with very little interaction. Those from Morann's crew huddled in their own groups, whispering among themselves, behaving like some kind of henchmen in an old spy movie. The clinking of plates on tables, and the scratches of knives on plates reminded Katsina of a restaurant, if a restaurant was set up as a waiting room in the mouth of purgatory. Katsina couldn't find Alice, even after checking behind every partition. Before resorting to returning to the bridge and subsequently keeping the new information that she'd learned to herself, a familiar voice pulled her back to where she was.

"...how about you back off, huh? I earned these just like you did..."

"Rutheo?"

She spun around, the entire cafeteria moving around her. The chairs and tables scratched off the floor, mumbles rising among the people moving the same direction she was. Towards the raised voices Katsina found a small but furious Rutheo, squaring up to a much taller and burlier Commander Kessler.

"What? you think just 'cause you got two more pins than me that makes you better? Touch my shit again and we're gonna have an issue okay?" Rutheo said.

"Watch your tongue, 'Ruthie', coffee is listed for upper command personnel only. Hand it over," Kessler said. Antagonistic as always.

His stature was that of a marbled rock. His shoulders reminded Katsina of a slope of a hill. He had two of his own men flanking him, and his arms were crossed. A spike in Katsina's chest signalled to her where the situation was going.

"I got my field promotion," she said, levity in her voice. "You've been pushing me around since day one, I'm sick of your shit. What do you want from me, huh?"

"Oho, there's a lot I want from you 'Ruthie'," Kessler said with a cheeky smile.

"It's Senior Specialist Rutheo McHugh to you. So come take it then?" Ruthio asked while she unclipped her tool belt.

She held her belt dangling to her side and dropped it to the floor. Leaving her right hand free. In her left, she held a commanding officer's ration pack. Similar to the one Alice had slipped Katsina the night before. A circle had formed around the tables, people pressed up against the partitions and standing on seats to see. Katsina moved as fast as she could, ducking around the poeple who gathered to watch the situation unfold.

"Hey, Hey!" She called, stepping into the circle. "That's enough."

"Aha, look at this, the betrayer herself. She stealing this stuff for you is it?" Kessler said, amused. He was just an inch taller than Katsina and three times the mass, certainly not her equal considering the two others he had by his side. The synthetic half of his grey face must have been itchy for him, Katsina thought about removing it.

"I'm perfectly capable of stealing for myself, not that I have to. Besides, Rutheo was promoted to senior engineer just three days ago and is entitled to these. So what's the issue here, huh?" She said, pushing her face into his, making the hubbub swell. Some criticized her, some even scoffed at her attempt to make him back down.

"Her promotion was made in the field, and therefore doesn't qualify her to the perks of the rank," said one of the other two men.

"Exactly, the Captain's guidelines are strict when it comes to these matters," Kessler said, his voice deep and commanding, just as Katsina had tried to sound.

"If that's it then I'm sure one of your MP's can sort it as a formal complaint," Katsina said. "Not this vigilante shit. If the captain has an issue with Rutheo's actions personally then he better get down here t-"

Katsina felt a soft squeeze of her wrist, and glanced down to see Rutheos hand. She turned back, and saw a defeated face, where one of confidence used to be.

"It's fine, I'll give it back," she said quietly. Katsina noticed her eyes, the same as they were before she had first brought her to Morann.

"Ruthie, you can't just let the-"

"Kat, I don't want to get in trouble," she said, her voice sounding smaller and shaken than before. Katsina glanced around, seeing similar scared faces among her crew. They were dotted between the jeering grins of Morann's people, who were ready to see what they came for. She frowned, the sight of her crew, broken as they were hit differently this time. She focused back onto Rutheo's dipped head.

"You won't get into trouble," Katsina said, before running her tongue over the cut in her lip. It was still sore as the day Morann beat it into her. "But I don't care for this anymore."

She reached down and snatched the rations box from Rutheo, and pushed her back into the circle of onlookers. Katsina saw a flash in her eyes, her rambunctiousness rearing its head, if only for a moment before Katsina fixed her gaze back to the mountainous Kessler.

"You think you can just throw Morann's name around and get people to do what you want? Is that it, Rendell?" She said with a sneer.

"That's how being a commanding officer works. So yes," he laughed. The ever growing crowd rumbled with different responses. "And it's Captain Kessler to you."

"Oh you want to go by proper titles now that it suits you? Fine, then you can call me *Captain* Katsina Lucas," she said, lifting her arms to either side of her. A swell of noise met her in response, jeering and booing at the sound of her captaincy. "But you won't pick out members of my crew to try and bully. Not on my ship," she replied, "If you want this faisaheßul ration so badly…"

A flash of Aardasini's memory clouded Katsina's mind

briefly and she saw herself, the barbarian on the hill.

"...then come and take it."

Kessler's eyes changed, widened slightly. The crowd around them had fallen silent. Katsina ran her tongue over her cut lip again, still remembering the pain, awaiting for it to happen all over again. Her breath spiked as she braced for his response. He was bigger, but she had fought worse, and never lost. Kessler stepped away from his comrades, entering the circle fully. An acceptance to a fight if Katsina had ever seen one. He began to circle her, lifting his hands to guard his face as he went. Katsina matched him after stuffing the ration pack in her back pocket, she took her stance, rotating around the arena. Kessler took his first jab at her, and missed. She ducked under his arm and shot back a jab into his chest. It felt like hitting a wall, not exactly the most pleasant feeling. She didn't have the liberty of a HUD to help her in her attack, leaving all her senses at a disadvantage. Already she could see Kesslers mind working, his speed increasing as she dodged his incoming swings. For as light as she was on her feet, eventually a punch landed. Kessler caught her on the left side, sending a shockwave up through her lower back. The punch was devastating, making Katsina stumble to one side before another hit connected with her lip.

Katsina hit the floor and rolled onto her side. She clutched at her lower back, feeling an aching bruise already beginning to form. The cut on her lip had opened back up. Kessler had no interest in pulling punches. She felt a hand grab her forearm, pulling her up from the floor, it was Rutheo. She helped Katsina to her feet before Kessler, who stood across from them, surrounded by the crewmembers of the Insurmountable. He was disheveled, his uniform out of sorts. It revealed the silver chain around his neck again, the one adorned with rings. Katsina wouldn't have noticed it, had he not hastily tucked it away under his shirt again. Katsina felt another hand on her shoulder, making her look around to see the faces of her crew around her.

"What's wrong 'Ruthie'?" Kessler gloated, "Can't stand up for yourself? Need your girlfriend to come save you? Need your crew to come save her?"

Rutheo's grip tightened on Katsina, her eyes seemingly frozen with fear. But it wasn't just fear Katsina noticed, it was shame. What happened to her?

"Shut it," Katsina said, spitting blood towards him' "You don't speak to her, you speak to me. What's with your weird obsession with her anyway? You too scared to face the real enemy out there so you have to make fake ones in here? The Yggs could be out there slaughtering every person you love right now, but instead of doing your job, you just want to torment her? Are you bored? Or just a coward?"

"Ha, the only coward I see here is the little girl who needs her captain to stand up for her," he said, feigning laughter. "You should tell her everything you said about her, Rutheo, everything you did to get out of being charged. I still think about it you know."

Katsina looked down to Rutheo, whose pain and anger had been completely replaced with red flushes of embarrassment. She stood deadly still, her eyes closed, her hand shaking. Katsina bent down to her ear.

"It's going to be fine," she said, before taking Rutheo's hand off her arm.

Katsina watched Kessler and his band of cronies, snickering in banter at what he said. It was clear to her that he had no intentions of acting properly, instead he just seemed to want to antagonise her people, particularly Rutheo. She couldn't allow it to go on. So she took a step towards him, lifting her hands to her face. She noticed she wasn't alone. Katsina glanced to her left to see a member of crisis response standing next to her, his arms raised. Next to him, a fighter pilot, arms raised. The list went on. And Katsina recognised every one of them.

"I don't need your help," she grunted.

"We know you don't, but we're ready when you are,

Captain," one of them said.

"t'Seiß ta schurul dzalm chusanichen?" Kessler said, his smirk falling away from his face.

"I don't think they are," Katsina said as Rutheo rejoined her at her side, "but I can only imagine that my ship is starting to run low on patience for you Kessler."

He stepped forward himself, squaring to the crowd that gathered around Katsina, but he did it alone. No one from the group around him stepped forward, making him look about, huffing in anger. He didn't advance any further, nor did he step back. Instead he just stared at Katsina and her band in confusion. The top of his head was cut off by Katsina's own eyebrows blocking her vision, a heat had swelled in her, and an old pain in the knuckles of her right hand throbbed with her heartbeat. The bald man took a step back as another voice entered the circle. Katsina felt the ration box slip from her back pocket, and turned about to see Alice enter the fray.

"I will be returning this to the ration stores," she said loudly, holding the box over her head, "and the Military Police will be monitoring the consumption and distribution of rations more closely. Mr. Kessler, you are confined to quarters until I believe you fit for duty. Leave."

"Alice?" Katsina said, snapping out of her inflamed state. The blond woman had stepped between her and the three men, keeping her back to her the entire time.

"Any more disruption during designated lunch times will be reported to the captain directly. As well as a disciplinary being written up by myself personally. Return to your food."

Kessler's eyes flared at the sight of Alice. Huffing in anger as he approached her. She didn't move back, instead she just tilted her chin upwards. The grey man towered over her, his leather like skin began to seep with sweat.

"Fine," he said, glancing a look of disgust in Katsina and Rutheo's direction.

The two opposing groups quickly dispersed, and Kessler disappeared in the crowd. Katsina looked about at Rutheo, who looked as confused as she felt. Alice turned to face them, revealing a new item that she was wearing. An Affix, clipped to the shoulder of her uniform, bearing the rank of first officer.

"Wow," Katsina said. "Two promotions in just a few weeks."

"Not something I chose," Alice sighed awkwardly. "I don't want to talk about it."

"That's fine, just, uh. Congratulations, Ma'am," Rutheo said, stepping towards them both.

"Ca- uhm, Kat, you said you had a coding issue you needed help with. Can you stop trying to get into trouble for five minutes?"

"I need the two of you to come with me and sit down, *I have to tell you something*." Katsina said as low as possible, motioning to a nearby table.

The three huddled together. Around them the cafeteria returned to normal, with the clinking of plates and chatter filling the room again. As they sat down Alice handed the ration back to Rutheo, albeit discreetly. Katsina delved into her experience in the archives, explaining what she'd seen to Alice and Rutheo, who listened intently for the most part. Rutheo ran her fingers through her wavy ponytail, while Alice scratched at her eyebrow. They had only pieces of the story from their perspectives, and were finally filled in by Katsina. The three were on the same page, Alice and Rutheo let out a deep sigh at what they had learned. Their responses were as grave as Katsina's tale, and were just as worrying.

"So you think he has it out for you because this lady followed you on the Alia moon?" Rutheo asked.

"Why wouldn't he?" Alice entered.

"Well it's not like Kat made his wife follow him, she made her own choice. Kat's not the one that killed her," Rutheo argued.

"Relax Ruthie," Katsina said softly, pulling her index

finger up to her lips.

"So what does this mean?" Alice asked.

"Morann has more than enough reason to dislike me, and I think he genuinely thinks I sold out the Delta Squadron. I got people killed before, so of course he thinks I did it again," Katsina said.

"But you didn't get those people killed, you led a ground offensive that won us a tactical advantage on the redemption wheel," Rutheo said.

"But why are her records not readily available for people to search? Surely if they are in the archives they should be able to be accessed by everyone on the network anywhere," Alice wondered.

"Exactly, why would they be only available under a different name?" said Katinsa.

"If somehow Morann altered the information, doctored records. That would support what I've been thinking…" Alice said vaguely.

"And what's that? Go on?" Rutheo egged her. She lifted her knees to her chest, wrapping her arms around her shins.

"This morning, Alice noticed a hidden signal in the ship's transmissions. It was similar to one that left the ship a few weeks ago," Katsina said.

Rutheo glanced between Katsina and Alice, her eyes wide. "Why didn't you report it? Alice?"

Katsina lifted her hand gently to Alice, she looked like a deer in headlights.

"Tell her."

"Well, I'm not sure, but I think if it's true that Morann has the capability of hiding the records of his wife the way he has, then he must be able to create and transmit messages like this as well. The quantum network doesn't mishandle information, Aardashini should have been listed under both her maiden name and married name. It also doesn't allow for untraceable comm links."

Rutheo's face contorted as she leant back in her chair,

clasping her hands behind her neck.

"Are you serious?" she asked.

"Yes."

Katsina leaned in, lowering her voice to barely a whisper.

"Either Morann genuinely believes I've done this because of Aardashini's death, and there is another player here behind the scenes-"

"Because you obviously didn't sell us out to the Yggs," Rutheo added.

"-Or Morann has put this conspiracy together himself to get back at me for Aardashini," Katsina concluded.

Silence set in, and the three of them looked at eachother. One of two narratives had been identified, and between the three, only one seemed to be the right fit.

"It explains the way he's been acting, forcing everyone against you. Making the ship suffer under your name, and his crew acting inappropriately. But it's hard to believe that someone would make up such an extravagant lie, one look at his memory core would expose him. The admiralty board needs to hear this," said Alice.

"Are you stupid? We can't send any messages without pre approval, Morann will know what we're doing. He has everyone being looked at, it's like living in a big brother house around here," Rutheo stressed.

"We don't have any tangible proof either, only two highly encrypted background noises in space," Katsina added.

"-and one deliberate tampering with the quantum archives. It's enough to raise suspicion," Alice said.

"Yeah, it's pretty sus like," Rutheo said.

"No, we have to keep this to ourselves until we learn more. If we can figure this much out so far, then eventually we can find more," Katsina said.

"Or even better," Rutheo added. "If he doesn't know that we know about these things, then eventually he'll do it again."

"And then we can pin him," Katsina concluded.

The three of them finished their rations, promising to tell no one of the discussion they had. Katsina walked back to the bridge with Alice, who seemed deeply disturbed by it all. Rutheo ended their lunch with a comment about staying safe. Which was all they could really do in the time they had on the ship. The rest of Katsina's work day was spent filing her data packets and finally finishing the work she had supposed to finish the day before. And just before her shift had ended, she found another set of data packets that were meant for decoding. She luckily dodged a bullet with Alice being promoted, even if it was unceremoniously, but it meant that her unfinished work wouldn't be reported to Morann. As the First officer, she was as high as those matters would go in the future, giving her a lot more say in things that happened on the ship. Katsina left her desk, awkwardly swapping with the man who would replace her for the evening shift. She found herself with some free time; so a trip to the tarmac felt like a much needed break from the dystopia aboard the Behemothis.

***

The only place on the ship that remained the same as always was the tarmac, ever present and always bustling with noise of work, machines and space ship engines. Over the few days since Katsina had left Botanica, warships of all shapes and sizes from the war effort had arrived on the Behemothis. Each with their own missions, and each with their own ailments. Katsina noticed one ship, which had one of its batteries completely torn from its hull. Another, speared multiple times with Electromagnetic Pulse, or EMP, rods. All around her as she jogged across the tarmac she saw pieces of ships that were no longer there, discarded to be recycled or broken down to be reused. The doors to the temporary housing units for those that arrived from the incoming ships were constantly opening and closing. With personnel returning to, or leaving, their scheduled leave as their ship would be repaired. Katsina made her way to her personal bay, and saw from a distance that the garage door had been left ajar. She remembered asking Howard to lock up for her, he wouldn't have forgotten.

Ducking under the door, Katsina once again found herself in complete darkness in her own garage. She couldn't control the lights from her HUD without being caught, making her have to go inside and find the manual controls. She didn't feel comfortable with entering, considering the afternoon she had with Kessler, so she reached to her right leg for her sidearm, forgetting it wasn't there anymore. She edged across the steel wall, clinging to it with her palms until she found a pad. Running her palm over it the garage finally lit up. Revealing a less than pleasant site to her. The Amber Eyes, just after Katsina restored it completely, was lying in parts all over the floor, the bare frame was all that was left hovering on the platform. Her ship had been looted, ransacked. The tablet fell from her hands, snapping shut on the floor. She approached the hull of the skeletal remains, lifting her hand to touch it. But she didn't touch it, instead her hand balled into a fist.

"Faisaheß," Katsina said aloud, kicking a toolbox across the floor.

She turned her attention to the screen behind her, and accessed the local security camera logs manually. It took a few minutes of rewinding to find the culprits.

"*What?*" she thought, staring at the footage of her ship slowly being put back together.

She slowed the video to normal speed, and watched Morann, a group of MP's led by Kessler, and Marshal entering her hangar. She turned up the volume on the display.

"-so I don't think we will find anything on this old thing. Physically and data forensically, there's nothing there," Kessler said.
"Strip the entire thing, it shouldn't even be in service anyway. Let me know if you find anything," Morann droned.

"Yes captain."

"Morann, wait a minute, he said he didn't find anything. What's the point in deconstructing the ship?" asked Marshal.

"I understand your captain doesn't keep many personal items, We found nothing in her quarters therefore every inch of this vessel must be checked. If you have a problem with that Captain Richmond, then I suggest you speak to the admiralty board about it. Otherwise, I expect this to remain between us. Only those I trust need know."

She watched Morann walk out of her hangar with Marshal in towe, then spent an hour or so watching the MP's strip her ships plating, its armor, weapons and even the interior linings of the seats. Tearing it to pieces before leaving again. Katsina stopped watching eventually, and instead of trying to clean up the mess they had made, she found herself a cosy spot under the belly of her ship's levitating frame, and closed her eyes. A pain welled in her stomach, gripping her diaphragm from within, Katsina tensed. Attempting to hold herself together, a sniff to breath every few seconds eventually forced her to let out a painful whimper. There was nothing more they could have taken from her, her ship, her fighter, her command, everything Katsina held dear.

"Kat? You alright?" a comforting voice said.

Katsina opened her eyes to see the last thing she expected, Marshal, his head peeking in under the ship's frame. He flourished a familiar and sympathetic smile, clearly an attempt to hide his own sadness. Katsina jumped at the sight of him, before noticing his somewhat ghostly nature. He was slightly transparent, the light of the screen on the wall shining through him. He was an AR projection, visible through Katsina's display.

"But how?" she asked, relaxing back into her fetal position.

"The little program I set up for us to talk," he said, crawling under the belly of the ship to sit with her. "It can let us see each other too, but just us."

"Such a bad boy, you are," Katsina smiled.

"Rules aren't as important to me as my friends are," he said, glancing around him. "I'm sorry about the ship. I wanted to tell you."

"It's fine, she can be fixed."

"Very true, never seen something you couldn't fix. It'll be back together in no time."

"Are you okay? What time is it there?" Katsina asked.

"It's been about two months, we're a bit ahead of you now timewise. It's been rough, we had a run in with a Yggdrasilian flotilla last week, lost two ships."

"I'm sorry. That must have been hard," Katsina said, her mind not entirely focused on his words. Instead she kept her eyes trained on his expression, which remained stoic.

"It's harder without having you here, Rutheo too," he sighed. "Morann's ship is ran so differently to ours. I know we are all military, but these people? Their high strung, Kat."

"It's hard not having you either," Katsina said, her voice cracking under the weight of her words. She reached her hand out, wishing to touch her closest friend, wishing to feel him in the same room. Marshal shuffled his weight to one side, lying down to face her. He placed his hand over hers, his image seemingly touching her.

"It's going to be okay, Kat. It's going to be okay," he said.

Katsina stared into his eyes, struggling to keep her own from welling up.

"No, no it's not," she managed. "I'm just so tired, I'm so tired."

"Then sleep, Kat," Marshal said, his voice barely a whisper. "I'm right here."

The two sat in silence together. Marshal remained watchful over Katsina while she let out the odd whimper. He was a compass that always steered her in the right direction, a voice of reason for her in any hardship. Even then, in a moment of defeat, he was there, as if he knew she needed him.

Marshal, unlike others, had an understanding of Katsina that she always wondered about. How was it that he knew what she needed, when she needed it. How could anyone dedicate such time and patience to another so selflessly? She felt a pang of happiness in that moment, finally, a respite. She felt a moment of solace. But deep in an unmapped region of space, away from home, Katsina paused and thought for a moment about her circumstances. She had every reason to, and every permission to, so she shrugged her shoulders, and fell asleep under the watchful eyes of Marshal Richmond.

THE LOG CABIN WEDDING

Two months had passed on the new and uncomfortable Behemothis. Most days Katsina spent working the best she could, while hiding from everyone that she could still see and hear as well as they did. Especially when it came to things that were said about her about the ship. The rumors were the hardest thing for her to restrain herself from reacting to. But over time the space carrier's change in captaincy was gotten used to by its crew. Or perhaps they just saw fit to not react to it anymore. The people around Katsina, apart from Morann's men, eventually accepted their fate; albeit reluctantly. Eventually, new rumors began to spread around the ship, stories from arriving ships and passengers. All of them were sharing the same narrative; a belief in Katsina rather than in the admiralty. Somehow there was more support growing for her innocence on other vessels. People whispered about Katsina's confrontation with Kessler and his antagonising of Rutheo had spread. Never had such an inappropriate set of actions been tolerated among the military and exploration fleet ships, so it was big news. Even on the Behemothis, Katsina noticed, over time, people treating her better; nothing more than a nod or a short smile, but it was more than enough for her after she'd lost the Amber Eyes.

Any spare moment she had was spent in the Amber Eyes; she still owned it, the garage, and all of the parts they'd stripped. Because she was never formally sentenced, her items and possessions couldn't be taken away under law. Even her captain's quarters were still hers. She just didn't bother fighting for them back. It was the only real space where she could use her HUD's full capabilities without scrutiny. It was a semblance of normal life, to live like everyone else; free to experience the entire color spectrum with her heightened senses. To not be afraid of judgement or having to face the prejudice outside the garage walls. The garage was her safe space, one that she so desperately needed. The Amber Eyes was still in pieces, but that didn't detract Katsina. Under the rear belly of the ship, Katsina wiped a drop of oil from her cheek, smearing it across her face. The Kugelblitz wheel housing, the fighters primary power source, didn't satisfy her in how it attached via the bolts and sockets that locked it into place. So she stripped and put it back together over and over- this was her third attempt in a row. Katsina cranked away at one of the loosened bolts, feeling a burning sensation in her shoulder as she worked on it. Eventually she winced, and collapsed down onto her back.

"Not complying today, are we?" she thought to herself before she tried to detach her wrench from the bolt. But the wrench wouldn't budge, and Katsina sighed in frustration.

"Faisaheß you then, be that way," she said aloud, rolling herself out from under the rear of the Amber Eyes.

After another full day of work, and another full evening of tinkering on her vessel, Katsina noticed a weight under her eyes. Grabbing a piece of the fighter's frame, she lifted herself to a slouching stand. She took a step back towards the edge of the room where Rutheo's coffee maker sat. Luckily for Katsina, the investigation into her activities hadn't damaged the vintage contraption; Rutheo would have killed her if it did. The machine buzzed with life and started to pour warm ground coffee into Katsina's cup while she plopped herself down on a nearby tool chest. Katsina looked back at her progress, licking her tongue over the scar in her upper lip. In her eyes' HUD she could see the full realtime layout of all the fighter ship's individual parts and pieces mapped over the real ship, showing her how much further she had to go. The coffee maker beeped, shaking Katsina out of her critical observations. Before picking up the orange cup, which was stained with more than a few layers of dried coffee, Katsina took one last look at the realtime schematic and noticed the time on her HUD.

"Lasine ui nyßolt'seich!"

The cup of hot coffee was left to go cold in the machine, as it was already time for her to make the sprint for her morning shift. She slammed the garage door behind her, leaving the hangar in a mess for the fifth day in a row.

***

Katsina barely had a moment to change in her quarters. Her jumpsuit, covered in oil and machine part stains, was dropped in the same spot in the corner by the door as it was in previous days. When she climbed over the bed upstairs, she felt something snag her ankle, causing her to fall forward into the mattress. The impact didn't hurt, but she cursed nonetheless. Before lifting herself out of her covers the bed seemed to take hold of her, a wave of sleep ran up her back, adding to the weight of her eyelids. Katsina fought the sensation and forced her hands into the mattress, pushing it away from her. She snatched her coat and rolled off the end of the bed. She stopped herself running down the stairs and looked back at the end of the bed to see what it was that caught her foot. It was one of the cables from the virtual headset, left under the bed when Katsina had moved into the quarters months before. She had almost forgotten it was there. With a twitch of her left eyebrow, a frown of curiosity formed on Katsina's face followed by a wide eyed flash of panic. She was still late.

***

The buzz of movement and activity on the bridge was uncharacteristically loud compared to the past two months, which had been a relatively quiet period in wartime. The war room doors continuously opened and closed, with people shuffling back and forth from their desks carrying tablets of data. Katsina used the commotion as a discreet opportunity to sneak to her desk, hoping to avoid the eyes of a superior officer. Moving quietly and hoping for impunity; Katsina kept on her toes, her head dipped low.

"Kat, Katsina," Alice's voice sounded off. "Kat, I am sorry but this is the third time that- t'sßolfé, Katsina."

She turned to face Alice, whose eyes had widened upon seeing Katsina's face.

"You look terrible. What have you been doing?" Alice asked, taken aback.

"What? Nothing, just working," she said, avoiding Alice's concerned gaze.

"You don't look like you've just been working. Are you eating? when's the last time you've slept?"

"Last night. Relax will ya? What's going on?" said Katsina, gesturing to the war room.

"We're tracking a suspicious heat signature in The Deep. The captain is mobilising a squadron to investigate. It'll be the first deployment since we-"

"Since we lost Mara," Katsina cut across.

"Yes," Alice replied in a somber tone, "that's correct."

Katsina felt her knuckles whiten as her muscles tensed.

"Assign me to deployment Alice. Get me out there."

"What? I can't do that. Your assignment is data retrieval an-"

"Yeah but as the acting first officer you can change my assignment without it going any further up the chain of command. I can-"

"No no, Katsina wait-"

"No, listen. I'm a lot more useful in a cockpit than I am here. I can finally use my HU-"

"You don't understand I'm under orders to ke-"

"Yeah I know, but you have authority, with your sign off I can get off the ground in a half-"

"A half hour? How do you plan to do that with no Amber Eyes, Katsina?" Alice said, causing more than one head to swivel in their direction. Katsina paused, took a calculated step back and looked Alice up and down.

"You been watching me, Alice?" Katsina asked, lowering her tone. "How do you know about the Amber Eyes?"

Many stopped to stare, others glanced from their screens every few seconds. Katsina didn't blink, instead she watched Alice's expression with cynicism.

"H-he told me to keep tabs on you for him. He wanted to have you followed but I told him I would take care of it b-"

"What?" Katsina snapped. "By following me and watching the security feeds of me yourself?"

"He would have had someone tail you if I didn't. It was the best I could do."

"And you asking me have I been sleeping, what's that? An attempt at info for him? If you've been watching me you must know. So why ask?"

"I don't have to explain my concern to you," said Alice.

"No but you better explain to me whose side you're on," Katsina said, closing the distance between them, keeping her eyes squared on Alice's.

"Y-you c-c," Alice paused, taking a breath. "You can't speak to me like that. As your superior officer I do not have to own up to you. I've tried to help, and I listened to you about him. You're acting irrationally and if you can't deal with the position I'm in, then I've no choice."

"What?"

"Petty Officer Lucas," Alice said in a prim and proper tone, lifting her tablet between them. "You are to report to the general practitioner service in the hospital to be assessed and placed on medical leave until you are fit for duty."

"You can't do that..."

"I am sure the doctor will recommend bed rest, and perhaps time to work on personal issues until you are able to return to your post."

Katsina stared into the eyes of her supposed friend, her mouth ajar with confusion. Alice stood resolute, their gaze locked in what looked like a renaissance scene between two powerful entities. She noticed a change in Alice, a crack in her statuesque glare. Behind it was the eyes of a pleading girl, begging for understanding.

"Take the leave," Alice said.

Katsina stepped back, bumping into someone who passed by on the way to the war room. Her eyes never left Alice, searching her for another glimpse into her true intention. Nothing could be found. On her tenth stride she finally broke her gaze, and passed the war room doors to leave. Glancing inside, she saw a large holographic map of the star cluster, emanating beautiful green and pink colors that bounced around the reflective surfaces of the room. Through the map, on the other side of the round table, Katsina saw a pair of eyes staring back at her. It was Morann. He had seen it all and he looked furious.

Katsina couldn't understand what had just happened. She had never fallen out with a friend like Alice before. She wandered the halls of the ship aimlessly, keeping her distance from others, turning corners to remain alone. She tried to think, to work out Alice's intentions in dismissing her. She had operated on less sleep in the past, which was something Alice regularly observed. She thought back to an early altercation when she first became captain, a four day conflict that kept her on the bridge coordinating three battalions of fighters with the assistance of two frigates in the theatre. Katsina had never left the captain's chair once, apart from the odd bathroom break. Alice had worked three separate shifts and one double during that encounter. By Katsina's logic, Alice had no reason to think exhaustion would interfere with her work. Katsina made it to the hospital entrance, and looked at the red cross on the glass doors. She never went inside.

***

Katsina considered returning to work on the Amber Eyes, but she couldn't focus on a single screw. She thought of visiting Rutheo in engineering by the reactor plant, but couldn't be bothered adjusting her body to the slightly radioactive environment. She circled her usual haunts on the space carrier, eventually finding herself back at the front door of Mara's quarters, her quarters. Staring at the open door frame, she contemplated that this would be the first time she would spend more than a few minutes in the quarters since she'd started sleeping under her levitating fighter. A tug in her abdomen made her hesitant while she stared at the shower across the room. A flash of that awful nightmare reminded her of what she'd lost, what Morann lost, and what she'd started to believe was really her fault. Before she let her mind meander any further, Katsina forced her right foot through the threshold, and marched her way up the stairs to the bed. She stripped to her tank top and underwear, and eased herself down onto the bed, mindful of her sore shoulder. She sat on the end corner closest to the stairs, head in her hands. She touched her elbows to her knees and stared at the floor between her feet. Her confused and frustrated expression began to relax as Katsina held a stoic and blank expression in its place. It was up to her to maintain composure at all costs, to never lose that composure, because for her, it was still her duty to hold the ship together. She wasn't going to do that without holding herself together first.

Katsina let out a deep sigh, another to add to the many she had been expressing in the preceding months, and fell back into the sheets. This time determined to sleep it off and reset, until she felt something tugging on her toe when she lifted her legs to get under the covers.

"For ts'ßolfé's sake," she thought, lifting her tired head to see what it was.

Katsina pulled on the wire that snagged her, and slid the VR helmet out from under the bed. Again she had completely forgotten to disconnect the cables and put it away somewhere. She plucked it up and gave it a once over, taking away the layer of dust she'd allowed to gather on it. The helmet visor must have been replaced more than once. The helmet itself had enough scratches and cracks in its pearlescent grey and orange coat which made it look ready to be completely recycled, but the visor looked good as new. On the left side a set of letters were etched into the paint: "MAJO X MIJO". The initials of Mara and her husband, Michael. Katsina pondered what made the helmet worth keeping for so long considering it's wear and tear. Why not replace it instead of refurbishing it? Everything in the universe was recycled, so Katsina couldn't think of a reason to keep it.

"Unless..." she said aloud.

Katsina dropped the helmet on the bed to her left and hopped down the stairs to the door. She plugged into it and scrolled in her HUD until she found the hard lock on the door and switched it on. With her privacy secured, she returned to the bed and ran the hardwire cable from the helmet to the back of her neck. She expected to see the drive of the helmet's computer pop up on her HUD, but nothing showed. A frown again creased her brow, and Katsina picked up the helmet to inspect the port the cable led to. It was connected properly, so what could have been wrong? She spun the helmet in her hands, searching for a fatal break in the housing of the helmet's computer, finding nothing, until she spotted a faint light emitting from the inside of the helmet itself. Katsina cautiously lifted the helmet to see what the light was, a blip on the inner screen of the helmet's visor. She couldn't make out the word that was spelled out, so she slid the helmet over her crown. Katsina shuddered as the helmet shuffled around her head, reshaping itself to fit her. It was a ticklish and goosebump inducing sensation around her neck and shoulders. The light began to glow in front of her, a phrase coming into focus:

Insert printed component.

Katsina pulled the helmet off her head, and turned it in her hands again, noticing an empty space in the modular computer system, a missing part.

"*Printed component?*" she thought.

She stood up, peaking over the balcony to the makeshift workshop that Mara had set up down below. The 3D printer was still there, one of the many flags that hung from the walls partially covering. She went to it, and pulled the flag aside. It was still on, with a half printed object inside the cabinet. Katsina pulled up the printer menu on her tablet, and tapped the *resume* prompt. The printer sprung to life, and the chip began to fully materialise. Returning to the helmet, she inserted the chip into the empty slot. She couldn't believe both the chip and helmet had been in the apartment, waiting the entire time. She slid the helmet back over her head. Katsina didn't see any manual controls on the screen for her eyes to select. The 'insert printed component' phrase had disappeared. Perhaps voice activation?

"Play."

Without warning a flash of light blinded Katsina's view, and she lifted her hands to block the glare. Upon adjusting to the brightness Katsina opened her eyes again, flinching at a blinding sunlight ahead of her as if she was driving on a clear winter's afternoon. She found herself in a place she never expected to revisit.

***

In a bright and colorful forest clearing, a cherry blossom tree climbed above a small log cabin. Its leaf petals raining down over the wooden single story structure. A loud *tweet* from her right hand side made Katsina jump to see a small bird zip past her, followed by another. Bluebirds. A nostalgic scent reached her nostrils, grass, roots, and clean woodland air. Katsina looked down to see that she was standing on the stone path that trailed to the front door of the cabin, and decided to follow it. Walking in VR wasn't a struggle, but it was a far cry from the quality she was used to. The resolution and frame rate on the old helmet was at least two generations out of date, but it amazed her regardless. Up the steps to the cabin door, framed by two antique gas burning lamp posts, Katsina heard voices and laughter. On the door hung a beautiful assortment of lilies and roses, an odd pairing, she thought, just as she had thought on the day she first saw them.

Katsina crossed the threshold and entered a beautifully decorated wooden hallway, with bows and streams of ribbons hanging from the ceiling. The floor under her feet *creaked* and *croaked* as she took each step, the heels of her boots knocking on the oakwood. At the end of the hallway, the wooden floorboards led to a white tiled sandstone floor, perfectly polished. She had entered the kitchen. A wood stove fire burned in one corner, while a whistling kettle on a bespoke cooker boiled away on another. Below the wide panoramic window sat a large and rectangular ceramic sink, deep and right angled all the way around. A Belfast sink, Rutheo had told her when she first saw it, a beautiful relic of the past. The cabin was adorned with mostly pre-spaceflight antiquities, making it next to perfect to be in a museum had it not been built in modern times. An incredible replica, replicated again in virtual reality. The sound of happy chants and cheers caught Katsina's ears again, and she followed the noise to the back door to a long and spacious patio.

Behind the Cabin, under another sprawling and tall cherry blossom tree, with the evening sunset lighting the atmosphere, Katsina saw too many familiar faces to keep herself contained. A gasp, followed by a broad smile, the first she had cracked in a long time. It was the crew of the spaceship Ralph Abernathy, which included herself, Rutheo, Mara, Michael, Marshal, Howard and many more. The crowd was arranged in a semicircle around the trunk of the tree, under which Katsina stood as Mara's bridesmaid. Mara, adorned in a snow white gown, held the hands of Michael, who wore an equally bright suit with an electric pink carnation clipped to the pocket. Mara wore a matching carnation as a corsage around her wrist. Her skin was slightly lighter than his, but with more scars.

He had no hair at all, while her dreaded locks were tied into a tight bun atop her head. Her button nose touched off of his nubian one, eskimo kissing. He was taller, but she wore heels. The two of them looked as happy as Katsina remembered them, with petals slowly being collected at their feet. Katsina walked down the stone wedding isle to get a better look, passing row after row of old friends.

She noticed the dress she herself was wearing, and still regretted letting Mara talk her into wearing the ugly salmon colored sparkling gown. She hadn't worn a dress since. She had just missed the kiss, but she remembered it well enough to not feel bad about it. After all, it was just a recording. Made from a memory. Left in an old helmet. But it didn't stop her feeling sad for just a moment. It was a beautiful day, and it was the last time everyone had been together before they were reassigned. The crowd started to move, and hugs and cheers were exchanged. She followed the crowd as it made its way back into the cabin. Trying not to bump into anyone, even though that wasn't possible, the older VR helmets didn't have neural feedback. Not like modern AR arenas, not to mention memories could not be interacted with unless modded. Katsina wondered why such a memory existed in Mara's VR helmet, why not just revisit it using her memory core?

In a wide, open living room, surrounded with pictures and artworks on the walls, the wedding party guests began sitting down in their chosen spots around a roaring fire. Above the tall hearth, a bogwood framed mirror hung slightly off centre. Reflecting a purple light into the room. A strange reflection in Katsina's opinion, it showed the age of the helmet's graphics card rather than the actual memory. Or maybe it was just modded? Katsina caught up with her past self, and listened in on the conversation she was having with the bride and groom.

"-ell, I'm sure it's just a briefing on where the ship is going next. I'd say the old girl will definitely need a full refit this time around," Katsina watched herself say.

"Oh come on, Kat," Michael chuckled in a deep bellowing breath, "I'm telling you now you're being brought in to get some kind of promotion. After the debrief you gave on what happened in the trenches up there? They can't not give you a medal."

"He's right, Captain. It's one thing winning a fight, but you damn near ended the war on that moon. Don't be surprised if you get your own Destroyer out of it," Mara teased.

"Sure, so we can all conquer the stars together?" Past Katsina said with a grin. "Look, we're pilots right? Pilots never get anything more than a frigate not to *mention*," she emphasised, "I wouldn't be able to stand sitting on the sidelines while everyone else got to go out and blow the Yggs back into the stone age."

Katsina noticed a difference in her past self, a confidence she barely recognised, but it was something more. She seemed callous, arrogant. The obvious difference was the missing scar running through her lips, but that wasn't it. Behind the confidence, in the back of her younger eyes, Katsina saw a painful look. Masked beyond recognition. A pain that she didn't realise she had carried around in full view of anyone who could discern it from her usual self.

"Is that what I look like?" she thought, looking herself up and down. Another memory came to mind, of her standing above the other soldiers on the Alia moon, the sadistic animal, ready to die for the cause.

"You guys talking about work already?" A tipsy Rutheo entered the conversation. Passing directly through Katsina as she joined the trio. "Gimme a, hic, break."

"Heeey, Ruthie, Kat was just saying she's too humble to accept her own ship command," Michael said, raising his glass to *clink* it off of Rutheos. His hands were incredibly large, requiring him to hold his scotch with just two fingers.

"Jeez you're not married five minutes and you guys need to talk about the war?" Marshal said, slapping Michael on the back as he joined in.

"Nothing wrong about discussing the sweet pleasure of kicking the enemy while they're down right?" past Katsina laughed. "They're off running; we pushed them out of our space now it's time to push them out of theirs."

"Who knows, Maybe they'll even surrender and we can get some peace and quiet?" Rutheo said, clapping her hands together and rubbing them excitedly. Her drink was already finished, she drank so much that evening.

"Peace?" Katsina said before letting out a rude scoff. "Honey, those bastards don't want peace. They want to take over the other 3 pillars of humanity and enslave the rest of us into their warped idea of a society."

"Yeah but, Kat, you can't deny it would be the best outcome. I mean no one wants this war to end more than you do right?" Marshal asked, lifting his arm to Katsina's shoulder. His voice was full of concern, a concern Katsina never noticed at the time.

"Is that so?" past Katsina said, raising her voice.

Katsina was taken aback, she didn't remember having snapped like that before, especially not during Mara's wedding. She watched her past self as she slapped Marshal's hand away from her. Spilling his drink and her's.

"Let me tell you something, Flight Lieutenant Richmond, the Yggs? They don't know what peace means. If they did, they wouldn't fry their own motor neurons every time we captured one of them."

"Kat, it's alright," Micheal said.

"No, no, let me finish. If they wanted peace, they wouldn't have developed weapons of mass destruction that sucked the souls out of their enemies now would they?" Past Katsina continued.

"Katsina, that's enough," Marshal said, raising his hands defensively.

"If they wanted peace, flight lieutenant Richmond, they would have left your family alive and not orphaned as a toddler. They wouldn't have shot down your ship, making your mother put you in an escape pod full of strangers without her. They don't wish for peace, they just have the longest list of death wishes I've ever seen."

She watched her past self, next to manic in her posture, as she necked the rest of her drink and stormed through a shocked room of people who'd heard her rant from the kitchen. Katsina felt all eyes on her, even though she wasn't really in the room to feel it. Her past self had left, and it was Marshal the room was staring at. Mumblings and whispers began to spread about the log cabin before Michael assured everyone that she hadn't meant what she said. That it was stress. The whispers grew louder and louder in Katsina's ear, making her close her eyes and clasp her hands over them to make it stop. The sound became unbearable. Her eyes lingered on Marshal, her trusted crewmate and second in command, his mouth pressed into a hard line. His eyes staring to the floor. How had she not remembered saying that? Katsina watched Mara approach Marshal, a solemn and empathetic look in her eyes.

"Are you okay? Will I go get her?" She asked him.

"Yeah, but not yet. There's something I need to talk to you about."

Before hearing or seeing anymore, Katsina pulled the helmet off her head, leaving the newly tarnished memory in the past again. In all her time as a soldier, Katsina had never thought she was any more or less patriotic to humanities interests as the next operator. Was she really hell bent on killing her enemy with such passion? Surely it was normal to be vicious towards one's oppressor? After every war humanity had fought in the name of race, religion, property, and freedom. After everything her ancestors experienced at the hands of slave owners, conqeurers, legal, social and economic discrimination. The disenfranchisement of an entire culture of the human race. Katsina had more than enough reasons to despise oppression considering her heritage, just as Rutheo did with hers. She thought of Marshal's face, and how he always spoke about his heritage. He knew how she felt about what happened to her people, what happened to Rutheo's, and even his. How could he say that the Yggdrasilians wanted peace after all they had done? Was it wrong to view the modern war mongers with vitriol and damnation? They were the warmongers. They were, weren't they? Would the Yggdrasilians really want peace?

"No," Katsina growled to herself. "No, they wouldn't."

INSOMNIA ASSESSED

Katsina sat at a glass table in a brightly lit aqua blue room, holding her chin up with the back of her hands. She stared out a ceiling-tall window at the augmented giraffes that strolled in the fields of the hospital's windows. The cold glass reminded her that she was still warm, regardless of how she felt.

The general practitioner's office was a clutter of thin tablets stacked in each corner and cables lying about the floor. In the centre of the room a tall pane of glass obstructed the space, bouncing reflections of the room. The only piece of paper in the room hung in a frame on the wall behind an old and rustic brown desk with golden adornments on its feet. A certificate of medicine, signalling twenty five years of education. Katsina pondered the award with a brief grin, wishing she had stayed at university for that long. Maybe she could have been a different person, maybe a better person.

The *whoosh* of the door signaled the doctor's entrance. Dr. Linda Foye was a tall and unmistakable beauty aboard the Behemothis. Her long black hair flowed past her petite shoulders and curled around her hips as silk would on an Egyptian bedsheet. What made Dr. Foye truly unique to see was that she was one of six hundred million people in the known human race to have vitiligo. Her Nubian skin tone was contrasted with patches of white across her arms, neck and face. vitiligo was easily treatable for those who sought it, but skin color and appearance had left the mainstream concerns of humanity long ago, meaning people of all races and skin tones lived equal lives. Though vitiligo wasn't necessarily cause for discrimination, it was fascinating to Katsina to see people proud of their skin, even with the ability to change it.

Dr. Foye made her way to her desk, but instead of

sitting behind it, she lifted herself onto it and sat on its edge. "How are you Captain?" she asked with a pleasant smile.

"Please, just Kat is fine," she said, leaning back from the table and running her hands through her locked hair.

"Sorry, Kat. It's a habit that needs changing for a lot of crew members I'd say."

"I can't imagine many people having trouble with it," Katsina said, keeping her eyes on the giraffes.

"So, in your dismissal, the acting first officer recommended you seek medical attention for sleep deprivation, bouts of anger episodes, and paranoia. I think it's bull, but I'm here to talk about it; if you're game?"

Katsina didn't take her eyes off one of the smaller giraffes, stretching as hard as it could for a tree branch that was just out of reach. Before she could grow concerned, a taller giraffe appeared from around the tree, pulling the branch down with its neck. She had never known a doctor to talk like Linda.

"Wow, the symbolism there is pretty good," Katsina said appreciatively.

"The designers of the hospital spared no expense," Dr. Foye replied.

"Yeah I see that. I've always loved the amount of work that went into this ship," Katsina pondered.

"Is that what's been on your mind? The ship?"

"Not exactly, I mean it always is. Just, not like it used to be."

"Because you're not the Captain anymore?" the doctor asked.

"Because I think I'm starting to see myself for what I really am, Linda," Katsina scratched her eyebrow and ran her tongue over her scarred lip, contemplating what she had been thinking for weeks: "A murderer, a stone cold one."

Dr. Foye slipped off her desk and joined Katsina at the glass table. She placed a tablet between them. Katsina wiped her palms over her cheeks, taking a deep breath.

"This is just going to take your dictation and record it

for my log, okay? Can you tell me what makes you think you're a murderer?" she asked in a kind and supportive tone.

"It's going to be a bit of a long story, I'm pretty sure you have better th-"

"I have all day, Kat. We've been working together on this ship long enough. I gave you those implants, remember? I have all day," the doctor reassured her.

It took most of the morning, but Katsina brought Dr. Foye up to speed with everything she had learned since Morann took over the Behemothis. It took multiple cups of coffee, Dr. Foye's home grown roast, and more than one lap around the room for Katsina to explain everything in order. By the time she had finished telling the story, Dr. Foye had taken off her white doctor's coat and her black pumps to get comfortable on the couch in the corner of the room. Over the course of the conversation Katsina stood by the glass strip in the middle of the room while Linda observed from the other side. The piece of glass acted as a filter, allowing Linda to see every layer of Katsina's body, her various implants, and even the folds of her mind. Katsina was healthy down to her skeleton and spinal fluid, her lack of sleep was simply a choice, her mind deciding to stay awake.

"So, your melatonin levels have been subconsciously suppressed by your own implants. Your mind came to a conclusion that you didn't need sleep, and you didn't notice the change in Melatonin release because you've been pretending to live without a HUD for so long."

"So you can prescribe me the regular use of my HUD again?"

"No, as a criminal awaiting conviction you're not entitled to it, but I will be installing a programme to help regulate your melatonin better so you don't have to consciously correct it. You'll just have to pretend you have no HUD a little bit longer."

"You won't tell anyone you gave it to me?" Katsina asked, pacing the room.

"Unless someone suspects me of doctoring the patient file, no one will know," Linda said with a grin.

"Aha, doctored, very funny."

"I thought you'd like that," she chuckled, before shifting to a more serious tone, "but Katsina, how you're feeling lately... It's not uncommon for soldiers to feel as though their actions during wartime are wrong because they wouldn't have done it under other circumstances. Feeling responsible for the lives of others is intrinsic to a command position like yours. You did kill people, yes. But not because you wanted to."

"And the memory from the wedding? If I didn't want to kill people then why would I say that? And how could I forget it?" Katsina asked, quickening her pace.

"Keeping the memories of the Alia moon and the subsequent emotions surrounding it at the back of your mind is a compartmentalisation method called dissociation. It's common among survivors of trauma and veterans like yourself," Linda explained.

"I'm not a 'survivor of trauma', doctor, I'm a deliverer of it. I did everything I did because I wanted to, acting as if I was right in doing it. And that's the question; was it right? Or wrong?"

"You know my answer to that; I think war is wrong Katsina. I took my Hippocratic oath to help others. So you know that's my subjective view. But for you the answer is more complicated because of your duties. And it's up to you to decide on what you think is right and wrong."

"So that's it? It's a moral dilemma?" Katsina asked, stopping at the window to watch the giraffes gallop across the savanna.

"It's more than that. It's coupled with a lot of anger towards our enemy. I think maybe reflecting on how you feel about them will help you reconcile a bit more."

"I thought you were a general practitioner? Now you sound like a psychiatrist."

"I did five years in psychiatry after university. Lifelong learner I guess. It took me a while to figure out what I wanted to be," Linda said before gently blowing on her steaming mug.

Katsina watched the smaller giraffes play, while the taller adults strolled about the trees in pairs. It really was a beautiful scene, even though it wasn't real.

"And here I am not having a clue about who or what I want to be," she muttered.

"My prescription to you is bed rest, Katsina. You've been here most of the day, maybe take the evening off from working on the Amber Eyes and do a bit of soul searching. Start with that headset you mentioned. You might find some kind of closure in seeing the memory again. There's nothing wrong with changing your views on yourself and challenging those views over time. You're not a bad person because you've had to do bad things. You're in your thirties, it's okay to not know exactly what you want at such a young age."

"Thanks Linda, and that melatonin regulator?"

"I'll have it issued as a temporary software update. Hanif at the front desk will give you a data stick to install it manually so you aren't seen using your HUD."

"Thank you. I'll appreciate the rest."

Katsina took one last look at the giraffes, and picked up her coat to leave. Before exiting she noticed her body still in the display on the pane of glass in the middle of the room. She noticed the new scar that added to her previous ones, sixty seven in total. In her mind each scar added to her story, just as every tattoo had added to Han Mao's family history. But she didn't expect such a small and insignificant cut that she'd gotten from falling down a set of steps to represent such a huge turmoil. Then again it was widened and lengthened by Morann; maybe that was the turmoil part. Katsina decided to take Linda's advice, and travelled to a place aboard the Broadsider than she had only seen once before.

The humidity in the room was almost like a different atmosphere. It reminded Katsina of a warm summer's day on the edge of a misty mountain. The spiraling columns that held the high ceilings above her were laced with golden cables and wires. All of which were for anyone aboard the ship to connect to, and learn from. About the room floated glowing orbs, just like those in Marshal's home. They changed colour any time Katsina approached one, a different hue each time before returning to their yellow warmth. Under these orbs were pockets in the floor for people to sit in and connect to the ship. The walls were adorned with beautiful glistening glyphs that moved and danced about the space, depicting humanity's past, its present, and a theorised future. In each scene, a figure, miniscule compared to the rest of the composition, stood watching over humanity. A guardian onlooker that secretly observed. A pale figure, with deep black lines etched into its skin. Eyes that glowed a beautiful enchanting gold. This figure was what the entire room was dedicated to. A figure only referred to as the Orchestrator, the leader of the t'sßolfé. The gods of human achievement. Kastina knew they weren't really gods, but instead an alien race that humanity had been searching for ever since it left Earth.

    It was long before the Sol exodus when human's realised that the search for alien life, particularly alien life that shaped its development, was the final great discovery to be made. In settling the four pillars, before the war with the Yggdrasil, the common goal was to make first contact. So far it still hadn't been achieved. The culmination of all religion into one scientific belief system was admirable, but earned no interest from Katsina. She'd never wanted to be in the exploration fleet, to search for alien life or other planets. She was a soldier, and her role in society didn't include having a religious belief system. But that was her personal opinion.

    Upon an altar in the centre of the room, sat an individual, a person; difficult to describe because few people were allowed to look upon them. Known as teachers, they were the conduits that remembered any and all information through their myriad of implants. Teachers possessed nothing, owned nothing, not even clothing. Their bodies were bare, pale, and thin. They knew everything there was to know, the entirety of human experience embedded in the multiple memory cores that adorned their spines. Before Katsina could approach the teacher, and step on the altar to connect, she noticed a shape in the corner of the room, a hulking shape. The only other person that was there. Her intention suddenly changed, realising that it wasn't the teacher she wanted to speak to. It was Kessler. He stood staring at one of the moving frescos, the back of his head wired into the ceiling above him. Katsina approached, albeit cautiously.

"I didn't expect to see you here, Lucas," he said with a rasp.

"Neither did I," Katsina responded, joining him at a distance in front of the scene. "I didn't think the church's teachings would mean much to a man like you."

"Just because I'm a soldier?" he asked.

"Because you seem hell bent on hurting Rutheo," Katsina said. "Surely the wealth of knowledge here shows you that that's wrong of you?"

"I won't argue with you here. This is a place of enlightenment, not conflict," he said, more docile than Katsina had ever seen him.

He never took his eyes off the painting, he almost didn't acknowledge Katsina at all. That was until he lifted his hand, gesturing for her to stand with him. Katsina didn't move.

"This picture here. I think you would find it interesting," he said. "Up here you see the Alia moon, its green glow sending a wave of light to earth. But what's missing?"

Katsina looked at the image of the moon, breaking into pieces and fixing itself over and over. The rest of the wall was a deep purple and black glitter, while a pale blue dot shone in the distance. She soon realised what was missing.

"There's no sun."

"Exactly," Kessler said. "How is it that humanity saw

the Alia moon from so far, when there was no sun to make it reflect its green light to us?"

"A great mystery, sure," Katsina said. "But we don't have the answer yet."

"We may not have the scientific explanation, Lucas. But we do have our belief. I believe the t'sßolfé generated a light, making the moon reflect it for us. Making us forget our petty squabbles. Forcing us to believe in something greater, something to find out here."

"Romantic," Katsina said. "Too bad the Yggs ruined that for all of us."

"I like to think that the Orchestrators knew we were struggling, and that's why they shone the light. They gave us direction so many times in our past, they will give us that direction again. That's what the crew of the Insurmountable believe."

"You think the t'sßolfé will help us end the war?" Katsina asked.

"Yes," Kessler said thoughtfully. "I think they will bring upon the Yggdrasilians a wrath like no other ever seen. They sealed their fate when they started this war."

Katsina watched him, weary of his demeanor. He was no longer the rock solid man she had fought in the canteen. A different side of him revealed itself to her in that moment as the purple light of the wall reflected off his grey skin. He wiggled his nose, and hung his head, no longer looking at the moon. He was flipping his ring over and over in his hands, slipping it on and off his finger. He couldn't have been, but Katsina could see it. She didn't believe it, but it was right in front of her. She finally stepped close enough to see his eyes, red and puffy. He had been crying.

"Kessler?" Katsina asked, confused at what she was seeing.

"The t'sßolfé helped us, because they love us. They're actions are the purest form of selflessness. One we can never achieve. Humans are too selfish, Lucas, even now. This war is the direct result of that. It's why we lost so much. Why I... lost so much."

It dawned on Katsina why he had so many rings that matched his own. They weren't all his.

"You lost your family, didn't you?" Katsina asked as her eyes widened.

"Six years ago, a blitz on the edge of the Crescent system. They all returned in bags," he sniffed.

"I'm sorry, I didn't know yo-"

"Don't," he snapped, ripping the cables from the back of his head. "Don't you apologize to me. You don't get to, you're working with them. Don't think because this is a place of safety that I will let you insult me. My job here is to make sure you stay in line, but I get to choose how. Your little rat in engineering told me all about you, how to get to you. And I will. Trust me when I say; your fate is sealed as well."

Katsina stepped away from him. His eyes grew wider and more deranged as he spoke, his anger taking him over. He didn't speak in complete sentences, instead spitting incoherent and angry thoughts at her. He was vicious, seething. He towered over Katsina, his threatening aura returning with a vengeance. His show of force made her think of Rutheo's willingness to comply with Morann, her fear of him. What had she told them? What was it that made Rendell Kessler so hateful of them both.

"I didn't mean t-"

"I don't believe you," he said. "You will pay for what you've done, for what they've done. To me and everyone else you've taken from. Leave, before I make you leave."

Katsina looked about the room, no one else was present except the silent and seemingly unconscious teacher. There was no one to support her, no one to back her up like the last time. It wasn't her space, she had never even been in it before. She was hardly going to argue with the man in the church. So she cut her losses, and backed out of the room, leaving Kessler alone again.

***

Katsina decided to pick up her rations packet from the canteen and bring it to eat somewhere else, away from Morann's crew and away from the noise of the rumors about her. She took a lesser travelled route around the ship through the peripheral maintenance catwalks that lined the ships outer shell. Between the walls of the interior and the ship's hull exterior Katsina found a different kind of noise. The sound of the Behemothis' massive hydraulic actuators *whirred* through the tremendous space lit by dim blue lights. The catwalks vibrated with the noise of the ship's engines, running an energy up through Katsina's spine. Her long walk brought her to a place she rarely visited, the edge of the ship's dome. On the other side of the interior walls, Katsina knew the crew of the bridge were operating as normal. But in the gap between the walls, Katsina could see out through the bottom of the dome, where ships flew to and fro from the flight deck. It was the best seat in the house, and Katsina took full advantage.

The ration pack was minimal as always, surely there was a case for malnourishment being the cause of Katsina's insomnia? Either way she ate it while watching a frigate class spaceship approach to land on the tarmac. In her eyes she lit up her HUD to scroll some of the Behemothis' social feeds. Keeping herself from commenting or participating was the most difficult part of the scroll. She took note of the cancelled social gatherings, peoples birthdays, and club meetings that she would have liked to attend had Morann not become the captain. Wishful thinking ran rampant in her mind as she endlessly scrolled through status after status. Katsina wasn't really looking at the feed, she focused more on the frigate coming to dock. It had multiple scars running along its port side, a winning battle most likely, the Yggdrasilians never left ships to limp home. The name on the side of the ship was Artifacterium, she had never heard of it. Most likely an exploration fleet vessel. Before it entirely disappeared into the bay door's of the Behemothis, Katsina glimpsed a post on her feed that caused a dopamine spike.

> Scientist find Amadellan Flu present
> in bodies of deceased Yddrasilian soldiers.
> Investigation underway.

Katina pinned the post before trying to read it. But before she made it past the first line, an uncommon clatter on the maintenance walkway made her close her HUD and turn to see the commotion. Down the walkway behind her she saw nothing. On the walkway below, empty again. A second clatter made her glance upwards to see a figure dip back into the shadows. Katsina thought back to the other day about what Alice said to her. Her claims that Morann would have her followed. She waited for another movement or sound, slowing her breathing to a deathly silence. Nothing moved, and neither did she. She kept her eyes solely trained on the spot where she'd seen the shadow's shift. It was a long and painful moment, where only the ship itself made noise. Katsina felt a knot in her stomach as she braced to move. Waiting for the opportune moment. Finally. A glinting pair of eyes opened in the dark, followed by a sprint in the opposite direction. Katsina took flight. She launched herself towards the nearest service ladder.

Climbing as fast as her body would carry her, Katsina made her way up to the walkway above, and hurdled after the sound of footsteps. Every so often ahead of her, about a hundred meters or so, a figure would appear in the blue lights that lit the cavernous metal space. She noticed the figure slow, and duck into a vent ahead of her. Katsina tried to keep an eye on the precise ventilation shaft, as there was one every 5 meters along the ship. She skid to a halt, and threw herself into the nearest vent, hoping it was the right one. The compact space wasn't lit, and was difficult to shuffle through. The walls pinned her shoulders together so that Katsina's momentum was stifled. Whoever it was that was spying on her, they must have been pretty small to make it through so quickly. Katsina pushed as hard as she could deeper into the vent, hearing the scurrying sounds of her stalker ahead; the popping sound of the shaft's metal sheets couldn't hide them from her. Whoever it was, they were quick.

Katsina continued forcing herself in, feeling the pressure build in her chest. Was the shaft getting smaller? She began to pant with the effort. Grunting her way until quickly slipping forward into a larger area. Katsina hit the ground hard enough that stars danced about her vision. They were the only bits of light she could see. A constricting pain crushed her abdomen from the fall, and Katsina gasped for breath while the footsteps grew further away. One cough after another and Katsina rolled onto her belly, dragging her legs up from under her and stumbling towards the sounds. She knew the ship inside and out, even in complete darkness; the spy was working back towards the engineering decks. Katsina found her second wind. At a quickened pace the footsteps ahead of her grew louder; she was gaining. Soon enough she could hear the person ahead of her breathing loudly, their shape materialising every so often as the ventilation shaft passed over rooms below them. They were getting tired, clearly not pacing themselves. She kept running until something tickled her face, fluttering ahead of her, streaming behind her opponent. Hair? Katsina launched herself forward and crashed into her target, making them both collapse through a grate and fall into an ocean of fluorescent light.

Katsina landed flat on her back with the weight of another person landing on her chest. The pain, more than she could contain, caused her to unleash a terrible groan while thrusting the spy off of her. Katsina could barely breathe, she felt as if a belt had been tied around her lungs, obstructing the air from entering her body. But to her amusement, she could hear the spy groan all the same. She slowly regained her breath, and rolled onto her side to see who it was, and realised she must have tackled the wrong person. The flowing mousy brown hair covered her face, but the pale forearms and greasy overalls of Rutheo were unmistakable. As was her sudden fit of violent cursing.

"Did you really have to tackle me like that? tS'ßolfe Faisaheß," she managed, rolling onto her back and hugging her own chest. Katsina felt her heart erupt, forcing her to move through the pain. She leapt onto Rutheo, pinning her to the floor.

"What do you think you're doing, Ruthie? Huh? Following me around? Like Alice is? Morann got you in his pocket now too?" she snarled.

The room around them came into focus, a boiler house for the ship's hot water supply. The various tanks around the walls emitted heat like no other interior of the ship. Katsina could already feel the beads of sweat build on her forehead and neck. The room was too humid an environment to see clearly to the exit. The steam filling it was erupting from a pipe above their heads; they must have ruptured it on the way down.

"Kat, get off. You're hurting me," Rutheo said, struggling under her weight.

"Hurting you? You're stalking me Rutheo. Faisaheß! Who the hell put you up to this one huh?" Katsina spat.

"What? No one. I just wanted to check on you, you've been missing," Rutheo responded.

"Pull the other one; it's got bells on it. You think I don't know how fast word travels on this ship? Don't tell me you didn't know I was dismissed, Morann's tS'eacheashin crew have probably been gloating about it all week," she said, feeling the anger build inside her.

"I said: Get. Off," Rutheo burst out, swiping Katsina with a right hook and knocking her back. "I didn't do anything to you. I've been doing everything *for* you. How could you say that?"

Katsina rolled back over and clambered to her feet to

face Rutheo.

"You've been so distant," Rutheo choked, "so reserved since you found the Amber Eyes. It's not my faisaheßul fault they messed up your fighter an-"

"If you aren't working with him then prove it!" Katsina yelled, raising her right hand, pointing at Rutheo's neck.

"What?" Rutheo asked, "No, no I'm not giving you my logs. I'm not some Ygg you're trying to get some data from. I'm your friend."

"If you can't prove you're not with him then how can I trust you? Huh?"

Katsina stared at Rutheo a moment longer, knowing that the one definitive question that she had to ask the engineer was on the tip of her tongue. She searched the eyes of her crew mate, trying to find a hint of deception in the woman's eyes. Rutheo, like everyone else, was never known to lie, and never known to cheat. She was vocal and eccentric, but forever loyal to humanity, and to Katsina. She felt her skin shaking all over, her legs weak from the sprint, her chest aching as she breathed so heavily.

"What did you tell Kessler and Morann about me?" Katsina asked.

"What?" Rutheo said. A new and unexpected defensive expression had flashed across her face.

"Answer the question. Kessler said you told him all about me. How to get to me. What did you tell him?"

"I didn't, I... I didn't-"

"Ruthie, just tell me what you said-"

"I wouldn't tell anyone anything to hurt you I-"

"Just tell me."

"I swear I-"

"Rutheo!" Katsina shouted. "What did you tell him?"

Katsina felt her nails dig into the palms of her hands. She impulsively stepped into Rutheo's personal space, making the short girl step back from her. Rutheo's eyes widened, and she thrust her hands into Katsina's chest. Katsina stumbled back before seeing Rutheo strain her face, revealing her teeth with a pained expression. Through the humidity in the room, tears could still be seen falling from her eyes. Rutheo fell back onto the wall behind her, cupping her head in her hands. Katsina exhaled sharply, and lifted her hands. Realising what she had done, she wanted to comfort her friend. Rutheo let out a sorrowful moan, and Katsina couldn't help but feel responsible. The two stood in a painful silence, before Rutheo finally spoke.

"I told him I loved you… You idiot. I told him I loved you… You ever thought of that? You faisaheßul bheibhen! I followed you on that tS'ßolzu'au moon, in the trenches, I even followed you to this ship when they gave it to you. I've been with you since they paired us up on the Abernathy. They were gonna give me the entire engineering deck on that ship, but no, I came out here with you! Because I love you."

Katsina stood stiff, rooted to the floor by what Rutheo said. She felt her knees shiver, and wished she had a chair to sit on. She didn't know what to say, how to respond, or what to do. It was a new and unfamiliar experience for her.

"You… You love me?" she asked.

"Yes, you moron," Rutheo stressed as she waved her hands in front of her face. "For years now…"

Katsina felt many things all at once. Confusion, flattery, shame, sadness, and happiness, all at once. To call it a torrent of emotions was an understatement. Above all, Katsina felt guilt. Rutheo had always confided in Katsina, and Katsina in her. Surely Rutheo could have told her this earlier. Or could she not have trusted her. Did Katsina do something to make Rutheo not tell her? A tingling sensation ran up Katsina's spine, and her eyes squinted as she fell short of breath.

"I'm sorry Rutheo…" she said. "I, I just don't feel the same way. Your one of my closest friends."

"You think I don't know that?" Rutheo said, huffing sarcastically. "I was never going to tell you. I know you don't feel the same way. I made peace with that a long time ago. Will it stop me feeling this way about you? No. But it won't get in the way of me being your friend either, Kat."

Katsina looked into the sorrowful eyes of the short mousy haired girl before her. Her closest ally aboard the entire Broadsider. A person who had never let her down before. A person she just tackled, practically assaulted, out of suspicion. Katsina tilted her head back and pushed her palms into her eye sockets. She sighed at the fact that she doubted Rutheo at all.

"Just because Morann freaks me out doesn't mean I'd do whatever he says. I know you think everyone is against you, but I just- ugh, wait a sec," Rutheo said, before gazing into the distance momentarily. "Can I get a maintenance team to boiler room six? We got a pipe rupture. Right, yeah. Thanks."

"Head of engineering can't fix it herself?" Katsina said sarcastically, walking past Rutheo to the control panel towards the door. A new and unbearable wave of defeat crashed over Katsina, making her resort to her dry humor. It wasn't appropriate for what she had just heard. But she had no other way to respond.

"Very funny," Rutheo said. She stood awkwardly behind Katsina, most likely contemplating her words. She clearly didn't know what to say or do either. "Kat, I know everyone's against you, but-"

"I know, Ruthie, I know," she admitted. Leaning on the panel, propping herself up. She ran her finger over the switch that controlled the alarms, giving them peace and quiet. "I just don't know if I'm even worth all this effort, from you, from Alice. What if it's true? And I am a reckless war criminal? Why would I deserve to be loved at all?"

"It's not true, Kat. If you're a war criminal then I'm a Ygg. And we all know you despise them; so we wouldn't be friends."

Katsina was still stunned, still wrapping her head around what she had heard.

"Kat, you've got to look in a mirror and know you're a

good person right? You deserve to be loved," Rutheo said, her voice cracking to shake off the confrontation.

"What? Wait, sorry, say that again," Katsina said, clinging to a distant idea that was fading quickly.

"What, you hate the Yggs? It's a jo-"

"No, no, that last part." Katsina said, spinning around. Her eyes wide.

"I, uh, just said look in a mirror?" said Rutheo with a confused look.

"A mirror... That's it. The mirror, Rutheo," Katsina blurted.

"What mirror?"

"Can't talk. Ruthie, you're a genius. I have to go," said Katsina, holding her hands up in a defensive stance.

She turned and slipped through the crack in the sliding door before it could fully open. Leaving Rutheo to fend for herself when the maintenance team arrived. She technically should have been on the way to the hospital, to check for something like a concussion, but her vitals read fine, apart from the apparent signs of stress indicated by her HUD's physiological data menu. But that was the last thing to matter to Katsina. What mattered was getting back to her quarters as fast as she could. She couldn't get there quickly enough. She passed the maintenance team on their way to help Rutheo, and spun around to yell at them.

"Tell Rutheo to come find me when you're done!" she called, she was met with confused and critical glances, but she didn't care. A new found fire began to burn in Katsina. Not one of anger, or passion, but of realisation. A breakthrough she had been fighting for the entire time she had been chipping away at the Amber Eyes, wallowing in her own downfall. She finally understood something.

Katsina knew why the last memory Mara was looking at was her wedding. She realised why Alice told her to take the time off. The entire time Kastsina had been questioning her circumstances. Whether or not she was a villain of war, was about to be settled. If Katsina was right, she was about to find the proof she needed to secure her innocence. The proof she needed to get Morann off her ship. Everything for her future was in the VR helmet, waiting to help her get back into her Captain's chair and end the war. But before she could end the war, she had to start another one. Her friends weren't her enemies; Morann was. He was the one that she was sure she had to defeat, and Mara's memories were going to prove it.

INFILTRATOR

Katsina stumbled up the stairs to the bed, weak from the excessive sprinting she had put herself through. If not being a spaceship captain anymore had made her anything new, it was soft around the edges. She felt a wheeze develop in the back of her throat, towards the middle of her chest. She couldn't tell if it was the fall from the ceiling, or being out of shape; either way she needed to hit the gym in the AR theatre.

Katsina stopped at the top of the steps to catch her breath, glancing ahead to see the helmet lying toppled on the floor where she had thrown it. She contemplated her excitement, wondering what it was she was really going to see, what Mara had left for her in the memory. Several deep breaths later, Katsina found her footing. She eased herself over to the bed, a burning pain in her thighs as she walked. She snatched the helmet from the floor, remembering the last time she ran to her quarters and picked up her own helmet. A sense of finality wasn't lost on her in the moment. It was time for her to get the proof she needed to end Morann's regime. She slipped the helmet on, and dived back into the virtual world, the dazzling lights blinding her again.

The sound of laughter and chatter filled her ears while the open fire *popped* and *snapped* in the background. The room came into focus, and Katsina found herself standing in the archway between the living room and the kitchen. She glanced around, and spotted Mara, still wearing her wedding gown, although a little more disheveled than earlier. The sun had finally set, leaving only the pink and orange streaks across the sparsely cloud patched sky outside. The cabin was lit warmly by candle and lamplight, no fluorescent electricity. It was a truly unique evening. Mara was laughing, joking with George, another crew member of the Abernathy. Though Katsina hardly remembered getting to know him. Katsina slipped away from the conversation, approaching the mirror. She could see nothing unusual, apart from its out of place purple tone. She examined it, looking for something to prompt an activation. Nothing happened. Perhaps an event had to happen to trigger the mirror to show her something. Maybe at a certain point in the memory. Nonetheless, the mirror was definitely modded, Katsina wished she had seen it the first time. Since memories couldn't be interacted with, Katsina decided to bide her time and rejoin Mara in the kitchen.

"Maybe you have a clue, huh, Bridezilla? Your wedding after all," Katsina said to the memory sarcastically. "Oh uh, don't mind me, George."

"Right, well, I better make the rounds; make sure no ones causing mischief in the cabin," Mara said, sidestepping George and working her way through the populated kitchen.

The sink was full of empty bottles, while the counter was littered with plates of food and half eaten cake. The cake had tasted impeccable; Katsina could still remember it. A hint of lemon curd throughout the sponge, while the icing was not too sweet, but perfect to combat the sour. Katsina stopped looking around, and made her way after Mara, knowing where she would be going. Out the back door and down the wedding aisle, past the cherry blossom towering overhead. Katsina noticed the warm lights of the cabin reflected in the stone, it had rained earlier.

"Kaaaaat, Katsina," Mara called, not knowing Katsina was walking with her.

"Yeah?" she could hear her past self call from a distance.

"Where are you?" Mara said, looking about the back of the tree trunk.

"I'm up here, join me!" past Katsina said jokingly, her voice sounding tipsier than Katsina remembered.

"In this dress? Honey, you can clamber your way down. I am not ruining my wedding dress for nobody," said Mara, laughing as she searched the branches above her head.

"Fine," Katsina heard her past self say before a gut wrenching thud sounded on the other side of the tree. "I'm okay. I'm fine."

"Oh, Kat, you okay?" Mara said, running towards a crumpled shape in the grass.

Katsina decided to take her seat by the tree, and watch the scene play out. She remembered the conversation, but had never seen it this way. Mara held out her hand, and helped the drunken idiot to her feet. Past Katsina had already changed out of her salmon dress, and instead wore her combat pants and a tank top. Katsina wondered how she had thought it was a good idea to always wear her military garb on almost every occasion. She never had a sense of wardrobe. Past Katsina began to spin about, holding out her hands to search for something.

"Aha, gotcha," she said, pulling a smoldering little object from the grass.

"Kat, what is that?" Mara asked.

"This? This is a cigarette. You never seen a cigarette before?" past Katsina jested.

"Kat, you know those kinds of pollutants aren't legal, right?" Mara said with a gasp.

"Says the girl who 3D printed gas burners and a wood-fire stove," said past Katsina with a cheeky smile. "Come on, it's a special occasion! We're war heroes now. Who's gonna stop us from having a cigarette?"

She held a small box full of little cylindrical white cigarettes out in Mara's direction.

"It won't kill you unless you smoke like forty a daaaay..."

"You're something else, Kat," laughed Mara, "Faisaheßul why not. It's my wedding night."

"Now you're talkin', babe," she said, pulling a small device from her pocket. "This is a lighter, you use it to-"

"Hey, I know how cigarettes work okay? I'm not stupid."

"Really? Cause that end is the filter, and it's supposed to be in your mouth."

"Oh, really? Okay, maybe I am stupid."

"Nah, just plastered darlin', I'll forgive that."

The two drunk women lit their cigarettes, and a past Katsina tossed herself onto the grass. Mara stayed standing, keeping her eye on the stars that started to appear in the summer's night sky.

"Marshal know's you didn't mean what you said," Mara said timidly.

"I know, Howard told me. He said it's what happens after a big fight like that," past Katsina replied.

"Maybe we had the wedding too soon..." Mara suggested.

"You kiddin'?" asked Katsina, propping herself up on her elbows. "It's the perfect time. Who knows where the Abernathy is gonna go next when she gets out of dry dock. Not to mention our assignments. They could change. This was the perfect time."

"Katsina, you still have shrapnel in your shoulder..." Mara said.

"True, but there's nowhere else I'd rather be."

"You should ta-ta-take a look in the mir-ir-ror inside."

Katsina shot up from leaning against the tree, hearing something she hadn't remembered. Mara was staring at her, directly at her. But something was off. Her body was facing one direction, her head the other. In the darkness of the evening the glow of the cabin reflected in her eyes, highlighting how different they looked to the rest of her face. Looking at her, she felt a pang of fear in her stomach. Mara looked disembodied, ghostly. Katsina lifted herself from the tree, and listened to see if she would say anything else. But she said nothing, not a sound. Even the wind in the trees had stopped blowing, the rustling of the leaves had fallen flat. The cheerful chatter in the cabin had died in an instant. Katsina took a step towards the uncanny representation of Mara.

"What did you say?" Katsina asked, feeling silly to think she could talk to such a glitch.

"You should ta-ta-take a look in the mir-ir-ror inside," it said, without moving or opening its mouth.

Katsina took a step back from the haunting stare of the figure, not taking her eyes away from it. I was too unnerving to turn away from. Something about it reminded her of that awful nightmare. As if locked in a distant staring contest, the figure would not look away from her; the eyes followed her all the way to the cabin as she walked slowly away from it. That was clearly it. The sign she needed. The mod that Mara, or someone, had installed in the memory program. Katsina finally broke her gaze with the figure, and found herself in a room full of frozen, statuesque party guests, as if time had stopped around her. It was clear the program was modded poorly, or perhaps quickly, or even by someone who didn't have experience. Whatever the case, it was time for her to return to the mirror in the living room.

The mirror reflected everything in a purple hue, the guests, furniture, and walls. How she hadn't noticed it was modded content the first time was beyond her. The room was silent, even her footsteps made no echo on the floorboards. Katsina placed herself squarely in front of the purple glass, unable to see herself in its reflection. After all she wasn't really there, just an observer. She didn't understand what she was meant to do to be able to see herself. She positioned herself closer, nothing changed, further away, nothing again. She dipped her head to a certain angle, hopefully able to catch her reflection, nothing. She stepped from left to right, angling herself further. Still nothing happened. She never appeared in the reflection, it was just the same wall. The same bottles on the dining table. The same eleven party guests in the room. Three at the archway, laughing together. One holding a bottle of unopened champagne. Another five littered along the large couch directly across from the fire. A couple, dancing at the window at the front of the room. And one sitting on a chair in the far corner. She couldn't see herself. Katsina spun about in frustration and began to pace the room. She tried to think of anything she could do. Nothing came to mind. Her forehead began to heat up. Her jaw clenched.

"Ugh what do you want from me?" said Katsina in frustration.

"You should ta-ta-take a look in the mir-ir-ror inside," said Mara's disembodied voice.

She jumped at the sound of the glitchy and scratchy sounding tone. Mara was not in the room, but sounded as if she was standing right next to her. Katsina stomped out to the kitchen, rested her hands on the edge of the sink and looked out the window to see Mara staring right at her. Her face was residing on the back of her head in the most unnerving manor. Katsina couldn't hold her gaze again. A shiver ran up her spine at the sight of her. She returned to the living room, wondering what it was she was missing. She thought maybe an object in the room might activate the mirror if she passed it. So she began running her hand through various things, the blowpoke, the rustic radio sitting on a marble top table. The decanter and glasses that sat in a corner display. The gas lamps, nothing changed. Every object and all of the ten people in the room didn't activate the mirror.

"Wait... ten?" she thought.

She double checked the living room, counting the occupants, the three in the archway, the two dancing together, the four sitting on the couch with one laying across their laps. Ten people. Katsina looked back into the mirror, wondering if she had imagined the eleventh person sitting in the corner. She wasn't. He was still there, but he wasn't dressed for the occasion. The man was wearing a grey jumpsuit with no shoes. How odd. His head was shaved around the sides, his black mopped hair on the top of his head tied into a bun. His head was dipped low, but his features were unmistakable. He was gaunt, and pale beyond anything she had ever seen. His skin almost translucent, his veins clearly visible. His tattoos, that drew harsh and dark lines across his arms and neck, made him stand out from everyone in the picturesque scene. Half of his skin was visible, while the other half was black ink hatched into him. Katsina looked away from the mirror, to the corner where he sat, there was no one there, it was an empty seat. Back to the mirror, there he was, plain as day. Katsina stepped forward timidly, trying to get a better look at the man's face. She pressed her forehead as close to the mirror as she could, trying not to pass through it. He seemed frozen like the rest in the room, but on closer inspection, Katsina could see a slow rise and fall in his arched shoulders. He wasn't frozen.

"Who are you?" asked Katsina out loud.

To her surprise the man lifted his head, making her step back as the room suddenly changed shape. The other figures in the living room disappeared, and the room's walls closed in as all the lights went out. She felt a pang of fear, her breath quickening. The furniture folded into the walls around her, the fire went out. And the wooden floor turned to concrete. The only light left was on the strange man, who sat under a purple glow that emanated from the ceiling. A beam rotated above him, as if photocopying his existence. Katsina had no idea what was happening as the seated man zipped across the dark room to sit right in front of her. The mirror fell away, and dematerialised from Katsina's view. She was in the room with him, and he had an answer to her question.

"I have nothing to say," said the black and white man.

"What? Who are you?" Katsina said.

"You have a lot to say to me, and to my friend here," another voice entered the room.

Katsina spun about to see none other than Admiral Krauss, her superior, enter the room in his dress blues. But his rank was different, he didn't look so old. His affix was that of a Rear Admiral, which had been his position for more than six years. He had only been Admiral for eight, meaning that this was a memory at least eight or nine years old. Krauss lifted his hand to his right, gesturing to the darkness. Where the all-too-familiar, smug, and arrogant face of Deacon Morann emerged from the darkness, his eyes reflecting the purple light of the room.

"I said: I have nothing to say," the black and white man repeated.

"Oh, I think you will," Morann said in a jolly manner. "You see, this funny little light here, it's going to keep you here with us. You won't be able to burn yourself from the inside out. This technology disables all of your artificial functions."

"That's not right," the man in the chair grunted. "You are violating Henry Dunant's Geneva Convention updated to include the use of cybernetic disruptors in the yea-"

"Don't you dare quote Geneva to me," Krauss said with a growl, smacking the man across the face. "My great grandfather was there; he campaigned for it. Not knowing what you would do to pervert it."

"Rear Admiral, I don't think our guest will respond to such things. These warmongering pests don't understand the basic rights and dignities of people in war," Morann slyly said.

"Agreed, Captain."

"So, tell us who you are, old chap. I'm sure with a little information shared we can come to some kind of agreement to return you to your system."

"I will tell you nothing. Not after what you did to us. You deserve no answers."

"Nonsense, seventy years ago your people ignited a war. You laid siege to multiple planets and space stations, killing millions. If history shows one thing it's that the Yggdrasilians decided to conquer the solar systems. We did nothing to you," Morann said quickly.

"Really? That's what you think? Is that what they're teaching you? You must not have even left the academy by the time this war started. You don't know a thing."

Morann crossed the room and bent down, pressing his forehead against the black and white man's. His breathing had gotten louder.

"I know enough about your kind, separatists, liars, deviants from the doctrine laid down when we settled these stars. Terra Yggdrasil abandoned the pillars, twisted it's way of life, using weapons that go far beyond humane," dictated Morann, as if a script was being read. Katsina couldn't understand what was happening.

"Weapons that *your* people made," droned the black and white man.

Katsina lifted her hand to her mouth to stay silent, forgetting that it was a memory and not reality. Morann stood back from the man in the chair, clearly taken aback himself. He joined Krauss on the edge of the light, whispering. Katsina took her chance and crouched in front of the Yggdrasilian man. He was tired, impossibly thin, the dark rings around his eyes showing signs of starvation and exhaustion. She took a step around him, and looked at the back of his neck.

"No military implants?" she mumbled.

"Right then," said Krauss, interrupting her inspection, "let me ask you the one question I know you're going to answer: Where are the spies that infiltrated our navy?"

"Why would I know that? I know nothing about the military."

"Lies, you were clearly an exploration fleet captain. Your tattoos and markings say that much. You've been fighting just like the rest of us."

"Defending," the Yggdrasilian said.

"What?"

"We've been defending. You have been fighting."

"Conjecture and nonsense. Your leaders must have really wiped your mind clean of reason," Morann interrupted.

"Shut it," Krauss growled, "this isn't a propaganda video, it's an interrogation, Morann. Get it together."

Morann fell silent at Krauss' rasp.

"Now listen to me," Krauss said, looking back to the Yggrasilian, lifting his head by the chin, "I know your ilk has nested in my fleet, at least one of you has been leaking information. Tell me how to find this person. A simple description, and I will grant your freedom."

"Rear Admiral, hah," laughed the Yggdrasilian. "Of the people in this room you should be asking, it isn't me."

"Explain," Krauss snapped through the laughter of the prisoner.

"Ha, haha, you people think I know the answer. I might, but I wouldn't tell. But I know who could," he said tilting his head to one side, looking around Krauss to find Morann.

"You of all people would know, Morann. Why interrogate me? You know. Haha, Hahaha"

The man fell into a fit of laughter, prompting Krauss to look at Morann with concern.

"What is he talking about, Morann?" Krauss said in a hushed tone.

"Morann, Morann, the man with a plan, if you want your spy then he's your man!" the prisoner chanted, repeating his words over and over.

Katsina noticed his laughter increase. He began to violently shake in his seat, as if seizing or fitting. She ran to his side. She tried to grab him, only to have her hands pass through his body. His skin began to turn a bright red. She watched as blood began to leak from the man's ears, then his nose, and finally a torrent of fluid spilled from his mouth. The captured Yggdrasilian was cooking himself alive.

"Damn," Krauss said, closing his eyes and exhaling slowly. "He was faster than anticipated."

"What is this?" Katsina heard Morann yell as men began to fill the room.

"Take Morann to interview room three, gentlemen," Kraus said as if further away.

Katsina looked around to see a commotion, but only saw darkness, and heard the sounds of a struggle fade away behind the walls of the room. She turned her attention back to the man in the chair. His eyes still open, staring at the lights above. He was still whispering something that Katsina couldn't understand, it sounded as if he was talking gibberish or a foreign language. Eventually his whispering stopped, and then his breath, and finally his seizure. The Yggdrasilian man had died, his eyes seeing nothing. Katsina could only hear the sound of her own breath, shaky and uneven. She slowed herself down, in through the nose, out through the mouth. Trying to regain a calm demeanor. She decided to step up back to her feet to watch the man fall away from her into the darkness. She found herself surrounded by laughter and cheer again. Katsina jumped at the sound of a bottle of champagne being popped behind her. She was back at the wedding party.

"Kat?" she heard echo in the room around her.

"Rutheo?" She responded.

"Kat, take that thing off would ya," Rutheo's distant voice said.

The implications of what Katsina had seen began to set in. She couldn't control her breathing much longer, a pressure began to mount in her stomach. Katsina lifted her hands and ripped the helmet away from her face, throwing herself back into the real world without ending the program. Before her was a kneeling Rutheo, her face pale and frightened. Her hands gripped on Katsina's shoulders, as if trying to hold her to the real world.

"Kat, your shaking," she said.

Katsina swiped Rutheo's hands away, and thrust herself off of the bed. She shoved past Rutheo, stumbling as she tried to navigate the stairs. She clapped her hands over her mouth, her clammy palms slipping across her lips. Eventually she made it to the kitchen sink, and puked. What she'd seen, coupled with the experience of being pulled in and out of a mod, a memory, and reality. It was all too overwhelming. She ran her hands across her cheeks, pulling her hair out of the way of her face, pinning it to the back of her neck. Eventually the regurgitation slowed to a halt and Katsina could rest her head on the end of the sink, her eyes watering with discomfort.

She opened her eyes, trying to steady herself. Standing

over her was 3 different Rutheo's, each holding a towel out to her. The nausea subsided, but the dizziness wouldn't go away. Katsina couldn't help but feel that the room was rotating, shifting the gravity under her feet. As if barrel rolling in the cockpit of an older fighter model. She forced her eyes closed again to keep the symptoms at bay, reaching out randomly to take the towel from Rutheo.

"You, uh, want to tell me what's going on now? First you tackle me, then you're screaming about 'taking sides', then you sprint off like a crazy person. And now you're vomiting in your sink?" said Rutheo, her voice pitching higher and higher with each sentence.

Katsina could feel an unpleasant mass in the back of her throat, forcing her to hoch and spit into the sink. Using the counter top as support, she slowly slid down to the ground. She reached for the fridge, trying not to make the room spin any worse. Rutheo opened the fridge for her, allowing her to snatch a flask of cold water.

"So? What's going on?" Rutheo insisted, while she slurped at the water.

"It's... It's Morann, Rutheo," managed Katsina.

"What about him?"

"He's an infiltrator," she said, taking another sip at the flask. "Morann's a Yggdrasilian."

GRAVITY BY DESIGN

Katsina remained seated by the fridge, focusing on her breathing and going over and over the events she had seen. The image of the man disintegrating in the chair continued to play in her mind's eye, distracting her from her HUD and even her outer vision. The only thing she could really keep focus on was Rutheo, who paced about the room her hands interlocked on the back of her neck. Rutheo had been silent for minutes at a time, trying to start a sentence and then stopping herself. There was a level of agitation in her eyes from learning what Katsina had found, but there was something else. The engineer looked out of her depth. Her typical sarcastic demeanour had fallen apart. It was replaced by what Katsina could only describe as petrification. She hung her head, feeling the nausea and shock fade away as she clutched the empty flask, touching the cap to her eyebrow.

"What do we do?" said Rutheo finally, her voice shaky.

"We have to stop him," Katsina replied, keeping her eyes on a smear of dirt on the kitchen floor.

"How did you know to look in the mirror? Where did Mara get the memory?"

"I don't know, the memory belongs to either Krauss or Morann."

"Or the Ygg…" Rutheo said, her tone more grave than she had ever sounded. Katsina flicked her eyes up to meet her gaze. "You said the memory ended when he died. That the room fell apart as he melted. What if the memory is his?"

"Then it makes me wonder how Mara could have gotten it. Ev-"

"What is it you brought me over here for Ruthe… oh."

Alice had entered through the door and stopped in between Katsina and Rutheo, becoming the elephant in the room. Katsina had no time to think, so she just acted. She jumped to her feet, crossing the room as quickly as possible.

"Ruthie, get the *door*," Katsina snapped.

Katsina snatched Alice's left arm with one hand, while running her other up her neck to the back of her ears. Alice recoiled at the encounter, cursing Katsina for touching her. Katsina felt the back of her earlobes for the little bump of her comm implant and subsequently pried it out from the port in her skin.

"What are you- how dare y- that's my-"

"Ruthie, her neck," Katsina said, snatching Alice up into a bear hug.

"Yah," Rutheo said before the sound of a loud *click* and *hiss*, "got it."

Katsina and Rutheo both stood back from Alice, who immediately searched her neck and ears for her implants frantically. She had probably never had them removed so suddenly and without preparation. Katsina held her hands up in innocence, while Rutheo took both implants and slipped them into her back pocket. Alice kept her hands around her empty implant ports, her eyes darting between them, her face wincing in discomfort.

"I'm sorry, we had to," Katsina said softly. "He could hear this through you."

"How dare you," Alice said, tears beginning to stream down her cheeks. "I dismiss you so you assault me is that it?"

"I'll be honest Alice; I didn't even know you were coming," Katsina said, darting a glare at Rutheo.

"I asked her to come help me check on you… I forgot I asked her, sorry," Rutheo shrugged.

"My eyes, it's so dark…" Alice mumbled.

"I know, I know. Alice, I really am sorry. I would never want to hurt you. This is important. I know it's uncomfortable now but you will adjust. Just keep your eyes closed for a few minutes. It's important that you listen to us," Katsina said, pleading with the distressed woman.

"Why are you doing this?" Alice asked, receding to the corner by the door.

"We're weren't trying to hurt you…" Rutheo said as she scratched her eyebrow.

"What is it you want? Tell me so I can have my implants back," Alice said, holding her eyes shut.

"We found something you need to hear, Alice," Katsina began. "Remember what we found? About Morann's wife? We thought that's why he had it out for me-"

"So?" Alice snapped. "What then?"

Katsina thought about what Rutheo had said, and considered Alice's actions thus far. She had to make a choice, to trust her crew, or to allow her paranoia push them away. Katsina didn't take much time to make her choice, and told Alice about the VR helmet and what she had seen. Throughout the story, Rutheo passed Alice another flask of water and refilled Katsina's. She made coffee for the three of them, but only she drank it. By the time Katsina finished her story, and shared her suspicion of Morann, Rutheo had drunk all three cups of coffee and went to the bathroom twice. All the while, Alice kept her eyes shut, flinching every time she tried to open them. But she listened patiently. Eventually her eyes opened, and Katsina escorted her up the stairs to see the memory herself. The three of them sat around the bed, the two watched Alice in the VR helmet before she eventually took it off. Katsina finished her story, and allowed Alice a moment to contemplate.

"Do you think this is all true, Rutheo? You think it's authentic?" Alice asked.

"She has no reason to lie…" said Rutheo. "If anything people have been lying about her. We thought Morann's motivations were to get revenge by ruining Katsina's career. But it looks like he's just trying to find a scapegoat to convince Krauss he's not the traitor."

"My thoughts exactly," said Katsina.

"Have you seen it?" Alice asked Rutheo, her breath uneasy.

"I don't have to. I trust her. Pshh Besides, I'd rather not see another person melt," She replied.

"I don't understand, the Yggdrasilian accused Morann of being the infiltrator. Why would he out his own man? Revenge for his capture?" Alice said.

"Probably because Morann stood back and let one of his people be interrogated like that. The Yggs avoid interrogation at all costs. I've never seen one captured," Katsina said.

"It's the first time I've ever seen one. Are they really that pale?"

"I don't know. Honestly, it's pretty disturbing to even imagine him," said Rutheo.

"So, what do we do? Could we bring this as evidence in your trial?" Alice asked.

"Níl is agaím," said Rutheo. "I've never even thought this was something that could happen. Besides, the Admiralty is in pieces. I hardly expect them to be worrying about convicting Kat right now."

"We have to get a message to Marshal," said Katsina.

"Ha, and how are we gonna do that. Morann has the comm's on lock, no messages in or out. We can't even write home. So, yeah, you find a way to do that then talk to me," Rutheo said, her eyes rolling in her head.

Her tone was laced in criticism, sarcasm, but not in her usual teasing nature. She seemed weary of Katsina, giving her a cold shoulder at every interval. Katsina shuffled on the bed, running her hands through her hair. Soon she could feel the eyes of Alice and Rutheo rest on her, they're expressions suspicious.

"Kat?" Rutheo prompted.

"Katsina?"

She wondered what it would mean to reveal her secret to them. To tell them that she had the ability to contact Marshal the entire time. She weighed her options. Marshal asked Rutheo to watch out for her, Alice was young, but Katsina had already made her choice. They were too far down the rabbit hole, if they were going to take Morann down, Katsina couldn't hide anything from them.

"I... uh... I have a way to reach him," she admitted.

The news didn't go down well. Alice was furious at the idea that Katsina had a way to sneak messages on and off the ship. Rutheo couldn't help but take it equally poorly, wondering why Marshal hadn't left her with a similar way to reach him. The three of them bickered about the morals of using such technology, considering the society they were fighting to protect was a society of truth. Alice felt that secrecy is what led to the war in the first place, but she was quickly shut down by Rutheo, who reminded her that they weren't the ones that started it.

"She's right. The Ygg's broke off from the rest of humanity. They stopped being truthful with us. Maybe it's time we use the enemies tactics against them," Katsina suggested.

"I still think we should run this up the chain of command, tell Krauss that we know what happened. Like, why would he let Morann go if the Yggrasilian outed him?" Alice asked.

"Morann has an extensive family history, his service to the fleet is also well documented. Maybe he's so deeply undercover that even his personal logs and data collected by his memory core exonerated him. But if they extracted it... Maybe they could have dug deeper," said Katsina.

"Other than that, what could expose him? I mean extracting his memory core would kill him; what else could you do?"

"Here's what we do; we pull his teeth out, one by one. Break each of his fingers, install a program in his implants to cause him neurological pain. That would make him talk," Rutheo said in a giddy tone.

"Yeah, we're not doing that," Katsina said. "What about a genetic screening? Surely the genes of Ygg's are different enough from ours?"

"They would have already done that when they

scanned his memory core. It must have shown nothing."

"Would a screening like that catch genetic engineering?" Katsina said.

"Kat…" Alice gasped. "There's… there's no way. Genetic engineering is against nature. Only used to help the severely ill-"

"Or help someone infiltrate an enemy power and tear it down from the inside," Rutheo said.

"A heinous lie…" Alice said.

"So unthinkable that we can't imagine it actually happening-" Katsina added.

"Meaning a generic genetic scan might not be looking for it," Rutheo finalised.

The lights in the room flickered, and a faint rumble ran across the floor of the room.

"The hell was that?" Rutheo asked, before the lights flickered again. Katsina launched to her feet to investigate, but immediately slipped and fell on her side. She slid across the floor, snatching at one of the cables attached to the VR helmet. She halted, and the cable cut into her hand for it. Rutheo tumbled over her, crashing into the wall to the left of the bed. Alice let out a scream, slipping off the bed and falling into the wall.

"Ruthie!" Katsina shouted, realising the entire room had turned on its side. She swung her right arm upwards, and tried to snatch the cable. She was too late. The cord snapped, slicing her hand open and causing her to fall. The room lit up red, signaling a shipwide emergency with alarms blaring. She landed with a crack next to Rutheo, who found her footing in the sudden gravity shift. Alice continued to scream, prompting Katsina to snatch the girl up into her arms.

"It's okay, I have you. I have you."

"Kat," she cried, "Kat, what's happening?"

"It's a faisaheßul failure in the inertial dampeners. Artificial gravity has shifted," Rutheo said.

"Ruthie," Katsina steadied herself, pulling Alice closer to her. "Get on to engineering. Who's supposed to be supervising the dampeners?"

"Uh, well, don't be mad okay?" Rutheo said timidly.

"Ruthie?"

"I was supposed to be on shift today, we were supposed to run a test on the dampeners and the gravity plating."

The room shifted again, pulling Katsina to her right. She crashed into Rutheo, knocking her legs out from under her. The three of them slid across the wall and crumpled into the kitchen cabinets over the balcony's edge. Katsina gripped the side of the cabinet, while the other two continued to fall to the other end of the small room. She swung her arm over the edge of the cabinet in a bid to catch one of them, but her attempt was in vain. Rutheo hit the wall first, with Alice smacking into her, the two of them becoming tangled in one of the many flags on the wall. Katsina heard an unnerving groan from the ceiling above.

"The bulkheads are straining!" Katsina shouted. "Rutheo, the bulkheads!"

Katsina shot a look down to see the other two, Rutheo was speaking frantically but not to Alice. Alice herself was fondling with her neck, trying to get her implants back into place. Another demented groan echoed through the walls. Katsina could only imagine the worst.

"Rutheo?" Katsina called watching a panel on the wall above begin to warp.

"Just a minute! I nearly got it."

"This is first officer Wesley. Can I get a report?" Alice said.

"-okay you have to reset the stabilizers and boot it again-" Ruteo could be heard.

"Rutheo?" Katsina called again. The panel began to peel away from the wall.

"-repeat I need a report from engineering-"

"-p and your nearly there ju-"

"Rutheo!" Katsina shouted.

Without warning the lights went out, and Katsina was pulled away from the cabinet. Her shoulder collided with another hard surface, causing her to cry out in pain. The red lights began to flash, brightly illuminating the room for a second at a time. A loud *pop* followed by a *smash* sounded just above Katsina's head, causing her to curl into a ball. Something rained over Katsina in tiny pieces, while another *crash* landed next to her. In the brief flashes, Katsina could make out the figures of Rutheo and Alice, who were in a heap on the floor a few feet away. The alarm halted, leaving them with only the sound of groans and strained breath.

"Rutheo?" called Katsina, "Alice? Ugh, Rutheo?"

"Yeah, yeah we're good. You hurt?"

The red flashes ceased, as the room's regular lighting flickered back on. Katsina rolled onto her back, looking back up at the ceiling. They were no longer on the walls. Katsina groaned as she moved, feeling more than one spot which was definitely going to bruise. She clutched at her chest with one hand and lifted herself with the other. She settled onto her knees, her arms wrapped tightly around her chest.

"Lasine uí nußolt'seich..." Rutheo said.

Katsina glanced to her left. A square sheet of metal was embedded into the cabinet she had just been clinging to. The floor around her was littered with splinters of wood and glass, while the food printer lay in pieces between her and the other two. Rutheo arrived at her side, grabbing her shoulder.

"You okay? You hurt?"

"I'm fine. I'm fine. Alice?"

"Y-you g-guys?" A shaky voice whimpered, making Katsina's heart jump into her throat.

They both shot up, arriving at Alice's side in an instant. She was leaning against one of the engine parts that had been strewn across the room in the shift. Her eyes fixated in shock.

"Alice, Alice, you okay? You hurt?" Katsina said, stopping herself from immediately lifting Alice into her arms.

"T-the… t-the…" she mumbled.

"Rutheo, a medkit, get a medkit," Katsina barked, making Rutheo sprint to the bathroom under the balcony. "Alice, Alice, it's okay. You just need to tell me where you're hurt. Don't talk okay? Just point where it hurts."

Alice continued to mumble. Katsina snapped her fingers in front of her to no avail. The girl seemed parilised had she not been shivering all over. Slowly Alice lifted her hand, trying to contort her fingers to point. She extended her hand away from herself, making Katsina turn around to see what she was gesturing towards.

"T-the, th-th-the helmet…" she said.

Katsina's stomach sank to see the VR headset lying in the corner by the door, smashed and crushed from being thrown around the room. The visor was missing and the ports were dislodged, it looked beyond repair. Suddenly Rutheo appeared beside them, fumbling with a white pouch bearing a red cross.

"Okay uh, I got burn gel or uh, an arm sling or a splint, what do you need," she said, panic in her voice.

"I'm fine, j-just. The h-helmet. Th-the memory."

"The memory can wait, Honey. Just tell me; are you hurt?" Katsina asked.

"No, no I'm okay."

"Kat," Rutheo interjected, "we gotta get down there."

"Yeah. Just, just give me a sec. Alice, can you walk?" she asked.

"Yes. I think so."

"Good, okay, good girl. You're okay," Katsina said, thrusting her hands under Alice's biceps, "Rutheo. you good?"

"Ready to go." Rutheo said.

"Whe-where are we going?" Alice said as Katsina lifted her to her feet.

"We need to get to engineering."

***

The painful jog to the engineering section took them all over the Behemothis, through corridors, service tunnels, and even people's personal quarters. The ship didn't feel severely damaged, but it looked awful. Katsina had only seen such damage on a ship twice before. To look at the Behemothis, in the state that it was in, brought back that old pain in her knuckles. Some sections of the ship appeared to be completely cut off by superficial debris, While others were covered in dislodged cables, panels, and in the residential areas, personal belongings. One person's house had been set up as an emergency medical tent for an entire housing unit, most of the people in the area being crisis response and nurses. Katsina found it while sliding between two panels that had been forced together in one of the hallways. On the sidewalk and in the living quarters, she saw rows of people, all injured. Crew members carried each other, treated each other's wounds. Katsina spotted a familiar face in the crowd, a person who seemed to be in charge.

"Dr. Foye!" Rutheo shouted.

"Kat, Ruthie... Alice?" Linda answered, looking them up and down. "What happened to you three?"

"Same thing that happened to everyone else. What's going on?" Katsina said, darting her eyes to the wounded.

"Three primary corridors collapsed in the direction of the hospital, this section is cut off so we're treating people here," Linda explained.

"The hospital? We just passed underneath it from my quarters," said Katsina, snatching Linda's arm and leading her out to the street, "See that crack? Through there, and up two flights of steps. Then you turn-"

"Katsina, I'm a doctor not a maze runner," Linda said.

"Yeah, those movies sucked," muttered Rutheo.

"Not now, Ruthie," Katsina said, "Alice, I need you to help some of these people back the way we came. Help them to the hospital and meet us in engineering."

"But my duty requires-"

"Your duty is to this crew," Katsina cut her off, "and they need you. See you in engineering."

Alice's eyes were wide, the entire day reflected in them. The chaos of the ship rebounding off of her pupils. She would be consumed by the disaster should she not focus on her immediate tasks. The first and foremost being the well-being of the crew.

"Dr. Foye, grab some of those crisis response people and get them to widen that gap. I can't stay," Katsina explained.

"You're fine, thank you, now go," Linda said with a faint but sincere smile.

Katsina brought her attention back to Alice, snatching the woman's shoulders up in her hands.

"Listen to me, you're the first officer. I know it's difficult, but now's the time to suck it up. Morann didn't make you first so he could control you, understand? He did it because you're capable. You can do this," Katsina said, staring into the blond woman's eyes.

"Okay, okay..." Alice said.

***

The engineering sections of the Behemothis were impressive to say the least, six nuclear reactors, sixteen kugelblitz wheels, 2 water refinement plants, electrical and power maintenance centres, multiple research and development workshops and much more. But the objective was the inertial dampener and gravity control department or IDGC, a vital part of the ship's function. Without these the ship's megastructure could tear itself open in an instant, the loss of gravity would cause otherwise stable beams and struts to shift, causing a weaker frame for the Broadsider should it enter a different atmosphere, or pass near an object with exceptional gravitational pull. Without inertial dampening, everyone in the ship would be subjected to the force of moving at high speeds through space. Without the dampeners dispersing this force, again, the ship would tear itself apart. Considering the day she had, the last thing Katsina needed was someone blowing the ship to smithereens in the middle of a systems test.

The control room for all the ship's major engineers was similar in design to the bridge; only it wasn't a full cone shaped dome structure. It was more of a semi dome made up of AR display screens. The semi dome stretched around multiple stations sunk into the floor, each with a set of 3 engineers on hand for individual functions. Maintenance and engineering field teams were deployed from their ready rooms below the semi dome. Most people referred to the control room as the orange room, as most of the AR displays were monochromatic to the naked eye. They only showed partial sections of information this way. However, with the extended AR layer of people's HUDs, the screens appeared multichromatic, as the HUD would fill in the missing information. This was a safety measure to allow people with special visual access codes the ability to work in engineering. Defending the ship from capture or sabotage.

The orange glow remained just that for Katsina, who, even with her HUD, didn't have access to see the full extent of the situation on the huge panoramic dome. But she tried to assess the situation in the room all the same. The lights had still not properly turned on, the red flashing alarm lights still spinning, casting shadows across the room in every direction. Each station in the room was divided by aisles, each aisle mapped with a colored strip to lead a person to an appropriate section. Katsina followed the flashing yellow line with Rutheo in tow. The room itself was a mess as people lay injured while medics treated their wounds. Scientists carried assistants in their arms towards the exits. A crack had formed on the panoramic semi dome itself in the top left corner, causing it to fold inward. A crowd had formed ahead of Katsina at the IDGC stations, another angry mob like the one in the canteen. She pushed through the crowd, forgetting it was probably faster to let Rutheo go first. After all, Rutheo did outrank her.

"-and where's Rutheo?"

"-eed a medic here-"

"-is reset and online sir, yes sir-"

"-as their fault! They knew what they were doing-"

Katsina made it to the front of the crowd to see the last thing she expected that day. Even less expected than seeing a real life Yggdrasilian. She halted herself at the top of the steps that lead down into the crater like station. Rutheo crashed into her, making her lose her balance for a moment. Their appearance made the arguing crowd hush as whispers began to be exchanged. Two men stood at the station, wearing military police uniforms, the same two from the group in the canteen. They each had their hands on the middle aged, grey haired, mustache sporting Howard Crawford. His forehead was cut, and his eye bruised, even in the orange light Katsina could see he was in pain. Standing before him, with an infuriating grin on his face, was Kessler. Leaning on one of the control panels, next to a frantic engineer working on stabilizing the ship, was Morann. Between him and the group of angered engineers was a barricade of men, all his own, bearing the brand of Military Police. His face didn't move, as if made of stone, completely unaffected by the sudden change in volume from the crowd. The arrival of Katsina didn't even make him look, he kept his eyes on Howard.

"Howard!" Rutheo screamed.

THE EXECUTIONER

"Howard! Howard," Rutheo squealed as she pushed past Katsina, jumping into the dome. Katsina tried to follow her, but was halted by one of the MPs.

"Finally, we can get started," announced Morann, clapping his hands together. Katsina felt a shuffle behind her, another two MPs strategically placed themselves on either side of her.

"Hey you okay? You get hurt?" Rutheo asked, her tone sweet but her eyes watering. She pushed past Kessler, who stood back from Howard, with his hands raised. She had Howard's cheeks cupped into her hands. The man looked brutalised.

"I- I did everything you asked me, Ruthie. But they told me to change the parameters of the test," Howard said, his voice croaked.

"Yes yes, whatever you say, Howard. Now ladies and gentlemen of the engineering department," Morann projected, walking around the concave station. "You're all probably wondering what happened here. Well, thankfully, Captain Kessler's prompt investigation has come to a close with the arrival of the culprit."

The crowd began to chatter, making Katsina peek around to ask Alice what was going on. She had forgotten that Alice was no longer by her side. Alice was with Dr. Foye and the emergency response team. A shiver ran up Katsina's spine.

"Now, from what I've been told, our chief of engineering, Rutheo McHugh, decided to assign the task of a gravity plate stress test, a highly complex and classified procedure, to a tarmac *mechanic*," he said, with a hint of glee in his voice. "As far as I'm aware this task is only to be performed by the head of engineering or an equally experienced individual, am I correct, Ruthie?"

Rutheo turned to face Morann, her nostrils flared, her cheeks red with anger bathed in an orange and red light. Rutheo's mouth hung ajar, her jaw cocked to one side, almost like she had forgotten what she was going to say, until she said it.

"What did you do to him you faisaheßul bheibhen?" she spat, causing a wave of hushed voices around the circle.

"Me? Ha, I did nothing. Mr. Kessler and I were simply here to inspect the stress test on t-"

"He knows exactly how to perform this test. He's been practicing for weeks to earn a new rank. He's been putting in extra hours like the rest of us, going above and beyond ever since *you* took over this ship. He *knows exactly* how to perform this test," Rutheo said, her voice scratching, spitting in anger.

"Hey! She's right. you're the one who has us on double and triple shifts all day!" an engineer from the crowd chimed in, followed by a mumbling amongst the others.

"Say, Mr. Rogers," Morann said, turning to the engineer frantically working at the screen next to him, "can you tell me how this test went wrong?"

"Y-yes captain," the thin, nervous engineer replied.

He was what Katsina would describe as wilted, strung thin, stretched, a man who clearly spent too much time studying and not enough time exercising. He was one of the few people who still wore glasses, which he adjusted with anxiety at having to answer Morann's question. His brown eyes were shaped by his frown, a flash of fear at having to speak directly to Morann.

"Out with it then," Morann said, a boom echoing from his voice in the room.

"The, um, parameters, sir. The equation required was unsuitable. The wrong values were entered. Causing the gravity to shift much more than the test required it to an-"

"And in turn threw everyone on this ship into a wall is that correct?" Kessler interrupted.

"Yes, sir."

Katsina noticed a stirring in the group around her, an anger she recognised. A flare for a conflict that could consume them.

"You evil, sniveling low-life. Your goons did something to him, didn't they? You have them threaten him? Smack him around?" Rutheo said, spinning on her heel and raising her hand. She drove her fist towards Kessler. Who, to her dismay, jabbed her in the chin before she got close. He snatched Rutheo up into his arms, wrapping his muscles around her neck, keeping her in a headlock. Her nose started to bleed.

"Hey! That's not right!" one man shouted.

"I saw them, they shook down Howard!" another added.

"You can't do that!"

As more voices added to the noise, Katsina decided it was time to make her move. She wasn't going to allow some walking boulder assault a single crew mate let alone two. She moved to enter the pit, only to realise she was held in place, snatched by more than one set of hands. One of the men behind her leaned over to her ear, his breath breezing against her hair.

"Captain said you're to watch," he whispered.

Katsina was outnumbered, and began to struggle, the grips on her arms and shoulders grew tighter with each move, until a metallic clank pulled her wrists together behind her back. Magnetic cuffs.

"Do not blame me or Mr. Kessler, my dear crew. The only person you need to blame for your circumstances is right there," Morann announced, pointing in the direction of Katsina.

All at once, for the second time in her life, all eyes were on her while she was cuffed. A feeling of unease worked its way into her mind. The room parted to make room for her, the circle turning into an oval.

"You see, had she not betrayed you all, betrayed humanity, we would not have needed to bring her to trial. If we didn't have to do that, she wouldn't have been able to get the Yggs to attack Los Ange. And if Los Ange wasn't laid to waste, well, you all see where I'm going."

The silence became uncomfortable, and the shadows in the orange and red light licked like flames around Katsina. She realised what was happening. And it made her feel sick. It was a witch hunt. Morann was trying to turn them.

"Now, I know that many of you may have heard that the allegations against your former compatriot are false, and that someone must have been mistaken. A dangerous rumour, we are a society of honesty, and lies like this must not be believed. Humanity hasn't lied in eight hundred years until your *Captain* turned up with her chasanuha of an engineer. You all are beginning to believe she is innocent. But how, may I ask, can you think that? How can you think that when she trusts hot headed troublemakers who assign dangerous work to imbeciles?"

"The only imbecile I see here is you!" Rutheo shouted, malice in her voice.

Morann paused, closed his eyes and opened them multiple times, as if confused by something. He lifted his hands, waving them about his face, taking a deep breath before closing the space between him and the detained Rutheo. He bent down slightly, matching his eye level to hers. A look of fear flashed across her face, one that Katsina had seen in her before.

"You have a big mouth for such a little c-"

"Captain, a report has been compiled," Alice interrupted, stepping down into the fray. She was holding a tablet out towards Morann, "I recommend we place Chief McHugh on administrative leave while Howard is moved to the hospital for his injuries. As is protocol. Also you're needed in the war room by request of Admiral Krauss. He awaits your call."

Katsina finally let out a breath as she watched the escalation in the room deflating. The tension was suffocating, and Alice had entered with a lifeline of fresh air. The crowd seemed placated for a moment to watch her. She noticed that, though her hair was tattered, her clothes disheveled and her affix was askew; Alice walked differently than Katsina remembered. Her chin was held high, her shoulders straight and rested. Her posture, even after being thrown around Katsina's quarters, was striking. Morann had closed his eyes at the sound of her voice. He peeled his lips back from his teeth, contorting his face in a strenuous way as his eyes rolled to the ceiling. His hands bent into claws, as if he was gripping onto his lost moment of unaccountability. He straightened himself, and turned to face his first officer with a smile.

"Ah, yes!" he beamed, "thank you Alice. I will look these over immediately. In the meantime, please remain here to oversee repairs and recalibrations of the Behemothis' systems. I will be in the war room."

"Aye captain. I'll see to it," Alice said.

"Good, good," Morann said aloud, before leaning into her ear. He muttered something inaudible. Katsina only hoped that her implants were reinstalled to record it. Morann lapped around the IDGC station, gathering his soldiers. Kessler threw Rutheo to the ground, with Harold thrown next to her. It was a barbaric display of force. He looked around the room, gauging the impact he left on the engineering team. The animosity could almost be tasted in the moisture of the air.

"Remember what was said here. Your circumstances are not the result of my actions. They are the result of an executioner. A betrayer to the cause. That executioner isn't me; it's her," Morann finished, pointing at Katsina before taking his leave. "Let's win the war."

A metallic click behind Katsina's back loosened her wrists, while the hands gripping her forearms and shoulders slid away. Morann's MPs dispersed into the crowd, following him out of the department. Katsina looked around the room, seeing hundreds of new threads connecting people to each other, the conversation over the network was exploding. The threads started to spread beyond the bulk heads of engineering, and many even attached to Katsina. Her HUD began displaying personal messages. But she had no time to read them. Katsina blinked her HUD away from her vision, and slid down into the IDGC station to get to Howard. He was lying by one of the control panels, his head rested on Rutheo's chest, a medic had arrived just as Katsina sat with him.

"Howard. I'm- I'm so sorry," Katsina said, holding her lip in a hard line.

"It's alright Captain, I shouldn't have listened to them. But they hit me a-"

"I know, I know. You did everything you were asked to do. It's not your fault," Rutheo said, cutting him off.

"She's right Howard. You were following orders," Katsina assured the older man, clasping his wrinkled hand into hers.

"Don't mind me, Howard. I'm just going to check your vitals before we move you." The medic said.

"That's fine lad. I know, Captain, but look, it's not all bad," Howard said, a smile growing under his mustache.

"Oh?" Katsina said, matching his smile. She felt her eyes well at the sight of his bloodied face. "Why is that then?"

"Look at them, they all believe now. He lied to them and they know it," Howard said, nodding his head in the direction of the crowd. "I can't see the connections they all share. I can't hear them like you can, but I know a consensus when I see one."

Katsina looked at the room without her HUD, seeing how the crowd exchanged looks of solidarity and agreement. Their expressions were grave, some even angry. But most of all, they appeared determined. Katsina immediately flashed back to the Alia moon, the last time she saw such a consensus. Alice, whose demeanour had fallen apart, stood with her head in her hands. Katsina never imagined her to take such a risk in confronting, even contradicting, albeit tactfully, Morann and his group of personal soldiers. Katsina could see her eyes, glassy and unresponsive to the commotion around her.

She felt for the woman and the role she had to play. But before she could decide what to do next, a faint squeeze of her hand brought her attention back to Howard and Rutheo. Howard, with the eyes of a loving grandfather, lifted his hand to Katsina's cheek.

"She did a brave thing Captain. Go to her," he said.

Katsina nodded to Rutheo, and returned Howard's compassionate smile. She let go of his hand and shuffled up from her knees, leaving them with the medic for the time being. The crowd began to disperse around them while Alice spoke to Engineer Rogers, who seemed to be the supervisor on shift. He seemed just as, if not more, shaken than she was. Their nervous natures seemed to bounce off one another, their conversation awkward to approach. Katsina noticed Alice's hand touch off his, pinching his pinky finger gently. Katsina didn't want to, but she had to interrupt.

"Uh, sorry, Rogers. I just need Commander Wesley for a sec."

"Oh, uh, yes captain. I mean uh… sorry I meant that uh," he stumbled over his words.

"It's alright, Mr. Rogers. Thank you for the update," Alice said, holding out her hand, directing Katsina to a vacant station for them to speak.

Katsina wanted to congratulate her on her actions, on facing her duty in a time of crises. But, looking at Alice she could see a difference and she decided that, considering the woman outranked her, that she didn't need Katsina's approval or praise. Not anymore.

"So, Mr. Rogers, huh? He's a nice guy, good scientist?" Katsina asked, looking at Alice expectantly.

"What? I mean, I don't know. We've been talking. He's really good at quantum entanglement and we like discussing it someti-"

"Alice, relax. I'm just teasing you," Katsina said. Alice flushed a bright red.

"He's just someone I've been spending my lunch times

with. The last thing I expected was for him to be here," Alice said, pulling her hair behind her left ear.

"Don't worry about it. But it must have felt nice to flex your muscles in front of him huh? His knight in shining armor. Did I ever tell you about the time I set Commander Richmond up with Sarah who used to work at the Energy distribution station?"

"You did? I mean you did that?" Alice said, a smile finally growing on her face.

"I did, but uh, everything kind of kicked off the day I finally got them to start talking. Sarah is on Botanica, she was on shore leave when we left the system."

"Her and half of the crew," Alice said. "It will prove problematic for what you need to do next."

"Yes it will, speaking of being problematic. What was it that Morann said to you before he left?" Katsina asked, losing the casual tone of the conversation.

Alice stopped momentarily, her smile faded as she looked Katsina in the eye.

"He said Admiral Krauss sent a shipment to us. It should be arriving in a week. Kessler is taking care of it and he doesn't want anyone to interrupt him. Admiral's orders."

Katsina closed her eyes, pinching her brow.

"What the hell could that mean?" she said.

"He expects me to keep it under wraps, and to not have it appear on the log until necessary. I think he believes I'm on his side. He's been leaning on me more and more, entrusting me with tasks while he spends all day in the war room talking to Krauss. I think he's beginning to trust me," Alice explained.

"Which is why I'm gonna have to ask you to do something difficult for me. If it's true that Morann listens to you, you're the only one I can ask."

"Whatever you need, *Captain*," Alice said with a grin.

***

Katsina returned to Rutheo, with Alice in tow. The three of them left the engineering department with Howard. He was being moved on a stretcher by members of the crisis response team, who stood out with their bright orange reflective jumpsuits, which contrasted with their blue colored harnesses and backpacks. Katsina took note of the faces she recognised in the engineering department before she left, seeing some that seemed out of the loop of communications. They were Morann's people. Thankfully most of the crisis response units were still made up of her people, which made it easy for her to have Howard moved to Dr. Foyes makeshift clinic instead of the hospital. Katsina needed to have him with someone she could trust, if he was going to have a chance to recover. Over the course of their journey the conversation was pointless but present to avoid suspicion. The real conversation happened in the eyes and ears of the four of them thanks to Marshal's private network. Katsina pretended to take disciplinary orders from Alice, while Rutheo pretended to argue over her administrative leave. The real conversation was much more serious.

"So you think you're up for it, Howard?" Rutheo asked, her hand still holding the old man's.

"Of course I am. I used to work on those things for breakfast," he said.

"Those schematics were installed on Mara's ship, you said? What makes you think they can be adapted to an older model?" said Alice.

"If anyone can do it, Howard can," said Katsina, her lips breaking into a cheeky grin.

"And what about the wounded? They will need somewhere to fall back to?" said Rutheo.

"That's why we're visiting Dr. Foye."

***

Dr. Foye's quarters continued to fill up with injured and confused crew members, even with the number that she had transported to the hospital. Katsina helped attend to some of the wounded, while Rutheo sat with Howard. Alice had liaised with the doctor over the current status of the patients, while looping her into the private network. Linda could not help showing her concern for what they were really talking about. Her eyes gave away the gravity of their true conversation. Luckily for them both, personal quarters weren't monitored, and Marshal's communication program was working like a charm. Katsina sat with an unconscious member of the spaceship repair team from the tarmac, picturing a vast railroad of connections that began to grow on the Behemothis. If subterfuge was to happen, she was at least glad it was for the right reasons. Morann had to be dealt with, but at the appropriate time.

"Katsina? A moment?" Linda said, taking Katsina's attention off of the unconscious woman.

"Yes, sorry, just wanted to give you guys a minute to talk. I'd say it wasn't easy hearing it all from Alice," said Katsina, as the two of them walked between the rows of injured people.

"It would have come as less of a shock from you I think, but from the first officer? This will be one for a history series," Linda said contemplatively.

"Oh yeah, we'll be living off royalties for decades."

"So, he called you an executioner? He really said that?"

"Yeah, he was really trying to make his point," Katsina said. "He thinks he has them in his hands because they didn't argue with him in engineering."

"That's because our crew are much smarter than that," Linda said with a smirk.

"Exactly, so you're in?"

"I am. I'll have the staff on alert."

"Thank you, and we need Howard on his feet. Do what

you can to help him. He may need protection," Katsina said, a frown growing across her forehead.

"Your concern is well intentioned but unnecessary. He will be back on his feet tomorrow morning. He has friends in ground operations who I'm sure will look out for him," Linda said, her eyes meeting Katsina's in a moment of understanding.

"Thank you. Rutheo is going to head back to engineering. Alice has her work to do on the bridge roster. I have to go as well."

"Where are you going?" Linda asked. "Aren't you out sick?"

"The less you know the better, you have my new comm. Talk soon."

***

The armory of a Man O'War class vessel could easily outfit a deployment of over 80 thousand troops. Its capability to print, assemble, and outfit an operator for combat in less than two minutes was a record breaking achievement for the war. The armory had access to every schematic for every weapon ever designed, with a backlog dating as far into the past as the first world war. Katsina had only ever been ground deployed once, and therefore only ever needed to be outfitted for a firefight once. Usually a fighter operator had their own personal equipment stored in their fighter, but Katsina no longer had access to her's. The armory of the ship had strict and selective access, Katsina couldn't get within ten meters of the door without being tagged by the ship's automated defense. But she had ideas on how to get around it. Katsina, along with Rutheo, figured that Marshal's program not only hid communications, but other selected processes as well. So she decided it was time to take her first drastic measure.

In the armory lobby, the walls were decorated with adornments of service operators who had sacrificed themselves for humanity. Every ship armory had some kind of memorial in this fashion. A reminder of the responsibility each operator carried with them as they received their weapons. For a split second, Katsina wondered why such dramatic imagery was necessary, before shaking her head. Instead of approaching the requisitions officer on duty, Katsina plugged into one of the automated request stations. These were easier for soldiers who needed quick access to standard equipment for fighter pilots, ground medics, infiltration teams, boarding units and more. Auto request stations had an operator's replacement gear ready to pick up immediately, while specialist equipment could only be requested face to face. But not for Katsina. Not this time. Katsina ran her finger over her port, leading the cable from the station to the back of her neck.

Cyberwarfare, particularly in space, was considered a heinous crime if used inappropriately. Most cyber defence programs would protect a ship from digital attack, flagging any foreign code and countering it with firewalls. In cyberwarfare, the only humane targets for people to hack were engine propulsion systems, any other sabotage could be fatal to an enemy ship. Thus, it wasn't permitted in the rules of engagement, not that the Yggdrasilians cared. The only people known to attempt to hack other vital systems of a ship, like its armory, weapons and environmental controls were the Yggdrasilians. Yet another reason Katsina despised them. She considered every other option she could, to not have to sink to the level of the enemy. Under the watchful eye of the requisition officer, she stood closely behind another person at the screen next to her, using him as cover.

"*Desperate times...*" she thought, as she began sweeping the system, activating controls to grant herself administrative access.

Marshal's program shielded her from detection, just as she suspected. It was proving its usefulness more and more throughout the day as she watched the red string of data connect her to the terminal. Katsina was granted the power she needed without suspicion brewing and made her request for the equipment she needed. She glanced over to the requisitions officer on duty, who was sitting at one of the glass booths at the end of the atrium. He turned around, noticing the printers in the warehouse starting to *whir* and *screech*. Before he could turn back to see her, Katsina ran. Katsina understood what she had done was wrong, but had very few options. Most of her day's activities were going to be reported to the first officer. Luckily the first officer was on the payroll of the Admiralty, not Morann or the Yggdrasilians.

    She returned to the makeshift medical tent to help Dr. Foye. Katsina used time there to help others while spreading the seeds she needed to cultivate her plans. Linda had most of Morann's injured crew moved to the hospital, while keeping as many of Katsina's people under her care. For the rest of the evening Katsina pondered whether or not Morann would suspect that his scheme to turn the crew against her had failed. Was he so confident that he couldn't see his own shortcomings? He'd tried to break her more times than she needed to count since he'd arrived on the Behemothis to arrest her. She realised that he nearly had, and that if he had just left her in her turmoil a little longer and had emptied Mara's quarters before giving it to her, he would have succeeded. His plan to surround her with her dead friends' possessions was cunning and especially cruel, but thanks to Mara and the information she'd had, it backfired spectacularly. While bandaging another crew member, who had recently been stitched up by a nurse, Katsina noticed a familiar cough in his throat. The man had a fever, but complained of being cold.

    "It's Amadellan flu," Linda said. "We still have a few cases here and there. Honestly, it's a hard one to shake off."

    "Yeah, I noticed an article yesterday about an investigation into some Yggs getting it. I still have to read it though."

    "Let me save you the time," Linda began. "They found a Ygg ship that crashed on one of the asteroids in the Riskus belt in the Crescent system. No one knows how it got there but it seemed to crash eight to ten months ago. Anyway the bodies were mostly frozen, everything corrupted and the neurons fried as always. But they didn't actually have the flu itself. They had antibodies for it. As if they had already had it before and recovered from it some time ago."

"Really? But the Amadellan flu is a new strain this season, how did they have it when it only kicked in six months ago?"

"Hence the investigation," Linda said.

"Weird, you think someone came in contact with a Ygg? Or maybe it was an attempt at a viral weapon?" Katsina asked.

"Bioterrorism isn't in my wheelhouse. I couldn't tell you, but what I can say is that they better solve that one soon. If the Yggdrasilian's could engineer Amadellan flu, then I don't want to see what else they can make.

"Yeah," Katsina said, distracted by her HUD. "Jeez, that *was* yesterday. I only saw you yesterday."

"And you didn't sleep did you?" Linda asked.

"I mean I thought the ship crashed. Or we could have been hit or something."

"Ha, well I guess so. At least the damage is minor. I'm pretty sure that's why you're still the captain to a lot of us."

"What's why you think I'm still the captain?" Katsina asked.

"Because you have no problem losing sleep over this ship," Linda said with a smile.

The night had begun to set in, and the Behemothis repairs were well underway. Linda and Katsina spoke at length about anything and everything that evening. Spending time together in a non-professional capacity felt familiar, and brought a sense of normality to the day that Katsina had. Before losing Mara, Katsina would spend time with each and every person she worked with, getting to know their families, their friends, even their interests. She realised that she had been missing out on a lot of that. Something she promised to rectify when all was said and done. Katsina had gotten too wrapped up in her own issues to see what else was happening with her friends. She didn't know Harold was trying to upskill, she didn't see or hear of Alice's new found relationship with Rogers, and she had to hear from Kessler that Rutheo was keeping something from her. All of which she brought up with Linda, who reassured her that she couldn't be the best at everything always, and that she would be forgiven for growing distant from everyone in a time of hardship. Through all their talking, Katsina's eyes grew heavy as the periodic sound of heart monitors on loop eventually made her close them. She didn't return to her quarters. Instead she fell asleep in the corner of Dr. Foyes makeshift infirmary.

WORLD DISCOVERER

The superficial damage to the Behemothis was easy enough to amend. Considering the ship was built to field repair and launch other ships, it wasn't a challenge for maintenance to fix it up quickly. The most costly repairs took place on the tarmac, where a lot of the floor plating was ripped from the ground and thrown out the hangar door into space. The building, fitting, and casting of each hexagonal tarmac piece meant that most ships had to transfer to be serviced by the Alchemathus, the Behemothis' second sister ship, on the edge of the Horizon system. Only the full attachment of fighter ships, assigned to the Broadsider, remained aboard. A far trek for a damaged ship to travel and a waste of military resources, all for Morann to have a power trip to discredit Katsina again, blaming the thorough repairs on her by association. Katsina had spent most of the five weeks since the gravity incident on the tarmac, volunteering her time off to help with repairs. Dr. Foye was generous enough to make sure she stayed away from the bridge with sick leave. Katsina expected Morann to care, but he hadn't been seen by many people since his display. Rumor was he spent most of the day in the war room, tracking an elusive Yggdrasilian ship across the deep.

Beads of sweat ran down Katsina's back as she straightened up. She ran her forearm over her brow, catching her breath as she leaned against the building site barrier. The tarmac was nearly back in order with just eight or so plates to be reattached to the floor. Katsina paused to look out the hangar doors at the darkness beyond the atmosphere.

The deep was a strange area of space in the galaxy. No one understood why it was as black as it was, but the exploration fleet was too busy running manoeuvres in the war to explore it to find an answer. Some suspected a problem with light traveling near the supermassive black hole at the centre. Others said it was most likely a cloud of cold rubidium atoms surrounding the area, capturing light or reflecting it back. Regardless of the explanation, looking into the deep was a sanity challenging ordeal. Many crew members were known to experience a severe bout of nyctophobia, depression, and anxiety as a result of staring into it for too long.

"Captain," a jolly voice called. Katsina turned to see Howard strolling down the tarmac, waving his meaty hands.

"Best not call me that so loudly. How are you today, Howard?" she asked.

"Oh I'm just fine, I finished up a little *project* of mine with my time off," he said, bobbling his head proudly.

"That's great, Howard. *Thanks for telling me.*"

"No problem. I'm off to visit some of the men in crisis response. They've been teaching me a thing or two about how they operate you know."

"Oh good, it's always great to learn new skills."

"Too right. I'll leave you to it. The tarmac looks great, so it does."

"Not as good as you do, Howard!" she said, waiving him off.

Katsina turned back to the worksite and joined the repair team in installing the tarmac plates, meanwhile she pulled up her HUD and used Marshal's program to secure an undetectable connection. A new window opened up before Katsina's eyes, a layer of red strands that stretched over the rest of the ship. Instead of seeing the usual comm links, she was seeing a new underground channel that allowed her people to communicate freely about the task at hand. The network was nicknamed "the red web" by Rutheo, who ran it as an admin while under house arrest. Katsina scrolled through many a digital conversation, hearing glimpses of normal life starting to happen again on the Behemothis, albeit in secret. Katsina never thought she would take to having a secret network of comms aboard her ship so easily. But it was better than the media blackout that Morann dictated. She created a new message, and sent it along the threads of the network.

The bird has a new set of wings.

Katsina picked up her rubber sledge hammer, and blinked her HUD away to continue hammering in plates, allowing the good news to spread. The rest of the evening was spent on the tarmac before Katsina retreated to Dr. Foyes quarters. Although no longer a medical centre, Linda's quarters were still filled with stretchers, first aid kits, and Personal Protective Equipment, or PPE. She had been stockpiling the haul for some time. By her kitchen stood over a hundred plates of metal and wooden boards collected from the gravity failure, blocking off her kitchen entirely. Instead she kept her food printer on the dining table, which still had a dent in it from that day.

"Wow, no one else could store the plates?" Katsina asked.

"Rutheo has another hundred and something so she can't. Alice is keeping nothing for obvious reasons, Howard said if he stored any more equipment in your garage you wouldn't be able to get into it. So I'll keep them for now. I just hope you're right about needing them," Linda said.

"We will, we will," Katsina said, plopping herself onto Linda's couch. The smell of printed coffee wasn't Katsina's idea of a good nasal experience. But she watched the doctor print her a cup anyway.

"Careful, that's hot. Now tell me something," Linda said, dropping down next to Katsina. "Are you doing alright?"

"Me? I think so. I'm doing okay."

"You've not had any other doubts about yourself? No... questions of morality?" Linda asked, looking at her expectantly.

"I think the reason I ended up in that place at all was because of him. He tried pushing me over the edge but he missed. And now he's about to go over the cliff himself," Katsina said.

"But what of the war? Do you still think you're a bad person for participating in it?"

"I won't know until it's over, I guess."

"But when will that be, Katsina? When every Yggdrasilian dies? You've sat on the tarmac working all these hours, people have seen you staring into the Deep," Linda probed.

"If you asked me that few months ago I would have said 'yes'. Now I don't know. That Ygg in the memory that Mara had. He seemed like a normal person like all of us. But all my life I've seen them as kind of inhuman. Surely they are still bad people for starting this war, but I don't think they all deserve to die for it," Katsina said, staring at the collection of green duffle bags stacked up by the door to the bathroom.

"Well that's a new point of view. One I didn't expect to hear from 'The Executioner', ha."

"I still can't believe he really did call me that. He's theatrical that way."

"Yes well, shall we call our meeting then?" Linda asked.

"Yeah, let's get it started," Katsina said, standing up.

Katsina and Linda stood at opposite ends of the coffee table and activated their HUDs. Rutheo and Alice appeared next to them, though they were only there in the AR filter. With Alice was Erwin Rodgers, the nervous engineer that she had grown fond of. He'd become invaluable for his knowledge of the ship's extensive electrical network of fuses, trip switches and power junctions, as well as his personal contributions. He expanded and developed the private network given to Katsina by Marshal, allowing it to spread to each and every member of her crew aboard the ship.

"Evening, everyone," Katsina began. "How are we doing? Ruthie, we'll start with you."

"Okay, all's looking good and on track. We're looking at numbers around the eighty percent mark when it comes to pledged participation."

"How are we doing with the armory? You mentioned you scored a man on the inside?" Alice asked.

"Oho, yeah, I did. I think you guys are going to like this one, adding him to the call now," Rutheo said, blinking her eyes.

Katsina watched a square jawed man with a tilted beret step into the conversation, his brown eyes staring directly ahead of him, his chin raised in attention. His broad arms were crossed and he had a great smile on his face, almost giddy looking. She couldn't believe he was actually on board, she didn't even realise he had survived.

"James!" she exclaimed, her smile overbearing as he waved to her.

"Commander James Garland reporting as Master at Arms, Captain," he said.

"Good to see you, James. The nausea getting to you yet?" Katsina asked.

"Surprisingly not, but the incident with the gravity threw me for six. That said, I found my space legs a bit since I got here. I've been mostly working in the armory."

"Garland, here, was part of the MPs before being reassigned when he made it on board, and has been taking care of outfitting our operators ever since. Everyone who pledged participation to our project will be suitably equipped thanks to his efforts," Rutheo said.

"With efficiency, Chief," Garland added.

"Good to hear, and my specialised order?" Katsina asked.

"Nearly complete, we will have most if not the entire crew well equipped. Considering a lot of them are inexperienced, this is understandably essential. As for the rest of your order, it was delivered to the tarmac this week."

"Good, Howard told us he finished up on that. How about the rest of the armory staff?" Dr. Foye asked.

"They're good, ready. They are all part of the original crew. None of Morann's men were assigned to the armory; I'm the only new guy. So there shouldn't be an issue."

"Okay, good work. Glad you're here James. Alice, how are things on your end?" Katsina asked, turning her attention.

"Well the rumours are true. We are tracking what looks like a Yggdrasilian vessel through the deep. We only know it's there because it's leaving a radioactive set of breadcrumbs."

"So it's been damaged. Any idea when we will intercept it?" Rutheo asked.

"Sometime tomorrow afternoon is when we'll have it in range."

"Great stuff, we can wait for that to be over before we do anything. We need to time this well if it's going to be effective; what's Morann's plan for the Ygg vessel?"

"He's been avoiding answering that. He just wants us to catch up with it. It really has his full attention since we spotted it on long range scans. I think it's what we've been tasked with looking for since we left Botanica," Alice said, her eyes dropping to the floor.

"You think it has something to do with Kessler's special delivery that came in?" Rutheo asked.

"I honestly don't know Rutheo. But Morann hasn't slept in days, he's fixated on this task. Admiral Krauss requests updates from him hourly."

"Thank you Alice. You okay?" Katsina asked.

"Fine, I uh. I just want this to be over soon," she said.

"It will be. You all know your own work has been cut out for you. I understand that nerves may creep in and try to take over. But trust me when I say we are doing the right thing, and it's about time we do it. Keep your eyes on the red web and expect to go ahead in a week's time. Rutheo, by then, see if we can get participation up to at least eighty five percent. Ride the lightning."

"Aye, Captain."
"Ride the lightning."
"Yes, sir."
The images of the other four fell away, leaving Katsina

and Linda alone. The room felt darker without them. Katsina let out a slow sigh, leaning on the edge of the couch, finishing her cup.

"You asked Alice if she was alright. But are you sure *you* are alright?"

"I think so, I just know there are more of them than there are of us. You'll be ready yourself? You have all the equipment you need?"

"I know you need them to believe that our chances of success are good, but we won't succeed if you don't believe it too. Have confidence in yourself," Linda said, talking the cup out of Katsina's hands.

"That's just it. I thought I was confident before, but it was just hubris, or arrogance. Now I'm trying to believe in what I'm doing without being that person," Katsina said, thinking of how she treated Marshal the night of Mara's wedding, of how she acted so selfishly when she chose to go after the Delta squadron herself.

"Just get me to him Katsina. And the truth will come out. You can do this and still hold onto this new found humility."

"Are you sure?" Katsina said, pulling her hair back from her face.

"I'm sure," Linda said, leaving Katsina to wash the cups.

"Alright. Great, okay. I better get sleep. Thanks for the terrible coffee."

"You're too used to the real thing. Decaf is better for you."

***

Katsina had solved her relationship with sleep since installing Linda's prescription. Only she went from not sleeping to sleeping badly. Which wasn't much of an improvement in her opinion. Her fears of repeating the nightmare she'd had in the shower clouded her mind any time she lay down. Luckily it wasn't that dream, but the others in its place were arguably worse. Each night started the same, an uncomfortable tossing and turning with the occasional feeling of falling. Katsina would jolt awake more than once before eventually falling asleep. And the same happened again the evening she returned from Dr. Foye's.

Upon a cosmic background Katsina stood in an infinite pool of black water, similar to her other dream. But instead of the black reaches of the abyss, sprawling nebulas and systems, laced about the spirals of the milky way, were reflected in the water. Without moving she could hear the trickles and splashes of feet around her.

"Hello?" she said, looking for the source of the noise.

The sounds of little feet jumping and running in the pool grew closer, accompanied by echoes of laughter. Sweet and soft sounds, the echoes of children. The water rippled about her feet but there was no one to make it move. In the distance, further away, a cry of distress. Katsina bolted towards the sound. As far as she ran, as quickly as she could, the sound never grew closer. If anything it seemed to stretch away beyond her reach. Before she could stop running, Katsina slipped and fell over the edge of the water, becoming drenched. Her fall slowly came to a halt and she floated. Katsina thrashed and spun, trying to find solid ground before noticing the droplets of water floating before her eyes. Glancing back up, she watched water fall from the edge of a pane of glass. She lifted a hand in front of her, inspecting the drops that slid away from her fingertips, rising and falling about her. The hairs on her skin stood up. The sound of the crying child had stopped. It was silent again. Katsina tried to speak, opening her mouth to call out to the sound of the child. The silence consumed her. Beyond the stars in the distance, she saw it again. The black shape emerging from the dark, carrying the darkness with it. A harrowing shiver ran up her back, swallowing her shoulders. It was coming closer to her. The slow and deathly howl of the shape filled her ears. The sound she could only imagine accompanied the souls of the dead as they fell into the abyss of space. Screaming for her to join them. Pale and unmoving bodies came into view around her, floating with her in the droplets. As they roasted and spun gently she tried to make out their faces, their eyes. But only one was close enough for her to recognise. His eyes glazed over, staring into the swirling stars overhead. Han Mao, the bullet wound still bleeding in his chest.

Katsina sprung up, flailing her arms ahead of her as she collided with the floor of her room. She leaped to her feet from the cold ground, spinning about to see where the shape had gone. She could hear her own breath again along with the ghostly echo of the shape. Something tickled her chest, a bead of sweat, she was soaked by it. Katsina closed her eyes; pushing the room away from her, she focussed on the image in her mind's eye. She immediately began recording the dream to her memory core. She turned to look for a towel nearby, noticing the wet smears on the sheets. Her legs felt weak at the sight. She racked her brain and memory core, thinking back to the day Los Ange was attacked. She thought of the moment she held Han Mao, and for the first time she remembered hearing the cries of a child in the distance. A detail she had forgotten. Katsina didn't think of why she'd dreamt about it; she thought instead of what it meant to dream about it. She pulled a towel from a drawer in the bedside table. A chill had begun to seep in, causing her to wrap herself in its folds while crawling back into the bed. Eventually Katsina's breathing slowed by means of her respiratory controls. Her willpower to control her own breathing without the help of her implants had diminished. She closed her eyes to return to sleep, but the sounds of footsteps caught her ears.

Katsina sat up and held her breath, freezing herself in place to try and hear the sound. She wondered had she just imagined it, or was she still dreaming? She almost couldn't tell in the dark room. But the footsteps sounded as if they were real. With them came the voices of people, and Katsina's eyes opened wide to the fact that something was wrong. A red flash lit up the room, and an alarm pierced the air, piercing into Katsina's ears. She threw the towel off, and snatched a pair of jeans from the end of the bed. The voices and footsteps grew thunderous. It was a ship-wide alert. Katsina slipped into her jeans, hopping up and down while pulling a tank top over her bushy unkempt bed head. On her HUD was a list of orders to all hands:

Report to stations, enemy contact.

Katsina flicked up her comms menu and linked to the encrypted red web, reaching out for Alice and Rutheo. Nobody answered. Katsina would hear from them eventually. Though she was still on leave, she knew what she had to do. She had to get to the bridge and find answers.

***

The main hall was flooded with people running in all directions, some towards the bridge, some away. Katsina darted left and right, weaving her way through the crowd to get to the steps. Before she made it that far, she stopped at the sight of Military Police and other operators lining the walls and the steps leading to the bridge balcony. They were all armed, their weapons unholstered and in hand. Katsina shifted her weight onto her right foot, and pivoted towards one of the stairwells to the lower deck. Her instincts had pushed her to the captain's position knowing full well she wasn't the captain. It could have gotten her shot had she not stopped herself. She could get to the bridge via the crew entrance lower in the dome. It was unguarded on the lower level, with crew members flooding in to occupy their battle station. Katsina slid through the door behind another crew member before it shut again and she immediately dipped her head behind one of the many metal struts that held the dome overhead.

The augmented reality image in the centre of the room was of a ship, its design unfamiliar to Katsina. At a glance it looked like a very old freighter or transport ship, but upon closer inspection its hazy shape was larger than anything Katsina had seen in service. Above her, on the balcony, Morann leaned over the edge, staring at the ship with malicious intent. He was unshaved and unkept, his jacket hastily thrown around his shoulders, his hair standing around his ears. The lines around his eyes had seemingly deepened since Katsina last saw him. On his left side stood Alice, her eyes wide with fear, her hair pulled into a tight bun. Katsina realised why she couldn't get a hold of her. She turned her attention to her HUD to see an audio message from Rutheo.

Kat, I don't know what it is but they have us ready to put all the power we have in reserve into the ship's rod launchers and the battery pylon. They're scrambling fighters too. I heard O'Keef say they're deploying all the auxiliary rail gun turrets. It's gonna be a fight. Stay safe.

Katsina blinked the audio message away to hear what was being said on the bridge.

"What range?" Morann barked down from the balcony.

"Within range now captain, dead ahead at twenty five thousand killometers," a skittish voice replied from the crowd working below.

"Get a message to the Insurmountable; we have engaged an unknown enemy vessel and need assistance. Do we have an ID on it?"

"No sir bu- wait, uh, Sir we have an estimate of mass. It looks like a Leviathan class ship."

A silence fell over the bridge, the only sound being the various computer displays beeping, and the ship's *humm* as it flew through space in the background. Katsina looked back up to Morann, whose anger had been replaced by shock. Outside the dome, the entire attachment of fighters the Man O'War could carry could be seen racing into the distance. Mumbles and murmurs began to sound about the bridge, before Morann cut into the chatter like a sharpened blade.

"There are no such thing as Leviathan class vessels," he boomed. "There were only ever three built, over five hundred years ago. There has not been a Leviathan class ship since. Now you get me an accurate reading of that ship or by the ts'ßolfé I will see you stripped of rank. Wesley, get them to ping serial numbers until you find one that fits."

"Sir, I don't know what serial numbers could be associated with a ship that size," Alice said.

"Don't you understand? The Yggs are trying to fool our sensors. Making it look bigger than it is. There *are* no ships that big. Helm, get us into visual range."

Morann was right. Katsina knew that not a single Leviathan class ship existed anymore. The first one had gotten humanity to the Redemption Wheel from Earth, the second led them to Yggdrasil, and the last had brought them to Botanica. The Behemothis, and its sister vessels, were the largest ships in space. There was no way the Yggs could have built something bigger without the military knowing about it. They had telescopes and sensors across the three solar systems. Even Katsina knew that the possibility of a Leviathan class ship was next to nothing. Unless it was the one thing that was completely impossible. Katsina ducked out from behind cover, and snatched a tablet from a nearby table. The person sitting at the desk began to protest, but quickly found silence when he realised who it was. Katsina held up a solitary finger to her lips, receding back behind her hiding spot. She knew using her HUD in the room near Morann was a risk, and didn't want to reveal herself unless she had to. So she began her archival search using the tablet instead. Eventually she came across the folder she needed, loaded it's contents and began to read. One file, a news cast over sixty years old. The one that Rutheo sent to her.

Of all the treasures lost to the depths of the galaxy, none were as tragic as the loss of The World Discoverer The last of three Leviathan class ships, the only three to exist. The ship had been dry docked and declared a historical preservation site in 2778. While the other Leviathan class ships were decommissioned and recycled, "The World Discoverer" remained in dry dock until its mysterious disappearance in 2810.

Katsina continued reading, finding historical documents and various travel logs of the ancient ship. Her eyes darted across pages and pages of information to find what she needed. Eventually she got it. Morann was pacing about his chair, while Alice zipped down the staircase to the war room, and back out onto the main floor. Katsina had no choice but to break cover, she had to get to a station. To her left she slid behind a row of desks, and kept her head as low as she could. She dipped between more rows, eventually catching up with Alice. She crept under a table, pushing past the legs of a crew member to edge closer behind the first officer. Letting out the odd *psst* to get her attention. She reached out to grab Alice's hand, close enough to pass her the tablet. But the tablet was snatched out of her hand before it could reach its destination. Katsina was grabbed by the wrist, pulled to her feet and subsequently thrown face down into a table top.

"Well, well, sneaking around the bridge are we?" Morann said, running his hand over Katsina's neck.

"Captain! Uh, sir. What is-" Alice said, spinning around.

"Silence, Commander, get Kessler in here. Miss Lucas has just been caught interfering in an enemy engagement."

"Morann, you faisaheßul idiot," Katsina managed.

"Trying to get to a comm terminal? Send out a signal to your friends?"

"Look at the tablet," Katsina said. "Alice, look at the tablet and ping the serial number."

"Shut it, you think you can fool her with your lies-"

Morann began.

Katsina struck his ankle with her right foot, tipping him to one side. She lifted herself from the table and struggled free of his grip, snatching the tablet out of his hand along the way. Morann let out a groan, leaning on the table for support while composing himself. His eyes shot around the room wildly, seeking support from the bridge crew. To his detriment, Katsina recognised every face around them, most of them were connected to the red web. Morann's face slowly turned red, his breathing became erratic. A vein bulged from his temple, his anger just ready to boil over.

"You dare attack me," he said, slipping his hand into his coat, drawing a pistol.

The entire room shifted, those behind Katsina ducked or stepped out of the line of fire, while others behind Morann slipped under their desks. Screams of terror and swears of shock echoed around them. Katsina stood still as a statue, unmoved by the sight of a weapon pointed at her. She wasn't afraid of being shot, there were more important things. So she held her hands up slowly, elevating the tablet for the room to see.

"I have the serial number that you need to ping to get identification of that ship," Katsina announced.

"Liar!" Morann shouted, strings of saliva spitting from his lips.

"That ship out there isn't a Yggdrasillian threat. Just ping it and I can prove it to you," said Katsina, attempting to reason with him. "Look at what you're doing, Morann. You know it's wrong."

"You'd know all about a Ygg threat wouldn't you? You traitorous chasanuha."

"Captain!" a small voice sounded from behind Morann. He spun his head, glancing behind him to find a culprit.

"What is it?" he said, but no one answered him.

Katsina looked behind Morann, searching the room for a voice she recognised. On the edge of the dome, in one of the helmsman's stations, Katsina found the owner of the voice, Aker Castle. He held his hand up to signal her attention.

"Captain Lucas," he said. "Ready to enter the serial number on your command."

WHERE LOYALTY LIES

Katsina couldn't help but smile. Though Aker Castle looked terrified, his bravery was beyond criticism. She noticed multiple strings of data dance about him as he waved to her, the entire red web was connected to him, watching Katsina just as he was. Morann didn't know it, but he was under the scrutiny of Katsina's people, and he certainly wasn't making the best show of himself.

"Belay that!" Morann shouted, keeping his pistol squared on Katsina.

"Serial number is-"

"Don't you dare!"

"L.. E.. V.."

"Stop," Morann said, running his thumb over the pistol's safety. The autoloader snapped back, loading a pellet into the chamber. The pistol began to charge.

"S... T... L... I..."

"I said stop! Cease and Desist!" Morann crossed the space between them, pushing the pistol up against Katsina's forehead.

"You're not going to shoot me Morann. Kill me now and you'll never get the conviction you want," Katsina said, looking down the barrel of the pistol into Morann's eyes. He squinted and his lips peeled back from his teeth.

"... dash... zero... two... X... ninety nine..." Katsina finished.

On the other side of the room, Aker's console beeped, and a new image popped up on the AR display above Katsina's head. It threw a new set of lights around the room, a layer of yellow over the dreary dark blue.

"Serial number confirmed, Leviathan class, 'LEVSTLI--02x99'. It's the World Discoverer, Captain," the helmsman called.

Morann glanced up at the image of a triangular prism, with rings embedded along its walls. Surrounding the prism were two hoops at either end, while multiple protruding arms of solar panels and satellite towers swung about the middle length of the shaft. The image matched the shape of the long range sensor scan by overlapping with the heat signatures. It was just over ten kilometers in length, making it truly the largest spaceship humanity had ever built. Housing ninety nine class one kugelblitz wheels, housing up to two hundred and fifty thousand people comfortably, while hosting an array of agricultural centers and much more. The ship was a feat of engineering that humanity had only attempted three times in its short existence. The image of the ship showed its age, with multiple worn plates on the hull, excessive scratches and dents from various objects impacting the superstructure; it even had one of its rings broken in half. Katsina glanced back down to Morann, who pretended that he hadn't taken his eye off of her the entire time. His glare would have made her uncomfortable before. But now she knew his mode of operation.

"Coming into visual range. Just over ten thousand kilometers," another helmsman called.

Morann finally dropped his pistol, slipping it back under his coat. He left Katsina, and walked towards the front of the dome. Ahead of the Behemothis was the leviathan class ship, a tiny glistening flicker in the distance. The fighter squadrons that had flown ahead maintained their distance from it, regrouping with the Behemothis as it approached. The AR display showed a more accurate image, as if the ship was right in front of them. Katsina couldn't take her eyes off of it. A piece of history, in front of her ship. Along its long hull small twinkles of light could be seen, but there was no light coming from its boosters. It was adrift, but it had power.

"Commander, I'm receiving an incoming message on a radio band," one of the comms specialists said.

"Bring it up on the AR display. Let's hear it," Alice said,

her mouth hung open since the ship had been revealed.

"Belay that," Morann finally said. "Any signal coming from that ship could be an attempt to gain access to military archives and secrets."

"Captain," Alice began, "the ship isn't armed, I don't think-"

"That's right! You don't think! This is a ruse, you ignorant woman. That ship was last seen on the planet Yggsrasil. It belongs to them."

"Yes sir, I am aware," Alice replied. She assumed a formal and confident tone, just like she had in engineering. "As protocol dictates, any quantum data packets are to be scanned, decoded and scrubbed for viral software, malware, or cyber warfare programs. However, radio signals do not fall under this level of security as the ship's cyber warfare suite can automatically scrub malicious data."

"Must you continue to cite protocol to me? I am in command here, not you," Morann barked.

"The rules of engagement are clear. Attempting to establish contact comes first, sir," said Alice, her face calm and hard as stone.

Morann paused, looking back and forth from Alice to the comm specialist. As if he contemplated denying protocol.

"Play the message," he said reluctantly.

A soundwave appeared over Katsina's head, it's glowing lines and spikes making up the audio she was about to hear. Like a mountain range reflected on an unmoving lake, a soundwave was a beautiful piece of data to see. She tuned her ears, not wanting to miss a word.

Man O' War vessel, please disengage your laser targeting equipment. My name is Shimon Ableson of the space colony Free Venture. Our colony currently resides on what is left of The World Discoverer star liner. There are over ten thousand men, women, and children aboard. Transmitting ship status logs now. We are adrift and in need of medical supplies and repairs to our remaining engines. We are travellers who wish to find peace and refuge from the war of the Yggdrasil. Please help us. This message will repeat.

The message played over, and then over again, and again a third time. In the background, beyond Shimon Ableson's voice, was the crying of a small child. Katsina couldn't believe what she was hearing. No one in the room appeared to move; they just listened. Katsina couldn't take her eyes from the audio waveform as it played from left to right over and over. It was the last thing she, or anyone on board the bridge, expected to hear. The voice of a Yggdrasilian asking for help, pleading for peace. Katsina felt stuck in place, her feet nailed to the floor. It was information she didn't know what to do with. Her mouth had gone dry from being open for so long.

"Get in here," Morann was the first to speak.

The doors in either corner of the room *whooshed* open, flooding the room with soldiers. Katsina spun around to see them on the balcony, aiming their weapons at the bridge crew. Green targeting lasers danced about, catching little particles of dust as they filled the room. One group of soldiers, surrounding a man in white coat and carrying a black case, entered the war room. Various members of the bridge crew were lifted out of their seats, their places taken by Morann's men. The already darkened bridge lights turned an even darker blue, matching the war room beyond the glass doors. Katsina saw a wall of soldiers, led by Kessler, who seemed outfitted for a castle siege, form between the bridge crew and the war room. She knew she had very little time to grasp what was happening.

"What is this?" Katsina turned to Morann.

"This is what happens when we find secret enemy vessels in the field. These people are Yggdrasilian. Therefore; they cannot be trusted," Morann retorted.

"You're mad, those people need help," Alice said.

"Oh, and you," said Morann with a sigh. "Consider yourself court martialed for gross misconduct in a firefight. Detain her and the traitor."

"A firefight?" Katsina asked.

"Excuse me?" Alice said, glancing around at the soldiers who approached her.

"Morann what are you doing?" Katsina said, dodging the hands of one of the approaching soldiers.

"Let the record show that a previously undiscovered enemy ship with advanced weaponry has been found. It was then engaged and subsequently destroyed by our purpose-built twenty-eight megaton implosion payload," Morann announced.

Katsina continued to bob and weave, punching one of the soldiers who swung at her. The message from the ship continued playing over loudspeaker. The words of Shimon Ableson echoing in Katsina's ears as Morann lifted his right arm, his palm wide open. Katsina tried to duck away from another soldier, but eventually collided with a blunt object to the side of her cheek. She stumbled, tripping over her own feet and falling into the arms of one of the three men who surrounded her.

"Katsina!" Alice shouted, followed by other rebellious voices on the bridge.

"Alice, what is he doing? What is he talking about?" Katsina said, desperate to understand before a hand clapped over her lips.

"On my mark," Morann said. Katsina's heart began skipping faster. She snapped her teeth into the skin of the man holding her, making him recoil.

"Prepare to fire."

"Stop this!" Katsina bellowed, freeing her mouth from the hand of her captor. "They aren't a threat. You heard their message!"

"Ah, there she is," Morann said gleefully, turning away from the glass to see her. "I knew for the longest time, and now you have shown everyone, even your crew."

Morann lifted his arms theatrically, fanning them

slowly around the room. A silence fell before him, the rebellious voices dying down as Kessler fired a round into the ceiling from his pistol. A gun had never been fired on Katsina's bridge, but she couldn't argue its effectiveness to maintain order.

"You see I knew the Yggs were hiding something out here. No doubt the weapon you described when you were first accused. It was a poor idea to mention it in an attempt to defend yourself. You just compromised your entire operation. It's clear now that your friends over there on that ship have that weapon. If they didn't, why hide? If they are innocent, why would you defend them? I knew I would find the link between you and the enemy. They didn't believe me for a time, but I knew," Morann paraded around a detained Katsina with a woeful smile on his face.

"You're insane!" Alice screamed.

"Me? Insane? That's a statement and a half to make coming from you. Half the crew on this ship is insane, thinking they could blindly follow a charismatic traitor to the end of this war. I'm not insane, Alice, no, no. I'm the only one who can see what Katsina Lucas truly is!"

Katsina saw a wild flare in Morann's eyes under the blue lights. He was transfixed, obsessed. She found it difficult to understand. Why go through so much trouble? He knew deep down that he was the traitor, not her. Yet his passion. She couldn't help but feel conflicted.

"I'm not a traitor! You think your little trial proved anything about me? Your attempts to get under my skin, to out me for what you think I am. You are delusional. Everyone on this ship who's loyal to our cause can see that you're a madman who would do anything to expose me!" Katsina said, her anger tearing through her vocal chords.

"Ah, you think I would do anything?" he asked with laughter; "But what about you? What would you do?"

"What?"

"What would you do to save your wretched band of Yggs over there, hmm?" he jeered.

"They're innocent people!" said Alice.

"Shut. Her. Up." Morann turned to his man in anger, waving his hands frantically. His fingers coiled into claws. His forehead turning a deep red.

Katsina watched as the soldier stuffed a rag into Alice's mouth and threw her to the ground.

"Bastard!"

"Now now, Katsina. This is war; we're all soldiers here. Disobedience is a serious crime that must be treated with equal, if not greater, severity," Morann said, stepping closer to her.

"You can't hurt those civilians. I won't let you," Katsina managed to get out. The pressure by the soldier's hand around her neck became slowly but surely unbearable.

"I know you won't. Because you're going to confess, right now," Morann said menacingly. "Confess to aiding and abetting the enemy through those people and I will spare them. They will be captured and processed for their crimes. But I will not harm them."

"If… I-if I confess?" she struggled.

"Yes, then this will all be over. Tell me the truth. And I will spare the lives of all those people. Surely you would want to save them?"

Katsina looked into Morann's eyes, behind his pupils, beyond his implants. She tried to see what it was he saw, what it was about her that maddened him. She could see her reflection in his eyes, the face of the savage woman atop the hill on the Alia moon. Katsina saw the reflection of the person she had grown to be, the spiteful and relentless warrior. Katsina saw what she was the day Aardashini Morann died, a remorseless killer. The blood harbinger of the Yggdrasilian people, something she couldn't be any longer, not if she was to save the innocent lives of those aboard that ship.

"Eventually you will have to own up to your true nature, Lucas. You will have to come to terms with what you are, what you chose to be. Look at what I offer you, the chance to save the lives of thousands, by admitting that you're the liar, the murderer, the heartless wretch we all know you to be," he said, pressing his forehead against hers.

Katsina struggled to breathe, the room dimming around her. She knew he was, in a way, right about her. She was a liar, a murderer, heartless. Sacrificing the lives of hundreds to take the lives of hundreds more. Katsina kept hearing the message in the background, knowing what she would have done had she heard it herself months before. She would have wiped out every last one of them. But Katsina, in her suffocation, felt something was different, she never would have defended the rights of a Yggdrasilian person before. A battle began to wage in her mind as her consciousness slipped away, the savage killer, tackling the righteous defender. Katsina's ears began to ring, with Morann's muffled voice speaking to her through the distance.

"Fine then, prepare to fire."

Katsina began losing touch, the tingling sensation in her extremities becoming numb. She had to do something. Anything. So she pulled up her HUD, barely able to see, and sent a message across the red web before trying to speak.

"Mor... ann..." She choked, "Mor... ann..."

"Ah, she's decided, good. Let her go, I want to hear it."

Katsina fell to her knees, drawing breath, returning to reality form her subconscious once again. Her eyes worked to correct themselves through the tears, her ears still ringing. She coughed and spluttered, straining to inhale the air. Her breathing was rattled, the pain in her neck blinding her still. She found the ground with her palms, gasping on all fours.

"Come on now, we don't have much time," Morann said, snatching her chin with her fingers. Katsina fell back on her knees, her head tilted back, looking at the glass ceiling. She took one deep breath. Steadying herself. She was ready.

"I am..." she said, her voice a rasp of what it could be. Morann squinted his eyes, looking down his nose on her expectantly.

"Yes?" He said.

"I am... the traitor," Katsina said, falling back onto her elbow. She closed her eyes and focused on her breathing, listening to the sound of the audio message. Morann crouched next to her, and pulled a strand of hair away from her face. He had put his pistol back into his coat, but it was loosely fastened, at risk of slipping loose. On his face was a compassionate smile, his hand felt warm on her cheek. He touched her face with the gentle nature she once felt from Marshal, the one person she needed. She shivered under Morann's gaze.

"Well done, Katsina. You have finally told the truth," he said before standing up again. "A confession!" he shouted, causing a disjointed eruption of cheers among his men.

Katsina could do no more. She had done all she could. She prepared herself to be taken away and locked in a cell for the rest of her days. The applause must have been music to Morann's ears. While the sound of the child in the audio message allowed Katsina to lay down, and accept her fate. It was over, there was to be no redemption, no proof that it was Morann instead of her. Only a memory, with nothing to back it up. Katsina sighed, her plans to redeem her name strangely felt selfish compared to sparing the lives of the Yggdrasilians.

"Now then, let's get on with it. Fire at will."

Katsina's eyes opened, her body lurched, she stumbled on her hands and feet. She could see nothing, hear nothing, but Morann. An awful hole felt as if it had been pushed through her chest. The Behemothis rumbled and groaned around her, Katsina opened her mouth, screaming for Morann to stop. But her voice was drowned out by the devastating sound of the ship's main cannon. The sight of the projectile falling away from the ship stopped Katsina in place, her arms fell limp around her waist. The popping sounds of the rail guns sent hundreds of minuscule strips of light after the payload. The white light that flashed in the distance consumed the Free Venture as a fireball grew. The initial flash blinded Katsina, burning its image into her eyes while the detonation continued. There was no shockwave, no sound, just the flash of light, and the Free Venture disappeared. Katsina lost her balance, light-headedness taking over her ability to stand straight. Her knees grew weak and she fell back to the floor as the sound of the radio message cut off from her ears. She felt her stomach curdle, her mouth salivating profusely. She had to regain control of her breathing if she was to make it through. She kept her eyes on the ground, the bright flash making it difficult to see her palms. Her face contorted in pain, and finally, Katsina felt a warm droplet run down her cheek. Her eyes welled, blurring her already limited vision. Soon the light receded, and the room fell back under its dark blue curtain. Katsina heard nothing else in the room but herself, her erratic breathing. She tried to sniff back the pain, swallow it if she could, but instead she watched the spatters of her own tears hit the floor under her. Her cries began to ring out through the bridge, to all that watched her weep at what Morann had done.

"Ah, Katsina, finally releasing all of that guilt for the things you've done," Morann said, standing over her, "but you are safe now child; I've cleansed your sins."

Katsina adjusted her HUD, and scrubbed the imprinted image from her retina. She sniffed back her tears, the shaking of her chest, the sobs. She tried to drag it all back inward to focus on her HUD. She accessed the red web, linking to everyone on the ship, drawing multiple connections over one another. AR images of hundreds of people began filling the room, their glow brightening Katsina's sight as she stood up. Her chest wouldn't stop writhing, as if her lungs needed to burst from her body. She stretched her lips over her teeth, gritting them to focus. The tiny strands of red connections lifted her to her feet. The sound of every crew member, every ally she had made, propped her up. Katsina knew what she had admitted to Morann, but she also knew what she told everyone on the red web. She wished she had had more time to prepare, to make it as painless for them all as possible, but that wasn't an option for her anymore. They were supposed to wait at least two more weeks. They were hardly ready. Katsina stepped carefully towards Morann, who looked at her with a sense of pride. She didn't look at him, rather she looked at her crew mates, physical or virtual, who stood watching her with sombre expressions.

"Well done, Katsina, well done," Morann said, his voice scratching at the last of Katsina's facade.

He held out his arms, placing his hands on her shoulders, a sick and demented smile stretched across his face. Looking on either side of him, Katsina counted one on the left, three on the right, and four behind her. She cleared her throat and dragged her eyes upward to meet his. He couldn't see it, but she could, the final connections to the web had been made, everyone was listening, waiting. The red web stretched to every corner of the Behemothis, entangling it in her message. Only eighty percent of her crew had accepted her request, less than she hoped. Her implants calibrated, preparing her muscles and secreting adrenaline throughout her system. Katsina stared into Morann's eyes and his expression dropped from gleeful happiness to horror. Katsina took a deep breath.

"Engage!"

She thrust her hand into Morann's coat as the lights went out. Her fingertips brushed off of his chest while her thumb clamped down on the grip of his pistol. The green targeting lasers danced around the room, creating a dance floor of decimation. But dancing wasn't the point of the exercise. Katsina ripped the pistol from him, lifting it to the last place she remembered seeing someone. Her HUD showed her the blue comm links in the room, labelling targets in the dark, it was strange to her how no one had thought that seeing everyone's connections to each other left rebellious and mutinous causes at a distinct advantage. The room began to light up with flashes, casting long and menacing shadows around her. Her ears had prepared for the gunfire that ensued, but it was still loud. She fired at her left hand side, the muzzle flash showing her target fall down. She dropped to one knee, and fired two more times, hitting the three to her right. Morann's face could be made out in the brief flashes of light surrounding them. He hadn't moved, his expression unchanged. Katsina snatched at his coat, pulling him to the floor next to her, she had to keep him alive.

The shouts of the wounded began filling the dome, forcing Katsina to drag Morann behind a desk with her. The gunfire became sparse and the flashes were few and far between. Katsina glanced around in the dark, using comm links and the dancing lazers to pick her targets. *Pop, pop, pop,* her pistol sounded as she scratched one, then two, and another in her sights. As far as firefights in the dark went, she didn't think it was going poorly. Her ears perked up at the sound of Alice's voice.

"Kat, Kat, where are you?" she whispered.

"Oh yeah, like I'm going to be able to answer that right now," Katsina said with frustration.

"We can't stay here much longer. We have to get him to Dr. Foye."

"I know, I know. Get on to Rutheo, get the lights back on and get me an extraction team."

"Aye, captain."

Katsina kept her knee pinned to Morann's thigh as he began to struggle with her. His shock seemed to wear off. His fist jabbed at her left side, throwing her off of him.

"Traitor!" he shouted.

Katsina heard an uninviting *sknit* on her left side, and tried to roll away from it. But she wasn't fast enough, Morann was fully up to speed. Another jab hit her left side, this time breaking something. The pain shot through her ribcage, making her writhe and kick out in the dark. Had the room not already been black, Katsina would have lost her vision with the blinding pain that erupted in her chest. Eventually her foot caught Morann, getting him off of her. She lifted the pistol and fired wildly in his direction, her shots ricocheting off desks and chairs as Morann dipped away behind them. The pain in her chest began growing, taking over her left side. She slapped her hand over the spot, feeling warmth and wet oozing the wound while a rubber and metal object protruded from her ribs.

"*Faisaheß*," she thought as a puddle began to form.

The lights in the dome began to flicker back on, leaving Katsina exposed under the AR image of the World Discoverer in the middle of the room. She had to find cover. Between her and a desk on her right side, she saw one of Morann's soldiers approaching. He didn't have line of sight yet, she had the element of surprise. She lifted the pistol, lined up her sights. *Click* it went, not firing anything from its chamber. The noise alerted the soldier, who turned to aim his weapon at her. Panic ran up her spine, she had an empty pistol and no extra ammunition. She had no time to think, only to act. Katsina fell onto her right side, using her elbow to get off the ground. The pain in her chest ripped at her. She took aim, and flung the pistol at the soldier. It connected with his chin, making him miss his shot. She barreled into him in his moment of distraction, pulling him to the floor with her. They struggled for a moment, Katsina trying to pry his gun from him. She grunted in pain, putting in all her effort while biting down on her own lips, but he was stronger. He snatched at the object in her side, pushing it further inward. Katsina let out a scream, letting go of his gun to pull his hand away. The muzzle of his weapon touched her cheek, making her flinch in fear.

Bang

Katsina fell to the floor, the weight of the soldier's body dropping off of her. She glanced around, wondering why she wasn't dead.

"Somebody call the cavalier cavalry?"

Katsina's vision began to blur, but not before she saw James Garland, leading a group of men across the bridge floor.

He was a sight for sore eyes. On top of his military garb, he wore a graphene chestplate and armor pads. A helmet sat atop his head with an external sensor system wired into the back of his neck. The soldiers around him fanned out, firing shots in all different directions. Their armor was more specialised, exactly what Katsina ordered. They were ironclad from head to toe, their bodies protected by the latest T4 ranger battle armor. Designed for ground and space operations, the T4 had flight capable booster jets, ceramic graphene woven plates, and an exoskeletal support system making the user light as a feather while being protected from external pressure, radiation and more. Katsina grinned at the sight, sputtering words in Garland's direction. The room began flooding with more of Morann's men.

"Captain, here to extract, where's the target?" James said, crouching down next to her. "Oh no. Captain?"

Katsina choked on fluid, trying to talk. She pointed down at the knife in her side. The pain became too much, and her eyes dimmed. Her HUD flickered away, and James' face faded. The last thing she could do was listen to the firefight, as if it was miles away. She cursed herself for it, but she couldn't help but slip away from consciousness under the pain of being stabbed.

IN BLOOD UNMADE

Lights passed overhead, while the echo of distant shouts and the sounds of war drummed against Katsina's ears. She struggled to stay awake, gripping to the reality that she found herself in. Her HUD flickered on and off, a warning flashing in her eyes every time it returned. It was a blood loss alarm, and a drop in lung pressure. Katsina could feel water in her throat, or at least, it felt like water. Trying to breath it just caused her to gurgle it, making her cough. The lights above her were the AR signs of the main hall, they had returned to normal. The colors danced on and off with Katsina's HUD.

"We have to get her to the Forward Operating Base," Garland shouted in the distance.

"Alert Dr. Foye, we have wounded," Alice replied.

Katsina opened her eyes, and tried to speak. Fluid spilled down her chin, and she started coughing.

"Mo... ra... nn," she managed.

"Captain don't try to talk, we need to get you to safety."

"Wh... ere... Mor..."

Katsina couldn't hold on, her attempt had failed. She'd had one shot to get at Morann, to take him down. To make him pay for the pain he had caused. She'd missed it. And instead he'd stabbed her in the chest. Katsina closed her eyes, and fell back into a deep sleep.

***

A ringing, like a bell or a chime reached Katsina's ears. Perhaps she had died? Could it be that she'd lost? No. Not her. She followed the sounds, as if rising from under a blanket of ocean. She resurfaced, a bright set of torches blinding her as she opened her eyes again.

"She's awake!"

"Get me a barrier, don't let her see it."

Katsina recognised the voices of Dr. Foye and the others. They were standing over her, their faces grave with concern. But the torch lights weren't being held by them, nor were they on the ceiling. Katsina struggled to focus, but eventually she recognised the sounds of robotic actuators, and the noise of a bonesaw. She lifted her head, glancing down at her chest, it was open. And bleeding. Katsina's brow curled, and her jaw fell open in shock. She felt a tremor in her side as the bonesaw cut into her.

"Captain, don't move, please," Linda said, cupping Katsina's cheeks in her hands. "Look at me. You're going to be fine."

Katsina kept her eyes on the mechanical arms digging into her body, their white coated joints spattered with red droplets. Her body and mind were numb to the pain, her tongue limp in her mouth. She couldn't feel the surgery, but she could tell it hurt.

"Katsina, listen to me. Look up here, look." Linda said, snapping her fingers. "Everyone is here. You're in the FOB. The surgical programme is nearly over. Just don't move."

"Whervs, Moooranb?" Katsina said, her tongue barley forming the words.

"He's still on the bridge," said Linda, lifting a sheet between Katsina and the surgical machine.

Rutheo leaned in, catching her attention.

"We have control of engineering, the tarmac, and the armory. But they have the bridge, hospital and most of the private quarters. They dropped the blast shield around the dome like you said they would," she said reassuringly.

"Lobsessss? Dub we hab Lobsess?"

"Losses aren't too high as it stands, Captain," James entered. "Considering the sudden engagement we didn't do ourselves any favors. Our fighters are engaged in a dogfight outside. They've been trying to punch a hole in the blast shield. But from where we are, we will be able to execute and retake most of the ship, just not the bridge. I have men and women ready to push. Just give me the go ahead."

"Nop… wiffou mbe…" Katsina managed.

"Kat, it's me, Alice. You're in no state to fight, if we removed the blade you could bleed to death. You have to stay here while the others push forward. I can command them from here."

"Then leeb it in."

"What did she say?" Rutheo asked.

"She wants to leave the blade in," Linda said, her eyes rolling to the ceiling.

"Sedate her or something; she can't be serious," said Alice, her voice panicked.

"James," Katsina sputtered, staring into the eyes of her former guard, "don't leeb me here. My Requisition…"

"Yes captain, it was assembled to specification."

"Good, thenb we're going," Katsina said.

She snatched at the cable connecting Dr. Foye to the robot, and plugged it into the back of her neck. Linda stepped back in shock while Katsina used the network to set new parameters for her surgery. Everyone but Morann and his people were using the red web now, giving Katsina an advantage over her enemy, and even her own team. She didn't want to deceive them, or to worry them in any way. But she didn't care what she wanted. She just had to get the job done. The smell of burning flesh hit Katsina's nostrils as the sound of sizzling filled the room. Everyone around the table, bar Dr. Foye, leapt away from the smell, leaving Katsina alone with her.

"Docter, I'm goinb," Katsina said, locking with Linda's eyes.

"I can't believe you. You won't make it Katsina. You're hurt too badly."

"I'm gonna need some implants," she said, feeling her voice return to her tongue.

"Faisaheßul ts'Solfé, you won't listen to reason will you?" Linda said with frustration, holding her fist to her mouth, as if wanting to bite down on her knuckles.

Katsina felt a gentile tug on her chest, and another. The tissue stitcher was putting her back together. *Clip* then *sizzle* the machine went as it worked it's way around her side.

"What implants do you need?" said the doctor, defeated.

"Local anaesthetic, adderall pump, and some stimulants," Katsina said.

"Aye, captain. Commander Wesley, help the captain up. She won't be staying." said Linda curtly as she walked away.

"What? Wait a minute you can't just let her walk out of here-" Alice protested.

"She refuses treatment. I have enough wounded who need that bed and that machine, so it's either let her go or waste time arguing," the doctor snapped, snatching an implant from a tray by Katsina's bed. "Implant this into the lower spine, it will replace the general anesthetic with a local dose."

Katsina lifted herself from the bed as the sheet fell away between her and the machine. The scars were brutal, and the cauterized flesh around the broken hilt of the blade looked worse. But for Katsina, as long as she wasn't bleeding to death, she could work. That was all she needed. Alice arrived by her side, helping her sit up in the bed. She took the implant out of Katsina's hands and bent behind her to place it in the socket on her back. Katsina began to feel pins and needles around her, the sensation of numbness receding. The pain of bruises and cuts returned, while the lower left of her chest remained numb. She ran her fingers over the bump, feeling the metal blade under her skin, embedded in her rib cage. The broken hilt didn't protrude out of her very far, meaning she could wear her armor without risking pushing the blade in any further. Katsina found another object sticking out of her left side towards her back.

"What's this?" she asked.

"You had a hemothorax, as a result of the knife wound," Alice said. "When you came in it was just tension pneumothorax but you began hemorrhaging badly. Basically you had a hole in your chest and it filled with blood and that collapsed your lung causing-"

"Alice, I know what a hemothorax is. So it's a catheter?"

"Yes, it's running a line into one of your lower back ports, recycling the blood from your chest cavity back into your kidneys."

"You ever considered being a nurse?" Katsina asked with a smile.

"I prefer space signals," Alice said, returning the gesture.

Katsina slid off the edge of the bed, using Alice for support. They were surrounded by a blue curtain, hiding them from the commotion outside. The sounds of heart monitors, moaning patients, distant gunfire, and surgeon machines filled the room around them. The curtain *slinked* back, revealing Rutheo. She closed it again quickly, tossing Katsina some clothes. Instead of her usual uniform, the light and shiny material was laced with a hexagonal pattern around a leotard. Along the limbs were nodes that matched the locations of Katsina's ports. While the front had a self adhesive fold on it in the place of a traditional zipper.

"Don't want people seeing the captain indecent now do we?" she said. "Get dressed."

Rutheo kept her eye on the screen showing Katsina's vitals, while Dr. Foye reentered with Katsina's requested implants. She had Katsina lift her arms, and she inspected the ports before inserting them. Katsina felt the cold of her hands running along her back, clicking the implants into place. Katsina's HUD registered them in her system, and they began working while she got dressed.

"The adderall stimulant pump will last you about eight hours before it depletes. I'm also giving you a procoagulant to help clot the wounds around the knife."

"Thanks Linda. I appreciate it."

"Just don't waste it," she said as she left through the curtain.

Katsina felt a ping in her chest, not a physical pain. It was guilt. She knew she wasn't doing anyone a favor by getting out of bed. But she had to. She couldn't let someone else take her place. The curtain opened one more time for James, who was carrying a black metal crate with a handle either side of the length. Embellished in gold on the case was the symbol of Katsina's affix. He handed it to her.

"You sure, Captain?" He asked.

"I'm sure," Katsina said, placing the case on the ground. "Step back."

The case opened, unfolding to reveal two plates in the shape of Katsina's boots. She stepped into it, and it clamped around her. She bent down, grabbing the two handles either side, and pulled the case upwards, unfolding it about her legs. She extended her arms upwards as the metal plates and pieces moved around her body, attaching to the nodes and ports on her bodysuit. A harness fell out from under the chest piece, attaching itself around Katsina's waist. A belt unfolded and attached to the harness, lining it with pouches and protective plates. As the armour pulled itself together, Katsina felt it pressurize around her body. She might have underestimated how tight it was going to be, but other than that, the armour fit perfectly. The grey and black plates produced a mask that pressed onto Katsina's face, while a helmet slid over her forehead from the back of her neck. On her shoulder, Katsina noticed a gun like object that moved to follow her eyesight, a feature she didn't remember ordering.

"Something new huh?" she said.

"Last minute addition, this laser targeter marks your enemies as you look at them. Making it easier for your weapon to land precise shots without having to lose time aiming down sights. It's useful in every situation apart from when smoke is involved. The laser can break up in it. It also has a friend/foe algorithm that reduces risk of friendly fire," Garland explained.

"Nice, that all?"

"It's, uh, also retractable if you prefer to trust yourself if you don't like it?"

"No, I like it. Honestly I might need it; good shout, James," Katsina said, loading her suit controls to retract the shoulder mounted laser.

"These flight suit specific variants of the T4 armor aren't on standard issue yet, so some features may not be compatible with what you need it for."

"Don't worry, Mr. Garland," Rutheo said with a smile. "We had Howard work that out."

"Speaking of which, James, get a team together. Were going to take down the blast shield and get Morann," Katsina said, her voice muffled by the mask.

"Aye captain," James said, detaching his rifle from his back and leaving them.

Katsina looked at Rutheo and Alice, both of whom had supported her from the very beginning. The two of them seemed unsure of what to do next, glancing about aimlessly. Rutheo looked as if she wanted to say something. She raised her hand slightly, opening her mouth before correcting herself.

"Speak your minds," Katsina said, "apart from trying to convince me to stay."

"Alright then," Rutheo said, clearing her throat. "You're such a t'sEcheashin sometimes, you take everything on your shoulders and have a hard time even trusting your friends. If Marshal were here, he'd slap you silly for even thinking this is a good idea."

"Not to mention that you're clearly devaluing yourself as a person because of your past, and you think stopping Morann will make you feel better, instead of reporting up the chain of command," Alice added.

"That too; you also treated me like a naysolye reiur and we're going to talk about it when this is over, not now," Rutheo said, her anger boiling over.

"I treated you like a bad smell? Ruthie, I-"

"I said: Not. Now. I'm mad at you still. You walked out on me after I told you I loved you, and you're not going to make it up that easily."

"She did what?" Alice said, her mouth falling open.

"Oh, and we're going with you," Rutheo finalised.

"Yes, we're going wi- wait what?" Alice said, glaring at Rutheo.

"If we're retaking the Behemothis, we're doing it together. This is our Broadsider too. We have just as much a reason to take down Morann as she does," said Rutheo.

"I-I uh, well I agree, but I never said I would take part in the conflict-"

"Shut up Alice, get a gun and a chestplate. You're coming. We need you to retake control of the bridge when we get there."

"Rutheo's right. I need both of you to get the ship back. It's not just me now," Katsina said.

"Told ya," said Rutheo before sticking her tongue out at Alice.

"Oh, *now* you'd rather not take everything on by yourself. Alright then. I'll uh, get a, uh, get a gun," Alice said.

***

Outside of Dr. Foye's quarters, the crew had erected barricades using the salvaged debris from weeks before. Either side of the street was blocked off, while one of the main stairwells was guarded by drones loaded with turret guns. The FOB itself had a quantum comms system, a rations station, and of course hoards of medical supplies and weapons. The base was sparsely populated, with more laying injured than standing able. Katsina met with James and his team, young ground operators that breached the bridge with him. They all saluted Katsina as she walked painfully out onto the street. The suit helped keep her standing, making her incredibly light and inhumanely agile on her feet.

"Not much of a turn out, James," Katsina said, returning her salute to the soldiers.

"We lost 4 getting you back, and many didn't have time to get here before the barricades went up. But thanks to Alice's roster, most people on shift together makes for a pretty dangerous set of resistance cells scattered around the ship. The odds aren't bad."

"Alright. Rutheo, did you get that maintenance tunnel closed up?" Katsina asked, gesturing down the stairwell.

"Yeah, also scrubbed it from live ship schematics and diagrams. As long as they don't see us using it they won't know we're in it."

"Good, down we go. Alice and Rutheo are staying in the middle, I need 3 in the rear, two flanking either side and another three to take point," Katsina said.

A panel on her suit opened up on her chest to reveal a pistol in an auto holster. Katsina unlatched the clip, allowing the pistol to land in her hand. She recognised it immediately, its golden grip smeared with dried blood. It was Morann's, retrieved along with Katsina during the bridge extraction. Katsina felt its weight, perfectly balanced. A fair trade considering Morann still had her affix clipped to his shoulder.

***

The sound of gunfire echoed up after every flash that lit the pitch black stairwell. They could have used traditional lighting, but Katsina refused, opting for them to use their implanted night vision lenses instead to avoid detection. The stairwell itself was laced with bodies, some Katsina's people, and others Morann's. Each body had an open pair of eyes that reflected what little light could be picked up, making them glow with an unnatural stare. Katsina made a point to stop at each one, collecting their ID chips along the way down. Many were nurses, unarmed, while Morann's were fully kitted operators. The match hadn't been fought evenly. The walls were dotted with holes, some spattered with blood. The team progressed down slowly, taking each corner and each floor cautiously. Eventually they came to a junction leading to a maintenance tunnel, one that ran across the ship from port to starboard. The tunnel was part of the hatched network that connected the upper half of the ship to the lower, with the tarmac directly below the tunnels.

"Alright, it's a tight space, stay sharp," James whispered over the comm link.

"What are we going to do when we get to the tarmac?" Alice asked.

"Yeah, you didn't actually fill us in on what the plan is here," one of the soldiers added.

"Assuming our fighters outside couldn't penetrate the blast shield on the dome, we need something a little heavier," Katsina said.

"Nothing short of a frigate cannon could pop a hole in that thing. We don't even have a cruiser," another soldier said.

"Don't worry, guys. Good ol' Howard made us something better," Rutheo said.

The maintenance shaft was hidden behind some makeshift wall paneling that Rutheo had a team install. Katsina had the group fan out to watch corners while Rutheo removed the bolts one by one. The sound of the drill was loud enough to echo through the corridor and down the remaining flights of the stairwell, where gunfire could be heard. Katsina changed the filters in her eyes, seeing through different light and wave spectrums to make sure nothing was hiding in the distance.

"Unnerving, isn't it?" James said.

"A little; I'm just surprised they have no one in this section," said Katsina, thoughtfully.

"Well they didn't have access to much equipment in the armory. We're better kitted than they are in some respects, not to mention we have most of the fighter pilots."

"You say that, but no one could have guessed that Morann had a plutonium implosion device on board. So if he has one of those, what else would he have?" Katsina said, keeping her eyes on the corners of the corridors. She glanced over at James, who's color had slightly drained from his face.

"You alright?" Katsina said.

"Yeah, just, woah. A nuclear bomb? That's unthinkable," he said. "If we knew about it earlier we could have stopped him."

"That's not on us. There's no way we could have known he would use such an ancient weapon design."

"It's just cruel. Killin' people wholesale like that."

"That's what war in space is, James, killing people wholesale is what we've been doing this entire time. He just did it illegally," Katsina said, clicking her tongue.

"My brother would have disagreed, he always said that all's fair in war, especially against the Yggs," James said, his brow dropping, his lips pressing together.

"Can I ask you a personal question?" Katsina said, glancing in his direction.

"Yeah."

"You said you didn't want to go to space, and that you remained on the ground," she said, watching his reaction, "but here you are. Did you sneak onto this ship?"

James sighed, closing his eyes in a moment of shame.

"I knew from the comm chatter that the entire court district was going to be lost, so I got on a shuttle, if I stayed…" he hesitated.

"If you stayed, you wouldn't have seen Jared again," Katsina finished his sentence.

"After this is over, when we get the ship back. I'm going to find my brother, find the Roverdendrom, and get him home," he said, his voice resolute.

Katsina paused, watching the former military policeman, a man who said he'd never go to space. She admired the lengths he planned to go to, and the lengths he already had gone to. He reminded her of Marshal.

"Booyah," Rutheo whispered in excitement, prematurely ending Katsina's heart to heart with James.

The team slowly bottle-necked into the claustrophobic space without making noise, which was tough for some of the more heavily armored operators. Their armor plates scratched the walls if they were not steady, making a dreadful screeching sound. Like nails on a chalkboard. Katsina kept her eye on the rear, watching the entrance they used shrink smaller and smaller as they went. She felt something catch in her throat, and coughed for a moment. The others began to cough with her.

"Smoke in the way. Must be a fire, masks on," James said over the comms.

The smoke eventually became thick, blocking Katsina's line of sight.

"How we doing up there?" she said, growing suspicious of her blindspot.

"Nearly there, just anoth- wait, wait, do you guys smell that? What t-?" the lead soldier said.

Katsina heard a loud *bang* over the comms, followed by a *sizzling* sound. The passageway lit up with gunfire behind her, while one of the soldiers at the front began to scream. He sounded in agony. Katsina was pulled back by James, who pushed her to the middle of the group with Rutheo and Alice. He disappeared in the smoke, only his silhouette appearing frequently from his muzzle flash. The sound of the screaming soldier eventually ended with a piercing set of chokes and gags. Katsina spun around, trying to see what was happening through the veil. The soldiers towards the front of the group dropped to one knee, giving Katsina a line of sight. The smoke kept her in the dark, so she just fired into the shaft, hoping against hope not to hit an ally. The floor and walls creaked, the metal below their feet popping and folding. The maintenance shaft shifted, causing the wires on the walls to snap, igniting the space with sparks. Katsina saw light pierce the metal floor, pulling the smoke out of the shaft.

"Run!" James shouted from behind her. "We have to get

out!"

Katsina looked down towards the hole in the floor, and saw the tarmac below. But around the opening, lay a smouldered and bubbling pile. Pieces of armor burnt and melted surrounded by a pungent odor. Inside the mess, she could make out what was left of a human face. Katsina, spun around, horrified by the sight.

"James!" she screamed, running back towards him.

Another bang shook the floor, and the flash framed itself around James. He fell back, smacking his head off the floor. Katsina watched as his armor began to bellow fumes from his chest. He started to scream, pulling at his helmet and face. In the distance, beyond the smoke, Katsina could hear a familiar jeering voice. It only called out one word, one name.

"Ruthie… Ruthie…"

"James, James, no!" she shouted, snatching at the clips of his armor, trying to pull it off of him. He wouldn't stop screaming.

"No! Kat, dont," Rutheo said, snatching her arm. "Don't touch him, it's acid. It's Kessler. He has them using acid."

Katsina ripped her arms from Rutheo's grasp and, looping them under James' shoulders, she tried to lift him.

"We have to get an evac for him, Rutheo," she said as she held him, his body twitching and writhing in pain. The smell of the corroding metal was repulsive.

"Kat-"

Another panel splintered under Katsina's feet, throwing her backwards with Rutheo in tow. Her hands slipped out from under James. She lost him. The acid had eaten away at the tunnel floors, causing them to fall. Katsina rolled in the air, snatching Rutheo up into her arms. She landed squarely on her feet, cracking the tarmac plate under her. The rest of the team landed equally as harsh around them. Katsina dropped to one knee, clutching at her chest in pain. Rutheo fell from her arms onto the ground with a thud. She inhaled sharply, the pain overbearing for a moment, the knife had moved. She lifted her head to see the other soldiers firing at the ceiling while standing atop the remains of a fighter ship. The maintenance tunnel had crushed it.

"Kat, Kat, get up!" Rutheo said before a bellowing sound deafened in the air above them.

A crescendo of railgun fire surrounded the small group. Fighter ships had entered the hangar, firing on one another. They chased each other about the massive space, some crashing into the walls, while others twisted into one another before falling to the ground. Katsina used her suit to lift herself off the floor, and looked to see where on the tarmac they were. They were too far back on the aft of the ship, so Katsina turned to the bow and began to sprint. Her eyes squinting away the pain that James had left her with. An acid attack. The savage dogfight overhead complicated Katsina's plan. She hoped the squadron holding the tarmac entrances were still there.

"Alice, lets go!" she shouted.

The group sprinted across the barren no man's land of tarmac, where ships fell to the ground while tungsten pellets rained about them. Katsina could see her garage, but her chest began to wheeze when she ran.

"Kat, I can't get a hold of anyone," Rutheo called from behind.

"What?" Katsina said, the noise above making it difficult to hear.

"I said, I can't get anyone on line. I don't know if they're still there," she said over the comm.

"Faisaheß, I need you to get some heavy weapons teams in here," Katsina said, trying to maintain her breathing.

"No promises!"

Katsina's garage was in sight, a makeshift set of barricades made of tires, plates and engine parts surrounded it. Flashing lights of rifles and cannons came from behind the line. Someone must still be alive behind it. A burst of fire above Katsina made her look up to see a burning fighter ship heading for the ground directly ahead of her and Rutheo. She made a quick decision, she stopped running, and lunged back at Rutheo. She pushed Rutheo with all her might, and activated her booster pack. The fighter smashed into the ground, tearing away the tarmac plates in its wake while it slid down the runway. Katsina tried to use her elbow to break her fall and let out a moan, only making her chest hurt even more. Her HUD lit up an emergency notification for blood loss. So she countered the pain with more of her stimulant to get up again. Her helmet was cracked, shards missing from its outer layer. She gasped for a moment, pressing her hands to her knees to balance herself. She slowly recovered, surprised that both she and Rutheo weren't dead. Katsina's eyes widened. She straightened up and spun about, looking about the wreckage to find her engineer.

"Rutheo!" She said, making her way through the smoke. "Rutheo!"

"Captain," Alice's voice sounded.

"Alice! Alice, you have Rutheo?"

"Captain, where are you?"

Katsina cleared the smoke, and found Alice to her left, covered in dirt and blood. Her hands were clinging to her helmet. Around her lay the bodies of the six men who'd escorted them, puncture wounds littering them while holes surrounded Alice on the tarmac. Katsina grabbed Alice's wrists, and retracted her own helmet to look at her.

"Alice, Alice look at me. Are you hit? Where's Rutheo?"

"I'm okay I just... she... she was right there," she said, pointing at the smoking crater Katsina had just passed through, "I saw her just there, before you pushed her."

"Alice, tell me she made it. She made it?" Katsina demanded.

"I don't know, I didn't see. I don't know."

Katsina's stomach felt as if it fell through her body, becoming an empty pit in her armor. Two more fighters flew overhead, throwing Katsina's hair around her face. The noise of their engines disappeared as they flew out the hangar doors, leaving the sound of flames and the smell of soot behind them. Water began to sprinkle onto the tarmac, soaking the battleground. Katsina saw a terrible pain in Alice's eyes, a remorse for following her no doubt. Katsina felt it as well, turning to the wreckage behind her in anger.

"Rutheo! Rutheo, you get out here right now!" she shouted, "Ruthie! Rutheo!"

Katsina launched her foot into a piece of ruble, kicking it into the smouldering wreck of the fighter. She smacked her helmet in her hands before bouncing it off the tarmac floor.

"Rutheo!" she shouted again.

Katsina began pacing as the flames around the fighter grew larger, and the puddles around her deepened. Her chest ached as she shouted for her friend over and over.

"Freeze! Disengage and stand down now!" a gruff and inelegant voice caught her off guard.

Through the smoke appeared a group of ten, materialising one by one. Military police officers, led by Kessler. Katsina reached for Morann's pistol, only to realise it was no longer there, she had lost it. A pellet from Kessler's gun rang off of her shoulder, throwing her to the ground.

"Hands up!" he shouted again.

They were too far from the barricade. The rest of the team was gone. They were surrounded. So Katsina raised her arms over her head and caused herself a considerable spike of pain. One of her protective plates fell away from her arm, clattering along the ground as it bounced. Blood began to spill from under her chestplate. She wouldn't last much longer. First Mara, Mike, and Aaron. Then the civilians of Los Ange, then James, and now Rutheo.

"Hands on your head! Slowly," Kessler commanded.

Katsina dipped her head and ran her fingers into her hair. She waited for one of them to approach her to make her stand, she wasn't going to be captured.

"You and your scummy rat caused us enough trouble, but at least she's out of the way now," he said, a smile stretching the synthetic skin on the side of his face.

He looked as if his muscles would tear themselves out of his skin, his veins bulbous under his temple, the scratches and soot marks on his arms were visible through his ripped clothes. The hulking Kessler was damaged, pushed to his edge seemingly. He fired another round at Katsina, cracking another plate of her armor, and then another, and another.

"Good thing you pushed her into that fireball for me, Lucas," he said. "I did want to have my way with her one last time, just to throw her around a bit, you know, Captain's orders. But I guess it's a bit more poetic this way, letting you kill all your own friends for us."

The sounds of the coup reached her ears from all across the Behemothis, people crying for help. Screams and gunfire. She wouldn't be captured while her crew died for the cause. Katsina braced herself, ready to be shot. Prepared to die for her failure. Kessler approached her slowly, keeping the barrel of his gun trained to her head.

"You should have just died at the courthouse," he said.

THROUGH STRENGTH ITSELF
WE BECOME

The pain would slow her down, her armor felt heavy on her shoulders. Katsina heard the footsteps of Kessler approach her. She waited to see the tip of his boot to move. There it was. Katsina lifted her leg, stomping down on his foot. But he was too fast. Katsina took a dig to the side of the head. She stumbled back, trying to recover, but another fist caught her in the chest. She spit blood from her mouth and crashed into the ground. She was at a disadvantage, considering she performed best in a cockpit.

"I was going to kill the rat slowly, you know, but I guess I'll have to settle for killing the great Katsina Lucas," he said.

A gut twisting kick landed square into Katsina's stomach. While another foot stomped into her leg. Katsina grunted at the pain, unable to fight back, her suit stopped responding to her thoughts, locking her inside of it.

"It was clever of you to have the armory. Honestly, I don't think anyone expected you to be this daring under the captain's gaze," he said, continuing his onslaught, "but of course, we can always improvise."

Katsina looked up at him, noticing the vials of clear liquid attached to the bandoleer around his chest. Each vial was marked with a corrosive warning symbol. Acid.

"It wasn't hard to find it in research and development. Engineering didn't put up a fight really, so you can cross them off your list of survivors anyway."

The kicking and punching continued from the muscular man while he recited his monologue, giving Katsina no chance until he paused. She heard the pop of a lid opening, and looked up to see the wild eyes of Rendell Kessler staring down at her, a vial of the acid in his hands. He tilted it, letting a drip fall onto Katsina's leg, setting her senses ablaze. She let out a scream as the droplet tore into her suit, leaving behind a wisp of smoke as it ate away at her.

"Did she ever tell you about our night together in the end?" Kessler jeered. "She told us all about you, everything we needed, and more. She would have done anything to have you spared the charges, lucky for her she didn't have to."

The *sizzling* began to drain away, replaced by a familiar whirring. The sound grew louder and a new set of lights flooded the tarmac before her. The pebbles on the ground bounced and vibrated, while gunfire flashed about the two of them. Katsina looked up through the hair in her eyes, watching Kessler step away from her. He reached for his own gun, before a tall cylindrical pole darted through his chest, pinning his body to the floor. The impact shook the ground, and the vials on Kessler's chest shattered, while the one in his hands spilled onto his forearms. He didn't scream like James did, he didn't have the chance, he just spluttered and choked, burning under the power of his own cruel weapon. A pair of hands grabbed Katsina's collar, picking at her suit. They were Alice's.

"Alice, I'm stuck," she said, watching the rest of the MP's fire their guns at whatever was above Katsina's head.

"I know, I know, Just a sec," Alice said, panicked. Another MP made his way over to them.

"Hit the emergency release quick-"

"I'm trying, I'm trying-"

"Alice, come on!" Katsina shouted.

Before the MP could make it to them, a lashing of lights and tungsten pellets ripped through him and the rest of the men. Alice slid into Katsina's chest, hiding herself from the barrage. The guns above their heads hummed as they fired over and over. Until she could see barely anything left of the ground, or even the men who stood on it in front of them. The rod that had been embedded in the floor fell onto its side, revealing nothing left of Kessler's body, bar a puddle of smouldering bones and goo. The gunfire ended, leaving them to the sound of the fire suppression sprinklers and the flames around them. A puddle of water began to build under Katsina. Alice struggled with the release cord, eventually pulling it from her collar with a *snap*. Her suit unfolded from her body, pushing her out of it into the water. It was a wreck behind her, unsalvageable apart from the shoulder plate adorned with the laser targeter. She sat up, looking into the blinding flood light coming from the craft that saved her. It slowly lowered itself to the ground, resting it's wheels on the ground above them. A pressurised hatch opened on the ship with a *psshhhhhh* sound, followed by a splash in the water. Katsina tried to stand up and meet her saviour. Alice lifted her left arm to help. She stumbled back into the water, struggling with the pain in her chest.

"Awe come on, you miss me or somethin'? Let's go."

The image of the little, pale Rutheo emerged from the smoke to stand over her, the woman's small hand stretched out to help Katsina up. Katsina lifted her arm, grabbing Rutheo and pulling her down to the ground with her.

"Woah, hey watch what your-"

Katsina snatched Rutheo into her arms. Forgetting the pain of her knife wound, instead she basqued in the relief from the pain in her heart.

"Uh, Kat, is everything okay?" Rutheo asked, sounding confused.

Another body collided with them both, Alice, crying.

"We thought you were dead!" she blubbered.

"We thought you were dead," Katsina repeated.

"What? Really?"

"Yes, you bheibhen, the crash. I tried to push you out of the way. I couldn't find you."

"But I just kept running. I thought you guys were ahead of me," Rutheo said.

The three of them sat in the pool of warm water together. Holding each other for a moment. Katsina didn't care for the explanation. No matter what, it felt like a miracle.

"I'm sorry, I'm so sorry Rutheo," Katsina whispered, "I

didn't know they beat it out of you. I didn't know. I'm sorry."

"Psh, it's nothing a bit of therapy can't sort out. Forget about it. Let's get moving."

Katsina eventually eased off, and let the other two lift her off the ground. The fighter ship Rutheo had used was the Amber Eyes, and Katsina had never been so happy to see it. It was completely refurbished and capable. With new railguns attached beneath the wingspan, a new EMP rod cannon and a series of new and unfamiliar striped and ribbed poles attached to the belly by a ring of winding gears. Katsina's secret weapon against Morann was ready to fly. She dipped under Rutheo's supporting arm, snatching at the shoulder plate of the ruined armor. She dropped to one knee, trying to leverage it from the rest of the suit. Rutheo lifted Katsina out of her way, and jammed a jagged piece of metal into the gap between the armor and the shoulder plate, ripping it out of place. The trio sloshed across the tarmac, dipping under the wings of the Amber eyes. Rutheo and Alice helped Katsina into the ship, and then into her chair. She couldn't fathom how they had made it, but they had. She pulled at her collar, unfurling her jumpsuit with a gasp, Rutheo looked at her chest, fiddling with the valve on her catheter.

"You gonna be okay to fly her?" Rutheo asked.

"Is that some kind of personal attack or something?" Katsina said, throwing Rutheo a sarcastic smile.

"Yeah, you definitely missed me," Rutheo said. "Strap in, Commander Wesley, we're going for a ride!"

Katsina paused to hear the joyful sound of Rutheo's voice. She leaned forward, pressing her palms into her eyes. The wheezing was not getting better. Her shoulders were heavy, her muscles battered. But the sound of Rutheo's voice brought her a peace she hadn't felt for a long time. Without her armor, Katsina had no chance in a ground assault. She couldn't face Morann alone. But she had to try to do something. The women behind her chuckled together, making Katsina crane her neck to see. Rutheo had bent to one knee, strapping Alice into her makeshift harness.

"I mean it's not a troop carrier so you have to be tied nice and good in there," Rutheo said.

"Are you always so good at tying people up, Ruthie?"

"Only to cheer them up after they thought I died, Commander."

"Consider me cheered then, Chief," Alice said with a smile.

Katsina wondered how Alice had ever gotten out of such a tight shell at all. Knowing her as the nervous and polite comms specialist felt like the distant past. Regardless if Morann chose her to be his first officer to control her, Katsina realised she was perfect for the job. A bead of sweat dripped down over her forehead, and her ears started to ring. It was time to go.

"Alright then. When you two are done flirting," Katsina cleared her throat, looking around her heads up display. "Mobilize."

With a jolt of energy that threw her back into her seat, the Amber Eyes kicked off of the tarmac. Katsina's seat kept its center of gravity, while the ship unfurled and spun around her, taking form for the fight ahead. Katsina raised her left arm, stretching her wounds, old and new. She felt the ship move with her as the cables linked to her ports. They were now one and the same. They cleared the smoke directly ahead, and Katsina drove the ship towards the end of the tarmac.

"Kat? Kat, the hanger door is behind us?" Alice said in confusion.

"Ha, we're not going out the hanger door!" shouted Rutheo.

"What?"

Katsina pushed the ship into view of the rear bulkhead and dropped the railguns from their housing. The bulkhead was only forty or so inches thick, so a true marksman could penetrate it. She lined up her targeting system, keeping her eye on the stringer bar running along its horizontal middle. Her HUD pinged, locked on to the target. The Amber eyes layed a bombardment down on the partition, sending sparks and shrapnel high into the air. Each cannon blast shook Katsina in her seat, the vibrations rippling through the hull of the fighter ship. *Pop, pop, pop,* went the railguns, eventually discharging an entire magazine of eighty-four tungsten pellets each before revealing a circular incision left in the bulkhead. Katsina detached the magnetic coils and let the rails fall away from the guns, each now useless after a magazine of use. The ship's autoloader attached a new set of rails and coils, and loaded a new magazine to each cannon while Katsian watched the smoke clear from the smouldering ring of metal.

"Uh, is that it?" Rutheo asked, her head appearing over Katsina's shoulder.

Katsina stared at the ring she had punched into the bulkhead in confusion. She doubled down on her mathematics of the situation, wondering why the ring hadn't punched a hole. Perhaps the angle was off, or one of the rounds didn't fully penetrate. She couldn't fire on it again, she needed the ammunition for the next hurdle. So she folded the wings inward to take the ship out of its static hover and tilted her head forward ever so slightly. The ship reacted in kind, tilting its nose cone forward, dead centre into the circle in the bulkhead. Katsina pushed the Amber Eyes forward, tapping the bulkhead with the tip of the nose cone. It rang like a bell in the cockpit, the vibration riveting her bones. It left a scratch on the tip of the cone, but it had the desired effect, the circle of metal Katsina cut into the wall slid backward and fell away. Leaving the gap she needed.

"How's that?" Katsina asked Rutheo.

"Not bad."

Katsina pushed the Amber eyes through her newly found portal and entered one of the Behemothis' nuclear plants, one of the more open air spaces of the ship to navigate. Each power plant was connected by a service elevator for the transport of heavy vehicles and equipment, giving Katsina the maneuverability she needed to get to the upper decks. Between the two cooling towers of the plant she flew the ship over a crowd of people, engineers, scientists, and the soldiers who stood with them. The fight hadn't made it to them yet, giving Katsina a pang of relief. She tilted the ship upwards, and found her exit to the level above by following the elevator shaft.

"So you punched through a bulkhead, but the blast shield around the bridge is barely scratchable with those guns. It's reinforced to a point where it may as well be the outer hull," Alice said.

"True, but we put something special together for it," Rutheo said, clapping her hands together.

"We don't know if it will work. It was a weapon's system that hadn't been tested in the field. And honestly I never fully agreed to the concept," Katsina added.

"Do you have a schematic?" Alice asked, "What exactly will it do?"

"Sending them now," Rutheo said, "Enjoy."

The three sat in silence, lying on their backs as the Amber Eyes ascended the rear of the engineering section. Alice read her schematics, Katsina adjusted the pressure in her chest, and Rutheo gazed out at the lights of the ship's power plant's, shimmering through the glass drenched in water. The lights danced about them as they flew, as if driving down a busy city street in the night. It was eerily calming.

"Is this kind of thing even legal?" Alice asked.

"Like I said, never fully agreed with it."

"It's beastly right?" Rutheo said.

"It's barbaric, this kind of thing surely goes against the rules of engagement in space?"

"It does, but we were ordered to install it on a ship and test it. It just never got tested," Katsina explained.

"What ship? The Behemothis?"

"No it's only applicable to fighters; we put it on one of

those," Rutheo mumbled, gazing away in the distance.

"Which one?" Alice asked. Katsina felt a stabbing pain of shame.

"Mara's," she said with discomfort, "we installed it in Mara's. She never got to use it."

"Oh, I'm sorry," Alice said, her voice devoid of its previous curiosity.

"It's okay. Rutheo, double check my combination keys and run a diagnostic on the EMP rod main gun. Just need to make sure we're ready. We're coming up on the operations center."

"Aye, Captain," Rutheo said, unstrapping herself from her seat.

The orange room was typically uneventful. But behind the semi circular dome laced with AR projections, Katsina could see flashes of light on the other side. The maintenance elevator they exited led to either a service corridor with no room for the Amber Eyes to fly, or the backstage area of the dome. So the only way out was through the semi dome.

"Kat, it looks bad on the other side, there's barely any red web connections," Alice said.

"Don't worry. We can have a look in a second," Katsina said, turning her attention to the Amber Eyes ceiling. "Engage full metal jacket."

They positioned themselves behind the semi dome, and the Amber Eyes folded inward on itself, its wings wrapping around the nose cone of the cockpit. Katsina loaded the images of the external cameras in her HUD, giving her full line of sight even with the nose cone covered. The semi dome was made of light aluminums, structurally supported by cables attaching it to the larger superstructure beams. So Katsina knew it would be easily rebuilt, which gave her full reason to drive the fighter ship directly into the wall, crashing through into operations. The ship immediately opened up to show the three of them the battleground that operations had become.

Rutheo unclipped herself from her seat, falling to the floor of the nose cone. She frantically looked from left to right, hoping to find something in the battle below.

"Howard won't be there, Ruthie," Katsina said. "He's been spending most of his time with crisis response. He should be safe with them holding the rear lines."

"I know- I know," she said with a shake in her voice.

"Captain, there's a lot of bodies down there," Alice said.

"I know, Alice. But we can't help them from here, we need to keep going," said Katsina as she glanced down to the scene underneath.

She turned on the floodlights of the ship, revealing the carnage of the coup they'd arranged, and the devastation that Kessler claimed he had caused. The individual stations had been outfitted as trenches, surrounded by makeshift barriers to hide from incoming fire. Swathes of water filled each station as the sprinklers flooded the room. Among the water filled pits, Katsina could see the backs of the dead floating face down, the water running red around them. Most of them wore jumpsuits, or white coats, barely any of them were outfitted for the fight. Only a few had body armor or vests. Among them were soldiers from both sides. Meaning whatever fight that waged, it was already over and they had missed it. No one on the ground could be seen to move, the room, and most inside it, looked dead in the orange glow.

"See the acid burns?" Rutheo whispered. "Just like Kessler did to James."

"We need to help them, someone has to be alive," Alice said.

"Alice, look at the network, can't you hear anything?" Rutheo snapped. "There's no one down there."

"Right, okay. I'm sorry," she replied, hanging her head.

"Let's just keep pushing. Strap back in Rutheo. We're going up."

***

On the main hallway, the fighting had never ceased; it only continued to get worse. The smoke that filled the upper atmosphere of the room made it impossible for Katsina to fly the Amber Eyes over the battle. She had to drop below the layer of smog, revealing herself and the ship to gunfire. The storefronts and cafes that lined the walls were in ruin, some even completely leveled by being shelled from the bow of the ship. The exchange of flashes and pellets seemed unending. Katsina had to get to Morann soon. She brought the ship level with the ground, and landed by the nearest allied encampment she could see with decent cover around it. The distance from one end of the main hall to the other was about seven hundred meters, a large part of it made up of craters and bodies. The various barricades and storefronts providing cover made it easier, but not achievable in Katsina's state. She clambered out of the Amber Eyes with the help of Rutheo and Alice, and made her way into a repurposed liquor shop. The door and glass windows had been completely removed, their frames and broken panes strewn across the floor, savaged by some kind of impact. The scorched walls and floor indicated a fire, but Katsina couldn't see where it came from. Fifteen people were inside, while four more guarded their posts at the entrance. On the floor were five rectangular black bags, each with an ID chip laying on top. At the cashier's counter, the men and women were working on a production line. One stuffing, one wrapping, one binding and one loading while the rest carted trolley's to the front door. The trolleys were full of alcoholic beverages stuffed with makeshift rags.

"What are those?" Alice whispered into Katsina's ears as she held her up.

"They're molotov cocktails," she grunted in response.

"Hey, you guys have any medics?" Rutheo said, slipping out from under Katsina's arm.

Alice helped Katsina sit down, unclipping her harness and jumpsuit as they went. Katsina flinched at the feeling of the material peeling away from her skin. Her vision was shaky as she looked down to see her skin losing its color.

"What's a molotov cocktail?" Alice asked.

"It's a vicious weapon. Used to set enemies and enemy controlled structures on fire," Katsina said, watching blood spill out from under her clothes.

"Surely we have more civilised weapons," Alice said with a frown.

"We did, until they started using acid and fire on us all," a new voice approached.

The voice was twangy, Southern American in tone. It was accompanied by a slim man, wearing a medics uniform, with bandages wrapped around the left side of his face and head. A lot of his uniform was missing on the left side, replaced by the sight of bare, broken, burned skin. Katsina couldn't make out any other defining features, apart from he looked as if he was near burned alive.

"I'm Doctor Martin Asher," he said. "Mind if I take a look?"

"I just need the chest cavity drained, I think." Katsina said, lifting her left arm over her head.

"Her left side isn't rising or falling at all," Alice added.

"Well okay, let's drain it," he said, examining the pump and tube keeping Katsina alive. He turned to Alice, "Can you ask that guy there to get me a bag."

Alice left them to it, and another soldier returned with a clear plastic bottle wrapped in a crinkly blue bag. Katsina turned her head away, trying to focus on breathing. A rattle had developed in her throat, fluids. She hoched, gurgling it into her mouth, and spat out a ball of phlegm and blood. She felt a tugging sensation on her lower back, followed by a light *pop* that caused the pressure in her chest to ease. Katsina gasped, finally feeling a relief from the suffocation.

"That should do it. You had a bit of clotted material in the pipe. You're going to need some more cellular stitching around this wound until you can be operated on."

"That's fine, who's in command here?" Katsina said.

"I am," Martin responded, "We were part of a support team aiding the soldiers ahead of us; they're gone. We're all that's left of the front."

"Sitrep then. Lets go," Katsina said, heaving her chest until it was under her control.

"They have fortified turrets, gas and acid vials. They're using some kind of old flamethrowers on anyone who gets too close. It all seems improvised, but they are capable with them weapons there. They have encampments that are forty men strong on either side of the bridge stairway. They're using some kind of light refracting particles in the gas so we have no line of sight. It's difficult to punch a hole," Martin said.

"Punching a hole isn't a problem, we have laser targeting tech that we can use to help the Amber Eyes get through. How many do we have behind us?"

"Enough to overwhelm them two to one, but a laser targeter won't pass through all that stuff up in the air."

"Good point, get Rutheo and Alice. We need to make a push past their line and mark the blast shield," Katsina said as she looked around for her companions.

"Sure, we just need a couple more minutes for you to get your breathing under control," Martin said, his voice sounding unsure.

Katsina turned her head back to him. He had stepped away from her, the other soldier also stood back on her other side, his auto holster unclipped. Katsina ran her eyes suspiciously around the room, no Rutheo, no Alice. Five or so of the people working on the molotov production line were gone, replaced by others. She activated her HUD's combat suite, marking targets around her.

"What is this?" she asked.

"Captain, please. We were asked to just distract you for a few more minutes," Martin said, his hands raised innocently.

A whirring sound came from outside, while the gunfire began to louden. Katsina pushed up from the counter she rested on, sliding her arm back into her jumpsuit. She ran to the exit to see the Amber Eyes hovering. Alice was in the pilot's seat. Katsina reached for Morann's pistol, forgetting she didn't have it anymore. Someone grabbed her, pulling her down under one of the barricades, it was Martin.

"Please keep your head down," he shouted over the sound of the engines above.

Sparks began to fly off of the hull of the Amber Eyes, as tungsten pellets smashed into its hull, bouncing around the main hall. Katsina pulled her arm out of Martin's hands, and snatched his rifle from his back. He didn't fight back, he just held his hands up. Katsina wasn't ready to deal with his deceit just then. She had to go after Rutheo. She peaked over the wall, using the scope of the rifle to see ahead of them. No sign of her.

"Where is she?" Katsina said, anger pulsating in her words. She turned her attention back to Martin.

"She said she was the only one who could get behind them. Something about the ventilation system."

Katsina knew what he meant, she had chased Rutheo through the vents already, she was small enough to get through them quickly. She used the red network, searching for a connection to Rutheo, but she never answered. She sent a ping to Alice, who also didn't answer. The fighter was too high above ground, laying suppressive fire on the enemy stronghold down the line. A worthy distraction. But Katsina felt fear in her chest replacing the pressure of her knife wound. Rutheo had gone ahead on her own, leaving Katsina with no way forward. She'd already thought she had lost her once. A soldier to her left fell to the ground, a hole punched in his neck, another one dead. A clanking of metal above her head made her glance up to see the Amber Eyes begin to change shape.

"We have to get inside," Katsina said. "We can't be near the Amber Eyes when it goes off."

She grabbed Martin's hand, dragging him to the body next to her.

"When what goes off?" he shouted in her ear, she didn't

reply.

Together they pulled the body with them back into the shop, followed by two others. The wings of the fighter split apart, creating four pointed petals around the belly of the ship. The gears holding the long poles that were attached to the body of the fighter began to spin, unlocking the weapons system. The poles fell from the belly of the ship, stopping in mid air. They began to float around the wingspan that began to slowly spin. The spinning grew faster while the tips of the levitating parts started to glow a bright green. The noise pulsed and boomed around Katsina's ears as tiny sparks and snaps of light filled the area around the Amber Eyes. The new weapons system was prepped.

"Alice," Rutheo said over the comm, "I'm ready. Fire at will."

"Rutheo, Rutheo, you have to stay at a safe distance, that thing will fry you if you're too close to the impact sight," Katsina said. She rubbed her palms into her scalp, scratching her nails into her temples.

"It's a risk you would have taken. I'll be fine," Rutheo snapped back.

"Captain," Alice said, her voice crackling over the soundwaves. "I'm ready, we're ready."

"Alice the ship could tear itself apart!" she shouted. "You're not supposed to be up there!"

"Sure, and I'm not supposed to be up here right?" Rutheo said, anger in her voice. "Kat, I know you wanted to do this alone. I get it. You feel responsible. But if I let you try this stunt in the shape you're in then I would've been breakin' a promise. And I'm not about to break a promise for nobody."

"Faisaheß!" Katsina shouted, snatching a glass bottle and chucking it into the wall in front of her. Katsina felt frustration taking her over, her anger at their subterfuge unleashed.

"Captain, it's alright. Just be ready to move up," Alice said, her voice calm.

"Fine, Okay," Katsina said, walking away from the shop window, leaving the Amber Eyes spinning in its beautiful green glow.

"Target marked," Rutheo said. "Engage."

"Engage," Alice replied.

Katsina watched as debris and rubble began to float from the floor surrounded by zaps and cracks of green lightning. Katsina ducked her head behind a set of shelves, bracing for it. Though she closed her eyes and clapped her hands over her ears, the light that flashed and the sound that it generated was too much. The shelves lifted from the ground. Katsina felt a shockwave throw her from her spot as the room lit up around her in a green and white flare. A burning sensation tore at her back and shoulders and she slid across the floor. Bottles smashed around her, the roof of the storefront fell inward. The great green flash drenched everything in Katsina's view before a shelf collapsed on top of her.

THE TRUTH, NOTHING ELSE

The destruction left in the wake of the plasma discharge had decimated the main hall. The center of the street still glowed hot red from the intense heat that melted metal and charred wood. The white steel buttresses and arches were blackened from soot while glass rained from the ceiling in shards. Katsina could barely make out the shape of anything around her as the entire area was blanketed in smoke and shadow. She had left the operators in the liquor shop to find Alice, but saw nothing left of the Amber Eyes outside. The world spun and shimmered around her, making her stumble as she tried to walk. She used the rifle she had taken from Martin as a crutch to keep herself upright, her hands shaking trying to hold onto it. She looked towards the bridge, seeing nothing but a green glow in the smoke. She couldn't find Alice, or anyone else, so the green glow was her next objective. She had to find Rutheo, or get to Morann. Either. Anything.

What was left of the main hall was smouldering, jagged piles of rubble. Not a single shopfront or restaurant was recognisable, each one just a hole in the wall. Katsina pushed one foot ahead of another, forcing her way up the glowing molten trail. She used the last of her adrenaline pump, and her final dose of stimulants. She could see fire burning, but couldn't hear the crackles of the flames. Everything was doused in a white film from Katsina's eyes, she could still see the flash burned in her retina. The smell of alcohol and burned hair was all her senses really picked up accurately. The rest felt like an impression. Katsina made it to the shattered steps past the remains of Morann's soldiers. Their line was wiped clean. Their bodies charred by the heat. Katsina looked around at each body, trying to find the corpse of a short individual. But none of them looked like Rutheo. Perhaps there was nothing left of her to find. The steps were a difficult climb for Katsina, although her legs had finally stopped shaking. She was more stable on her feet, but that didn't make it much easier. She knew she had little time before Morann's men would regroup. Katsina pushed herself towards the glowing green ring and threw herself into it, leaving the smoke and flames behind.

***

The bridge was dark, the only light source being the green glow from the hole the Amber Eyes had cut. Katsina wheezed. It would probably alert anyone to her presence, but nothing else on the bridge seemed to move, the entire area was static. Katsina pulled up her HUD, which was badly offset, making it difficult to focus. Multiple warnings flashed, one of them for her shallow heartbeat. She used her visual settings to lighten the room, showing her what was left to see. Just bodies, and little else. Morann was nowhere among them. Instead there were soldiers among soldiers. Scattered, bleeding and burned by the blast. Katsina made it to the Captain's chair. Her eyes darted in every direction for Morann, but she saw nothing. Her only chance was to reset her auditory implants and get her ears working again. Without a doctor, that wasn't going to happen. Sparks and flashes dropped from the ceiling of the dome, glistening the various computer stations in light briefly. Katsina dropped into the chair, gasping from her five hundred metre limp. Her chin and neck tingled with a warmth that made her spit out whatever was leaking from her face. More blood. She found the Captain's neural link, and connected to the intercom of the ship.

"We... we have the bridge. Anyone loyal to the war criminal Deacon Morann will lay down their arms. It's over."

Katsina disconnected the intercom, hoping the ship could hear her words, even if she couldn't. Her vision seemed to fade in and out of her control. The orange hue of her HUD flickering away, she felt she could sleep for years to come. But there wasn't time. She still had to get up and finish it. With no way of resetting her hearing, she lifted her hands to her left ear and began to unscrew the auditory implant completely. She felt warm blood on her ears and fingers, making her wonder how much of her was left uninjured. Eventually a sound echoed in her ear as the small metal implant *clinked* on to the floor. She started on the second one. Her natural hearing was dull, ringing, and difficult to make sense of. With both auditory implants unscrewed she could at least hear something. It was barely anything. She could hear her own breathing, the sound of the flames behind her, the cracks of sound each time a spark lit up the room. She lost her ability to hear the connections around her, the comm, the red web, all of it. But she gained the sound of something else. Footsteps to her right, coming closer. Katsina leapt from the chair, just missing the blow of a dark figure that approached. She reached for the rifle, but missed it. It was kicked away. Leaving her to fend for herself. Katsina felt fingers run through her hair, pulling her back and throwing her. She dipped, and threw herself into the person who had her. They both tumbled, and the sound of smashing glass accompanied their fall. Katsina landed on the figure, who grunted in pain, giving her a chance to roll off of them. She finally caught a glimpse of her attacker.

"It's... over... for you... Morann..." she heaved.

Morann lifted himself from the ground, shrouded in his long and tattered captain's coat. He was scraped and burned over his left eye, which was swollen shut. His facial hair was missing, along with one of his ears. He had escaped the plasma blast with his life, but without half of his face. He stumbled to his feet, ripping one of his own sleeves from his arm. Katsina stepped back from him, searching one of her pouches for the device she needed.

"For me?" he grunted. "You think it's over for me? You Yggdrasilain lasine uí nyßolt'Seich."

He wrapped the sleeve around his thigh, nursing a

wound in his left leg. He seemed badly hurt, which permitted Katsina to plan ahead. Her only thought was to get a drop of his blood, to prove he was Yggdrasilian. The drop of blood was all she needed. It was what was going to end it. Morann rose to his feet and lifted his hands, preparing himself. Katsina found the small blood test meter, and held it out for him to see.

"There's no point hiding anymore, Morann. I've lost enough good people because of you. I'm not the traitor here; you are. And *you're* going to pay for it," she managed.

Morann looked down at the meter in her hands, a flash of anger and confusion in his eyes. He looked back to her eyes, a glare of malice radiating from his own. Katsina saw no point drawing it out any longer, she gave him a chance to bind his leg, to surrender. He didn't seem to want to. So she had to make him.

Katsina scraped her foot along the floor, taking up her stance against him. He charged. The two began to dance. Katsina gave him a wide berth, ducking away from his jabs and swings. She looked for an opening in his onslaught, unable to find one without her HUD working. He had the advantage of his HUD and strength. But she was light as a feather in comparison, giving her the advantage of speed. Eventually her breath failed her, and she let herself misstep. Morann connected with her, and the two of them locked into a struggle for the blood meter. Katsina kicked at his leg, pushing him to the ground. But he had his hand around her neck, so he pulled her to the floor with him. She jabbed at his eye with her fist, making him groan and flail. His fist impacted her jaw, causing a *cracking* sound. He jabbed and jabbed again, knocking into Katsina's head, throwing her onto her back. He eventually landed on her, his hands gripping her neck. She threw jab after jab into his chest, but he didn't let go. She tried to get the meter to an open wound, but he refused to let it touch him. They continued to struggle as the sound of footsteps and the sight of flashlights entered the room, they were surrounded. Katsina's throat began to fill with fluids, her breathing had begun to fail.

For the moment she accepted her fate, giving in to the dark that began to cloud her vision. Morann had the support of his men, and the upper hand in the fight. She wouldn't win. The next moment, she gasped as the pressure on her throat lifted away. She coughed, the weight on her chest eased, leaving only the pain of her wound behind. Rolling onto her side, she tried to escape the lights and sounds of the people surrounding them, but she was snatched by a pair of hands, and turned over to see a set of lights in her face.

"Captain," a familiar voice said. "Captain, can you hear me?"

"She has no audio. We need to-"

"Get your hands off me, you traitorous swine! I will see you shot for this," Morann's voice shouted.

Katsina slapped one of the flashlights out of her face and propped herself up to find Morann. She was surrounded by her own people, including Dr. Foye. Around the room navigators and comms specialists had taken up their posts, taking back control of the ship. Katsina heard their voices chattering, bringing each other up to speed with the ship's status.

"Captain, don't move. Your hurt an-"

"Get... get out of my way," Katsina said.

She rose to her feet, using the shoulders of one of the medics as a support. She pushed past Dr. Foye to see Morann. He was on his knees, each of his arms held behind his back. On either side of him, Katsina recognised two faces. One was Rutheo, covered in dust and ash. The other, Alice, her arms covered in burn marks, but otherwise unscathed. A wave of pins and needles ran throughout Katsina's body, a relief she didn't expect. Her moment of solace was cut short by the sound of Morann's laughter. It brought her back to the situation at hand.

"Happily reunited then eh? A pack of traitors and murderers," he said.

"You can shut it!" Alice snapped.

"Ohoho, Alice, such backbone. Ha, I underestimated

you, so I did."

"Kat, do it," Rutheo said. "Let's get this over with."

Katsina still had the blood meter in her shaking hand. She didn't hesitate. She swiped at Morann's neck, sticking the sharp end of the meter into him. The small vial on the side of it filled with blood as Morann scoffed at her. She pulled it away, waiting for it to tell her what she already knew.

"Ouch, you should put some pressure on that," Rutheo said sweetly. "Don't want it to bleed too much."

"Go to hell," said Morann.

Katsina watched the meter load the results, ticking over the little hourglass icon. She relaxed her chest, knowing it was all over. He had nothing to cover his actions now as the lights began to flicker on in the bridge dome, his genetics alone incriminating him and providing enough evidence to pin him to his crimes. But the evidence never turned up. The meter beeped with the test result. No genetic alteration. No biological masking agent. Not a single strand of DNA out of place. Katsina's heart skipped a beat in her chest. She was wrong.

"Kat?" Rutheo asked, "Kat, what does it say?"

"Captain?" said Dr. Foye, joining Katsina's side.

Katsina felt frozen in place, her eyes locked onto the little meter in her hands.

"Captain, what does it say?" Alice asked, her voice in a panic.

"Ha, looking for something that isn't there, are we?" Morann teased.

A heat filled Katsina's mind, an anger she had rarely felt. She dropped the blood meter, and drove her fist into Morann's nose.

"How?" she shouted in his ear.

"How what?" he groaned, a smile still on his face.

"How could that Ygg point to you as the infiltrator? He told Krauss it was you, I saw it!" Katsina said, desperate to understand.

"Oh you witless woman," Morann said, "I don't know how you saw that. But someone lied to you to get to me."

"Lies, you liar!" Katsina said, striking him again.

"You think you can beat it out of me Katsina? Krauss already tried. Don't tell me it didn't cross your mind already. He checked my background, my genetics. I was imprisoned longer than I could remem-"

Katsina punched him again, sending a shooting pain up her hand. "The truth," she said, "now."

"They could have just said it was me you know, just like you're trying to do now. But that wouldn't have stopped the information being leaked," Morann said, blood dripping from his cheek. "They cut into me for days. Trying to get an answer I didn't have. The Ygg lied to them."

"Then why me?" Katsina asked, "was it because of Aardashini?"

His face changed. His smile disappeared. His anger returned with a venomous hatred.

"Don't you *dare* bring my wife into this," he spat.

"You wanted it to be me didn't you? After losing her, because she followed me on the moon," Katsina said, antagonising him. He struggled in Rutheo's grasp.

"You twisted liar! We have had evidence against you since that day. Krauss told me I had one job, to find the infiltrator. To flush it out, or he would have me shot. I saw what you did on that moon, no one could have made an accurate calculation as to the Ygg's ability to fight back. But you knew. You knew their numbers, their forces, their munitions. And you turned on them to cover for yourself. But it didn't work. That's when I knew," Morann ranted to the room.

"Liar," Katsina said, turning away from him.

The room was near silent, no one seemed to move an inch. They were all listening to Morann, hearing his reasoning. The tension had frozen them all in place. Katsina could see it in their faces, had they done the right thing? Seizing the ship. Had they put their faith in the wrong person?

"Then the Roverdendrom, lost to a superior Ygg force after being serviced by the Behemothis a month before. You knew it was going to The Deep. That was my next clue," Morann continued. "So I had Krauss give you the task of getting it back. I told him it would make you reveal yourself for what you really are. And it did."

"What are you talking about?" Katsina said, doubt began to consume her.

"You sent the Delta squadron out to find it before sending your hidden signal out into The Deep. You told the Yggs where they were. You had them slaughtered. The second last clue."

Katsina turned back to him, looking into his eyes. He had no malice, no anger. He wasn't gloating or even exaggerating. His eyes told the truth. He believed he was telling the truth.

"The second last clue?" Katsina asked.

"And the second last nail in your coffin," he said.

"What was your last one?" Dr. Foye's voice interrupted, making them both look at her.

"The Amadellan flu," Morann announced. "The epidemiologists of Terra Horizon traced the outbreak of the flu strain to this ship. They thought patient zero was aboard this vessel. That was until we found some of your comrades' bodies in the Riskus belt. They had it before we did, before your ship did."

Katsina stared at him, stunned. She was taken aback by the influx of information. It all made sense to her, however incriminating it was.

"But we were told it was spread from a colony transport," Dr. Foye said. "Why not tell us this before?"

"What? So she could realise we were on to her? I was too close, I just needed her to make another mistake. She contracted the flu from her Yggdrasilian friends, brought it aboard her own ship and infected hundreds of thousands of our people. She acted as a weapon for them, spreading the virus and weakening the human element of the fleet, every contact trace we ran led us to her," Morann said, freeing his hand from Alice's grasp, pointing it at Katsina.

The room fell silent to Morann's accusation. His revelations stopped their coup attempt in its tracks. Katsina could feel the minds around her changing. Her own people wondered, just as she did, if he was really telling the truth. Alice stepped away from them both, looking at Katsina with fear. Her jaw had slacked. Her mouth hung open and she lifted her hands to cover her shock. It wasn't possible, Katsina knew who she was. She knew what she believed in. She wanted peace for humanity, to end the war, to rid the universe of the Yggdrasilians. She wasn't one of them. She wouldn't be one of them. The sound of footsteps pricked her ears, and Katsina turned to Dr. Foye. She approached cautiously, staring at Morann with concern. Katsina could see what was happening.

"You make a convincing argument, Morann," Dr. Foye said.

Katsina felt a wave crash over her, a finishing blow. She had lost the support of her people. Morann twisted them against her, making her out to be the one that betrayed them.

"But... you missed one crucial fact..." Dr. Foye continued. "Katsina wasn't the person who brought the Amadellan flu aboard the Behemothis. She wasn't the first case on the Broadsider."

Katsina's heart felt as if it had stopped, restarted and stopped again. Her eyes darted to Rutheo, then to Alice and back to Dr. Foye.

"What?" she said.

"You weren't the first case aboard the Behemothis."

"You liar," Morann said. "You think you can protect her? Create a scapegoat?"

"Doctor," Alice said, her voice small compared to the rest of them, "if Katsina wasn't the first case, then who was?"

All eyes and ears had shifted to Dr. Foye. The room was hers. She gulped at the attention, preparing to share her knowledge. As she opened her mouth, another voice interrupted her.

"We have incoming!" one of the navigators shouted. "Dead ahead!"

Katsina turned to see the blast shields of the dome retract, revealing the black backdrop of the deep. In the distance a single light appeared, growing and growing until it filled the view of the ship. Out of the light, the Insurmountable charged into view, arriving directly in front of the Behemothis. It halted its approach, and one of the comms specialists stood up to Katsina's right.

"We have a comm request from Captain Richmond for Captain Morann," the specialist said.

Katsina turned to Alice, who was looking at her in confusion. She nodded to her, letting her make the decision on her own.

"Put it on loudspeaker please. Set up a visual connection," she ordered.

Above her head, Katsina saw the image of Marshal projected into the glass of the dome. He was alone, the space behind him looked like his captains quarters. His calm features immediately contorted to confusion and concern, the comms specialist had connected him to the view of the bridge.

"Kat," he said.

"Marshal? What are you doing here? What's going on?" she asked.

"I believe he has something to tell you," Dr. Foye said. "Don't you, Captain Richmond."

Katsina darted her gaze to Dr. Foye and back. Dr. Foye watched him with suspicion, her eyes squinted while her brow creased. Katsina watched Marshal's face fall into contemplation, then doubt, and then acceptance. He sighed heavily.

"I wanted to tell you under better circumstances…"

"What is this?" Katsina asked, her breath running short. Dr. Foye joined her. She placed her hand on Katsina's back.

"First Officer Richmond was the first case of Amadellan flu that was diagnosed on the Behemothis."

***

The wheezing became difficult to control, making Katsina prop herself up against one of the navigation desks. Her mouth and nose insisted on bleeding regardless of how long she held her hand to it. A tingle in her side made her realise she had very little time left before needing surgical attention. She couldn't take her eyes away from the projected image of Marshal, he looked ashamed, like a child caught stealing from a candy shop. He looked everywhere but at Katsina.

"So your shore leave?" she said, "where did you go?"

"I wanted to tell you…"

"On shore leave, where did you go?" she repeated herself.

"To go see my parents, Kat, they lived on the Free Venture," he said, a sadness grew in his eyes.

"Parents? The signals into the deep? Telling the Yggs about our movements? Mike and Mara were your friends!"

"I did send messages into the deep, but not to the Yggs. To the colony. I swear."

"How was I so blind…" Katsina whispered, glancing to her right.

Morann kept his eyes on the ground, most likely licking his wounds. He was just as wrong as her. Alice kept her eyes on the image of Marshal; tears streamed down her cheeks. Rutheo paced back and forth behind Morann, ashes falling out of her hair as she walked. She still had a pistol in one hand. That hand was shaking.

"I want the truth, nothing else," Katsina said, clearing her throat. "Have you been collaborating with the Yggdrasilians?"

He hesitated again, knowing the entire Behemothis would hear his words. He sighed heavily.

"Katsina... I *am* Yggdrasilian..."

She exhaled sharply, losing control of her breathing. The dried dirt and blood on her face cracked and broke. She contorted in pain. Her eyes no longer contained the events of the previous months. Everything she had done, everything she had worked towards. Gone. In an instant. Her efforts were wasted. She thought back to the day he returned, the day the Behemothis began to get sick. She thought of his home outside of Los Ange, the dust that layered every surface. The messages he could send her, the technology they used to build the red web and take back the ship; Yggdrasilian technology. His people's technology.

"Fine," she said, closing her eyes.

"Kat, I'm not a traitor. I want this war to end just as much as you do and I can-"

"What was the weapon?" Katsina cut him off.

"The weapon?"

"The weapon the Yggs used to displace our fighters and throw Mara and Aaron into a black hole. What is it?"

"I - I don't know, I've been searching for it, like you have."

"Your filthy race has weapons of mass destruction more dangerous than anything else. Surely you wouldn't lie about that." Morann's voice entered.

Katsina turned to him. A flash of fire raged in his eyes. A manic and unsalvageable hatred. A hatred she recognised, a glimpse into her past. The savage warrior atop the hill.

"Our race has only done what it could to defend itself from the onslaught of the other pillars," Marshal said.

Katsina could feel the sweat dripping down the dried dirt on her brow. She was in awe at what she was hearing, what she continued to hear, but she had to dig deeper, to find more answers. She thought back to that evening, with the fine wine they shared, to all the times they had shared before that, years of her life.

"Marshal," she managed, shaking off her uncertainty,

"I'm sorry about Free Venture. I tried to stop it. But please, I need you to tell me what it is. What did they use to wipe Delta squadron off the map?"

"I know you tried, Kat. I can see what happened here. The truth is, we don't know what it is. Our planet has never seen something this brutal either. It's not ours."

"Liar!" Morann spat, "Ygg scum!"

His shouts were met with supportive phrases of some of the men and women that surrounded them on the bridge. Katsina's own crew. Her people.

"Are you lying?" Katsina asked, pressing her lips together, maintaining her composure.

"No," he said, "I have no reason to hide anything anymore, my home, my family... They're gone. Once the men, women and others of the Insurmountable find out, they will try to take me. I can't go willingly, you understand."

Katsina hung her head, rubbing her fingers over her eyes, wiping away the muck. Never had a Ygg willingly allowed themselves to be captured, to have information about them taken or discovered. They would rather die. Katsina understood that. A loud and regular *beep* sounded from the sensor array station across the room. She looked around to see a shocked face on the woman standing at the station.

"Captain, uh, something out there, I-I don't know what it is."

"Describe it then. Spatial anomaly?" Alice said, walking towards the station.

"It's, it's just dark..." she said.

Katsina felt a pull in her gut, a reminder of her dreams. The death horn. The creature that stalked her nightmares.

"If it's not theirs, and it's not ours, then whose is it?" Katsina asked herself under her breath.

"We have an incoming signal. It's coming from that thing!" Alice said. "Kat, I think it's a ship."

THE CLEAVER

The room around her shifted, and Katsina was pulled from her spot by Rutheo. People jumped to stations, dropping their weapons in favour of getting the ship moving. Morann was held by two operators, handcuffed to a chair on the far right of the dome. Katsina, held up by Rutheo and Dr. Foye, climbed the stairway to the captain's chair, where they met Alice. She stood ready at her post as First Officer. At the helm to the right of the captains chair stood Aker Castle, his eyes trained ahead of him, his face strained.

"Aker," Katsina said, "let's run her smoothly today."

"Aye, Captain."

"Ride the lightning," she said, clapping her weary hand on his shoulder.

"Ride the lightning," he smiled.

Katsina eased into her chair with Rutheo's help, and a medic arrived at her left side. The young man immediately began working on her knife wound, applying fresh gauze and cleaning the area around it. Alice settled into her seat, Rutheo stood behind her. The bridge was still a mess of damage and bodies. Dr. Foye couldn't help but protest Katsina's presence considering her condition, but Katsina connected to the ship anyway. Marshal had disappeared from the overhead projection. He had to mobilise his ship too. Katsina didn't know what she was going to do with him. But it had to wait; they had a transmission to answer. The medic to her left began fondling her ears.

"No auditory implants?" he said.

"They were damaged - Alice, get me a sitrep from every section of the carrier and scramble whatever fighters we have left - I had to take them out."

"Okay, uh here, take these; they aren't the best, but

they will do," the medic said, handing Katsina a set of stubby rubber plugs. He was caked in ash, his high-vis overcoat torn and burned. Katsina could barely make out any details on his face under all of the soot.

"What are these?"

"Temporary audio receivers, like your implant, but just not implanted. They sit in the ear canal instead of under the skin. Standard med kit stuff for loss of hearing."

"Weird. Thank you."

"Aye, Captain."

Katsina pulled up her HUD, still displaced and blipping in and out of her vision. She felt her connection to the buds in her ears, and used it to get to the red web. She had to reach Marshal. Messages began to pop up on the tablet handed to her by Rutheo, status reports from around the Man O'War. She skimmed over them, waving her index finger around in a circle at Aker. The Ship began to groan, and Katsina could see it turning away from the Insurmountable.

"Alright, I want all hands at arms. Get the guns prepped," Katsina said.

"Transmission ready to be opened, Captain," A comms specialist shouted

"Keep them on hold for a minute," she replied, focusing on her own communications. "Marshal, you there?"

A voice crackled across the airwaves, reaching Katsina's ears. She didn't hear his voice like she normally would have; instead it came from the audio device in her ear, not in her mind itself. It was an odd feeling.

"Yeah, I'm here."

"Whatever this is, we're going to deal with it. Then I'm going to need you to answer a few more questions," She said, lacing her voice in false confidence.

"I can do that, no problem."

"And Marshal, no more secrets."

"No more secrets."

He still sounded the same to her, his voice, his inflection, his image on the screen before. Everything about him was Marshal. Her closest ally, her First Officer. Katsina couldn't bring herself to see him differently. Because she knew who he was, even if he did lie. Was it possible for her to be friends with a Yggdrasilian? It became apparent to her that she always had been. If Yggdrasilian people were anything like he was, then perhaps there wasn't as much of a divide as she had been taught.

"Alright people, lets keep it tight. I want full coordination with the Insurmountable," Alice called out to the room. "We don't know what it is, so let's stay on our toes."

Katsina looked over to Alice, once again appreciating the girl's new found confidence. She was never going to tire of seeing it; the turtle that finally came out of her shell. She turned her attention back to the glass of the dome.

"Alright, connect the transmission. Put it on the dome for the whole ship to see."

Katsina hadn't prepared for it; surely it wasn't real. The image displayed on the glass ahead of her, it was the old face of Admiral Krauss. He stood resolute, unmoving. His chin tilted slightly towards the ceiling, his eyes bearing down on Katsina. He squinted suspiciously, his lip twitching at the sight of her. Behind him, a set of columns that were adorned with golden filigree laced cables, and dancing frescos on the walls. They reminded Katsina of the chapel aboard the Behemothis.

"Well done Lucas." he said, his voice reminding her of sandpaper.

"What for sir?" she asked.

"I had tasked Morann with finding the infiltrator. It appears he failed. I didn't believe him at first, when he claimed it was you. You are an exceptional soldier after all, but his evidence was sound. That said, he was wrong; instead you completed his task for him. So again, well done."

"Sorry sir, I don't have any ideas about an infiltrator. You're mistaken," Katsina said, building a cool and collected bravado in place of her injured and stressed face.

"Really?" Krauss began, "you think I don't know about Captain Richmond? As if I didn't have the same information you do? This is my fleet, Lucas; I know everything."

Katsina leaned to one side, looking through the broken glass of the balcony to see if Morann was still there. He was still with his guards, so Katsina sent a thread to them on the red web to remove his implants.

"We have an unknown object thirty five thousand kilometres above our port side. I'm assuming you are aware of that too?" Alice said, cutting across Krauss.

"Ah, yes I am. I thought it was finally time for you all to see the latest addition to our fleet."

A schematic loaded onto the screen above them all. A long, flat shape, with a sharp edge on either end. The semblance of an ancient steam liner, but massive in scope. It had no windows, no ports, no hangar bay doors. Just one surface.

"Rutheo, give me a rundown on that thing," Katsina said, trying to hold back a painful sigh while the medic continued to patch her up. He was changing the tubing and filters in her lower back. It was an odd and uncomfortable sensation.

"Oh there's no need, Lucas. We thought it best to give you a demonstration. You see the hull we've developed makes her invincible, nigh impenetrable. She doesn't require guns, pellets, or rods. Instead, she *is* the weapon. We call her: 'The Cleaver'," Krauss said menacingly.

"Captain that thing is picking up speed," Alice said.

"You see, we had to flush out the infiltrator. We knew the Ygg was aboard the Behemothis. So a level of *provocation* was required. I originally thought you would have called upon the Yggdrasilians to aid your Delta squadron, which would have made this a lot easier."

"What?" Katsina said.

"I guessed that you wanted to conceal yourself, letting them die to keep your secret. But that was my mistake; I had bad intel."

"You? It was you?" Katsina asked, her right hand began

to shiver.

"It was an unfortunate miscalculation, but your delta squadron died for a noble cause..." he trailed off.

"And the attack on Los Ange... My court day... You wanted me in Selvin's office," Katsina mumbled, her eyes growing wider.

"A captured Ygg ship, I had it spun up. You had too many supporters for us to convict you. I had to make a decision; you were too dangerous. But now you and I can finish this together, cut out the cancer that is the Yggdrasilian threat. That Ygg has the Insurmountable; I'd rather see it scuttled."

"But those are *my* people, Krauss!" shouted Morann.

"I'll deal with you later, Morann. Your people knew what they signed up for. Shame to lose them like this but we know what the infiltrator is capable of."

"You can't do that sir," Katsina said. Her mind was clouded by shock. Surely he was a man of reason? Perhaps the man was insane. "It's wrong."

"This whole war is wrong, Captain Lucas. My father didn't want to bomb the hell out of the Yggdrasilian fleet, because he knew it was wrong. But without the wrong thing happening, humanity can't do the right thing to move on. That's what he believed."

"What is he talking about?" Rutheo asked. It was the first time she peeked her head up from staring at the schematics of the Cleaver.

"The Yggdrasilian fleet attacked us, how can it be wrong to defend ourselves?" Alice asked.

"Because they didn't attack us, Alice," Katsina said. Her voice began to crack under the weight of her realisation. She thought back to what the Yggdrasilian man in the interrogation room had said. "We haven't been defending ourselves."

Katsina receded into her mind, falling into a black pit of shame and despair. Her own admiral, Krauss, had taken her friends away. In the name of the war. Her fellow captain, Morann, had taken the lives of thousands of innocent souls. In the name of the war. Her own people, the pillars of humanity, stripped her of her innocence, her status as a citizen. Her fellow soldiers, using inhumane weapons against the enemy and even her crew. In the name of the war. A war she didn't start, but one she was raised and taught to finish. A war of hatred, pitting humanity against itself after hundreds of years of peace.

"Kat, Kat, you there?" A voice reached out in the dark.

"Yeah, yeah, I'm here…" she thought.

"My parents told me once that this war is being fought in the names of those who can only benefit from its waging," Marshal said.

"Is that why you infiltrated us? Took advantage of our trust? My trust?"

"I had to keep the people of Free Venture safe. I couldn't do that any other way," he said. "If the people of Free Venture wanted military secrets and intel on your weaknesses from me. They'd have them. But they don't. We don't want them. We don't want to hurt anyone."

"Then what do they want? What do you want?" Katsina asked.

"To take the power away from the beneficiaries. We want the cycle to end."

"Do your crew know?"

"Yes, but they see what the bigger threat is right now," Marshal said.

Katsina paused, knowing what she had to do.

"So do I."

Katsina opened her eyes, rejoining the room around her. She snatched up the tablet to her right and stood up, gauging the situation for herself. The medic at her side quickly followed her, pulling her bodysuit back over her shoulder. The Behemothis, the Insurmountable, and the much heavier Cleaver; oriented around each other like points of an equilateral triangle in space. The Behemothis was damaged by the coup, but functional in most aspects. Not many fighters remained, and by the look of Alice's arms, the modified Amber Eyes destroyed itself getting through the blast shield. Katsina considered the entire armament payload of her Broadsider, wondering would a battle of attrition save them from such a monstrosity. Before deciding, she considered Marshal's words, labouring over the idea of someone benefiting from their efforts to kill each other. She linked to the rest of the red web, asking them for patience. Krauss was still unaware of the red web, so she used it to her advantage.

"Sounds good to me, Admiral," Katsina said, prompting judgemental stares from the crew around her, "but before we do take care of the Ygg scum that has the Insurmountable, can I ask you something?"

"I knew you would come around; go ahead then. What?" Krauss said with a smile.

"That ship is impressive, but I never saw plans or construction allocations in our long term strategy. How did we get it built under such secrecy?" Katsina feigned her curiosity.

"Ah, well spotted. It was a gift actually, the Guardian Church built it specifically to defeat the Yggs and end this war once and for all," he explained gladly.

"Exploration fleet huh? Guardian Church built?" she said, raising her eyebrows. "I understand."

Katsina stood still for a few seconds. Allowing herself to feel the aches and pains left on her from the fight. But not just the coup, the entire fight. The old scar on her shoulder, the line that ran up her face. The various scrapes and burns she had dotted about her skin from the years she'd spent killing others. She looked back at Krauss' face, barely a scratch on it. She had never seen him fight in person. She had never heard of him taking part in a space battle, he always remained in the rear. His church pendant keeping him safe throughout the war. It still hung around his neck, Katsina could see the gold chain. His affix was still adorned with church medallions. Perhaps he also believed what Rendell Kessler did before he died.

"All engines ahead, release all artillery and fire up the

battery pylon," bellowed Katsina. "Tear that god damned ship to pieces."

Krauss had disappeared from the screen, but not before a flare of anger appeared on his face. His skin stretched in a strange way, withered and pulled tight over his bones. Katsina curled her hands around the balcony rail as the Behemothis roared to life under her feet. What was left of the fighter squadrons darted away from them, already firing on the Cleaver ship. The Insurmountable spewed fighters from its hangar doors, allowing them to join Katsina's group. The darkness of the deep began to light up with the flashes of the Insurmountable's artillery while Katsina waited for the words she needed to hear.

"Weapons locked. We have a firing solution, Captain."

Katsina smiled. Finally she'd found the enemy she had searched for her entire life.

"Engage!" she shouted.

The thumping kicks of the Behemothis' guns sent shockwaves around the bridge, lifting the broken pieces of glass ever so slightly up from the floor. Katsina felt the ship growl at her fingertips, it's fury matching her own. An ever growing build up of noise made her retreat to her chair, strapping herself into the harness. The noise and its vibrations peaked, and Katsina watched the cascade of fire erupt from the barrel of the battery pylon. It drove a tungsten missile across fifteen thousand kilometers of deep space at 15 percent the speed of light. Not a single spaceship, meteorite, or small moon could withstand the devastating effects of the two megajoule impact.

"Rutheo, I need a serial number on that ship. Broadcast the specs across all wide band and quantum entangled frequencies," Katsina said, watching the trails of light ahead of her.

"Aye, Captain."

Katsina shielded her eyes from the flashes of light erupting in the distance, the impact of the tungsten rods lit their enemy as bright as a small sun. Blinding at first, but beautiful through the broadsider's filters.

"Direct hit on its starboard side! Ship's computer has a second firing solution," called one of the petty officers below her.

"Hit em' again!"

The Behemothis fired its battery a second time, leaving nothing to chance. A shiver ran up Katsina's spine, a satisfaction that she had been needing for the past months. The revenge she'd promised the court when she was publicly dragged.

"Insurmountable has confirmed two hits with their battery pylon," an ensign said.

"Get us in range of the Insurmountable," she replied. "Send word to evacuate any and all civilian vessels and to prep every military vessel they have on the tarmac. We need to run a salvage operation on that thing and collect as much evidence as-"

"Captain! It's still flying!"

Katsina shot her eyes in the direction of the cloud of hot plasma left in the wake of their attack. Through the cloud, larger than before, the Cleaver ship came.

"What the hell..." Katsina said under her breath.

"Captain," Rutheo called, "we have a serial number, MON-001x01. Monstrosity class vessel. That hull, we barely made a dent..."

"Get me a visual from our fighters. Show me the impact site."

An image blipped onto the dome, showing them what the camera aboard one of the few fighters had seen. A crater, seven meters deep and surrounded by plasma scorch in the starboard bow of The Cleaver. The structure itself remained standing, no collapse had occurred in the hull, no struts had been buckled. The Cleaver zipped past the fighter at incredible speed, as if lunging in the direction of the Behemothis.

"It's coming right at us!" Rutheo said.

"Mr. Castle, evasive maneuvers!" Katsina said.

From where she was sitting, staring out the dome into the deep, Katsina could see the black shape growing. It was coming for her, just like in her dreams. As if her unconscious culmination of treachery and corruption had manifested in The Deep. The Behemothis spun, throwing Katsina to her right side, making her grip the chair. Her harness kept her in place as the ship lunged downward to avoid the incoming attack. But a sudden and devastating crash could be heard in the walls of the Broadsider. Katsina was thrown forward in her seat, reaching for the tablet that was thrown away from her. A dizzying ache ran up her neck. Katsina felt like she had just been in a car crash.

"Damage report!" she said, clutching at her neck.

"Bow Starboard Quarter, they impacted one of our Kugelblitze wheels," Alice replied while tapping relentlessly on her tablet. "It's disabled. Compensating."

Katsina unclipped her harness briefly, making her fall out of her chair. The entire ship was in a spin, and the inertial dampers didn't seem to be working correctly. Katsina made it to her tablet and returned to her seat. She had to crawl on all fours to get past the motion sickness. She loaded back the image that the fighter took of the impact site on the Cleaver, and casted her red web connection back to Marshal.

"You see that?" Katsina thought.

"I see it," he said. His voice was hollow in her mind, he sounded as if he was shivering.

Katsina flicked her eyes over the many filters the camera could show her, radiological scans, heat signatures, alloy density. Krauss hadn't lied to her; the hull of the ship was thick, thicker than anything she had ever seen. And it was fast when it lunged the way it did, as if it defied physics.

"Rutheo how deep do our rods penetrate a graphene weave ceramic armor plate?" Katsina said, staring at the hole on the screen.

"Uh, about, uh three meters? Impact velocity can penetrate that kind of armor at 3 meters."

"How wide is that ship at its minimum?"

"Twenty eight meters thick at each point. One Kilometer at its widest." Rutheo said.

"Then we need to bore deeper. Assume it's got at least 14 meter thick armor. How many rods do we have?"

Katsina didn't hear a response, making her crane her neck to look at Alice. The woman's face was cemented in fear, along with everyone else around Katsina on the bridge. Katsina didn't have to be told how bad the situation was, it seemed futile already.

"Come on, Alice, please. How many do we have?"

"We only have eight left... We've never had to use more than one..."

"It's coming about," another voice called.

Katsina turned back, wishing she hadn't. The Cleaver was heading straight for them again, its sharp end aimed right at the bridge dome.

"Give me a burst on the starboard bow boosters, drop us underneath its belly, Mr. Castle," Katsina said, reclipping her harness. She braced for another impact.

The entire ship rumbled around the crew as the Cleaver passed overhead, the Behemothis groaned with the sound of metal grinding along it's back. Katsina looked above her, watching the lights flicker and shake in their sockets.

"Damage report?" she said.

"It just scraped us, but we have a wide hull breach and we lost some heat shield tiles," said Aker.

"You can tell?" Rutheo asked.

"Course I can, I fly this thing nearly every day, I know how she feels," he said with pride.

"Can you keep us out of range of that thing?" Katsina asked.

"Aye captain, it's as fast as us, but we can turn faster. We can keep away from it, but we can't lose it. With one of the Kugelblitz wheels gone I can't lose it."

"Alright. Keep it up Mr. Castle. Rutheo, Alice, war room," Katsina said, unclipping her harness again. She understood why it was there, but Katsina grew to be annoyed by it. Surely an automatic harness system would be on the drawing board at some stage. Why she thought of such a random irritation in such a moment, she couldn't tell. It certainly didn't fit with the rest of her thought pattern. Perhaps Katsina's mind wanted to think of anything else.

***

The war room was a mess of bodies and smears. A clean up effort was already being made, with crisis response operators removing the dead, tagging their ID's as they went. Katsina sighed heavily at the loss of life they had sustained. She wondered if it was the right thing to take the ship back in the first place, considering Krauss wanted to destroy the Insurmountable, she had to assume it was for the best, since there was no way to change her actions. She awkwardly eased herself into one of the seats around the table while staring at the glitching AR image hanging above them.

"Just a sec, I can fix that," Rutheo said, ducking under the table.

Her legs remained dangled out from the hatch she'd entered, and her voice echoed from inside the table itself. The image became clearer as she struggled with the computer system underneath. The crater they had made in the Cleaver came into focus, together with the specifications of its design that Krauss had given them. They had just enough information to know how dangerous it was, but not enough to kill it. The blue light of the war room felt cold. It was the first time Katsina had been in the room since Morann had taken her as his prisoner. The AR feild began to expand, and Marshal's image appeared next to them at the table.

"Okay. So, we can't punch a hole," he said. "We can't run away, and help is too far for us to wait on."

"There has to be something we can do to figure it out. It must have a weakness-" Katsina began.

"Uh, excuse me?" Rutheo echoed from under the table. "Can I just point out that if it wasn't for *him* we wouldn't be in this mess."

She crawled out as she spoke, and stood with a righteous glare, looking directly at Marshal.

"I know you're upset Ruthie. I lied to you, but right now we-"

"Lied? Lied? You put every one of us at risk. Katsina was implicated as a war criminal. Morann laid waste to everything that used to make this ship home for us. You and your selfishness have us trapped in the Deep with a ship that they designated a monstrosity class. That's insane. Does anyone else not see how much this is his fault." She said, her voice pitched higher with each word.

"Marshal, you betrayed us all. Ruthie, you're upset about it," Katsina said as she leaned forward in her seat, "but right now we have to focus on the task at hand. What's going to help us get rid of this thing?"

"Katsina is right, Rutheo. Let's fix one thing at a time. What do we know about this ship?" Alice said.

Rutheo sniffed and wiped her eyes dry. She eventually took her eyes off of Marshal and relaxed her anger. She began pacing, shaking her hands around her, rotating her shoulders.

"So monstrosity class. That's new; somewhere between Man O'War and Leviathan class I guess. Stupid name. The hull armor is immense, between ten and fourteen meters thick at its weakest by my estimate. It works off of one Kugelblitz wheel, which means the black hole drive would be huge and therefore it would be at the center of the structure. Its surface temperature is hot because it has no vents to eject heat. Its propulsion system is unknown, but we can rule out the use of boosters and aerospikes like ours. It's rough tonnage would be maybe sixty million. That's all I got."

"Good assessment," Marshal said.

"Faisaheß t'Sei," she snapped, all the while keeping her gaze on the ceiling.

"Alright Ruthie, so it's thick hull would require the combined arsenal of our EMP charged tungsten rods. Can we focus our fire on a single point to penetrate it?" Alice asked.

"No, even getting past the hull, the superstructure would remain intact and they would just use emergency bulkheads to seal the decks that are exposed to space. That's if it even has decks."

"Could we discharge some of the plasma from the railguns as we fire? Use it to melt some of the way through?" Marshal asked.

"Again, no. The surface temperature seems resistant to plasma scorching."

"We could create a barycenter? Keep the ships orbiting it, matching its turns so it cant hit us. At Least until help arrives?" Katsina proposed.

"Then we would have to go where it goes. It could easily take us out into deeper space and wait for us all to starve. It's engine is huge, and it seems to only run the propulsion and life support systems. It can last longer than we can," Rutheo said, her voice sounded defeated.

"I have an idea," a new voice entered the conversation. A gruff and ragged tone, the last thing Katsina needed to hear.

Through the sliding doors, surrounded by guards, his hands behind his back, Morann crossed the threshold to the war room. His head was still bloodied, but his wound had been treated. He was just as beaten as the rest of them. He had a slight limp in his right foot as he walked. His captain's coat was missing, leaving him only with a shirt, trousers and boots. He didn't seem as imposing before, no longer a threat to the lives aboard the ship. For once he radiated humility and not theatrical bravado. His chin was no longer held in the air as it always was, his eyes no longer judgemental and cunning. The only thing that gave him a semblance of his former self was his grin; it was the one thing that remained.

"t'Sei befir chasanichen nwan t'Sai," said Rutheo, waving her hand dismissively.

"But I can help-"

"I don't care! You're just as bad as him," she said with vitriol, pointing at Marshal. "Liars, warmongers. Evil, rotten men."

"Rutheo!" Alice said, taken aback.

"He can't help us. He treated us like dogs, worse than dogs. t'Sen ir'ru schural dzalm chusanichen! Your wife should be rolling in her grave! Tá súil agam go ndéana an diabhal dréimire do chnámh do dhroma!"

She switched languages as she spoke, bouncing from traditional and modern speech, leveling insults at Morann in any manner she could.

"Rutheo he's not taking anything, the devil isn't going to make anything out of his spine, and he's going to die just like the rest of us if we don't have a solution soon," Katsina said, raising her voice to a familiar level of authority. Katsina stood up, feeling the ache in her chest as she rose. The knife he had put in her was still there, the tip of its blade resting against her lung. Rutheo was right about him, perhaps not about Marshal, but she was right about him. But for Katsina, the most important thing was to keep them all alive. Meaning Morann's cooperation, however unwanted, had to be welcome.

"What's your idea?"

Morann approached the table, making Rutheo step back out of his way. The guards by his side kept their weapons trained to his memory core at the back of his neck, as if waiting for the chance to end him permanently. Perhaps they wanted him to make a move on one of them, perhaps they needed the satisfaction.

"I heard what you said, about boring a hole in the hull. The little rat is right, it would make no difference, unless you have something to put in that hole…"

Katsina squinted her eyes in suspicion. Her fingers

began to tap on the table while she stared him down. She wondered what he meant.

"If you let me, I can tell you what I told these fine soldiers here," Morann said, raising his eyebrows. He held his palms to the ceiling, shrugging his shoulders. As if bartering. Katsina didn't like where the conversation was going.

"Go on then," Marshal said, "what do we put in the hole?"

THAT WHICH THE DEEP CONSUMES

A pin could be heard hitting the floor in the war room had it not been for the rumble of the ship's engines. The inertial dampeners weren't calibrated after the coup, and the rumbling of the ship reminded Katsina of their situation's fragility. Trapped in space, in a long metal maze, preyed upon by a superior force, Katsina couldn't help but feel slightly claustrophobic. She had stopped tapping her fingers on the table, instead she joined the rest of her crew in their wide-eyed stares directed at Morann, who stood proud at what he had just explained to them. His proposal was terrifying.

"You brought more than one of those things onboard?" Alice asked, her voice shaking.

"Under orders from Krauss, himself. He probably thinks we detonated them both since he didn't ask you about the status of the second one."

"So let me get this straight," Rutheo said, her arms crossed as she paced, "you want us to bore that hole, hoping it will get through to a compartment behind the armor of Krauss' ship. And then you want to fire a big faisaheßul chur bomb into that hole, and disintegrate everything in a six kilometer fireball?"

"I think that summarizes my idea, yes," Morann said.

"The hubris…" Alice muttered.

"What kind of man would think of detonating two weapons of mass destruction in one day?" Marshal asked.

"It may not even work," Rutheo added.

"I'm open to other ideas if anyone has them," Katsina said to the room, "anyone?"

The silence returned, giving Katsina a moment to consider her options. Morann, the narcissist and the newly infamous war criminal, had the only option that was worth considering. Katsina felt the cold on the back of her hand, she needed a hospital. She snatched it away from the table as her breathing stalled, frightening her momentarily. She couldn't condone the use of such a weapon, regardless of the good it would do. What Morann proposed was immoral.

"Don't you see, Lucas?" Morann said, his voice lower than before. He spoke only to her.

"See what?" she asked.

"It doesn't matter how war is fought; it's always been an atrocity. There is no right or wrong way to kill other people," he said.

"You would know all about that," Marshal barked. "Those were my people, my family you wiped off the starmap."

"And what about her?" Morann asked. "What about Katsina Lucas? The great war hero, the longest list of confirmed kills of any pilot, any ground operator."

"What's your point?" Katsina asked.

"My point? It's simply this: you've killed more with much less. The weapon is irrelevant."

Katsina paused, her face hardening into a blank stare.

"Alice, have our computers sync up the targeting parameters of the Behemothis, the Insurmountable, and all remaining non-Man O' War class vessels inside it. Rutheo, select where you believe the armor on that ship to be the weakest so we can determine a firing solution. Morann, I will need your launch codes-"

"You can't be serious-"

"Katsina, I don't think-"

"Captain, there has to be-"

"My decision is made; that ship has to be stopped," Katsina commanded. "It killed our own people and the ts'ßolfé know how many others. Krauss has perverted the rules of engagement and assigned lower ranking officers to tasks amounting to genocide. He decided to stop fighting fairly first. Not me."

Katsina felt eyes all around her; she was exposed. Her voice cracked before she could finish. Her emotions got the better of her. She ran her tongue over the scar on her lip, lightly biting it in frustration. She took a deep breath, and another, over and over until she felt composed. Her lip stopped quivering.

"You have your orders. After this, there won't be any more fighting. If you think differently about me for doing this, then so be it. But we are doing it."

She had no more to say. In her mind, she felt she could be content with never saying anything again. Katsina had finally learned something that she hadn't realised she'd been thinking about in all the time she had spent fighting for the cause. That she was never going to be redeemed, that there was nothing heroic in fighting a war. Perhaps the Yggdrasilians could be considered heroes, defending themselves initially. But at some stage, the fighting had to stop. For Katsina that stage was here, now, against Krauss. She had no false narrative driving her anymore, no multifaceted lie to make her follow what she was told. Her promised reward of a peaceful life and a warm bed on a safe and happy planet had never been in reach.

Her left shoulder still felt off without her Affix sitting on it; for the longest time, she'd wanted it back.

"I'm just going to have to learn to live without it," she muttered.

Katsina turned to Morann as the others left the war room.

"I'll need the launch codes for that weapon," she said.

"Ah, that's the part we will have to negotiate on," Morann said, leaning his head forward, jeering.

"No we don't," Katsina said, holding out her left hand to the guard behind Morann, "because I'm only making one offer."

A cold metal object landed in her hand, its grip and weight familiar. The glimmer of gold on the grip was smeared with dirt. She had lost it earlier but was glad to have it again.

She unlocked the safety and pushed the dangerous end into Morann's temple.

"You give me the launch codes, and I won't let the countless souls aboard this ship have their way with you when this is over," she said, her voice laced in lustful anger.

"Ooooh, I see," Morann said. "So no protections or pardons for helping you deal with the rogue Admiral then?"

"I don't see any reason to repeat myself."

Katsina pulled back the autoloader switch, making the slide of the pistol jolt back and forth, placing a round into the chamber.

**

The bridge was no longer a center of operations for the ship. Instead, it had shifted its shape, forming a new area where the captain's balcony sat at the front of the dome. The dome itself had raised its blast shields, and the glass started to mirror what the external sensors showed them. The color of the room changed, darkening as the threat level increased. Soon it looked a lot closer to Morann's lighting preferences than Katsina's. She tried to ignore the similarities between her actions and his. The room felt uncomfortable for making her think about it. A lot of the crew had departed the bridge, leaving only Katsina, Lieutenant Castle, Rutheo, Alice, Morann, and his two guards.

"Captain, the Combat Information Center is ready and the automated firing system is primed," Alice said.

"Alright, good work," Katsina said, her mind further away than it should be.

"Uhm, we just need the launch code for the payload. I can enter it here," she said.

"No," Katsina said, snapping back to reality. "I mean, no Alice, it's alright. I can do it."

Katsina looked out at the empty reach of space, knowing that Krauss was just behind them. It was peaceful until humanity had interfered. She dipped her head and looked at the display on the console.

There were five blank spaces, each to be filled to activate the launch sequence of the warhead. Katsina lifted her finger, her voice groaned solemnly. "I.. D.. D.. Q.. D.. Engage."

Morann's words from the days before echoed in Katsina's mind as she gave her orders:

Eventually, you will have to own up to your true nature, Lucas. You will have to come to terms with what you are, what you chose to be. The liar, the murderer, the heartless wretch we all know you to be.

The Behemothis drove itself into a turn at the hands of Lt. Castle, prompting them all to find their seats. The external sensors showed them all they needed to see as if they'd attended a theater to watch the carnage unfold. The Cleaver ship narrowly missed them, scraping its sharp end off of the blast shield, bending it inwards to crack the glass of the dome. The impact threw Katsina to one side, only her harness kept her in place. The main gun whirred to life, while an echoing *clank* signaled the loading of a tungsten round in its chamber. The Insurmountable appeared underneath them, its main gun lined up neatly to theirs. On either side of the ship, Katsina could see the wingtips of fighters, frigates, anything that was housed in the Insurmountable. Ready to aid them. The crosshairs ahead of her showed the center mass of the Cleaver coming into view. The ships around her moved as one.

"Captain, we have the firing solution locked."

A few more seconds passed.

"Fire!" She said.

The ferocious waves of energy that ran through the ship shook the bridge as she watched every vessel around her unload into a single target on the port side of the Cleaver. The tungsten EMP rounds and rail gun accelerated pellets battered the middle of the ship, which tried to turn to make another pass. Katsina wasn't going to let it.

"Mr. Castle, match that ship's pivot and keep us on par with the broadside. We're not letting it turn until we punch a hole amidship."

"Aye Captain."

The main gun fired again, causing the pain in Katsina's left side to spike as the ship rumbled. Her nails dug into the leather of her seat, keeping her grounded as she forced her way through it. Another blast, and another. It continued punching her back into her seat every single time. The lights ahead could have been confused as a firework show; Katsina had never seen so many ships laying down fire on a single target. Just as she had gotten used to the lights and sounds beating into the Cleaver ship, it all ended. The lights disappeared back into the dark, and the noise left only a ringing in Katsina's ears. How she expected her body to recover from it all, she never knew. It was mostly a blind hope that she could heal one day. But that wasn't her concern for now.

"Status of the enemy vessel?" she asked.

"Waiting for it to clear the plasma cloud," Alice said.

The plasma cloud was the only light remaining from the guns. Trails and wisps of glowing ionised gas that had the most beautiful colours. The purple and yellow clouds lit up the ships around them. Katsina wondered how something so violent could make her so awestruck. She closed her open mouth, snapping her teeth back together as the cloud began to fade, revealing the Monstrosity class ship emerging from behind it. It was aiming to strike them again.

"Get some floodlights on that ship. Mr. Castle, get us back on its broadside. Let's go," Katsina said, leaning forward to see if they had penetrated its hull.

The Behemothis moved, flying over the Cleaver ship to dodge its incoming crash. An unholy eruption from behind her made Katsina throw her eyes over her shoulders. But she saw nothing, she could just hear it.

"Hull breach on G deck in crew housing. Emergency shielding in place. Crisis responders en route," Rutheo said.

"Mr. Castle, get us out of range and someone get me some surface scans of its hull," Katsina said, flicking through the torrent of images she was receiving from other ships.

Eventually, she found a detailed image, 80 terabytes in size, a large panoramic by a survey cruiser that was docked inside the Insurmountable. Katsina pushed the image from her mind, displaying it on the screen overhead.

"Bollocks..." Rutheo said.

The image showed the long charred hull of the Cleaver, with a crater six hundred meters wide, but barely any deeper than they had cut before. With all the ammunition they could muster to support the only chance of escape they had left, Katsina had failed to put a hole in the Cleaver.

"How is that possible?" Alice asked the room.

"I don't know. I just, I just don't know," Rutheo said, defeated.

Katsina sunk in her chair, her hands rested on her forehead, pulling on her brow as hard as she could. She had no other ideas. The way the Cleaver lurched at them was unlike anything she had seen, it was too difficult to dodge. As if it was being pulled through space with an unstoppable force, unable to slow down once it started. Its momentum was terrifying.

"Captain, we have a deserting vessel. A fighter ship just left formation," Lt. Castle shouted.

Katsina's head snapped out of her hands and she looked at the screen to see a tiny shape speed away from the collection of ships they had amassed. At the same time, a blip popped up on her HUD, a voice comm. She answered as quickly as she could, realising what was happening.

"What the hell are you doing?" she said, terror in her words.

"Kat, he wants me. So I'm gonna let him have me," Marshal said, his words soft as a pillow for her to lay on.

"No, no, no you can't do that. We can beat him. He's going to try to take you and then kill us all anyway. If you come back we can try and beat him. We can try-"

"Kat, look at the plasma trail. Look at what it's doing," he said, making her shift in her seat.

The last wisps of glowing plasma trailed away from them. Like paint being smeared on a canvas, it was dragged across the backdrop of the deep as it faded.

"The rules of the universe apply to everyone, Kat. We can make gravity on the ships sure, but we can't get away from it. The Behemothis is correcting for gravitational pull every minute. But that doesn't mean it's not there."

His voice cut out of range as the fighter got smaller and smaller in the distance.

"Get him back. Rutheo, put him on the long range dish and get him back," Katsina said, panic-stricken.

"Kat… that was the long range dish…" she croaked.

"The Ygg abandoned us, huh?" Morann said. "Anybody a believer? I guess we could pray, or we could chant? Hold a prayer circle or something. How about Mass?"

"Can't you just shut up!" Rutheo said.

"Wait, Rutheo. Wh-what did you say?" said Katsina.

"What? I'm just saying we're all going to die. A prayer or something might work out," Morann said.

"No, you f-, ugh ts'ßolfé. Mass! He was talking about Mass!" she shouted.

"What?" Alice asked.

"Ruthie, you have size and shape, what's the approximate mass of a ship that size?" Katsina said excitedly.

"Uh, níl is agam. It would be like-"

"It doesn't matter! It's got more mass than us right?" Katsina asked.

"Of course it does," entered Alice.

"And gravity affects all mass right?"

"Yeah… where are you going with this?" Rutheo asked.

Katsina looked back at the screen to see the Cleaver

push itself away, following Marshal's wake through the cloud of plasma. Katsina realised where he was going, and it was a ludicrous idea. She let out a grin. There was only one place the wisps of plasma would lead them in the Deep.

"Krauss is following Marshal. Castle, get us on the tail of that thing. Let's go!"

"Aye captain, going intersolar," Lt. Castle said.

"Mobilize," Katsina called.

The lights bent and warped away from them as they left the rest of the ships behind. They launched further into the Deep, following the chase of the millennium. Katsina's heart pounded in her chest, pulsating her new injuries to the point of severe discomfort. But she gritted her teeth and ignored it. Apart from themselves and the other ships around them, there was only one other thing in the deep. A celestial body thought to have taken up the entire mass of the region, but it was in fact relatively small. The Behemothis fell out of intersolar speed, causing the warped lights to disappear in an instant. They were replaced with the only light that penetrated the deep. For something that was considered small by science and nature, Katsina couldn't bend her head around how massive it was. The head of anyone who looked at it too long would hurt. The physics behind them infinitely difficult to understand. But the Behemothis arrived in its domain, and Katsina stared into the eye of Comedenti. The stellar black hole that resided in the center of the deep. The disk of light and burning matter that flowed around it was immense, its optical effects boggling to look at. Even after all of man's advancement, Comedenti, and other black holes, were still mysterious.

"Found them Captain, far edge of the accretion disk," Lt. Castle said.

"Jaysus," began Rutheo, "any closer and he'll be trapped."

"Not if he pulls off an Oberth maneuver," Katsina said.

"You think he's going to slingshot around?" Morann

asked.

"-And let Krauss get trapped in the pull of Comedenti as he tries to follow him," Katsina finished. "That ship can't arrest its speed when it lunges, it will get stuck."

"But… why isn't he moving?" Rutheo asked quietly.

Katsina looked at the display screen, noticing a halt in the Cleaver's trajectory, both of them orbited the accretion disk, facing each other. Katsina frowned in confusion, the astronautics projection must have been mistaken. She pulled up her HUD to link with the ship, forcing it to open the blast shield of the dome. Light began to bleed through into the dome, beginning as a strip between the panels that retracted around them. Eventually, the glare was compensated for, and a tiny dot was visible on the edge of the disk ahead of them.

"Get us in range, Mr. Castle," Katsina said.

"Captain, any closer and we would be caught in the disk. We won't be able to leave it," he replied.

"We have to get him. His engine must have been stalled…" she said.

"Kat," Rutheo said, her voice soft and caring, "he can't come back out."

Katsina's chest tightened at the sound of Rutheo's words. Her eyes began to well, her cheeks burned as she swallowed back the excessive amount of saliva that began to build on her tongue. Surely his plan wasn't to sacrifice himself, a slingshot would have saved them all. Was that not his plan? Katsina understood the mechanics of gravity. She knew nothing could come out of a black hole that wasn't hawking radiation.

"Do… do we have uh, do we have a comm link?" Katsina asked the room.

"We do," Alice said in a somber tone, "but it's unstable. We would only have a few minutes."

Katsina pulled her cables out from the back of her neck and lurched out of the chair, turning her back on the dome and the rest of them.

"Mr. Castle, maintain our orbit and correct for any deterioration. Alice, connect me to him. I'll take it in the Captain's quarters."

"Aye, Captain."

The captain's cabin was all but trashed. It resembled the back alley behind a junk store or a thrift shop. Morann's family trophies were in pieces, strewn across the glowing orange panels. Katsina didn't pay attention to the mess as she walked towards the far corner of the triangular space. The pointed end of the room was to the bow of the ship, giving her a perfect view of what was below. She approached an old trunk that was in that corner and pulled it out of the way so she could sit down. She placed her hand on the glass and it began to change color, slowly shifting to white, then fading transparently to allow the light from the outside in. The glass was cold on Katsina's shoulder as she slowly slid down onto the floor, easing her weight onto her left thigh. The glass corner pinched her head slightly as she leaned into it. She stared down at the black hole below. It's darkness consuming all things. Even her.

"Kat.." a strained and static ridden voice entered her ears, "Long time no see."

"Hey, you okay?" She asked, staring down at the small black dot, knowing he was near it, somewhere, falling infinitely.

"Better than you'd think. It's been a few weeks for me since we fought Krauss. Time-"

"-dilation was a bitch," Katsina said with a sniff. "You always say that."

"Ah, I know. It's true though. I had to wait ages for you to turn up. I was bored out of my mind here."

"Maybe if you actually did the slingshot you wouldn't have been waiting so long. Besides, it was only 30 seconds..." Katsina said, trying to feign sarcasm. She did it poorly.

"I did, but he got me, pushed us both in when he did though. Either way, same effect, the job is done and we can all go home. I mean, I can't but uh... Well, you know what I mean..."

"I know, I know. I'm..." Katsina whimpered, the tears became uncontrollable as they fell down her nose.

"Don't say you're sorry now. I'm the one that lied. I thought that if I told you what I was doing then you'd hate me, Kat," Marshal said warmly. His voice low as a whisper.

"I know, but not anymore. I don't hate you," she said.

"That's good to hear. I'd be so pissed if I had to die with you hating me."

The glass under Katsina began to turn red, she was still bleeding. Her right hand looked pale as she pressed it against the pane. She tried to convince the universe to give him back to her through sheer will. But gravity was unforgiving.

"How much oxygen do you have left?" Katsina asked, her voice struggling to leave her throat.

"Ah, a few days. But it's getting pretty hot in here. I turned off all the major systems to keep the oxygen recycler going and the comms online," he said, seemingly cheerful. But sniffing, struggling, just as Katsina was.

"I'd be so pissed if you made me wait this long to talk. Ha"

"There's no point in being angry anymore, Kat. We found out who took our people from us. It probably wasn't the answer you hoped for, but I can't be angry anymore. I don't have the time to be..."

"I'm sorry about your parents, I... I tried to stop him..."

"I know you did. Rutheo kept me up to date with everything. She's a great kid."

"That great kid would kick your ass for calling her that, Richmond," Katsina joked.

"She would, yeah, that's why I love her. And why I love you, hell the whole crew you put together. The people we've worked with. Despite everything we've done, least I know we were good people," he said, beginning to pant.

His breathing seemed labored, his lungs struggling to

keep him talking. Katsina knew all too well the feeling. A cockpit boiling slowly as it was bombarded with heat. A sob or two left her chest, her will to keep her control finally diminishing.

"Are you scared?" she asked.

"No, actually I'm hopeful..." he said, his voice laced with static and interference.

"Why?"

"Because I never thought I'd see you grow the way you have; only hoped. You've always been a good soldier, Kat, and a better leader. Your compassion for the crew was always unique to you, and now? Now I see your compassion reaching not just to your side of the war, but to my side as well. We've always wanted peace... I think now... we can finally have it."

Katsina listened to his voice and the hope it radiated. The idea of a future she couldn't see clearly yet. A future he would never see. The glass began to fog, the condensation of her breath obstructing her view. The static grew louder in her ear, as did her weeping. The pain, the immense pain, it finally began to eat her from the inside. Katsina felt something leave her as the string through space that connected them both began to flicker away.

"Marshal?" She whispered.

"Yeah... Ka... here..."

Eventually, the static stopped, and Katsina was left with the ringing sound in her ears, accompanied by her intermittent sobs. Her shoulders shook against the solid glass which had turned warm from her touch. Katsina considered her circumstances again. She paused, floating deep in an unmapped region of space. She thought about shrugging her shoulders. She had every excuse to do it. She thought about hanging her head, succumbing to the end. She could if she wanted to, no one would think less of her. Sitting in a red pool, beaten and shaken, Katsina considered it to be easier if she just stopped existing. Something she had never thought about before. But, if what Marshal said was true, that was the last thing she could do. Katsina lifted her hand from the glass, and stood up in the face of the black hole. The all-consuming giant that, to her, seemed to want her to give in while it swallowed Kraus and Marshal's ships. But she didn't. Katsina struggled to her feet for the last time and turned her back to the war she had waged her entire life.

THE FIRST OF MANY

Katsina had never spent so long writing up an after action report in her entire career. Pages and pages of digital text, illustration, and multiple memory files were needed from many crew members to complete her transcripts. Though she had been asked many times by Dr. Foye to rest and sleep, she found it difficult to do the latter. So instead of sleeping in her assigned hospital bed, she used it as a makeshift office for ship personnel to come and go. Like her ship, though she was injured, she still had work to do. The Behemothis was damaged almost beyond field repair, just short of being crippled by the beating it had taken from the Cleaver. The coordination efforts between the Insurmountable and the Behemothis had shown a new, cathartic change to cooperation between the men and women under Katsina's command and Morann's. An outcome Katsina didn't expect.

Out the window of her temporary office, a playground bustled full of life. Children and parents of all shapes and sizes played together, smiling. The far off sound of laughter filtered through the projection, accompanied by the sounds of birds and even the odd bark of a dog. Katsina took time each day to enjoy the sounds and sights of the imagined landscapes that lay outside the windows, making a note of details that made her particularly happy while she recovered. The wound in her side had finally been operated on and closed once and for all, though shrapnel still remained. The scarring left over from the broken blade felt bumpy and uneven under her fingers, its impact left on her for good. Synthetic tissue regeneration and blood replacement enhancers made recovery easier, but in all of humanity's advances, the mind was still the hardest to heal. Katsina's particular effort was to process as much as she could, leading her to the only conclusion she could reach, to keep going. That was why on the third day after the Cleaver attacked them, she had a visitor she didn't particularly want to see. But needed to see.

Through the sliding glass door, supported by a wooden cane, his jacket draped over one shoulder, entered Morann. His bruises seemed as bad as hers, one of his eyes still swollen, his face in a constant flinch. Katsina hadn't seen him since that night on the bridge, knowing that seeing him before she was ready would set her recovery back a few days. She didn't have time for that, neither did the Behemothis. Morann remained standing next to an open seat, opting to drop a satchel into it instead. Katsina adjusted herself in her hospital bed, squaring her shoulders and keeping her chin trained to the ceiling.

"Ah, don't look at me like that. I come in peace," he said, his voice drained of his usual dramatic flare.

"Commander Wesley informed me you had something you wanted to say. I'll listen to it, then you will return to your own room until we return to Botanica," Katsina said, her voice still hoarse.

"Yeah, well, I'm not a stupid man. I'm not a smart one either, that part I've recently learned. My men recovered these, they were left on the tarmac of my ship. I thought it best you have them."

Morann rummaged in the satchel with his free hand, leaning on his cane as he bent down. From it he produced an ID chip, and a golden affix. He tossed them into Katsina's lap.

She pulled the various tablets and cables out from under the affix, and looked into the medallion in it's center. It bore Marshal's name, rank and signature. The ID chip was listed with his serial number and a glowing relief of his thumbprint. Katsina stared at the thumbprint, running her own thumb over its grit. Her bottom lip quivered, making her instinctively bite it, reminding herself who she was with.

"Thank you for this. Or thank your men, I should say. I didn't realise he left them behind."

"Apparently before leaving he traded his captain's Affix

for his old first officer's one. That's what I'm told," Morann said.

"Alright, anything else?" Katsina said with a sniff. She avoided looking at him, keeping her eyes on the playing children on the projection.

"Yeah, I brought you this," Morann said, tossing another heavy item into her lap, "Hindsight is twenty twenty, or uh, six six as they Europans say. I know now that I should never have taken this from you. That's all I have to say."

Katsina heard him turn on his foot as she looked down at the second affix in her lap. Much more worn and scraped than Marshal's. It was hers. The click of his cain on the floor made her glance up to look at him. A broken and defeated man with nothing left to offer her, but Katsina had something to offer him.

"Wait a moment," she said with a sniff, making him pause at the door. "I read the ship's logs the last few days. Over the last six months the work you have done aboard this ship was nothing short of dehumanising, malevolent, and borderline cruel. Particularly toward my crew. However, I see from your command prompts, as well as corroborating information from Alice, that you received strict instruction to perform the way you have from Admiral Krauss. He instructed you and your crew to act in an adversarial manor towards my people. Is that correct?"

Morann tilted his head back, a deep sigh leaving his chest.

"It's no excuse, orders or not. I did what I did. If I had known that Krauss arranged the execution of your team to flush you out I would have shot him myself. He used what that Ygg in the interrogation room said against me. He used the fact that my wife left to fight with you against me. He threatened the destruction of my ship, to strip me of rank without trial. We attended church and read together many times. We were close because of it. I should have looked past it. But I followed him, knowing what he was like."

"According to your crew they had never seen you act this way before. They say you're a great captain, they trust their lives to you and the late Captain Kessler," Katsina said.

"And your point?" Morann said, turning back to face her.

"I have determined that your crimes have been a direct result of the influence and incitement of the rogue Admiral Krauss and as such you are to be pardoned on certain counts for this reason. When repairs are finished you will be returned to the Insurmountable and escorted home to aid in my debriefing of the admiralty board," she said, albeit with difficulty.

"You don't have to do that…" Morann said, his eyes trained on the floor, avoiding her gaze.

"You acted the t'secheashin," Katsina clipped. "This is not a full pardon, when you return to Botanica you will serve penance for what you've done. But, the help and aid that our ship received in the past three days was only given under your orders, or so I'm told. Which means there is a good man in you somewhere, I saw it first when you stood up to Krauss that night."

"You say that, but I don't see it. You and your ship found the real threat to humanity. You did what I was tasked to do and you did it better than I could have. The Ygg… Uh, Captain Richmond, saved the lives of my people as much as he saved the lives of yours. Personally I never thought I'd owe my life to one of them. But here we are," he said, turning back to the door.

"Morann…"

"What?" he droned.

"I'm sorry about your wife. I didn't know her. But, from what I saw, she was a fine soldier," Katsina said, bearing compassion in her words.

"She wasn't just a fine soldier," said Morann as he opened the sliding door. "She was the best of us… I think that's why she followed you."

Morann slipped out of the room without another word, his shame left in his wake. Katsina's eyes remained on the door as it clicked shut, his words remaining in the room with her.

***

More days passed, and Katsina's report was taking shape. Soon she would be able to leave the hospital and not have to listen to Dr. Foye's advice about receiving therapy. Katsina had all the therapy she needed thanks to Rutheo, who visited her every day, providing every ounce of entertainment for any weary soul aboard the broadsider. Had there not been a war, Rutheo could have been a thespian in Katsina's mind. She never could sit down for more than a few minutes, but when she did, it was on the end of Katsina's bed or on a table instead of an actual seat. Her jumpsuit lay on the floor in the corner, she sat in a tank top and a pair of shorts while she took a break from her work repairing the ship. Her hands-on approach to being the chief engineer always left her filthy, like a pig in mud; she loved it.

"So then he said, 'Oh, they went to the moon? What they thought we had land up there too?' The man was hilarious!" she said, hunched over with laughter.

"I don't get it?" Katsina said, confused.

"Cause you know, colonialism and all that? It's a Cherokee joke; the context is the time period I guess."

"Fair, ancient history was never my bag," Katsina said.

"Yeah, well we all know you prefer astro trajectories and interstellar physics so it's fine," Rutheo said, the happiness draining away.

Katsina leaned forward, pushing her bedside tray out of the way. She reached out to Rutheo, who jumped off the bed after noticing her approach.

"It's fine," she said, wiping her nose. "Just hard is all."

"I know Ruthie. I feel the loss too. I'm torn up as well."

"I'm not torn up. I'm *mad* Kat, I'm so faisaheßul mad.

He could have told us everything. We knew him, he fought against Yggs with us. He could have told us and we could have helped him," she said frantically.

Katsina couldn't imagine what she had to say at that moment. Rutheo thought so well of her that she assumed Katsina would have done the right thing before. But she couldn't even tell herself, if she could do the right thing; in her mind she didn't know. The silence was a sudden departure from the jokes and laughter, Rutheo as always, suffering more than her exterior could show.

"He would want us to talk about it, Rutheo," was all she could manage.

"Yeah…" she sniffed, "I know. But not yet. I want to get the tarmac finished first. Couple more days and we should be good on that front."

"Second major replating of the tarmac in just a month; never thought I'd see that."

"Yeah. Well, you did go all nineteen sixteen on the place. Looked worse than the Easter Rising when we started cleaning up."

"Ah, now there's a reference I can relate to," Katsina said with a smile.

An old song came to her mind, one that Rutheo had taught her many years before, she began humming the Irish tune. Rutheo even chimed in.

Katsina watched her face change, a painful frown followed by a realisation. Followed then by an accepting nod, and a toothy smile that could beat all others at a beauty pageant.

"You know, that report could end up being a great book," she said, glancing down at Katsina's pile of disheveled tablets.

"Ha, maybe I would go as far as a dissertation. But a book? I'm no author."

"You never know," Rutheo said, pulling up her jumpsuit and zipping it back on. "The story of the warrior who learned to love her enemy? I'd read it."

"Rutheo, you hate reading," Katsina said.

"True," she laughed, "I'll watch the movie though."

"Alright, back to work grease monkey."

"I want some royalties though, and that actor, whatsername with the black eyes and the cool tattoo? She's playing me," she said, throwing a pair of finger guns at Katsina as she backed towards the door.

"In your dreams!" Katsina called after her. Making Rutheo pop her head back through the door.

"She's in them like *every* night," she said before sticking out her tongue at Katsina.

She disappeared, leaving Katsina with a smile on her face yet again. As close as she was to Marshal, she knew Rutheo looked up to him. In a way, it probably hurt her more than anyone else. Katsina returned to her work with a much brighter attitude that day.

***

If Katsina could appreciate anything in the universe, it was the advancement of modern medicine. She didn't need pumps or multiple surgeries to fix her body, her implants and core function did it for her. The feelings of throbbing bruises and burned skin slowly fell away, literally, as her old skin began to shed. But some scars would never leave her, like the one on her right palm from the gravity shift, the one that split her lip on the day that Los Ange was sacked, and the cluster of scars in her chest. They all remained as the rest of her injuries faded away. Soon she could get out of bed and perform her usual routine of exercising, though she still couldn't leave the hospital. She couldn't do as many push ups as she used to, but her strength slowly returned. Each day the burning sensation in her muscles took longer to set in. Eventually Dr. Foye brought her the news she needed.

"No rest for the wicked huh?" she asked, watching Katsina bounce up and down off the floor.

"How, is, the, crew?" Katsina huffed while doing her push ups.

"Good, we have no cases left of Amadellan flu, all bullet punctures, knife wounds and acid burns that could be healed are done. Few people still remain in observation but most are discharged with bed rest and a prescription of family time."

"Do we have a final number of casualties?" Katsina said, resting herself to the floor.

"Yes, a total of eight hundred and twenty nine souls lost aboard the Behemothis, and one from the Insurmountable. No casualties on the three frigates that were on the Insurmountable," she said.

"Eight hundred and twenty nine..." Katsina repeated.

"Yes."

"Seems low considering we lost over ten thousand last week," Katsina said, a hint of sarcasm in her tone.

"Casualty reports and the investigation into Morann's nuclear strike are still ongoing. Alice should have a report for you on that soon."

"Alright then, if that's all?" Katsina said, lifting off the floor back into her push ups.

"Actually no, it's not. This is for you," she said, dropping a tablet onto the bed.

Katsina lifted her knees, and popped her elbows onto the bed, pulling herself off the floor. The tablet displayed a list of medications, instructions on taking each, and a discharge letter. Katsina huffed at the sight, a smile crept under her nose.

"Freedom at last, eh?" she asked.

"Freedom at last, Captain," Dr. Foye said, "but on one condition..."

"What's that then?"

"I read and watched everything I could find on what happened during the coup. I saw what happened to you and those men on the tarmac. I also saw what Morann made you do before he blew up that ship."

"And? What does that have to do with my going home?"

"Kat, a while back you were all over this ship causing trouble, lashing out at your friends, having nightmares, and when I asked you what you thought of that behaviour, you told me it's because you're a murderer and that you wanted to kill Yggdrasilians."

"Okay," Katsina said as she sat down, "I'm listening."

"Morann made you say the same things you said to me. Only he made you say it about your own people, and not the Yggdrasilians. You said those things about yourself because he said he would spare those people. I think that says a lot about how you really feel."

"I know you mean well, I just, I'm struggling to see what you're saying. I mean I'm listening I just… I don't…"

"It takes a strong individual to challenge their misdeeds, Kat, to learn from their actions and to change. When you strolled into this hospital before, you were too stubborn to look inward and assess your actions. My point is this, and it's part of your care plan I have written down there, Morann did the wrong things in the name of doing the right thing. Marshal did the right things even though many could see them as wrong. You seemed to struggle with figuring out where you fit into all that. And now I think you need to decide once and for all."

Katsina stared at the tablet, ignoring everything but the words "return to active duty". She could finally do something more useful than lay in bed. Something she had never been fond of. The doctor's words weighed on her after she was left alone, thinking about what she had done for the war, for her people.

The day went on, and Katsina gathered her things. She had over a hundred get-well-soon tokens in her bedside drawer, each from multiple crew members with messages of support and well wishes. The small coin-like tokens added up to a hefty weight, but Katsina put them all in her backpack anyway. Her model enterprise sat on the window sill, it's nacelles haphazardly glued back on by Rutheo. Some of her clothes, laundered and folded, sat on the chair across the room. She could finally change out of her hospital gown. Her tank top was riddled with holes, while the jeans and shoes, though clean, were ragged and battered. At least she could thank Rutheo for bringing her new underwear and socks. By the time she was fully packed, multiple helium balloons and the head of her Riley bear hung from her overflowing bag. She would have had to make more than one trip, had Alice not sneakily appeared by the door before she left, making Katsina jump.

"ts'ßolfé," she said, "could you not knock?"

"Knocking is old fashioned, surely you could see me coming?" she said, gesturing at the blue and red strands around them, connecting everyone.

"I was distracted."

"You? Caught up in your thoughts? No way," Alice said cheekily.

"Rutheo must seriously be rubbing off on you," said Katsina. "Whats up?"

"I uh, well, I have uh," she began timidly, "I have something you're going to want to sit down for."

Katsina caught her change of tone, and cocked her head to one side. She rotated her shoulders and dropped her backpack, pointing Alice towards the bed. She closed the door behind her.

"Lay it on me."

"Okay, so I know you wanted a definitive number of deaths on Free Venture, the logs of the ship list about ten thousand, two hundred and twelve souls. Morann, after returning to the Insurmountable, began aiding in the containment effort of the space debris left over after the attack on the ship. Rutheo has the tarmac ready, the ship is fully operational again, and we are ready to make our way as soon as you are," she said, her speech well rehearsed.

"Okay, what's the catch?"

"Well I can't get you an accurate number of lives lost on the Free Venture because Morann and his crew found this..." She said, handing a tablet to Katsina.

She flicked it open, and synced it to her HUD. She loaded a series of images from the tablet to her eyesight. It showed the wreckage of the vessel, the entire amidship sections missing, while the bow and stern floated in space, in pieces.

"What am I looking at here?" she asked.

"Look at the infrared images," Alice said, her voice peaking with an underlying excitement.

Katsina pulled up the infrared images on the file, and saw multiple orange dots inside the blue bulbs of the debris field. All of it was back dropped by the Deep, which was black, no matter what way they could look at it. The image was laced with radiation wisps that made it unclear to see what the small orange dots could be. The fallout from Morann's attack was visible in the photo.

"Weird, surely the debris would have cooled down by now?" Katsina said, curious about the meaning of the small orange dots.

"Morann recovered this as well, we would have missed it, but he had a hunch."

An audio file appeared on Katsina's HUD, its format was unfamiliar to her.

"The hell is that?"

"He used an old receiver to listen for an alternating current on the lower end of the EM spectrum. It's a set of radio waves. Listen, listen," Alice said, her excitement beginning to bubble over.

Katsina accessed the audio file and heard a familiar voice:

> Man O' War vessels. This is Shimon Ableson of Free Venture. We require assistance and aid. Our lifeboat shuttles cannot leave the deep unassisted. This message will repeat.

She shot her eyes to Alice, whose teary smile and flustered cheeks mirrored the essence of joy that Katsina herself felt erupting in her chest. A shimmer of goosebumps ran up her arms, before a sudden realisation took her excitement away, and replaced it with a grave new resolution. Alice's happiness turned to concern, she dipped her head to meet Katsina's wandering eyes.

"Kat?" she asked.

Katsina weighed the options in her mind, knowing the implications for those left alive. What awaited them should they be saved. They'd ran and hid from the war for a reason. A reason Katsina was beginning to understand. They're only champion was dead, their home destroyed, and there was very little Katsina could do as a captain enlisted in the fleet. She took a deep breath.

"We have work to do tonight. Assemble the crew on the tarmac. And get Morann on the comms," she said, leaving the room and her things behind. There was something more important than moving her possessions home that day.

***

It was late, probably the latest any captain had addressed a crew; Katsina struggled to remember any other similar situation. The tarmac was once again brand new. The paint on some of the tiles were still drying behind cordoned off lines. Katsina could have easily addressed the crew from the war room or even the bridge. But something made her do it in person. A new and strange calling, pushing her in a direction she didn't think she could go. The crowd that filled the bow end of the tarmac stood impatiently, arguing with each other about why they were there. There was no podium, no stage to garner their attention towards. Katsina clambered atop a nearby shuttle to stare down at the expectant faces. She recognised most, many of them friendly faces she had served with, some others had shot at her in the past week. She tried to not focus on them. What she mainly recognised was that, unlike before, Morann's people did not stand divided from her people. Instead they gathered together, as they could have done before, if not for Krauss' influence. Katsina cleared her throat.

"Thank you all for coming," she began, searching for her inner confidence. "I've uh, always been known for making speeches. I'm sure you all caught my most recent one, telling the admiralty board to suck it."

She caught a few laughs, even a whistle or two from her crowd. But the attention of four hundred or so was not enough considering there were four thousand listening.

"Anyway, you have all read the logs, seen the footage of what happened here this past week. It's a lot to process for everyone, myself included. One day this will be an interesting war story, but for now we have to wait for it to be over before we can start telling it. And what I want to say is that it's not over yet. Due to the combined efforts of you all, and the many crew members on each of the ships with us, the Behemothis is fully functional and ready to serve the people again. But, our ship, and the others, would not be here if it weren't for the sacrifice of our own Captain Marshal Richmond, who, as you now know, was Yggdrasilian."

Whispers and hums began to spread around the crowd, people showing their distaste. Anger and even hatred. Only a handful showed little or no adversity to her words, most of them her crew, some of them Morann's and even Morann himself. Which was surprising. Katsina continued to speak, regardless of the whispers.

"His participation in our military was not founded out of espionage, teachery, or thievery of knowledge. It was an act of protection, which I'm sure you can all understand. He joined our fleet to protect his people, other Yggdrasilians, who would have been killed for going home, or killed for coming to us. It was a level of bravery, that I don't think a single one of us could have mustered. Marshal Richmond sacrificed his life in more ways than one in service to not just our people, but his people as well. Which is what brings me here before you now."

She paused, looking at the settled crowd, who became more and more interested as she continued. Some that whispered were struck to silence, others who seemed uninterested began to pay attention. Katsina had considered her options, but knew there was only one thing she could really do. But before she could do it, she had to tell them. Not because she needed permission, but she needed to give others permission. The tension around them began to swell, some of them knew what was coming.

"In the early hours of this morning a team of fighters, led by Captain Morann, discovered that there are survivors aboard shuttles from the Free Venture. They are trapped in the deep, irradiated, and most likely starving to death."

The last of the doubtful and the few whisperers fell silent. Leaving only the hum of the space carrier left to listen to.

"The number of survivors could be in the thousands. With no homes, no food, and no one to protect them anymore. Which is why the Behemothis will not be returning home. It will be staying here, in the Deep, where it can keep these people hidden from the war and provide them with the home that we took away from them. Captain Morann has agreed to take anyone who does not want to stay back to Botanica. He will be submitting a false after action report, giving us the opportunity to hide from this war and help these people find peace. He has also agreed to do everything he can to aid us in the future. You are welcome to leave, no one will stop you. But myself, the chief, the commander and the other officers are staying to begin a rescue mission to aid these people. It would be the least we could do to repay the man who saved us all."

The room remained dead silent, not a person shifted, not an eye blinked. They all stood frozen.

"Anyone who wishes to leave may do so now," she said, awaiting the mass exodus.

Morann stepped out of the crowd, followed by his people. They moved to one side, forming the group that intended to leave. Katsina watched the rest of the crowd, waiting for others to leave it. But enough time had passed, and no one moved. She rubbed the back of her neck, wondering had they even all heard her. She looked to Rutheo, Alice, and Dr. Foye. Even Aker Castle remained. Still no one moved, until a distant hand shot up into the air.

"So when do we start?" a voice called from the back of the crowd.

***

It is an inarguable fact that most people believe in a reason to exist, whether it be a religion, a personal goal, or a responsibility to another person. For Katsina Lucas, it wasn't just her ship with every person on board, it was more than that. Her reason to exist was to serve, not just her people, but all people in need. In a deep, now mapped, region of space, a new and independent Pillar of Humanity was born. In the years that passed, the war forgot about Katsina Lucas. Very few people ever saw her ship again during that lifetime. Eventually, people stopped looking for it at all, believing it lost to the Deep. Instead of searching, they remembered the glory of the Behemothis and what it stood for. Eventually, the story of the broadsider became legend.

GLOSSARY OF TERMS AND TRANSLATIONS

t'ßiensorta is the language that most people speak in the future. Below is a list of common and exemplary words that a person would say.

t'ßiensorta phrases:
Faisaheßul and Faisaheß - A general and widely adaptable curse word with no English, Irish, Korean or Chinese translation.
Zehu'uo - Cursed.
Bheibhen - A word to refer to a person's rectum.
t'Secheashin - A word that describes a person who has no family or friends.
t'ßolu'ou - God forsaken or cursed.
Chasanichennwan t'sai - An insult that tells a person to go away. There is no English, Irish, Korean or Chinese translation.
Lasine ui nyßolt'seich - Child of a bad parent.
Chasanuha - Loser.
Schurul dzalm chusanichen - A phrase that describes someone acting rudely sarcastic.

t'ßiensorta Root Words:
Tayë - Yes.
t'Sanu - No.
Bayet - Mother.
Aichin - Father.
Lachien - Parent.
Behts - Rock/Earth.
Ichen - Water.

t'ßiensorta pronouns:
tSaï - I.
tSeï - You.
tSen - He.
t'tSu - She.
dZalm - It.
tSeh/ tSun - They/Them.
tSeiß - You's.

MORE READING

If you enjoyed the story of Katsina and the Behemothis, and would like to read more from this fictional world, then there is much more for you to discover! The 'Orchestrators of The Universe' blog is updated regularly with writing content and free science fiction stories from different times and places along the timeline of Broadsiders narrative. On the blog you can read about how Mara and Delta Squadron were lost to the deep, how AI was first merged with humans, and what life was like on earth before humans left the planet for good. These stories and many more are added to the ever expanding story regularly. Also available on the blog is updated about future novels, artwork, and insights to the writing process.

You can find 'Orchestrators of The Universe' on Facebook and Tumblr.
To review this novel you can visit it's page
on Amazon and Goodreads. You can also submit a
review to the Facebook and Tumblr pages.
You can follow me, the author, Lilith Antoinette on Instagram and Twitter by searching the username: @justlilytbh.
For business enquiries, please email orchestratorsoftheuniverse@gmail.com

Printed in Poland
by Amazon Fulfillment
Poland Sp. z o.o., Wrocław